Landry opens the car door and steps out into the garage.

But there are shadowy corners where someone could be concealed, watching her.

The call is coming from inside the house.

The line from an old slasher movie barges into her brain.

Her legs wobble as she starts moving across the floor, expecting someone to jump out at her with every step she takes.

Addison's bedroom door is ajar.

Landry hesitates, wondering if she should push it open and walk right in. Tucker's closed door is just down the hall.

The rain is falling hard on the roof. She waits until the next clap of thunder and knocks.

No reply.

She pushes the door open, crosses the threshold . . . and screams.

By Wendy Corsi Staub

THE PERFECT STRANGER

WENDY CORSI STAUB

HARPER

An Imprint of HarperCollinsPublishers

This is a work of fiction. Names, characters, places, and incidents are products of the author's imagination or are used fictitiously and are not to be construed as real. Any resemblance to actual events, locales, organizations, or persons, living or dead, is entirely coincidental.

HARPER

An Imprint of HarperCollins*Publishers*
195 Broadway
New York, New York 10007

Copyright © 2014 by Wendy Corsi Staub
Excerpt from *The Black Widow* copyright © 2015 by Wendy Corsi Staub
ISBN 978-0-06-222240-4

First Harper mass market printing: August 2014

HarperCollins® and Harper® are registered trademarks of Harper-Collins Publishers.

Printed in the United States of America

Visit Harper paperbacks on the World Wide Web at
www.harpercollins.com

10 9 8 7 6 5 4 3 2 1

Turn your face to the sun and the shadows fall behind you.

—*Maori Proverb*

Acknowledgments

With gratitude to John Strawser, Bridget Kubera, and Lisa Taylor-Phelpps and her "stinkerdoodle"; to my editor Lucia Macro and her assistant Nicole Fischer and the many amazing people at HarperCollins who had a hand in bringing this novel to print; to my agents Laura Blake Peterson and Holly Frederick, and to Mina Feig and the team at Curtis Brown, Ltd.; to Peter Meluso and to Carol Fitzgerald and the gang at the Book Report Network for keeping my Web sites up and running; to the gals at Writerspace for wrangling the newsletter; to David Staub and Stacey Sypko for all things tech or trailer-related; to Mark Staub, business manager, creative advisor, proofreader, and oh, yeah, love of my life. My glass is raised to my family and friends for careening along with me toward yet another deadline—and being there, always, to toast the end. Finally, I offer heartfelt appreciation to booksellers, librarians, and readers everywhere—because without you, I could not wholly be me.

THE PERFECT STRANGER

Prologue

When the doctor's receptionist called this morning to say that they had the results, it never dawned on her that it might be bad news.

"Hi, hon," Janine said—she called all the patients "hon"—and casually requested that she come by in person this afternoon. She even used just that phrasing, and it was a question, as opposed to a command: "Can you come by the office in person this afternoon?"

Come by.

So breezy. So inconsequential. So . . . so everything this situation is not.

What if she'd told Janine, over the phone, that she was busy this afternoon? Would the receptionist then have at least hinted that her presence at the office was urgent; that it was, in fact, more than a mere request?

But she wasn't busy and so here she is, blindsided, numbly staring at the doctor pointing the tip of a ballpoint pen at the left breast on the anatomical diagram.

The doctor keeps talking, talking, talking; tapping, tapping, tapping the paper with the pen point to indicate exactly where the cancerous tissue is growing, leaving ominous black ink pockmarks.

She nods as though she's listening intently, not betraying

that every word after *malignancy* has been drowned out by the warning bells clanging in her brain.

I'm going to die, she thinks with the absolute certainty of someone trapped on a railroad track, staring helplessly into the glaring roar of an oncoming train. *I'm going to be one of those ravaged bald women lying dwarfed in a hospital bed, terrified and exhausted and dying an awful, solitary death . . .*

She's seen that person before, too many times—in the movies, and in real life . . . but she never thought she'd ever actually *become* that person. Or did she?

Well, yes—you worry, whenever a horrific fate befalls someone else, that it could happen to you. But then you reassure yourself that it won't, and you push the thought from your head, and you move on.

This time there is no reassurance, no pushing, no moving. The image won't budge.

Me . . . sick . . . bald . . . dying.

Dead.

Me. Dead.

The tinny taste of fear fills her mouth, joined by bile as her stomach pitches and rolls, attempting to eject the tuna sandwich she devoured in the carefree life she was still living at lunchtime.

Carefree? Really?

No. Just last night she lost sleep over the usual conflicts involving money and work and household mishaps. When she woke this morning, her first thought was that there would be too few hours in the day ahead to resolve everything that needed to be dealt with. She actually welcomed the call from Janine the receptionist, thinking a detour to the doctor's office would be a distraction from her other problems.

How could I have thought those problems were problems?

Stomach churning, she manages to excuse herself, lurches to her feet and rushes for the door, out into the hall, toward the small restroom.

Kneeling and retching, she finds herself wondering if this is what it will be like when she goes through chemotherapy. You hear that the harsh drugs make patients sick to their stomachs.

Me . . . sick . . .

Dead.

How can she possibly wrap her head around that idea? If only she could magically escape to her bed right now, where she'd be alone to cry or scream or sleep . . .

But she can't. She has to pull herself together somehow, make herself presentable and coherent enough to walk back down the hall to the doctor's office . . . and then, dear God, the nurses and Janine and a waiting room full of patients still lie between her and solitude.

I can't do this. I can't.

I need to be alone . . .

Five minutes later, shaken, she emerges from the bathroom, returns to the still-ajar door marked with the physician's name.

As she crosses the threshold again, the doctor looks up, wearing a nonplused expression that makes it clear this isn't the first time that a patient on the receiving end of a malignant diagnosis has behaved in such a manner. "Feeling better now? Come on in."

"I—I'm sorry," she stammers, making her way back to the seat opposite the desk, where the anatomical diagram still sits like a signed, sealed, and delivered execution notice awaiting final action.

"It's all right. Here . . . drink some water."

She takes the paper cup the doctor offers. Sips.

As the lukewarm water slides along her throat, left raw from retching, she nearly gags again.

"I'm sorry," she repeats, and sets aside the cup.

"No need. Would you like to call someone?"

Call someone . . .

Would you like to call someone . . .

Unable to process the question, she stares at the doctor.

"A friend, or a family member . . . someone who can come over here and—"

"Oh. No. No, thank you." *I just want to be alone. Can't you see that?*

"Are you sure?"

"Yes. I'm . . . I'll be fine. I just needed a few minutes to . . ."

To throw up my lunch and splash water on my face and look into the mirror and try to absorb the news that I have cancer and what if I die?

Me . . .

Dead?

It's unfathomable that her worst fear might actually come to fruition after all these years, but then . . .

Isn't it everyone's worst fear?

We're all mortal, aren't we?

I wouldn't be the only person in the world who's ever lain awake at night, tossing and turning, terrified that I'm going to die, only to have it actually happen.

No. But it becomes second nature to reassure yourself that it's not going to happen—not really, or at least, not anytime soon. You almost believe you're safe, that you've escaped the inevitable, and then suddenly . . .

"I know it's difficult to hear news like this," the doctor is saying, "but the important thing is that we caught it early. We're going to discuss your treatment options, and there are many. New ones are being developed every day. The bottom line is that the survival rates for a stage one malignancy are . . ."

Treatment options . . .

Survival rates . . .
Stage one . . .
And here she is, right back to *malignancy.*

Jaw set grimly, she wills herself not to cry, but the tears come anyway.

Part 1

Saturday, June 1

Sixty Is the New . . . Oh, Who Am I Kidding? Sixty Is Old!

I can't recognize a single musician on the cover of Rolling Stone, *I can't remember my user names and passwords if they're not saved in my laptop or phone, I can't see a blessed thing without my bifocals, and if they're not on my head, chances are I have no idea where I left them . . . Still, faced with the prospects of old age and senility—or not sticking around long enough to grow old and senile—I'll take the prior.*

—Excerpt from Meredith's blog, *Pink Stinks*

Chapter 1

Nightgown on, glasses off . . .

About to climb into her side of the bed she shares with her husband, when he's not up in Cleveland tending to his elderly mother, Meredith Heywood winces and reaches back to rest a hand against her spine.

The ache is even worse now than it was before she took a hot bath, hoping in vain that it would relax her muscles. An entire Saturday spent working in the yard—followed by a few hours hunched over her laptop, writing about the garden she just planted—had been inarguably good for the soul. But for her middle-aged, cancer-tainted, bones . . . eh, not so much.

"Why don't you wait until I get home to do the planting?" Hank had asked on the phone this morning when she told him of her plans. He'd always liked to do things with her—and for her. Now, more than ever.

It's not just her illness; he was laid off from his job as an airline mechanic a few weeks before they got the news that her cancer has spread.

It's almost been a relief to have him away. When he's here, he hovers, trying to take care of her.

There was a time when she enjoyed that kind of attention. That was in another lifetime: a younger and thus occasionally emotionally insecure lifetime that was, at the same time, a physically self-sufficient and healthy lifetime.

A lifetime before cancer.

"I can't wait until you're back to do the garden," she told Hank. "It's getting too late."

"It's not even summer yet, Mer."

Had he really interpreted her statement to mean that it was too late in the season?

Or maybe . . .

Was that really what she'd meant, in a momentary lapse with reality?

Too late . . . too late . . .

Those two words have taken on a whole new meaning now.

"We usually get the vegetables in over Memorial Day," she pointed out to Hank. "That was last weekend."

They'd been planning to do it then, but Hank's mother took a bad fall the Thursday before, and he had to jump into his truck and head to his hometown. He's been there ever since, trying to convince the most stubborn woman in the world that at ninety-three she's too old to live alone.

Mission accomplished—finally.

"I can handle the planting," Meredith assured him when he mentioned that it may be at least a few more days before he gets his mother acclimated to her new nursing home and cleans out her condo so the realtor can list it. "It's going to rain for the next couple of days, so this is the perfect time to get the seedlings in."

"Why don't you call the kids to help you?"

"Maybe I will," she lied.

Their daughter and sons, all married and scattered within an hour or so drive of this small middle-class Cincinnati suburb, have their hands full with jobs, young children, household obligations of their own. She wasn't about to bother any of them to come help her.

Especially since . . .

Well, they don't know yet that her cancer has returned a third time and spread. And she doesn't want them to suspect anything until she's ready to tell them. No need for anyone to worry until it's absolutely necessary.

Only Hank is aware of the truth. He's having a rough time with it.

"There are so many things we've been waiting to do until I retire," he said one night a few weeks ago, head in hands.

"We'll do them now."

"Now that I don't have a job and we're broke?"

"We're not broke yet. Don't worry. You'll find another job."

"Where? Not here. And how can we move, with—" He cleared his throat. "I mean, you need to be near your doctors now that . . ."

Now that it's almost over.

But he didn't say it, and Meredith, who has spent decades finishing his sentences, didn't either.

She just assured him, "You'll find something here. Some other kind of work."

"With decent pay? And benefits? If I don't find something before our medical insurance runs out . . . I can't believe this is happening to us."

"Not just to us. Teddy's in the same boat, and with a baby on the way," she pointed out. Their firstborn, an accountant, lost his job and health care last year and has been struggling to keep a roof over his family's heads and food on the table. Hank and Meredith have been giving him whatever they can spare—but that's now gone from very little to nothing at all.

"Yeah, and then there's my mother . . ." Hank was on a roll. "No long-term care insurance and she can't keep living alone. And of course I get sole responsibility for her since my brother fell off the face of the earth."

Hank's only sibling stopped speaking to both him and his mother after a family falling out years ago.

It would have been easier if the old woman hadn't fallen last weekend, accelerating the need to get her out of her condo and into the only available—though not necessarily affordable—facility.

Easier, too, if Hank's mother wasn't so damned adamant about staying in Cleveland. They could have moved her to Cincinnati years ago to make things easier on Hank—though certainly not under their own roof. Even if Meredith were healthy enough to be a caregiver—as opposed to facing the eventual need for one herself—her mother-in-law is downright impossible.

"She's never living with us, no matter what happens," Hank said flatly many years ago, when his mother was widowed shortly after their engagement. At the time, Meredith found the statement unduly harsh and started having second thoughts, wondering what kind of man would say such a thing.

That was before she got to know his mother—in small doses and from a distance, thank goodness.

"She's probably going to live to be a hundred," Hank says frequently—and dismally.

He's probably right. But whenever he brings it up, Meredith duly points out that he's lucky to have her, having lost her own mother when her kids were young, and now facing her own mortality at this age.

"I know. I just . . . I'm worried about having to deal with her while I'm trying to find a job, and worrying about health care . . . In the end, it always comes down to money we don't have. Story of our lives, right?"

Money? In the end it comes down to money?

He doesn't realize what he's saying. That's what she told herself. She knew he was just stressed, knew he loved her, knew that deep down his priorities were straight. He's only human.

But—being only human herself—she couldn't help

saying, "Hey, you can always push me off a cliff and collect on my life insurance policy now instead of later. I mean, I'm a goner anyway, right? Why not put us both out of our misery—the sooner the better?"

His jaw dropped. "What kind of thing is that to say?"

"I'm sorry. I was kidding. Come on, Hank. Look at the bright side."

To his credit, he didn't say, "What bright side?"

If he had, she might have broken down and cried.

Instead, he'd hugged her and apologized. "I just want to make sure that we do everything we ever said we were going to do. No more putting things off—not because I don't think you're going to be around, but because . . . well, I don't like to waste time. That's all."

Right. Because she doesn't have time to waste.

Why dwell on the past when you can focus on the future?

That was the title of an optimistic blog post she wrote back when she was in treatment, still assuming she was going to beat this disease.

The piece was met with a mixed reaction from her followers, depending on their stage of the disease. Those who were in remission shared her mind-set. Those who were not—those with very little future left—didn't want to think about what might lie ahead. They found comfort in reflecting upon happier times.

Now I get it. Now I'm sorry, so sorry. I wish I could have told some of them . . .

But it's too late.

Too late . . . too late . . .

Meredith arches her back, stretching, trying to work out the kinks as a warm breeze flutters the peach and yellow paisley curtains at the window.

Through the screen she can hear only crickets, a distant dog barking, and the occasional sound of traffic out on the main road. The houses in this neighborhood may be of the no frills, cookie-cutter architectural style, but they're set far apart on relatively large lots.

It was the quiet, private location that drew Meredith and Hank here well over three decades ago, when they were living downtown in a one-bedroom apartment with two toddlers and an *oops* baby on the way. This seventeen-hundred-square-foot house—with an eat-in kitchen, three bedrooms, and one and a half baths—seemed palatial by comparison.

They felt like they'd be living in the lap of luxury and promised each other they were going to grow old here.

But they'd outgrown it by the time the kids were teenagers with friends coming and going at all hours, and the house was showing wear and tear.

With three college tuitions looming in the near future, they couldn't afford to add on or buy anything bigger. Not on Hank's salary and what little she made working at a local daycare.

Somehow, they survived the old plumbing and wiring and constant repairs; the crowds of kids, the lack of privacy and closet space. Eventually their sons and daughter moved on, and although their finances aren't terrific—thanks to the economy and a series of bad investments—at least Meredith and Hank grew back into their house.

It may be shabby, but it's home.

Now, the mere idea of growing old anywhere at all . . . that in itself is a luxury.

"Ouch," she says aloud, wincing again as she rolls her shoulders.

It's going to take a hell of a lot more than stretching, a hot bath, or even lying down on the memory foam mattress they splurged on last September when Macy's had a sale. That was when she was assuming their old, saggy mattress was causing the dull ache in her back. Hank's back ached, too.

"I think it's from giving the grandkids piggyback rides," he said, "not the mattress."

"Well, I haven't given anyone piggyback rides. Trust me. It's the mattress."

The pricey new one was their early Christmas present to each other, along with the bright, cheerful paisley bedding and curtains that at least made it look like springtime in here all winter long . . . even after she found out the memory foam wasn't going to cure her hurting bones. Nothing was.

She wishes now that she'd allowed her doctor to prescribe something for the pain during her last visit, but she was afraid she'd become dependent.

"That's crazy," Hank said when she told him. "Why would you think that?"

"You hear stories—all those celebrities addicted to prescription pain medication . . . and some of my blogger friends have had issues, too."

Hank shook his head. "Next time you go, let them give you something. Why suffer?"

Suffer—such a strong word. Especially since she isn't truly suffering. Not yet, anyway.

There will be plenty of time down the road for Percocet or morphine or whatever it is that doctors prescribe in the final stages . . .

Plenty of time—please, God, let there be plenty of time.

She's not against pain medicine, but even now, while they still have insurance, their prescription plan isn't the best. Her medications have already cost them a fortune out of pocket—and a lot of good they did.

Plain old ibuprofen might help, but Hank must have packed the Advil they keep in the master bathroom medicine cabinet. She just looked for it and it wasn't there. She's too tired to go hunt for another bottle.

What she really needs right now, as much as, if not more than, medication, is a good, stiff shot of Kentucky Bourbon. There's plenty of that downstairs, courtesy of living a stone's throw from some of the world's finest distilleries.

In the old days—well, in the few years' window after the kids were grown but before Meredith got sick—she and Hank spent some deliciously decadent weekend afternoons with fellow empty nester friends, sipping their way along the Bourbon trail that lies in the bluegrass hills south of Cincinnati.

She was never a big drinker; just a social one. But that came to a complete halt after her breast cancer diagnosis, when she became hypervigilant about everything she put into her body. She lightened up a bit after five years in remission, but last year a routine test betrayed a resurgence of microscopic cancer cells in her remaining breast tissue, and she went right back on the wagon. Not a drop of liquor, no soy products, only organic fruits and vegetables . . .

I don't know about that, one of the other bloggers commented on a post where Meredith outlined her stringent habits. *What good is being alive if you sacrifice all the fun stuff?*

I'm just trying to improve my odds. To each his own, Meredith wrote back.

The blogger—that's right, now she remembers, it was Elena—Elena wrote back: *My mother was a health nut who did everything right, and she was hit by a train before her thirtieth birthday. I did everything right, and I was diagnosed with cancer right after mine. I have to admit: I'm sick of being good.*

Meredith understood how Elena felt. But she hoped Elena understood why she herself wasn't—*isn't*—taking any chances.

Certainly not now that the cancer has metastasized to her bones. But of course, Elena doesn't know about that.

"How long do I have?" Meredith asked the oncologist matter-of-factly when she first got the news.

"Don't jump the gun, there," said the doctor, a straight shooter. "It's a relatively small spot, and we're going to treat it. Radiation, chemotherapy . . ."

Yes. She knows the drill.

They treat it until everything stops working, and it continues to spread.

That, she suspects, is where they're headed now. A few weeks ago, the morning after an idyllic Mother's Day spent cooking outside with Hank and the kids and grandkids, the doctor gave her some discouraging test results, then told her they're going to try this current treatment—which she knows is basically her last hope—a little longer and take some more tests to see whether it's working.

She has a feeling it isn't.

All those needles—God, how she hated needles, even when they were lifelines—endlessly poking into her, delivering medication, drawing blood . . . all for what?

There are no more lifelines.

She's been doing her best to prepare herself for what lies ahead—if not in the immediate future, then at some point down the road.

Sooner or later she'll be told to call hospice and get her affairs in order.

Even then, she knows, many doctors aren't able—or perhaps aren't willing—to provide a time frame.

She's seen it happen to her online friends time and again, and now it's going to happen to her. Maybe not this year, maybe not even next, but eventually this damned disease is going to get her.

She's privately told one or two of her online friends of her situation, but not everyone. Eventually she'll have to write an official blog post about it. The moment it goes live, she'll become *that* person—the doomed friend everyone rallies around.

I'm not ready. I don't want to be her. *Not yet. I want to be* me *for as long as I can.*

There's only one way to do that: pretend this isn't really happening.

The lyrics to an old Styx song—one she and Hank used to listen to on vinyl back in their dating days—keep running through her head.

You're fooling yourself . . . you don't believe it . . .

She'll get through her days staying busy so that she won't have to dwell on the future—and get through her nights the best she can.

Right now she'll have to settle for over-the-counter pain relievers without the courtesy of Bourbon to numb the pain in her back—or the disquieting, morbid thoughts that sometimes strike at night, especially when she's here alone.

With a sigh, she leaves the lamplit bedroom and flicks on the hallway light. As she makes her way to the stairs, she hears a whisper of movement below.

"Hank?" she calls.

No answer.

Of course not. He's in Cleveland. She spoke to him a half hour ago on the phone, although . . .

He could very well have just *said* he was in Cleveland. Maybe he was really on the road, headed home early to surprise her.

"Hank! Is that you?"

Absolutely still, poised mid-flight with her hand on the banister, Meredith is enveloped in complete silence.

"Is someone there?"

No.

And yet—she did hear something before. Or perhaps it's more just a sensation of not being alone in the house . . .

Or did you just imagine it altogether?

For a long time she stands there, listening—one moment certain she can feel someone there, the next, certain she's losing it.

Just last week she blogged about this very scenario. Not about things that go bump in the night, per se, but about getting older and potentially senile.

That entry stemmed from Hank's report that his mother suspected her neighbor—a distinguished widowed professor—of sneaking into her condo in the wee hours, trying on her clothes and taking perfumed bubble baths in her tub.

Her blog entry was written entirely tongue in cheek, as so many of them are. Even during the darkest days of her cancer treatment, she's always managed to find a humorous angle.

She'd started the blog at the suggestion of her therapist, who knew she'd dreamed of graduating college and becoming a writer before marriage and motherhood set her on a different path. Even the title of the blog page—*Pink Stinks*—is meant to be an irreverent poke at the breast cancer awareness movement.

Determined to keep her latest diagnosis to herself, she wrote a blog post last week about the inevitability of aging and the many signs—now that she's past her sixtieth birthday—that the process is well under way.

That post was greeted by a barrage of positive, amusing comments from her regular followers and a couple of newcomers who have since stuck around. Someone—who was it?—said that she was wise and had a tough outer shell, like a turtle, and turtles are known for their longevity—*So I'm sure you're going to live a good long time!*

From your lips—rather, fingertips—to God's ears, Meredith wanted to respond to whoever wrote that, but of course, she didn't.

Standing on the stairway, listening for movement below and wondering if she should go back to the bedroom for the baseball bat Hank keeps under his side of the bed, she mentally composes the opening of a new blog post she'll write tomorrow.

So there I was, armed and dangerous in my granny nightgown . . .

Oh, geez. She really is losing it, isn't she?

And her taut posture as she stands clenched from head to toe, clutching the railing, isn't helping her back pain.

Either turn around and go to bed, or go downstairs, get what you need, and then go to bed.

Meredith opts for the latter. She flips a wall switch at the foot of the stairs, then another in the living room, and the one in the dining room, reassured as she makes her way through familiar rooms bathed in light. As always, she notices not just the threadbare area rug, the worn spots on the furniture, the chipped paint on the baseboards, but also the clay bowl Beck had made in Girl Scouts, the bookshelf lined with Hardy Boys titles Hank had handed down to his sons and newer picture books Meredith had collected for the grand-children, the faint pencil marks on the doorjamb where they marked their growing kids' height over the years . . .

It's a good house. It's been a good life here.

Whenever Hank talks about selling it now, she shakes her head. "This is home. I don't ever want to leave."

In the kitchen cabinet where she keeps her daily vitamins and the medications prescribed to keep cancer at bay for as long as possible, she finds a bottle of drugstore brand pain-killers.

Having left her glasses upstairs on the nightstand, she can't quite make out the label. It looks to her like they ex-pired last year, but they're probably fine. Fine, as in safe to swallow, if not as effective as they might have been.

She takes three, just in case they're less potent. Washing them down with tap water, she wonders how long it will take before the pills ease the tension in her muscles.

It really is too bad she can't take something stronger.

Not medicine. Just a nip of something that will warm her from the inside out, and let her sleep.

She glances longingly at the high cupboard above the fridge where they've kept the booze since their firstborn, Teddy, reached high school.

Ha. As if keeping the stash out of arm's reach would deter him and his friends from getting into it. It didn't work, they discovered belatedly, when Hank realized that one of their offspring—by then, all three were in college—had replaced the contents of a bottle of Woodford Reserve with iced tea.

Still, they were good kids, Meredith remembers as she sets the empty water glass into the sink. Spirited, but good. She's blessed to have watched them grow up and give her grandchildren—three grandsons so far between Teddy and Neal and their wives, with another little stinkerdoodle on the way this fall.

That's what Meredith calls her grandchildren, just as she always called her own children: a nice batch of stinkerdoodles.

Everyone is hoping for a girl this time.

Everyone but her. Secretly, she worries about passing the cancer gene to a new generation.

Men get breast cancer, too, one of her blogger friends pointed out when she wrote about that concern.

True. But it's not nearly as common.

She can't help but worry about the health of her daughter and future granddaughters. She's been warning Rebecca that she needs to do self-exams and start her yearly mammogram screening in another couple of years.

Beck, of course, waves her mother off. She's too young and full of life to worry about illness.

So was I at her age. I never thought something like this could happen. No family history . . .

You just never know.

It's been over a year now since Beck married Keith. They'll probably be starting a family, too, soon.

Meredith has so much to live for. If only . . .

Shaking her head, she turns off the light and leaves the kitchen, never noticing the cut screen on the window facing the newly planted garden out back, or the shadow of a human figure lurking in the far corner.

Tragic News

This is Meredith's daughter, Rebecca, writing. I don't know how to say this. There's no easy way. I'm still in shock. But you all meant a lot to my mom, and she would want our family to let you all know that she passed away this weekend.

—Excerpt from Meredith's blog, *Pink Stinks*

Chapter 2

The news reaches Landry Wells on the sort of picture-perfect summer morning when it feels as though nothing can possibly go wrong.

It's warm—southern Alabama in June is always warm—but not yet too steamy for sipping hot coffee on the second-story porch swing. A gentle breeze stirs Spanish moss draped in the live oaks framing her view of Mobile Bay, and the world is hushed but for chirping birds and the staccato spritzing of the lawn sprinklers below.

Still unshowered, wearing the shorts and T-shirt she threw on to walk the dog after rolling out of bed, Landry sits with her bare feet propped on the rail, laptop open to the Web page that bears the shocking news.

News that struck out of nowhere on what promised to be another precious, precious ordinary day.

Years ago—after a routine mammogram gave way to the sonogram that led to the biopsy that resulted in a cancer diagnosis—she couldn't imagine ever living another ordinary day. But the women to whom she turned for support—an online group of breast cancer patients and survivors she now counts among her closest friends—assured her that normality would return, sooner or later. They were right.

Every night, when she climbs into bed, she thanks God

for the gift of a day in which she carted her teenagers around and did loads of laundry and sat sipping coffee with her husband; a day filled with reading and writing, weeding the garden, feeding a family, watching good television and decadently bad television, grumbling about crumbs and clutter and mosquito bites but never really minding any of it.

She watches a monarch butterfly alight on a pink rose blossom in her sunlit flower bed below and thinks of Meredith.

She had been doing so well. Yes, Meredith had reported a recurrence well over a year ago. Her oncologist found some suspicious cells in her breast, and after a radical mastectomy and radiation, pronounced her clear again.

That's what she wrote, anyway, in one of her typically cheerful blog entries.

Was it a lie? Was she shielding them all from the grim fact that her cancer had spread; that she was dying? Was she trying to avoid the familiar shift in interaction they had all witnessed on other cancer blogs?

Landry considers the inevitable scenario that commences whenever a fellow blogger reports, in a post laced with incredulity, bravado, false cheer—or all of the above—that her doctors have run out of treatment options.

There's always a prompt outpouring of support, prayers, hollow optimism, and talk of miracles. Eventually—too often overnight—the blogger's posts will begin to detail alarming symptoms, hospital visits, hospice arrangements. Attempts at breezy humor fall flat; entries become increasingly graphic and sporadic, infused with sadness, weariness, fear.

Then come the final posts written by someone else—a daughter, a husband, a friend—sometimes chronicling the blogger's final days or hours, often reporting that the patient wants her Internet friends to know she's thinking of them; that their comments are being shared with her in her lucid moments. Once in a while the blogger's own last entry—sometimes intended as a farewell, but often not—is followed by just one other: a loved one's terse report of the death and funeral arrangements.

With Meredith, there's been none of that. Her daughter's post had struck out of the blue.

Bewildered, Landry scrolls up to the previous blog entry. Bearing Saturday's date, it was written by Meredith herself.

Having read it when it first appeared, Landry is already familiar with the buoyant account of Meredith's weekend morning spent planting a vegetable garden in her Ohio backyard.

Her husband was still away, she wrote, so she had to dig and lug heavy bags of fertilizer herself. But it would all be worthwhile, she said in closing, a few months from now when she got to enjoy *my favorite treat in the whole wild world: home-grown tomatoes, heavy with sugar and juice, eaten straight off the vine, sprinkled with salt and still warm from the sun.*

The woman who wrote those words seemed to be looking ahead to August without reservation. Was she deluding herself, or trying to fool everyone else, writing about arduous physical labor when she was in fact confined to a hospital bed in the final stages of her disease?

This is crazy. It can't be real.

Maybe it's some kind of practical joke, or . . .

Maybe Meredith's blogger account was hacked, or . . .

Maybe it's real and she just didn't want us to know.

Feeling vaguely betrayed, Landry opens a search window, types in the name Meredith, and stops to think for a moment.

She knows her friend's last name is Haywood—or is it Heywood? Heyworth? Something like that. And she lives in a Cincinnati suburb . . . but which one?

Funny how you can know someone intimately without

having that basic information; without ever having come face-to-face in the real world.

She types Haywood into the Google box and presses Enter.

There are a number of hits for *Meredith Haywood*—none that fit.

But when she replaces *Haywood* with *Heywood,* she finds herself looking at a death notice from the *Cincinnati Enquirer,* accompanied by a familiar photo: the head shot Meredith uses on her blog.

It's real.

A lump rises in Landry's throat, but she pushes it back and reads on, dry-eyed.

There was a time when she cried over Hallmark Christmas commercials. She wrote about that on her blog last December. Turned out that a surprising number of her followers did the same sappy thing.

These days it takes a hell of a lot more than a sentimental advertisement to bring tears to her eyes. She got used to holding them back in the wake of her diagnosis, not wanting to frighten her children, or depress her husband, or feel sorry for herself. Perhaps, most of all, she was afraid that if she allowed herself to start crying, she'd never stop.

But this is no Hallmark ad. It's a death notice—albeit a brief one, not a full-blown obituary. Details are sparse, funeral arrangements incomplete.

Shaken, Landry closes the laptop and stands. Resting her elbows on the wooden railing, chin cupped heavily in her hands, she gazes out over the water.

Just beyond the boardwalk, in the shallows close to shore, a pair of kayakers glide in parallel symmetry. Farther out: the usual array of fishing boats, plus a cluster of sailors taking advantage of the morning breeze. Not a cloud in the sky; the forecast calls for a beautiful day.

Again, Landry is struck by disbelief.

I need to talk to someone. I should call someone.

But not her husband.

Rob left for the office less than ten minutes ago, kissing her good-bye as she poured her coffee and reminding her that it's Wednesday, golf day, and he'll be home late. Right now he's driving, somewhere on the road between here and his law office in Mobile.

Anyway, he doesn't know Meredith—though he knows *about* her, of course, along with the other bloggers Landry counts among her closest confidantes. Bound by a common diagnosis, they found their way into each other's virtual worlds by chance and settled in with the camaraderie of old pals. She shares things with her online friends that she would never dream of telling anyone she knows in real life, other than Rob.

Oh, who is she kidding? There are some things Landry can't even bring herself to tell Rob, yet somehow she's comfortable putting it all out there on the Internet—hiding behind a screen name, of course.

Some bloggers just go by their first names, but her own is much too distinctive to ensure anonymity. She devoted nearly as much time to choosing a screen name as she had to baby names when she was pregnant with her children, ultimately deciding to go by BamaBelle.

"BamaBelle?" Rob echoed when she first shared it with him. "Bama as in Alabama?"

"What else?"

"I don't know . . . Obama?"

"No. B*aaaaa*ma. Not B*ahhh*ma."

She wanted him to congratulate her on her cleverness, not critique it—but he was Rob. He wasn't just nitpicking—he was protecting her, being cautious.

"I don't think you should share anything specific online about where you are, Landry."

"That's not specific. This is a huge state, and it's not like anyone's going to figure out exactly where I am. Or care."

"How about just 'Southern Belle'?"

"Too cliché. Rob, it's BamaBelle. Too late to change it. It's already out there."

He scowled, unaccustomed—back then, anyway—to her being short with him.

These days, thanks to the residual pressures of her illness, along with his job stress, and raising temperamental teenagers, they're much more prone to snapping at each other, or bickering—usually about little things.

For the most part, though, they get along. He's Landry's best friend and soul mate. He loves her and has her best interests at heart.

But he's not the person she needs for comfort right now, when she's reeling from the news of Meredith's death.

No. I need . . .

She gazes at the monarch butterfly below, still perched on the rose petals. It flutters its wings as if contemplating liftoff.

I need to talk to someone else who knew Meredith. Someone who will share my grief; someone who might know what happened.

Unfortunately, she can't just pick up the phone and call one of her blogger friends. Nor can she even text. She doesn't have their phone numbers. The only way to get in touch with them is online.

Returning to her laptop, she opens an instant message window, then sits with her fingers resting over the keyboard, once again staring into space, wondering whose screen name she should type.

Ordinarily she'd reach out first to Meredith, the unofficial matriarch of the group, but . . .

Something flutters in the air just beyond the balcony rail. The monarch butterfly. She watches it flit away, backlit by the sun against a brilliant blue morning sky.

Landry swallows hard, shaking her head, and types the first name to come to mind.

Awakened by the tone indicating that an instant message just popped up on her laptop across the hotel room, Jaycee opens her eyes to darkness.

Certain it's the middle of the night, she glances at the digital clock on the bedside table and sees that it's a little after 5:00 A.M.—an hour that may not technically be the middle of the night, but doesn't necessarily qualify as morning when you crawled into bed at three after a long flight, a late dinner, and too much champagne in a suite down the road at Chateau Marmont. It was almost like the good old days for a little while there, before her life derailed. She could almost forget . . .

Almost. But not entirely. She'll never forget. They won't let her.

Whoever is trying to reach her—probably Cory, oblivious to the time difference—will just have to wait until a decent hour.

With a groan, Jaycee rolls onto her other side—and gasps, seeing the silhouette of a woman across the room.

Dear God, she's back!

Terror sweeps through her even as common sense attempts to remind her that it's impossible. She can't come back, because—

With a burst of clarity, Jaycee realizes it's just the silhouette of her long blond wig sitting atop the tall bureau across the room, draped over its wig form.

Of course it is.

And of course she can't come back, because she's dead, because . . .

Because I killed her.

With a shudder, Jaycee pulls the pillow over her head, desperate to escape into a deep, blessed sleep, where the nightmare—the one that continues to haunt her waking hours—can't reach her.

Standing in front of her classroom filled with first graders, Elena writes the name of today's dinosaur on the board, sounding out the syllables as she goes.

"Steg . . ."

"Steg," her students echo.

"O . . ."

"O."

"Saur . . ."

"Saur," they say—well, eighteen of them do.

The nineteenth, Michael Patterson, shouts, "Ms. Ferreira! Ms. Ferreira! Your computer just dinged!"

"Thank you, Michael. Come on, people. Saur . . ."

"Saur . . ."

"We already said that one!" Michael protests.

Elena clenches the whiteboard marker in her hand. *"You* didn't say it. Join us, Michael. Saur . . ."

"Saur . . ."

"Us."

"Us."

"Stegosaurus! That is our dinosaur of the day, boys and girls. Can anyone tell me—"

"Ms. Ferreira! Your computer! It's dinging again!"

God, give me strength, she prays silently, *to deal with this kid for another . . .*

She glances at the big black and white wall clock. It's only a quarter after eight. The school day has barely begun.

Okay, God. I need strength for another six hours and forty-five minutes.

Wait a minute—today isn't an ordinary day. There's a staff meeting after school, followed by Activities night, when her first graders return with their parents to tour the classroom display of their culminating projects and present a musical skit. She won't be free to make the half-hour drive home until well after nine o'clock.

And after that she'll still have to get through seven more days before summer vacation begins.

Well—two more full ones after this. Beginning on Monday, they have a week of half days before the school year trudges to an end at last.

It's not that her current students are such a bad bunch of kids. For the most part they've been spirited, avid learners. Over her decade of teaching in this small Massachusetts town, Elena has only had one—maybe two—groups where the challenging kids outnumbered the pleasures. But the long Memorial Day weekend—a cruel teaser of a break, she has often thought—always marks the beginning of the end. Everyone is fidgety and no one feels like being in school for almost another month. Especially when the gray chill of New England spring gives way to warm, sunny days that create restlessness in the kids and a greenhouse effect in the un-air-conditioned classroom.

Elena's computer, on the carrel by the window, sounds another alert. Darn. Someone is trying to instant-message her. That's not unusual—just distracting. She usually keeps the volume muted while she's teaching, but she turned it on this morning before the students arrived and forgot to turn it off again. Her friend had sent her one of those funny You-Tube videos in an e-mail—one that was totally inappropriate to watch in an elementary school classroom, with or without the kids present—but it's June. Everyone at Northmeadow Elementary School is slacking off. Even the teachers.

"Ms. Ferreira! Your computer just—"

"Thank you, Michael. Right now we are not worrying about my computer. We are worrying about the stegosaurus. Or are we? Does anyone know whether the stegosaurus would want to eat us if we ran into one? Would we have to worry about that? Raise your hand if you know."

"We can't run into one," Michael blurts as several others raise their hands, "because humans and dinosaurs can't be alive at the same time! Dinosaurs have been dead for sixty-five million years!"

The kid is smart as a whip. If he weren't so darned disruptive, she'd be more willing to appreciate his intelligence.

With a sigh, she agrees that humans and dinosaurs did not coexist. "But if they *did*," she adds patiently, "humans would have nothing to fear from stegosauruses because they're herbivores. Raise your hands, please . . . who knows what an herbivore is?"

Naturally, Michael does. After defining herbivore—without raising his hand—he asks if she's going to check her computer.

"Not right now," Elena tells him, the patient smile straining her cheek muscles.

Just six hours and forty-four minutes . . .

And then just seven more days . . .

The moment Kay Collier sees the message pop up on her computer screen, she knows what it must be about.

Meredith.

She's been sitting here thinking about Meredith in her small home office off the kitchen ever since she got back from her rainy morning walk a little while ago. That's when she got online and spotted the blog entry written by Meredith's daughter.

A china teacup filled with jasmine tea has long since grown cold beside her keyboard as she struggled with how—and whether—to post a comment in response. No words of comfort she's conjured so far seem even remotely appropriate for such an overwhelming tragedy.

But BamaBelle's brief query demands nothing more than a simple, *Yes, I'm here.*

After Kay types the three words and hits Send, there's a long pause, as if Bama is trying to figure out how to word the tragic message she needs to deliver.

Sparing her the ordeal, Kay writes, *Terrible news. You saw?*

This time, the answer is instantaneous. *Yes. So upset.*

Me too. What the hell happened?

Then, realizing she might have just offended BamaBelle, one of the more ladylike members of the blogger network, she adds, *Sorry. Pardon my French. I just—*

Bama's response pops up before she can finish. *I didn't know she was sick again. Did you?*

No clue. Guess she didn't want anyone to know.

Feel so helpless.

Me too. Have you talked to anyone else?

No. You?

No.

Kay stares glumly into space, trying to think of something else to say.

Grandmotherly Meredith was everybody's friend, the heart and soul of their online group. She was always there when you needed her, the first to pop up with a comforting word or a virtual hug—indicated by multiple parentheses around a person's name.

((((((((((((Kay))))))))))))) was the last thing Meredith ever wrote to her, in final response to a heartfelt private message exchange just last week.

She sounded normal in the post she wrote Saturday about gardening, she writes now to BamaBelle. *Did you read that?*

Yes. That's why I'm so freaked out.

Me too.

Kay pauses. Waits.

BamaBelle, too, seems to have run out of things to say.

Kay types, *GTG.*

Shorthand for *got to go.*

NP is the response; shorthand for *no problem.*

That's the nice thing about these online friendships. You pop in and out of each other's lives with much less ado than in real life. There's no obligation to provide detailed explanations about why you're coming and going.

IM me if you find out anything, Bama writes. *Or call if you want to talk. I'll give you my number.*

Kay responds to Bama's offering with her own cell number, but she's not sure how she feels about that, because . . . because . . .

Because the walls are coming down.

Until now she's felt so safe with these Internet friendships. When you're shy and accustomed to maintaining your privacy, there's a certain comfort to keeping people at arm's length—in real life, anyway.

Now that her mother is gone and her old schoolmates and neighbors have moved away or moved on, caught up in lives of their own, there are no real life friends. There are no longer even colleagues: she was laid off from her job as a guard at the federal prison in Terre Haute a few years ago, thanks to budget cuts.

Kay spends most of her time alone, unless you count people she's never even met in person.

Her online friends are her family. The only people in the world she cares about; the only ones who care about her.

A final message pops onto her screen from Bama: *I wish we all lived in the same town so that we could help each other through this.*

Me too, Kay replies automatically, though she doesn't really wish that . . . does she?

The bloggers have had an ongoing discussion about getting together in person sometime. Recently, someone suggested organizing a meeting to coincide with breast cancer awareness month in October, or joining forces for one of the Making Strides walks around the country, or for a march in Washington, D.C.

Kay isn't sure whether to be disappointed or relieved that it's never managed to get beyond the wishful thinking stage.

In real life relationships, there's always pressure.

If her online friends met her in person, they might expect her to be something she isn't. Or they might turn out to be something she doesn't want them to be.

Then I'd lose everything.

That can't happen. It's too special—sometimes it's the only thing that keeps her going. She loves these people and she needs them, now more than ever . . .

She pushes back her chair, stands, and gets halfway across the room before pausing to straighten a framed photo that doesn't really need straightening.

It's an old black and white portrait showing her parents on their wedding day, circa 1962. They were together two decades before Kay was born, then separated before her first birthday.

Her mother never forgave her for that; or for being born—which was, after all, the reason he left.

Mother never came right out and said her conception had been an accident, or that they hadn't wanted children, or that it was Kay's fault the love of her life had walked out, leaving her a struggling single mother.

She didn't have to say it.

It was obvious from the way her mother looked at her, the way she treated her, the way she cried over old photos of him . . .

Especially this one.

In it, her parents are standing on the steps of a church that used to sit a few miles from this house where Kay has lived all her life, in the western suburbs of Indianapolis. She remembers when the church was torn down, about ten years ago, maybe fifteen, to make way for a now-defunct shopping plaza. Yes, at least fifteen years ago, because Mother was still alive, she had recently been diagnosed with cancer, the *Indianapolis News* was still the evening paper, and business was still booming in this neighborhood.

Mother tore out the short article with its side-by-side black and white photos—before and after, from brick church to pile of rubble—and showed it to Kay.

"This is where Daddy and I were married," she said, as if Kay didn't know; as if that man had actually been a "daddy" to her.

As old age and illness got the best of her, Mother was increasingly delusional.

"I always thought I'd have my funeral there," she said wistfully. "Now where will it be?"

"Please don't talk about that, Mother."

"I have to talk about it. It's not that far off, you know."

Yes. Kay knew.

She stares at the picture of her parents on their wedding day over fifty years ago, looking into each other's eyes with blatant adoration. Her mother, in dark lipstick and a puffy veil, and her father, in a dark suit with a skinny tie, are obviously madly in love.

The photo sat upstairs, framed on her mother's bedside table, until the day she died.

All her life, Kay had hated looking at it. Yet when the time came, she couldn't bear to throw it away.

Maybe it was better to hang onto it, she decided, as a reminder never to get too close to any man. You'd only end up alone and brokenhearted.

"The old saying is wrong. It's not better to have loved and lost," her mother used to rasp in her cigarette voice. "Believe me. If you don't love, you can't lose."

Kay took those words to heart. In her formative years, she had casual friendships, even a date here and there . . . but managed to avoid the risks that come with real relationships. Now, when she wants companionship, she finds it online, and when she needs a creative outlet, she posts entries on her blog.

That's how she met Meredith and BamaBelle and the others—how many years has it been now?

She used to be able to keep track of things like that. But a lot of details about the past have become fuzzy lately.

Too bad she can't choose which memories to keep and which to let go. There are a few that persist in haunting her waking hours and dreams, and she'd give anything to banish them forever.

You left me! Why did you leave me?

I didn't leave you, Mother! I've been right here by your bed!

Kay turns away from the photo and leaves the room.

Even with the windows closed, there's a depressing chill in the air this morning, just as there was on the gloomy spring morning her mother died. Now, as then, the house is filled with rainy day shadows.

Kay forces herself to turn on lights to brighten the rooms as she goes downstairs. Meredith, a true believer in the physical healing benefits of an optimistic attitude, frequently wrote about surrounding yourself with positive energy.

In the dining room, Kay stops and turns on the old tabletop radio, tuned to the upbeat oldies station. Meredith wouldn't want her to wallow in the gloom.

After flooding the kitchen with overhead light, she dumps her cold tea into the sink and turns on the flame to heat water for a fresh cup.

Waiting for it to boil, she reaches for the orange prescription bottle on the windowsill and shakes out the pill she takes daily to keep cancer at bay.

Meredith, whose cancer, like Kay's, was hormone fed, was on the same chemical regimen. They used to compare notes. She never dreamed the drug had stopped working for her friend until Meredith shared the news with her privately not long ago. Her cancer was back, Meredith told her, and spreading. Her days were numbered.

Kay was stunned. She knew her upbeat friend had her share of problems. Meredith had written blog entries about her husband's job loss, about never having enough money, that sort of thing. She always made light of her troubles. But this, she'd kept to herself.

Please don't tell the others, Meredith wrote to her. *I'm going to reach out to them one by one, here and there . . . but I'm not comfortable sharing with everyone just yet.*

I won't say anything. I promise.

Kay kept her word. She didn't tell, and she won't tell, not even now that Meredith is gone. Not even if it means lying, the way she did just now when she was messaging with BamaBelle.

She turns on the faucet and lets the water run, a lifelong habit.

"You never know what's lying around in these old pipes," Mother used to say when she was a little girl. "Don't take a drink from the tap until you've washed it all away."

"Washed all what away?"

"You know. The toxins."

Kay wrote a blog about that once. About Mother, perpetually veiled in a cloud of cigarette smoke, wasting time worrying about negligible issues, devoting not nearly enough energy tending to the things that were actually within her control.

That post generated more comments than most; her online friends related to the irony.

Kay grabs a tall glass from the cupboard above the sink. She fills it, turns off the tap, and swallows the pill, along with a couple of ibuprofen.

She has a headache again. It happens a lot lately. In her

levelheaded moments she assumes it's probably just middle-aged eye strain, spending too much time on the computer. Maybe she needs a stronger prescription for her reading glasses.

But other times, paranoia and pessimism get the best of her and she's sure it's the cancer—that it's back, spreading tumors into her brain.

After all, the preventative medication didn't prevent cancer's death march through Meredith's body. It didn't work for Mother, either, during her own brief remission, or for Whoa Nellie or countless other bloggers who had lost their battles.

Why should it be any different for her?

But if the cancer ever does return, it's not going to ravage her until she draws her last anguished breath. No, she'll put an end to it before that can ever happen. She has the means, tucked away upstairs in her nightstand drawer. It could all be over in a flash.

Please, please, let it have been that way for Meredith . . .

With a trembling hand, Kay sets the glass into the sink and goes back to glumly waiting for the teakettle to whistle.

The Day My Life Changed Forever

It was a Wednesday: August 24, 2005.

Rain was pouring down as I drove to the doctor's office after dropping the kids with a sitter. I was about to get the results from a routine biopsy that had been done after a routine mammogram showed something that was probably nothing, according to my doctor.

Probably was the key word there, but I wasn't really worried. Not even when they called me in to get the results in person.

I wasn't worried, either, when I heard on the car radio that the tropical depression out in the Atlantic had been upgraded to a tropical storm and named Katrina. I remember that the meteorologist reported that it would likely impact the Gulf later in the weekend, and that he had that breathless anticipation of a child discussing the prospects for a white Christmas.

Looking back, I'm struck that I paid so little attention to the forecast; that I failed to interpret the gloomy weather as a harbinger of catastrophe looming out on the water, much less inside the obstetrician's office.

—Excerpt from Landry's blog, *The Breast Cancer Diaries*

Chapter 3

During the height of her cancer battle, Landry learned that sometimes going through the motions of a normal day can almost convince you that you're living one.

So she forces herself to embark on her morning ritual: take a shower, get dressed, make the king-sized bed, and transfer the contents of the master bathroom hamper into a wicker basket.

With every task, she thinks about Meredith. What happened to her? How can she be dead?

She was so content with her life. It was obvious from every post she wrote that she loved every minute she had on earth.

So what wasn't she saying?

After her electronic conversation with A-Okay earlier, Landry had gone back through Meredith's blog posts for the past several months, trying to read between the lines. This time she thought she detected a bit more wistfulness than usual; perhaps a melancholy undercurrent here and there . . .

Maybe she was just seeing what she needs to see, though, in her retrospective search for rhyme and reason.

A-Okay didn't have any details, either, and Landry couldn't get a response from the other two bloggers she'd tried to reach.

Jaycee, who writes *PC BC*, lives in New York City. Elena, whose blog bears the irreverent title *The Boobless Wonder*, is somewhere in New England—Rhode Island, maybe, or Massachusetts? Knowing it's an hour later on the east coast, Landry figures she must not have caught either of them before their workdays began. Elena is an elementary schoolteacher, while Jaycee . . .

What does Jaycee do, anyway?

Some kind of business—maybe finance? She travels a lot, Landry knows. But Jaycee doesn't spend much time writing about her personal life on her blog, and was the only one of the regulars who didn't write a post about the day she received her initial diagnosis when they all decided to share their stories a few months back. She doesn't even post a head shot on her page, just a pink ribbon with a circle around it and a slash across it. As her blog title indicates—PC as in Politically Correct—she's one of the more politically aware bloggers, concerned with what she calls the Cancer Industry rather than day-to-day, postdiagnosis details. She's only been around for a year, maybe a year and a half.

Carrying the basket of dirty clothes, Landry makes her way along the upstairs hall, her mind settling on her children.

Just five minutes ago, it seems, they were toddlers: blond, blue-eyed Tucker the picture of his handsome daddy yet with his mama's laid back demeanor; Addison resembling Landry, with her delicate features, pale green eyes, and silky dark hair, but motivated and energetic as Rob from the moment she could walk and talk.

Now Addison is going to be a high school senior and Tucker a sophomore. Soon he'll be driving, and she'll be off to college. Life is careening along, a blessed string of ordinary—and extraordinary—days.

Addison's door is open. The white plantation shutters are parted so that sunlight splashes in through the windows. The quilt, in patterned shades of Caribbean sea foam, is neatly spread over the white iron bed, pillows plumped just so. A pile of magazines aligns at right angles with the edges of the nightstand, and the toiletries clustered on the bureau are precisely arranged as always. Stacked on an adjacent worktable are half a dozen compartmentalized plastic containers that hold the colored glass and metallic beads Addison uses to make jewelry.

Ambitious and goal oriented, with a lifelong flair for aesthetics, Landry's daughter is already certain about her future: she's planning to apply to Savannah College of Art and Design this fall, and intends to build a career in architectural or interior design.

For now, she works a few days a week in the gift shop over at the Grand Hotel. She's off Wednesdays, but she likes to get up early anyway—unlike her brother, who just started at the hotel as a summer busboy.

Across the hall, Tucker's door is still closed, but his alarm should be going off any minute. Not that he'll hear it.

Landry knocks on his door, then opens it a crack. "Tucker? It's almost time to get up."

No response. She crosses the shadowy room, stepping over piles of clothes on the floor, and opens the shutters. Daylight falls over the mess—not just clothes, but soda cans and snack wrappers on every surface, CDs and video games lying around without their cases, stray electronics cords and chargers tangled like heaps of black and white spaghetti on the desk and floor.

"Tucker?"

No movement from the lump beneath the covers. Only a few tufts of dark hair are visible between the quilt and the pillow.

"Tucker . . . "

"Tucker."

"TUCKER!"

Finally, a muffled sound from her son.

Balancing the laundry basket on her hip, Landry marches over to the bed and pulls the covers away from his face. "Come on. Up."

He throws a tanned, muscular arm across his eyes, and she notes the fuzz in his armpit and on his upper lip. Her little boy is becoming a man. A man who often acts like a little boy.

"Aw, come on, Mom," he rumbles. His voice changed months ago, but sometimes the low pitch still catches her off guard. "My alarm didn't even go off yet."

"It's about to. Get busy. This room is a mess. You have a lot to do before you leave. Get it? Got it? Good."

That's their thing: *Get it-got-it-good.* She and Tucker have been saying it to each other, usually to add a hint of lightheartedness to no-nonsense conversations, since he was a little boy. It used to make him laugh. Now he doesn't crack a smile.

She gives him another nudge and then another, waiting until his gigantic bare feet are squarely planted on the hardwood floor before heading downstairs.

The large living room is her favorite spot in the house. White woodwork contrasts with wide-board hardwoods and walls painted a muted, mossy shade of grayish green. Couches and chairs with cushy upholstery in soothing earth tones are clustered into several seating areas: near the fireplace, facing the flat screen television, and in a cozy nook lined with bookshelves. Paned glass windows and doors line the back wall, opening onto the lower level of the double-decker porch overlooking the landscaped yard and, beyond, the hundred-year-old boardwalk and the bay.

Landry crosses into the dining room, passing the formal table they use only on holidays and the built-in cabinets holding china that's been in her family for over a century.

On the wall is a gallery of family photos. Some are vintage shots of ancestors who settled around Mobile before the Civil War. Others are more recent: hers and Rob's wedding day, the kids' baby pictures, toddler and elementary school shots, a couple of family portraits. The four of them with her parents—one of the last snapshots before her father's fatal heart attack a few years back. The four of them with Rob's parents, his brother Will, and his sister Mary Leigh and her husband at their Christmas destination wedding in the Caribbean.

Landry doesn't like to look at that one. In it, her smile is forced. So is Rob's, and the kids', too. Not just because they were all jet-lagged after flight delays, or because no one wanted to spend the holidays away from home, or because they weren't crazy about Mary Leigh's new husband, Wade—but because breast cancer had struck just a few months earlier.

At the time, she was miserable and terrified, and so were her husband and children.

She really should take down that picture. Maybe some of the others as well. Make room for new memories. Happier ones.

Landry continues on into the kitchen, with its custom-built cherry cabinetry, sleek stainless steel appliances, and slate floor. They had just finished remodeling it when she was first diagnosed, and one of the first things that popped into her head in the doctor's office that day was that after all the renovation stress, she wouldn't be around to enjoy the new space.

We probably shouldn't have wasted all that extra money on the gourmet six-burner stove and double ovens, she'd thought, since no one else in the family even cooks.

She kept that regret to herself, of course, not wanting the doctor to think she was shallow.

When she later blogged about it—about the crazy thoughts that run through your mind in those first few moments when you assume you're going to be dying of, and not living with, or after, cancer—she found out that she wasn't alone.

Her online friends shared similar initial reactions to their diagnoses. One confessed that she was irrationally concerned about having just booked a nonrefundable timeshare; another said she rushed to cancel an expensive salon treatment, saying it felt wrong to waste time and money on hair that was just going to fall out anyway.

Though Landry had long since forgiven herself for fretting about her fancy appliances in the wake of the doctor's bombshell, it made her feel better to know that she wasn't alone.

It always does, doesn't it?

Yes. It helps to know there's someone out there who can say, "I know exactly what you mean!" or "Wow, you too? I thought I was the only one!"

So often, Meredith was that person, and now . . .

" 'Morning, Mom." Landry's firstborn is sitting on a stool at the granite-topped breakfast bar, eating a container of Greek yogurt in front of her open laptop.

" 'Morning," she returns, finding comfort in the sight of her daughter. Addison is just a kid, but there's always something reassuring about her presence in a room.

"She's an old soul," Landry's friend Everly likes to say. When her marriage ended, she developed a fascination with New Age philosophy. Sometimes—like with her observations about Addison—her groovy insight feels dead on. Other times it's out there. Waaaay out there.

Addison's damp hair hangs long and loose, tucked behind her ears to reveal beadwork earrings that match her bracelet—all handmade, of course, by Addie herself. She's wearing a pair of cutoffs that bare her toned, tanned legs and a tank top that barely covers her taut midriff.

Oh, to be sixteen going on seventeen again. Oh, to look like that . . .

Again?

No. At that age, she might have had the same coloring, hairstyle, and build, but her daughter has a confident poise that she herself lacked. Addison is Rob, through and through.

Addie glances up from the computer screen, then takes a closer look at her mother's face, and immediately asks, "What's wrong?"

"Why?"

"You look upset. What happened?"

"I got some bad news this morning." Setting the laundry basket on the slate floor, she quickly explains about Meredith.

Addison digests the information, then reaches out to touch Landry's arm. "I'm sorry, Mom. I guess it doesn't help to hear that her suffering is over and she's in a better place?"

"No, it does . . . I just . . . I wish I'd known in the first place that she was suffering."

"Maybe she wasn't."

"Maybe not."

But she doesn't believe it. She's seen it happen among her online friends too many times to think that there's an easy way out.

"Meredith never even mentioned that she was sick again," she says, more to herself than to Addie.

"Really? Well, then, maybe she wasn't. Just because she'd *had* cancer doesn't mean she *died of* cancer. Maybe something else happened to her. A car accident, or a heart attack, or—" Addison cuts herself off abruptly. "Sorry. I guess that doesn't make it any better. But you said it seemed sudden, so . . . I don't know. I was just looking at it logically and thinking maybe it *was* sudden."

"You're right. I'm so used to assuming . . . you know. Cancer."

"I know. But so many people survive it, Mom. Look

at your grandma. She had it, was cured, and then died of old age."

"Meredith wasn't old enough for that. She'd just turned sixty. But her daughter did say . . ." She hesitates, trying to remember the wording of the post. "I think she said she was still in shock."

Seeing the troubled shadow cross her daughter's green eyes, Landry remembers that she's the adult here and Addie's just a kid, old soul or not.

She abruptly changes the subject. "What are you going to do on your day off?"

"I'm not sure yet. Maybe I'll go shopping. I need a new bathing suit."

Ordinarily, Landry would offer to go along, but today she's not in the mood. Instead, she offers her credit card and use of the car, then carries her basket full of clothes toward the laundry room off the kitchen.

A few minutes later, as she's pouring detergent into the washing machine, Addison calls out urgently from the next room.

"Mom? You need to come in here. Hurry!"

Landry doesn't bother to start the washer, hurrying back to the kitchen to find her daughter still seated at the breakfast bar. The yogurt container is pushed aside on the counter and she's leaning over her laptop, delicately arched eyebrows furrowed as stares at the screen.

"You said your friend's name is Meredith and she lives in Cincinnati, right?"

"That's right. Why?"

"I plugged that and her age into Google—is her last name Heywood?"

"Heywood. With an e. Yes. Why?" she asks again, already leaning in to look over her daughter's shoulder.

"This is from a Cincinnati newspaper. It was just posted. I'm . . . I'm really sorry, Mom."

Addison points at a headline.

Landry stares.

LOCAL WOMAN MURDERED IN APPARENT
HOME INVASION

"Is that . . . is that—" She can't seem to get the words out.

Addison points mutely at name in the lead paragraph.

Meredith Heywood.

"Dad?"

When her father, sprawled in the leather recliner where he spent the night, doesn't turn around, Rebecca Heywood Drover crosses into the den and reaches out to gently touch his shoulder.

He jumps, and jerks his head to look at her with wide, red-rimmed eyes. "Beck! You scared the hell out of me."

Three days' worth of beard shadows Hank Heywood's lower face, and his brown hair has gone mostly gray since Beck saw him before all this—before he left to take care of Gram in Cleveland, before Mom . . .

"Sorry," she tells her father. "It's just . . . Detective Burns is here, with another detective. They want to talk to you."

He nods dully. "You can send them in here."

"You don't want to . . ." Beck trails off, trying to figure out how to put it delicately.

Pull yourself together isn't very delicate; nor is *make yourself presentable.*

If Mom were here, she'd make him shave and change out of the rumpled Miami University Red Hawks T-shirt he's slept in for the past couple of nights at the hotel—if he's slept at all.

Mom isn't here, though.

Mom will never be here again.

Beck still can't believe that she's gone.

Years ago, when her mother was first diagnosed with breast cancer, she'd imagined what it would be like to lose her. Even last year, when she had that recurrence, Beck had once again allowed herself to consider that her mother might not be around for years to come. Waiting for test results for days, weeks, she found herself imagining various excruciating scenarios.

But then the tests came back clear, and Mom had beaten the disease again, and the worry faded.

She'd been caught off guard when her father's cell phone number came up on her caller ID Sunday afternoon. She knew right away something was wrong. He was not the type to call just to chat.

"Beck," he said, "I'm still in Cleveland and I can't get ahold of your mother. Do you know where she is?"

"Nope. I talked to her Friday night, and she said she was going to putter around all weekend. She's probably outside or something."

"It's supposed to be pouring there. It has been here, all day."

"Here, too," Beck told him, glancing at the rain streaming down the windowpanes.

"I've been calling the house and her cell phone since this morning, and texting her, and e-mailing and IMing, too. She hasn't responded. That's not like her."

It wasn't. Mom may not always answer the house phone, but she's pretty reliable when it comes to online stuff. Ever since she started her blog, she's developed quite a reader following and made friends all over the world.

Beck found it ironic that the woman who didn't know a Web site from a campsite a few years ago now spends many—if not most—of her waking hours on the Internet.

Spends?

Spent.

Mom is gone.

Swallowing hard, she looks at her father and says,

"Maybe you should go in there and talk to the detectives. They're waiting in the living room, and . . ."

And I need to be alone for a second to pull myself together.

"Yeah. Okay."

She watches him push himself out of the chair and shuffle out into the hall, hunched over as if he's aged a couple of decades in as many days.

Beck sinks into the seat he vacated and buries her head in her hands, wishing her older brothers were here to help her deal with this.

But they finally returned to their respective homes to sleep last night, after spending both Sunday and Monday nights at the nearby hotel where the family was holed up while the house was off-limits as a crime scene investigation.

The police released it late yesterday.

The last thing any of them wanted to do was walk through the door into the house where Mom had been killed, but they knew they'd have to do it sooner or later. No one could spare the money for more nights in a hotel, and Dad didn't want to leave town to come stay at one of their houses in the midst of all this.

So they came back here and did their best to clean up the disorder left in the wake of the investigation.

No one had opened the master bedroom door and gone in. A professional cleanup crew had been in there, and the man in charge came to the hotel to assure Dad—delicately—that the room was now "fine." Dad just looked at him, and shook his head. For all he cared—for all any of them did—that door could stay closed for as long as the house remained in their possession.

Beck and her brothers have privately discussed the situation and agreed that Dad will have to sell it as soon as possible. It's not what Mom would have wanted, but she had no way of knowing what would happen to her here.

Last night they sat glumly around the kitchen table, trying to make memorial service arrangements while choking down a meal prepared by a well-meaning neighbor. Neal and Teddy took turns taking repeated phone calls from their wives.

"You guys should go home tonight and be with your families," Beck urged them afterward, as they all did the dishes. "I'll stay here with Dad."

She knew it was the right thing to say. Her brothers both have kids, and Teddy's wife is pregnant. Unemployed, he had a promising job interview lined up for yesterday. Mom would have been so upset that he'd missed it. She worried about all of them, but lately, especially about Teddy, with a baby on the way and no medical benefits.

Beck's brothers took her up on the offer to go home, promising to be back first thing this morning. Of course, they assumed that her husband, Keith, would remain here with her and Dad.

But he drove back home to Lexington not long after her brothers left, saying he needed to go check on the house, get the mail and papers, and should stop in at the office today to make sure things had been running smoothly in his two-day absence.

He's on the research faculty at the university. One summer session just ended and the next is about to begin, but things are relatively quiet at this time of year. Beck works on campus herself, as a lab technician.

"You really don't have go to check in at the office," she told Keith. "They don't expect you to do that in the middle of a family crisis. You can call in and check your e-mail from here. And the neighbors can keep grabbing our mail and newspapers and they'll keep an eye on the house for a few more days."

"It's less than a hundred miles away. I'll be back here tomorrow night."

"Why leave at all?"

"Because I have to," Keith said tightly.

"No. Because you *want* to."

Dad, still sitting at the table with them, barely seemed aware of the discussion, and hopefully didn't see the look Beck shot Keith when he pushed back his chair and ended the conversation with a curt, "I'm sorry, but I have to go."

"Fine," she said. "Go."

She did get up and walk with him to the door, but only because her father might have noticed if she didn't. The last thing she wants right now is to let him know that her marriage is in serious trouble and has been for months. Grief-stricken and devastated, facing life as a widower, Dad doesn't need anything else to worry about.

Anyway, who knows? Maybe, when this is all behind them, she and Keith will manage to work things out.

Maybe he'll have a change of heart or change his ways; or maybe she's been wrong about him, about what he's been up to behind her back . . .

But probably not.

Mom always liked to say, *if it looks like a duck and it walks like a duck—*

"Ms. Heywood?" Detective Burns, an attractive, middle-aged African-American woman, is standing in the doorway.

Technically, Beck is Mrs. Drover, not Ms. Heywood, but then . . . maybe not for much longer. Without bothering to correct the detective, she says, "Yes?"

"I just wanted to make sure you stick around. And you said your brothers are on their way back here now?"

"Yes."

"We're going to need to talk to all of you again, too, after we speak to your father. And the rest of the family as well."

Something in the woman's tone makes Beck look more closely at her face. When they first met, on Sunday, she seemed much kinder, more sympathetic—although her memory is admittedly fuzzy.

That was such a terrible, terrifying time.

She was the one who'd called the police.

After talking to her father and then also trying unsuccessfully to reach her mother, she got into her car and drove through the rain up to Cincinnati, arriving at the house in the late afternoon. All was quiet. Mom's car was in the driveway.

As soon as she walked around back, intending to let herself in with her key, she found the cut window screen and knew something was terribly wrong.

She has very little recollection of the two uniformed cops who showed up. It's all a blur now, like a nightmare after you wake up in the morning, when the specific details have faded but you still remember the horror, and the gist of what happened.

What happened . . .

What happened was—

After she handed over her set of keys, the police officers went into the house, and she stood there waiting beneath the overhang above the back door as the rain poured down, drowning the newly planted seedlings in the vegetable garden in the yard.

Then the police came back out and they told her—

"Ms. Heywood?"

"Yes." She blinks, looks up at Detective Burns. "Yes, it's fine. I'll . . . I'll be happy to talk to you. No problem."

"Thank you."

Beck gets up and starts to follow the detective into the next room, but the woman holds out her hand like a traffic cop.

"Not yet," she says. "If you can wait right here while we talk to your father, I'd appreciate it."

"But—"

Wait a minute. Are the detectives here to *talk* to them, or *interrogate* them?

When they showed up today, she assumed it was with an update on the case. They've been in close contact ever since Sunday, regularly coming and going from the hotel where the family was staying. They promised to keep them apprised of any developments; to find out who had broken into the house sometime late Saturday night or early Sunday morning and left Mom dead on the floor beside her bed.

Do they have a suspect now?

Or do they think—

The terrible thought fully forms in Beck's mind. She bites her lip to keep from blurting it out.

"Is there a problem, Ms. Heywood?"

"No. No problem." She shrinks back. "I'm sorry. I misunderstood.. I thought you wanted me to— Never mind. I'll wait here."

"Thank you."

The detective steps out of the den, reaches back and pulls the door closed after her.

Feeling like a caged prisoner, Beck wonders if she should call her brothers—or, perhaps, a lawyer.

She's watched enough television crime shows to know that homicide investigators always look closely at family members—particularly spouses. Why didn't she realize sooner that this was going to happen?

Because you're still in shock, and because it's ridiculous that anyone would even imagine that Dad might be capable of . . .

She pushes away an unwanted memory.

Ridiculous.

Anyway, Dad was 250 miles away this weekend—they must know he was in Cleveland when it happened.

Or maybe they don't know. Maybe that's why they're here now.

They were here on Sunday, but maybe they arrived on the scene after Dad did.

She thinks back, but the timeline is fuzzy. Her father was on his way back from Cleveland, she remembers, before she even left Lexington. When she called him from her car as she was driving up to Cincinnati, he said he was on the road, too, heading home to check on Mom.

She told him not to bother; that she was already going; that she'd let him know if there was any reason to worry—

But of course there was already reason to worry.

Did she begin to suspect then, as she raced north up Interstate 75, that something was going to be terribly wrong at the house?

The drive, like everything that happened afterward, has become a blur in her mind.

She'd just had yet another fight with Keith. That, she remembers.

He wasn't thrilled that she was leaving so abruptly in the middle of a Sunday afternoon when they had plans that evening to sit down and go over their finances.

That was what he claimed, anyway, calling it "a meeting." The year was almost half over, he'd said that morning, and he was concerned about his job stability amid funding cuts to the university. He thought it was time that they made some decisions about their future; about whether they should look into selling the house, moving into a smaller place . . .

Or separate places.

He didn't come right out and say it, but she knew it was going to come up. It wouldn't be the first time. But it might have been the first time she might be willing to go along with it. She'd already done her homework, talked to a lawyer.

Her feelings were muddled. One moment she was sure she still loved him, and the next, she wanted him out of her life.

Sunday afternoon, as she threw some things into a bag in case she wound up spending the night in Cincinnati, he followed her around the house asking why she couldn't have someone else check in on her mother—a neighbor, or one of her brothers.

"Because I can get there quicker than my brothers can, and I can't reach any of their neighbors," she lied.

The truth was, she wanted to go.

Not—to her shame, in retrospect—just because she was worried about Mom.

Of course she was, but she really didn't think, at that point, the situation was going to be dire. She was mainly going because she wanted to get away from Keith for a few hours. She thought the drive might bring some clarity.

"But what about our meeting?" he asked as she picked up her keys and, with the bag over her shoulder, opened the door.

"It'll have to wait till I get back."

"When will that be?"

She didn't answer him, just splashed through the driveway puddles to the car and drove away.

The next time they spoke, she was calling him, hysterical, to tell him that her mother had been murdered. To his credit, he made the ninety-minute trip in less than an hour and stayed by her side until last night.

Now he's home, ostensibly checking on mail and work—but more likely on his mistress.

Meanwhile, the homicide detectives are talking to Dad, and they want to talk to her, and again the unwanted memory is trying to barge in, but she won't let it; no, she won't let it, because . . .

Because it means nothing.

Absolutely nothing.

Relax.

No one is ever going to know the truth.

And even if they do figure it out—that Meredith's murder wasn't some random home invasion gone bad—they'll never in a million years suspect that you, of all people, had anything to do with it.

At first—in the wee hours of Sunday morning—those self-assurances brought a measure of comfort.

But in the three days since, it's been increasingly hard to remain convinced that everything is going to be okay.

You dismiss one nagging *what if*—what if my finger-prints somehow came through the gloves?—only to have another pop up.

And then another.

What if . . . ?

What if . . . ?

Sleep has been all but impossible; interminable nights spent tossing and turning as fresh waves of worry seep in.

And for what? Every detail of Saturday night was well-planned in advance.

Okay—not that far in advance.

The spark of an idea ignited a while back, but opportunity to act on it didn't present itself until about ten days ago, Memorial Day weekend, when a senile ninety-three-year-old woman happened to take a nasty fall in Cleveland.

It was Meredith herself who set things in motion by blogging about how her husband had gone up to his hometown to take care of his aging mother. The whole world now knew she was alone in the house every night for the foreseeable future.

Maybe not the whole world—but anyone who happened to stumble across her blog online.

You didn't have to be a seasoned detective to figure out where she lived. Anyone could piece together the personal details she'd posted in her official bio and scattered through-out her blog archives.

It's not inconceivable that someone—some stranger—might have done just that. Not inconceivable that the evil predator might have slipped into the house in the dead of night with nothing more than robbery on his mind.

The house, after all, was found ransacked.

Some valuables were missing.

One thing was left behind—for good luck.

But no one is going to notice that, in the grand scheme of things.

And Meredith—Meredith's body was left crumpled on the floor, as if she'd gotten up to investigate a noise and surprised a prowler.

Right. It all makes perfect sense. The police are looking for a prowler, a predator, a stranger . . .

Not for you.

No one would ever in a million years guess that it was you. All you have to do is be smart and stay quiet—but not too quiet—until the whole thing blows over.

Strength Training

Battling cancer demands a certain level of forti-
tude. Not just physical stamina to endure symptoms
and treatments, but inner strength to handle the shit
storm of emotions that come your way. Getting a
cancer diagnosis is like being asked to go, overnight,
from couch potato to the Olympics. No, not asked—
told. Because really, what choice do you have?

Your only option—unless you have a freaking
death wish—is to fight. And fighting takes strength.
Physical strength, yes—and you supposedly build that
by taking vitamins, getting plenty of rest, exercising,
and eating that crap otherwise known as health food.
But emotional strength is just as important. How do
you build that? Through daily challenges that include
not just fighting back tears, but also counting your
blessings, living in the moment, taking small setbacks
in stride . . .

— Excerpt from Elena's blog, *The Boobless Wonder*

Chapter 4

Landry's cell phone rings as she again paces the length of the master bedroom with it in her hand.

It's about time.

Over an hour has passed since she e-mailed her number, along with a link to the Cincinnati newspaper article— LOCAL WOMAN MURDERED IN APPARENT HOME INVA-SION—to the three remaining online friends with whom she communicates most regularly: Elena, Jaycee, and A-Okay.

She also tried to call A-Okay at the number she'd provided earlier, but there was no answer; it went right into an automated voice-mail recording. She hung up without leaving a message. Now, looking at the caller ID to see which of the bloggers is calling back, she sees a 310 area code. That, she knows, is Los Angeles.

Guess it's not one of my online friends after all.

"Hello?"

A vaguely familiar voice says, "Hi. I'm looking for . . . BamaBelle? Is this you?"

"It's me. Who is this?"

"It's Jaycee. You know—*PC BC*. Hi."

"Oh! Hi. I'm—I guess I should tell you my name. It's Landry."

"Landry? First, or last?"

"First. It's Landry Wells."

"That's pretty. And unusual."

She quickly explains that Landry was her mother's maiden name; that last names as first are a southern tradition.

"I love that," Jaycee tells her. "Did you follow it when you had your own kids?"

"Well, my own maiden name is Quackenbush, so . . ."

"No?" Jaycee laughs. "At least, I hope not."

"Well, my husband used to joke that we could always call them Quack or Bush for short, but in the end we went with names from his side of the family," Landry tells her.

Then her smile fades as she remembers the reason for the call, and she turns the subject to Meredith.

"I don't even know what to say," Jaycee tells her. "I'm shocked. This is horrible."

As she talks on, Landry tries to focus on what she's saying and not on why her voice had initially sounded so familiar. It's low-pitched, with a distinct, husky note, and her words come at a measured cadence not very typical of New Yorkers. Not the ones Landry had known in college, anyway. She always had trouble decoding their rapid-fire speech and accents. Jaycee doesn't even have one.

She mentions that she's away on a business trip and just woke up a few minutes ago, so she wasn't available when Landry was trying to IM her earlier.

"I'm just so stunned and sick about this. It was a robbery?"

"That's what it sounds like. All I know is what's in the newspaper. Someone must have broken in, and she must have woken up and confronted whoever it was."

"She must have been so scared."

"I know." Landry shudders at the thought of the terror Meredith endured in her last moments alive. It happened late last Saturday night or early Sunday morning, while Landry and Rob were at a charity ball in Mobile with some of his colleagues.

To think that at the very moment Landry was blissfully sipping champagne or spinning around the dance floor in her husband's arms, Meredith was—

"Have you been in touch with anyone else yet?" Jaycee's question shatters the macabre vision taking shape in her brain.

"I chatted online with A-Okay . . . that sounds weird, doesn't it?"

"What does?"

"To refer to someone only by her screen name. But I don't even know what her real name is, do you?"

"No. And by the way, I know I shouldn't be saying it at a time like this, but your accent is so sweet."

Taken aback by the abrupt shift, Landry says, "Well, thank you—I guess?"

"Oh, I meant it as a compliment for sure. I love southern drawls. Somehow it never occurred to me that you must have one, but of course it makes sense. You live in Alabama, right?"

"I sure do. And since you brought it up . . . I guess I'll admit that I thought you would sound more like a New Yorker."

"Yeah, well, I usually *tawk* like *dis*," Jaycee replies with an exaggerated tough guy accent, "but I didn't wanna, ya know, scare you *awf*."

For the first time today, Landry laughs. "So what are you doing in L.A.?"

There's a pause. "Did I mention I was in L.A.?"

"I think—no, you said you were away," she remembers, "but I knew it was L.A. because of the 310 area code. I saw it on caller ID."

"Oh. Right. Well, I'm calling from the phone in my hotel room, so . . ." Jaycee clears her throat. "Actually, you know what? This is probably costing a fortune, and it's on my company's bill, so . . . I should hang up."

"Do you want me to call you back there from my phone? Or do you have a cell?"

"I do, but—what time is it? Oh, wow—I have a meeting to get to anyway. Let's talk later, okay?"

"Sure. Do you want to give me your cell number?" She looks around for something to write on, and with, coming up with an old grocery receipt and a Sharpie.

Jaycee gives the number, then hurriedly hangs up after asking Landry to keep her posted if she hears anything else.

She didn't even have a chance to get Jaycee's last name or home phone number, or bring up the prospect of going to Meredith's funeral.

That's something that occurred to her earlier, when she was talking to Addison in the kitchen. Her daughter asked if she was going, and wanted to know why not when she said she probably wouldn't.

"Because I have you and your brother to take care of, and—"

"Please, Mom, we're old enough to take care of ourselves! Dad's always going away on business and on those golf weekends with Grandpa and Uncle Will and Uncle Wade. Why shouldn't you go away, too, for once in your life?"

"I don't know . . . I've never met Meredith's family—I haven't even met *her*. I might feel like I was intruding."

"That's crazy. It's a funeral, not some party y'all are crashing."

True.

But the thought of confronting this loss head-on, in person, doesn't sit well with her . . .

Which is precisely why she should force herself to do it.

Strength training, as Elena likes to call it.

This isn't about herself, though. It's about Meredith. About paying respects to a friend who met a tragic, violent death.

If something happened to me, Meredith is the type who'd rally the troops and come down here to see how she could help Rob and the kids. I owe her the same.

By the time Jaycee called her, she had decided it would be a good idea if they all went. Together. For Meredith. She was going to ask how Jaycee felt about it, but Jaycee was in such a hurry to get off the phone . . .

That was strange. One minute she was kidding around, the next she was abruptly ending the call. Why?

Maybe because I asked her what she was doing in L.A.

Jaycee seemed taken aback that she knew where she was, almost as if . . .

Maybe she didn't want anyone to know.

But why not? What do I care where she travels on business?

Oh, well.

Maybe she's paranoid about sharing too much with someone she doesn't know very well. Maybe that's why she doesn't post a photo on her blog.

At least Landry now has a voice to go with Jaycee's name . . . a familiar one, at that. Jaycee definitely reminds her of someone. She just can't remember whom.

"Mom?"

Addison is in the doorway. She's changed into a corn-flower blue sundress and white sandals, sunglasses propped on her head and a purse over her shoulder. She's added a necklace of blue and silver beads that complement the neck-lace and earrings she put on earlier. As always, she looks perfectly put together in an easy-breezy way, so that you'd never guess everything she's wearing was carefully coordi-nated to create a very specific overall effect.

"I'm ready to go shopping. Can I have the car keys and . . ."

"Bathing suit money?" Landry smiles. "Sure. Come on downstairs and I'll find my purse."

About to shove her cell phone into a pocket, she realizes that the gym shorts she threw on earlier don't have one. The battery is running low anyway—and she's had enough, for now, of talking about Meredith's death. She plugs the phone into the charger near her side of the bed and walks downstairs with Addison.

"Did you figure out what you're going to do about your friend's funeral?" her daughter asks.

"The arrangements haven't been posted yet, but when they are, I'll send out a group e-mail to the other bloggers to see if they want to meet in Cincinnati."

"What if they don't want to?"

"What do you mean?"

"You're still going either way, right?"

Landry hesitates. The last thing she wants is to give her teenage daughter the impression that you should reconsider whether to do something just because your friends aren't doing it.

But it would be hard to go alone.

When was the last time she traveled far from home completely on her own?

The semester abroad she did back when she was an undergrad English major at the University of Alabama?

Those four months in London felt like a stepping-stone to a future spent traveling the world. But then it was over and she was back in Tuscaloosa, and the next thing she knew, that, too, was over. She graduated and found herself back at home, where she spent the summer sending out résumés for jobs in London, jobs in New York, Chicago, L.A. . . .

A few weeks later she met Rob, and almost simultaneously was hired as an assistant in a tiny PR firm in Mobile. She decided that everything she wanted and needed—for the time being, anyway—was right here.

"Mom?"

"Hmm?"

"You're going to Cincinnati, right?"

"Of course," she tells Addison. "Of course I'm going."

And somewhere in the back of her mind, a flicker of anticipation accompanies her apprehension.

"Hi, you've reached Landry Wells," drawls a pleasant, recorded voice. "Please leave a message and I'll get right back to you. Have a great day!"

Elena hesitates, then hangs up without leaving a message. By the time Landry returns the call, this brief lunch break will probably be over. Better to wait until she gets home tonight and try her back then.

She looks again at the headline on her computer screen, the one that made her heart pound when she first clicked on it. The kids were still in the classroom then, so she couldn't react. Now they're in the cafeteria, and the salad-filled Tupperware container she brought from home is sitting untouched on her desk.

LOCAL WOMAN MURDERED IN APPARENT
HOME INVASION

There isn't much detail in the article. It doesn't report how Meredith was killed or where she was in the house when it happened. Standard procedure, Elena guesses, to leave out certain details. It's an active police investigation. No mention of suspects, and anyone who can provide a lead is asked to call a special crime hotline.

"Elena?"

She looks up to see Tony Kerwin, the gym teacher—*again*. The guy manages to find his way into her classroom several times a day, and she's not exactly in the mood for him right now.

Really, she's *never* in the mood for Tony.

Ironic, because when he walked into the first staff meeting right after he was hired here last fall, she was immediately drawn to him. So was her friend Sidney, a fellow teacher and recent divorcée.

When Tony introduced himself, it turned out he was in his early thirties, like Elena. He had grown up south of Providence, just as she had—he was from Cranston, she from neighboring Warwick.

Over drinks after the meeting, Sidney mused, "The new gym teacher looks like what's his name—that hot actor who was in the movie we watched on cable last weekend . . ."

"Mark Wahlberg?"

"Yup. Do you think he's married?"

"Mark Wahlberg?" Elena chose to deliberately misunderstand the question, buying herself a moment to decide whether she wanted to admit to Sidney that she, too, found him attractive. If she did, Sidney would probably back off in her intended pursuit.

As a statuesque, slender blonde, Sidney has no shortage of dates and—to her credit—is well aware that men gravitate toward her instead of relatively short, curvy, brunette Elena when they're together.

"I don't care whether Mark Wahlberg is married!" Sidney said. "I'm talking about the new gym teacher."

"Nope. Not married—unless he is and he doesn't wear a ring."

"You looked?"

She grinned at Sidney over the rim of her pinot grigio glass. "Oh, I definitely looked."

With that comment, Elena knew, she'd sealed the unspoken deal. Sidney would let her have the first shot at Tony.

It's hard to remember, now, that there was a time when she thought of him as potential dating material . . . let alone that she actually went out with him.

Just once, back in September.

Once was all it took for her to realize that the guy was an

opinionated jackass. Sidney was welcome to him—except by then she didn't want him, either.

But he wanted Elena. He persisted in asking her out, so clueless that she finally resorted to inventing a fake boyfriend to get rid of him.

That was Meredith's advice; Elena had confided in her about the situation. Confided in her about almost everything, really.

Tell him that you're seeing someone else, Meredith wrote in an e-mail after Elena told her she couldn't shake Tony.

You want me to lie? I can't believe it! Elena wrote back teasingly. *And here I thought you were a fine moral character.*

Where did you get that idea? was the response, followed by ;-)—the Internet emoticon symbolizing a wink. *A little white lie never hurt anyone. Trust me.*

Meredith was right. It did the trick.

"I hope he makes you very happy," Tony said about her fictitious boyfriend, and every time she saw him after that—which was every single weekday—he'd give her a sappy, sad little smile and ask how things were going in her relationship.

It took him a few months to stop asking and stop sad-smiling. In February he overheard Elena asking Sidney if she wanted to go to a singles night, and he asked if she'd broken up with her boyfriend.

Forced to say yes, she braced herself for him to start asking her out again, but it turned out he was dating someone else by then—or so he claimed. Sidney thought he was just trying to make her jealous, ostensibly playing hard to get.

"Either that," she said, "or he's seriously delusional, because I can't imagine why anyone in her right mind would go out with him."

"I did."

"Once. And anyone would, once, because he's gorgeous."

The strange thing is, Elena barely notices the *gorgeous* anymore. It's too hard to see past the *desperate* and the *crazy*.

"What's up?" Elena asks him now, not in the mood for small talk.

"I got your note about the collection for a retirement gift for Betty Jamison."

"Mmm-hmm."

"I don't think it's fair to ask everyone on the staff to contribute the same amount. Some of us barely know this woman."

It's impossible for anyone to be employed at North-meadow Elementary for any length of time and not have regular contact with Betty Jamison, head secretary in the main office, and the most beloved person on the staff.

But Elena opts not to waste time saying any of that to Tony. "Just donate what you think is fair, then."

"That's the trouble. I don't want to come across as cheap if everyone else is donating more. What I think you might want to do is reword the memo so that . . ."

He drones on.

Elena's hand clenches around the computer mouse. She looks again at the computer screen, thinks again about Meredith.

Thinks of her lying there, lifeless.

She never knew what hit her.

The line fits, but the voice in Elena's head isn't referring to Meredith.

No, she's remembering what her father said to her uncle after her mother was killed. It happened twenty-five years ago, when she was an eavesdropping seven-year-old, but she remembers the conversation like it was yesterday.

Her father was repeating what the police had told him about the accident. Apparently, the signal at the railroad crossing had failed, so her mother had driven onto the tracks into the path of an oncoming train . . .

"She never knew what hit her. That's what they told me, Louie . . ."

"You gotta admit, Bobby—it's not the worst way to go," her uncle had said.

"What are you talking about?"

"No drawn-out suffering—not like Ma." The brothers had lost their mother, Elena's grandmother, not long before that. Cancer.

Of course, cancer. Always cancer . . .

Well, not always.

"Are you saying my wife was *lucky* to be hit by a friggin' *freight train*?" her father yelled at Uncle Louie.

"No! No, I just mean that if she didn't know what hit her . . . well, that was a blessing."

"I lost my wife! My kids lost their mother! You're saying that's a *blessing*?"

Pop threw Uncle Louie out of the house, and Elena listened to him sobbing, late into the night. She heard it that night, and every night thereafter, for a long time. Months. Maybe years.

They hardly saw Uncle Louie after that. She and her brother no longer got to visit anyone, not any of the aunts, uncles, or cousins. After spending the first seven years of her life surrounded by a close-knit family, Elena basically spent the rest of her childhood listening to her father cry, or watching him drink himself into a stupor while she took care of the house and her younger brother.

For years she forgot all about the argument she'd overheard between her father and her uncle after her mother's death.

She's forgotten a lot of things she's seen, and heard, and done over the years. She's always been good at that. If a painful memory tries to work its way into your consciousness, you learn to push it right back out before it can fully form.

But the decades-old family argument she'd overheard came barging into her brain out of the blue on the day she herself was diagnosed with breast cancer, and she was too shell-shocked to defend herself against it.

"I know it's a shock," her doctor was saying, "especially at your age."

Just thirty years old.

Yes, it was a shock.

She never knew what hit her . . .

The phrase landed in her head that day, and try as she might, she's never quite managed to get it out again.

Maybe because it resonates now. At last, she understands what her uncle was trying to say.

That if you have to die young—or die at all—maybe it's better that way. Better not to suffer, and linger, and waste away. Better not to fear a looming death for weeks, months. Better for it to be over with in a flash.

"What do you think?" Tony's voice reaches her, plucking her out of the past and depositing her, with a thud, into the present.

She blinks. "About what?"

"About putting this new policy into place for the next school year? No gifts. None at all. Not even cards. No more passing them around for everyone to sign, no more collecting for people's wedding showers and baby showers and retirements . . . no more. Done. Finito."

She stares at him, thinking about cancer. About Meredith. About her mother. About never knowing what hit you . . .

"Otherwise, where does it end, Elena? Elena?" Tony passes a beefy, hairy-knuckled hand in front of her face. "Are you even listening to me?"

"Sorry."

"Are you okay? I've noticed there are a lot of times when

you seem like . . . you know, the lights are on but nobody's home."

She clenches. "I . . . listen, I need a minute alone right now. And I'm fine. Okay?"

"Did you even hear what I said about the gift for—"

"I heard."

"Good. Just so we understand each other."

We will never understand each other, Elena thinks. Trust me.

Finally, she musters that fake smile. "Absolutely. See you, Tony."

Alone again in her classroom, she clicks on the *X* in the corner of the newspaper article onscreen, closing it out. Then she starts typing: P-I-N—

Thanks to her regular visits to the address, the full name of Meredith's blog pops up before she goes any farther: PINK STINKS.

She hits Enter and is transported to the home page.

After reading the post from Meredith's daughter, she scrolls back up to the top of the page and stares at the photo. In it, Meredith is smiling, looking as though she hasn't a care in the world.

Her last few posts were about her garden, about cooking healthy meals for just one person with her husband away, about a novel she was reading . . .

Not a hint of dread or sorrow; no clue that these were her last days on earth, no drawn-out good-byes, no pain and suffering.

Yes.

In the end—if there has to be an end—it really is better that way.

Hearing voices in the hall, Elena clicks the mouse again, and the screen goes black as her first-graders bound back into the room.

* * *

Slowly, Beck climbs the stairs to the second floor, thoughts spinning.

The detectives are still down there, now behind closed doors with her oldest brother, Teddy. Her middle brother, Neal, is on his way. Her sisters-in-law are scrambling to find child care because the police want to speak to them again, too.

And Keith—they've summoned Keith as well. He couldn't have been pleased.

Beck hasn't spoken to him directly, but he texted her to say that he's on his way back from Lexington to be interviewed again by the police.

Are there new developments?

Are they closing in on a suspect?

Is it . . .

Do they really think it's one of us?

Or do they just think someone knows something, or might remember something?

They asked so many questions.

Beck was careful to look them in the eye when she answered, not wanting them to suspect that she had anything to hide.

Because, of course, she doesn't.

None of them do.

Beck's hand is tight on the banister as she reaches the top of the stairway, greeted there by the closed master bedroom door.

What if the police don't believe them? What if they have to take lie detector tests or something?

If that happens, she might be so nervous she'll fail. Not because she's lying, but because . . .

Well, lying, and not revealing something you know—something no one has asked you about—that's not the same thing, is it?

Just a little while ago, you thought that it was, she reminds herself. *When they told you about Mom being sick again.*

It was the female detective who brought up her mother's illness, addressing Beck in a straightforward fashion that made her uncomfortable.

"Can you tell us about your mother's cancer treatment?"

"She'd had surgery, and then chemo and radiation. She went through that twice," Beck said, pretty sure they'd gone over this already, "and she's been back in remission since last year . . ."

At that, Detectives Burns and Schneider exchanged a glance, and that was when Beck realized.

Her first reaction was that Mom had lied.

Now that she's had some time to digest the information—and to compare it to her own situation, to the fact that she'd neglected to tell the police every single thing she knows about her father . . .

Well, it's not like I ever came right out and asked Mom if she was sick again.

If I had, and she'd told me she wasn't—well, that would have been a lie.

But I didn't ask her that, so she didn't tell me.

And today . . . the police didn't ask me certain things, and I didn't tell them.

That's not lying.

Protecting, maybe . . . but not lying.

Beck cried when the detectives informed her that her mother's cancer had come back a few months ago, and spread.

They were uncomfortable relaying that news, she could tell. Dad must have told them that she and her brothers were unaware, but the detectives had apparently decided it was time that they knew the truth.

After they were done questioning her, Beck found her father back in the den, staring into space once again.

"Dad," she said in a choked voice.

He turned toward her, said nothing. She couldn't read his expression.

"Mom was sick again?"

Still he didn't speak, just nodded bleakly.

"So you knew? Why didn't you tell us? Why didn't she?"

"You know your mother. She didn't want you to worry."

Yes. That makes sense.

She wasn't lying. She was protecting.

"So it was . . . was it terminal?"

Again her father nodded. She saw tears in his eyes.

Maybe the revelation should be, in some bizarre, twisted way, a source of comfort. Mom was spared the dreaded ordeal of an extended terminal illness. That's the last thing she would have wanted.

And this? Would she have wanted this?

Beck turns away from the closed door and heads on down the hallway to her childhood bedroom, with the cheerful blue and yellow decor she and Mom had chosen together years ago.

She sits on the bed and opens her laptop. Clicking on the recent browsing history, she brings up Mom's blog site.

The detectives had mentioned that they'd seen the entry Beck posted there last night.

"You had to have the password to do that," Detective Schneider pointed out. "Did your mother share that kind of information with you?"

"No," she said. "I just guessed it."

A few months ago she'd helped Mom change the PIN number for her new ATM card.

"I always use our phone number and my initials or Dad's whenever I need a password for something," Mom said.

"Bad idea. Too easy for someone to guess. You should use something else."

Mom waved her off. She never worried about things like

identity theft, or hacking. Until, of course, her personal e-mail account was hacked, not long after the PIN number conversation.

She told Beck about it on the phone, and Beck advised her to close that account, set up a new one, and again encouraged her to make up a unique password no one would guess.

Remembering that incident last night as she tried to figure out the blog account password, she nailed it on the third try. It was her father's initials followed by the four-digit home phone number in reverse order.

When the detectives asked her for the password, she gave it to them, reminding herself that it isn't a violation of her mother's privacy.

This is, after all, a homicide investigation. They're trying to get a search warrant for the electronic records, but that process takes time.

"Do you know your mother's password for her most recent e-mail account?" Detective Burns asked. "Or did you try to guess it?"

The answer was no on both counts. But she mentioned that both passwords were most likely saved on Mom's own laptop and cell phone, which were among the electronics that had been stolen in the robbery.

"Are you sure the passwords were there?"

"I assume they were because my mother mentioned a while back that she was having trouble remembering things, and that it was a good thing she didn't have to reenter her passwords every time she wanted to check mail or write a blog. She said she always used some combination of initials and the phone number, and I told her she should use a made-up word you wouldn't find in the dictionary, not a name or initials. Or that if she did use a dictionary word or initials, she should substitute a zero for an O, or a symbol for a letter—the *at* symbol for an *A*, or a dollar sign for an *S*. I also said she should put the phone number in reverse so that it would be harder for someone to guess, and she said—"

Beck had to break off to compose herself before she could go on with the story.

Now, her mother's wry words echo in her head: *These days, Beck, I'm lucky if I can remember the phone number forward—forget backward. And by the time I'm Gram's age, I won't know my own name.*

They laughed together, and Mom later mentioned the incident in a funny blog she wrote about getting senile.

But she must have known even then, Beck realizes, that she wasn't going to live to be a little old lady.

Swallowing a lump in her throat, Beck clicks the Sign in tab on her mother's blog, then enters the user name—meredithheywood—and the password she'd guessed the other day.

Whoever has Mom's laptop and phone can access the account . . .

But so can I.

Maybe there's some clue there. Something the police wouldn't have picked up on.

She logs in and is about to start searching when she remembers the e-mail account.

She should check that, too.

She switches over to the Web site for the e-mail service her mother uses, enters the address, then tries the password that worked for the blog account.

No luck.

She tries another combination of the same letters and numbers—forward, backward. She substitutes the @ symbol for an *A,* the *$* sign for an *S* . . .

Nope.

This, she realizes, might take a while—thanks to her own brilliant advice about coming up with a word you wouldn't find in the dictionary; something no one would ever guess . . .

Including me.

There must be very few people on this earth who after taking someone's life wouldn't spend the immediate aftermath, at least, endlessly replaying the scenario.

But even now, days later, the events of Saturday night are inescapable; a relentless mental movie set on a continuous play loop.

Crickets chirping.

Silver sliver of moon.

Aching legs, after all this time crouched in the bushes clutching the cast iron pan wrapped in a towel. It's a small pan, but it weighs enough, brought down with enough force, to crush a skull.

A bag, stashed nearby, contains a couple of new pillows and an orange and yellow bedspread identical to the one Meredith wrote about on her blog, conveniently including a photo and mentioning that she'd bought it at Macy's.

All the lights in the house extinguish one by one until everything is dark except a pair of bedroom windows.

It seems safe, after a reasonable wait, to make a move and slip into the kitchen. Safer than waiting outside, where someone from a neighboring house might spot the shadowy figure in the yard and call the police.

Get inside. Go. It's time.

Open the folding knife, the one with the tortoiseshell handle.

Slice through the screen.

Crawl through the window.

Tiptoe, tiptoe, across the linoleum, one measured step at a time.

No turning back now.

But wait!

Footsteps overhead.

Creaking stairs.

Move back toward the window to escape.

Don't run. Slow and steady, slow and steady.

The footsteps have stopped.

Meredith has paused halfway down the stairs. Why? Does she sense something?

Wait . . .

Wait . . .

Footsteps again, descending.

Meredith comes into the kitchen, turns on the light above the sink, opens cupboards . . .

Don't move. Don't breathe.

Stay in the shadowy corner of the room, hiding in plain sight, a turtle lurking beneath its shell on a rocky landscape.

Wait . . .

Wait . . .

Meredith turns.

But she doesn't see. She isn't wearing her glasses.

She goes back up the stairs.

Wait . . .

Wait . . .

At last, there hasn't been any movement overhead for at least an hour, probably longer.

Only then is it safe to creep up the stairs clutching the towel-wrapped cast iron pan, a weapon chosen after careful research because it would have been, *should* have been, merciful.

Not as merciful, generally speaking, as an injection that would simply stop her heart from beating, but that would be needlessly cruel. Meredith hates needles.

Not as merciful, either, as a simple gunshot to the head, but . . .

I don't have a gun. And I can't get one—legally or illegally—without involving someone else.

And so, in the grand scheme of things, this was the best choice. An everyday household object as a weapon.

Flashlight beam swings across the shadowy bedroom.

Meredith, lying in her bed with her eyes closed.

She appears to be sleeping . . .

I thought she was sleeping! Really, I did! But she surprised me—again.

Meredith's eyes open.

Only for a fleeting second, perhaps just long enough to see a human shadow standing over her, but . . .

There's a chance that she saw me. That she knew.

Even if she saw, though, there would have been no time for her to comprehend.

It's over in the next second.

The towel swishes over her head, her face . . .

Not for the purpose of covering her eyes, but to contain the inevitable spatters caused by the pan crashing down on her skull.

Blunt force trauma to the head.

She isn't dead yet. Just unconscious. She has a faint pulse when she's moved to the floor.

The towel comes off and the job is swiftly finished with another strategic blow.

It had to happen, and yet . . .

It's hard to see her lying there like that when it was over. So hard . . .

But there's no time for remorse.

The plan. Stick to the plan.

It can't appear as if she'd been attacked in her bed while she was sleeping. No ordinary robber would do something like that. That would be a red flag for the police that the motive for the break-in had been murder.

It has to look as though Meredith interrupted a robbery, provoked the intruder.

The headboard is clean, thanks to the towel, but the bedding has to be changed.

The sheets are replaced with a clean set from the cedar chest at the foot of the bed. A brand new pillow and identical bedspread—purchased just yesterday at Macy's—are swapped for the slightly bloodied bedding. There's a small spot of blood on the mattress, too, but bleach takes care of that.

When they investigate, they'll have no reason to strip off the spotless sheets and test the mattress for blood, will they?

Will they?

Too late to second-guess now.

The plan. Stick to the plan.

The soiled bedding is hastily packed into a garbage bag, to be tossed into a Dumpster a hundred miles away.

The final touch: a new necklace to replace the thin silver chain visible beneath the open placket of Meredith's nightgown. That one had a heart-shaped locket with a photo of her three children when they were young.

It's tempting to leave it on, but that might arouse suspicion. Meredith conveniently informed the blogosphere that she always sleeps in her jewelry, but two necklaces?

No, she just needs one.

For good luck.

"It's going to be okay. You'll be at peace now, and someday we'll see each other again . . ."

Off comes the locket. It goes into a bag, along with the contents of the jewelry box on the bureau, and—of course—her laptop and phone.

Those are key. The files need to be purged of any damaging evidence, communication that might prove incriminating down the road, if things don't go according to plan.

The plan.

Jewelry . . . electronics . . .

What else might a burglar want to steal?

There aren't many valuables in this modest household.

Slowly, steadily, the crime scene is staged.

Slow . . .

Steady . . .

At last, it's over.

Only now are nagging details popping up, triggering second thoughts.

Only now does the necklace left around Meredith's neck, with its small cameo made of delicate tortoiseshell, seem like a bad idea.

It was a vintage piece. Rare. Valued by collectors.

Only the most discerning eye would know that, but still . . .

It was a risk, leaving that final gift behind with Meredith.

Looking back, perhaps it was a foolish one.

But it was a risk I had to take. I had to protect her.

And now . . .

Now I have to protect myself.

"We Need to Go Beyond a Cure. We Need to Stop People from Ever Getting Breast Cancer in the First Place."

The title of this post is a quote from Dr. Susan Love. Fitting, because today, October 1, the Dr. Susan Love Research Foundation is launching HOW, the Health of Women Study. A worldwide, long-term online study open to women and men eighteen years and older with or without breast cancer. By compiling and studying answers to questions about one's health, family, job, and other topics, researchers will gain a better understanding of breast cancer and its possible causes.

By registering online at HOW you can help put awareness into action. There is no cost or permanent obligation. Once registered, you'll receive periodic questionnaires that you can fill out at your convenience. If you'd rather not participate at any point, you can opt out of further communication. There's no down side. Your privacy is protected and your answers may contribute to the future prevention of breast cancer.

For the most part, breast cancer takes us by the hand and leads us down a path of its own choosing. We stare it down with treatment and surgery, hoping for many more years, but by participating in HOW, we're doing something more than waiting.

We're actively helping researchers figure out a way to stop breast cancer once and for all.

So no one need look over their shoulder ever again.

—Excerpt from Jaycee's blog, *PC BC*

Chapter 5

It's been a long day and a longer night, with Rob golfing after work and the kids out of the house. They both left right after gobbling down the pizza Landry ordered for dinner. She herself couldn't eat a thing. Her stomach has been churning all day.

After rattling around the place alone for a few hours, unable to lose herself in mindless housework, magazines, or TV, she decides to see if a good book might make her forget about Meredith for a little while.

Curled up in the corner of the living room, in a lamplit overstuffed reading chair, she picks up the e-reader Rob and the kids bought her for her birthday in March.

Until then she'd resisted digital books, insisting that she preferred to hold good old-fashioned bound paper pages in her hands.

"Come on, Mom, get with it. You've learned how to do everything else electronically. You're even blogging!" Addison pointed out. "You've come a long way from the person who couldn't figure out how to check our elementary school homework assignments online."

That was true. And while she continues to buy print books as well, she's been surprised to find that the electronic device has come in handy for reading in bed on restless nights or when Rob turns out the light earlier than she'd like. Even better, it allowed her to pack a pile of beach reads into her carry-on for Easter week in Playa Del Carmen.

The thought of that trip brings to mind, yet again, the prospect of traveling up to Cincinnati for Meredith's funeral.

She manages to resist the urge to check the Web for updated information about the arrangements, or updates on the investigation. She's been looking every so often—more often, perhaps, than is healthy—and so far there's been nothing.

This afternoon she had a brief e-mail from Elena, who thanked her for sharing the grim news. She said she has to work straight through until tonight and will call if it isn't too late when she gets home.

There's been nothing more from Jaycee. She'd tried calling A-Okay again right before she ordered the pizza. Once again the line went into voice mail.

Forget it. Stop thinking about it for a few minutes, will you?

She focuses on the e-reader. Last night she'd left off in the middle of a trashy celebrity tell-all she'd been too self-conscious to buy in Page & Palette, her favorite bookstore in Fairhope, where everyone on the staff knows her name and probably expects her to purchase more highbrow literature. She's been fascinated by Hollywood gossip from the time she was a little girl playing Movie Star dress-up games in her mother's closet.

But tonight, distracted, all she can think about is Meredith. Meredith frightened, Meredith hurt, Meredith dying.

It's so wrong, so unfair.

Come on. Who are you kidding?

Violent death at the hands of someone else is always, *always* wrong and unfair. But for it to happen to someone who's been through cancer—someone who already stared the prospect of terminal illness in the face, not once, but twice, and won—it seems even more cruel.

On the table beside her chair, her cell phone rings.

Landry pounces on it, hoping it's one of her blogger friends at last.

But the number in the caller ID window belongs to her cousin Barbie June.

Their mothers are sisters and they'd grown up like sisters themselves, born just ten months apart and raised right across the road from each other. They looked so much alike they were often mistaken for twins. They ran with the same crowd in high school, became roommates in their college sorority house, maid of honor at each other's weddings and godmother to each other's firstborns.

Ordinarily, Landry would pick up her cousin's call, but not tonight. She just isn't in the mood to try to explain about Meredith to someone who won't understand—and there's no way Barbie June will understand.

Her cousin has lots of great qualities.

Subtlety and empathy aren't among them.

"I know you're scared," Barbie June told Landry when she opted for a preventative mastectomy over a lumpectomy, "but why put yourself through major surgery? Why disfigure yourself when you don't have to? How are you going to wear that darling strapless dress you bought last month at Dillard's?"

Landry bit back her anger and frustration, explaining why it was the right choice for her, despite the fact that her cancer was stage one—microscopic cells limited to one breast, with relatively low odds for a relapse.

There were no guarantees even with the surgery, but she had a husband and two young kids who needed her, and she intended to do everything within her power to take control and perhaps further reduce her chances of a recurrence.

Barbie June just didn't get it.

"But look at Grammy," Barbie June said. "She didn't do anything so drastic, and she was just fine."

Their maternal grandmother had been diagnosed with breast cancer a good forty years ago. She'd survived it with just a lumpectomy, minor treatment, and faith that God would let her live to a ripe old age. He did.

Unfortunately, she passed away just a year before Landry's diagnosis. The quintessential steel magnolia, she'd have been a godsend: a fellow wife and mother who knew what it was like to face your mortality one day out of the clear blue sky.

That was why it was such a relief to her when she found Meredith and the others.

Naturally, Barbie June had since made her share of comments about her blog and social networking in general, hinting that it was for people who don't have anything else to do.

Landry had always thought pretty much the same thing—until the day she went searching online for information about reconstructive surgery and stumbled across an irreverent breast cancer blog on the subject.

Back then, she barely knew what a blog was.

"I think it's a sort of online daily journal," she explained to Barbie June when she made the initial mistake of telling her about it.

When she described the post—an account of nipple reconstruction that managed to be simultaneously poignant and hilarious—her cousin reacted with an incredulous, "Why on God's green earth would any halfway decent person put something like that out there in public for just *anyone* to read?"

"I don't know," she'd said. "I guess for the same reasons people keep diaries. Because sometimes it's cathartic to write about things you can't find the nerve to talk about. It's an outlet."

"Yes, but you write a diary for yourself. Not for perfect strangers to read."

"Well, then, maybe they do it to help other people cope.

Or maybe because they're shy, and they can hide behind anonymity online, or because they're lonely and socially isolated . . . who knows?"

Undaunted by her cousin's disdain, Landry began to follow the cancer blogs daily, along with the usual barrage of comments from other readers.

Like a would-be pledge wistfully eavesdropping on a chatty cluster of sorority sisters, she noted not just the easygoing banter among the regulars on Meredith's blog, but also their genuine compassion for each other. Nearly all were fellow breast cancer patients or survivors, and many were bloggers themselves. Landry clicked their links and began to follow their posts as well, on blogs that had clever titles like *Yes, Ma'am(ogram)* or *Making the Breast of It.*

Finally, she worked up her nerve to post a comment somewhere—was it on one of Meredith's entries? Or Whoa Nellie's?

She no longer remembers the details, only that she was welcomed so warmly that her shyness evaporated—kind of like the first time she stepped over the threshold of her college sorority house.

Barbie June didn't understand that reference either. She knew her cousin would never understand why she was initially drawn to the online community, or why she was still there. Barbie June has asked, time and again, why she "still bothers" with her cancer blog now that she's "cured."

"Don't you want to put the whole nasty thing behind you and move on?"

Landry sighs. How do you answer a question like that?

"I think she's in denial," she confided in her friend Everly. "She's afraid that if it happened to me, and to our grandmother, then it could happen to her, too, and she doesn't want to face—"

"Oh, please, she's just jealous," Everly cut in, "same as she always was back in high school whenever you got invited to a party without her. She wants to be front and center in your life, just like the old days. I've always thought it's a wonder she doesn't resent me—or resent Rob, even, for taking you away from her."

"Don't be silly," was Landry's response, though Everly had a point.

Barbie June's possessiveness had occasionally reared its head during their formative years whenever Landry spent time with other friends, or when she had a boyfriend and her cousin didn't. But by the time Rob came along, Barbie June was already engaged.

Now, she and her husband live in a waterfront home less than a mile away with their two children, a son and daughter born in reverse order of Addison and Tucker but almost exactly the same ages. The new generation of cousins isn't nearly as close as their mothers and grandmothers had been, and their husbands aren't particularly fond of each other, but despite traveling in different social circles with disparate lifestyles, Landry and Barbie June have maintained a connection over the years.

If she picks up the phone to talk to her cousin tonight, there will be no concealing the fact that something's wrong. And if she were to tell Barbie June what happened to Meredith, she's certain she wouldn't be met with much sympathy.

The phone goes silent, and after a long pause, it beeps to indicate a new voice mail message.

Moments later the home phone begins to ring.

Barbie June again. If her cousin doesn't get an answer on one number, she always tries the other—and sometimes she'll even call Rob's phone, trying to reach her.

Landry ignores the ringing, letting it, too, go into voice mail.

Guilt settles over her as she tries to go back to her book. What if the call was about a family emergency rather than the usual chit-chatty check-in?

Worried, she reaches for her cell phone to listen to the message.

"Hello there, darlin'. That was a divine picture of you and Rob and the Sandersons in the paper on Sunday, and I've been meanin' to call you ever since I saw it. I know it's Rob's golf night so I figured you might be lonely. But—you're not pickin' up. Where the heck are you without your phone? I'll try you at home. Buh-bye."

Ah, the usual chit-chatty check-in—laced with a slight hint of accusation.

Landry deletes the message.

Beck leans back, rubbing her eyes.

She's just spent hours sitting at the kitchen table on her laptop, alternately reading every entry and subsequent comment on her mother's blog and still trying to figure out the password to her e-mail.

She's tried every combination of her parents' initials, plus her own and her brothers', along with various symbols and phone numbers and birthdates in chronological and reverse order . . .

Nothing has worked.

She's been keeping track, at least, on a yellow legal pad, so that she won't waste her time on duplicate guesses. Now she flips the pages, scanning the list of everything she's tried, feeling as though she's missing the obvious.

Hearing a floorboard creak in the next room, she looks up. It's either her father or Keith. Her brothers again drove back home for the night, promising to come back first thing in the morning.

After they left, Keith said he was going to bed and disappeared up the stairs, ever-present phone in hand. Since there's only a twin bed in her old bedroom, he's sleeping across the hall, in one of the bunk beds that once belonged to her brothers.

Dad adjourned to the den around the same time, presumably planning to spend the night in his recliner once again. Beck had offered him her room, pointing out that she can sleep in the other bunk in the boys' room where Keith is, but Dad turned her down.

That was fine with her—and not just because she understood how hard it would be for her father to climb the stairs to go to bed, no matter which bedroom he was sleeping in.

She's just not eager to share space with Keith right now, and she's pretty sure he feels the same way.

"What did you tell them?" she asked him after he spoke to the detectives this afternoon.

"What do you *think* I told them?"

"I have no idea. Why do you *think* I'm asking?" she said aloud.

To herself, she thought, *Jackass.*

Thank God she never confided in him about her father— about what she saw, that one time.

The incident did nag at her for a few weeks after it happened, and at the time she considered telling Keith about it, but she kept it to herself in the end.

Thank God. Thank God.

The floorboard creaks again.

"Hello?" she calls.

As much as she hopes her father is finally getting some sleep, she'd prefer to see him pop up in the kitchen doorway right now, rather than her husband.

"Dad? Keith?"

No reply. She's just starting to think she imagined the creaking when a shadow falls across the floor.

Keith.

"What are you doing?" she asks.

"Why are you still up?" he asks, simultaneously.

He's still dressed—or perhaps dressed again—in jeans and a T-shirt. And he's wearing shoes, she notices.

"I'm hungry," he says with a shrug. "Is there any more of that chicken casserole from dinner?"

She looks from his face to the phone in his hand to the fridge.

"Help yourself."

He crosses over to the refrigerator and opens the door. "So what are you doing up, Rebecca?"

He always calls her by her full name, unlike her family and friends. That never really bothered her until now. In fact, when she first met him she thought it was sweet and refreshing.

But lately—especially here in her childhood home, where she's been referred to as Beck all her life—her given name, particularly on her husband's lips, seems stiff and formal.

"I was just rereading my mother's blog," she tells him.

And trying to hack into her e-mail account . . .

But Keith doesn't need to know that. For some reason, she feels like he might not approve.

"Why?" he asks.

"Why, what?"

"Why are you reading her blog?"

"I was just looking for . . ." She trails off, watching him lift a corner of foil off the casserole dish in the fridge, peer inside, and fold it back down.

"What were you looking for?" he asks.

"I was just looking to see what she'd written lately. That's all. It makes me feel close to her."

"Oh." He opens the crisper drawer, takes out an apple, closes the fridge.

"I thought you were hungry."

"I am. I'm having an apple."

"I thought you wanted that chicken casserole."

"So did I, but . . . it's congealed."

"You can heat it in the microwave."

"No, thanks. This is fine."

You weren't hungry at all, she thinks, watching him wash the apple at the sink.

In all the years they've been married, he's never been a midnight snacker. If anything, she's the one who gets up and roots around the fridge in the wee hours.

Besides, when she served the chicken casserole the neighbor dropped off for their dinner, he picked at it. The recipe was probably straight off the label of a can of cream soup, and Keith—who works for the department of animal and food sciences at the university—isn't big on packaged foods as ingredients for anything.

She'd bet anything that he has his car keys in his pocket. He was probably going to sneak out of the house like a wayward teenager, probably thinking he could rendezvous with . . . *whoever* . . . and be back at dawn.

Sorry, pal, she thinks, watching him crunch into the apple. *Guess I foiled your plan.*

At last Landry hears the garage door going up.

Rob is home, thank goodness. He might not understand about Meredith, but he'll listen patiently, and he'll care. Or at least pretend to.

"Which one is she?" he'll ask, never able to tell her online friends apart when she talks about them.

If Landry explains, "She's the older woman who lives in Ohio," or "She's the one who writes the *Pink Stinks* blog," he'll murmur as if he knows who she means, but he won't. He'll be sympathetic, though he won't understand how the loss of a woman she's never met can hit so hard.

That's how he reacted in January, when Nell died.

She, too, was a blogger. She lived in England.

"Whoa Nellie died today," Landry told Rob when he walked in the door that night.

Concern immediately etched his face. *"Who?"*

"My friend Nell. *Whoa Nellie*. That's the name of her blog."

The concern dissipated and she could see the wheels turning: *No one I know. No one in real life.*

Landry can hear him in the kitchen, going through his nightly ritual: electronic beeping as he sets the alarm on the panel beside the door, water running as he washes his hands at the sink, the fridge door opening and closing as he grabs a bottle of water, footsteps creaking the wide old floorboards as he makes his way through the dining room, calling, "Anybody home?"

"In here."

He walks into the living room. Tanned, lean, and handsome, he's wearing khakis and a golf shirt, carrying his briefcase and a garment bag containing the suit he'd worn to work this morning.

"What's going on?" he asks, setting the bags on a chair and walking over to her lamplit reading nook. "Where are the kids?"

"Tucker's playing video games at Jake's. Addie's at a movie with her friends. She's going to pick him up at ten and drive him home."

"So you're here all by your lonesome?" He perches on the arm of her chair and kisses the top of her head. "Why are all the shutters closed?"

She follows his gaze to the wall of windows facing the bay. Ordinarily, they don't bother to draw the plantation shutters at night. The boardwalk is sparsely traveled after dark, and though anyone out there would ostensibly have a clear view into the house, it's not, typically, a troubling thought.

Tonight is not typical.

"I just . . . I didn't want to sit here thinking that anyone could see in," she admits to Rob.

"You feeling okay?"

"Not really."

Feeling him stiffen, she reads his mind, quickly saying, "No, not that. Physically, I'm fine."

"For a second I thought—"

"I know." He thought cancer. "It's just . . . I got some bad news today about one of my online friends."

"I'm sorry. What happened?"

She hesitates, remembering the first time she'd ever introduced him to Meredith—online, of course.

She remembers how Rob studied the photo of a smiling woman with grayish blond hair and glasses, and read over the brief bio beneath it.

"How do you know that's really her?" he asked—of course he did, because as an attorney, he rarely accepts anything at face value.

"Because this is her Web page."

"No, I mean . . . anyone can post any picture online and claim it as their own. For all you know, this Meredith person might actually be a twenty-year-old tattooed jailbird."

"She's not. This is her."

"You don't know that."

"I do."

Meredith's entries resonated too sharply to be anything but authentic.

"What happened?" Rob asks again, and he strokes Landry's hair while she tells him the tragic news, shaking his head and wearing a grave expression.

"So her husband was away on business when it happened?"

"Not on business—he was out of town taking care of his mother."

"How do you know that?"

"She told me."

"She told *you*—or she wrote about it online?"

Realizing where he's going with this line of questioning, she bristles. "She blogged about it."

Rob shakes his head but says nothing.

He's always worrying about what the kids are doing online, equating social networking Web sites with letting them walk into a room filled with predators.

Landry opens her mouth to tell him that Meredith wasn't murdered because she blogged personal details about her life, then closes it again.

Oh, really? How can you be so sure about that?

She'd been assuming that her friend had been killed by an intruder who randomly broke into her house . . .

But there *is* a chance—however slight—that Meredith might have been targeted by someone who knew her, or at least, knew that her husband was out of town, leaving her alone and vulnerable.

Maybe he overheard Meredith talking about it at the supermarket, or in a restaurant, or . . .

Or maybe he read it on her blog.

It's not very likely—but it could have happened, she supposes.

"Her husband must be devastated," Rob says.

"I'm sure he is. And she has kids—they're grown and married. Two sons and a daughter. There are grandchildren, too. Three, I think, with another one due in October. She called them her stinkerdoodles." She smiles, remembering the affection Meredith had for her growing family.

"She wrote all of that on the Internet?"

"Yes, but . . . it's not like that. We're basically just friends who share things online, just like friends do in person."

"But in person, we're careful about what we say when other people can overhear. Online, it's easy to forget that there's an audience. People shouldn't post anything they wouldn't be comfortable sharing with millions of perfect strangers, including opportunistic rapists and murderers."

"I would consider rapists and murderers *imperfect* strangers, wouldn't you?" she quips to lighten the topic.

He offers a sort-of smile, but he's still shaking his head. "It's just basic Internet Safety 101. You're inviting trouble when you—"

"Are you saying Meredith brought this on herself?" she cuts in. So much for lightening things up.

"No. I'm just saying . . . I'm worried. I've seen social networkers post way too much personal information."

"So have I. But I've never put down our last name or even our first names, or where we live . . ."

No, but many of the other bloggers—Meredith included—do share all those details. Rather than calling her spouse and children DH, DS, and DD—widely used Internet shorthand for Dear Husband, Darling Son, and Darling Daughter—Meredith referred to her family members by their first names. Hank was her husband; her kids were Neal, Teddy, and Beck, short for Rebecca. She occasionally posted photos, too . . .

Landry feels sick to her stomach remembering that Meredith had proudly posted pictures of her master bedroom last fall, with the new king-sized bed and bedding and curtains she'd just bought on sale at Macy's.

And then there was a more recent picture accompanied by a caption: *View of our home, sweet home from the street with the lilacs in full bloom.*

There were plenty of compliments in the comments section from the usual followers: *Pretty! . . . Love Lilacs! . . . Ooh, wish it was scratch and sniff!*

But how many other pairs of eyes had also seen the photo of the modest house? How many silent lurkers had noticed the dense shrub borders along the property lines, which, as Meredith had cheerfully pointed out to her online friends, offered privacy and shielded her house from the neighbors' views?

Landry thinks back over her own posts, wondering if she's inadvertently been just as careless.

"You didn't write on your blog that I'm going away on a golf outing Father's Day weekend, did you?" asks Rob the mind-reader.

"Of course not!"

She did, however, mention it to Meredith in a private message exchange just last week. They were going back and forth about how having a husband away can be a mixed blessing—more so, Meredith thought, when you have kids still at home.

It's kind of lonely when you're the only one rattling around the house day after day—well, mostly, night after night, Meredith wrote, almost echoing what she'd written in her blog.

Exactly—don't think I'm a big baby, she wrote back, *but sometimes I still get scared at night when Rob's away!*

Now, remembering that exchange, she feels a twinge of guilt. It was only Meredith—but what if it had been someone else? Someone she trusted, but shouldn't have?

Rob is looking a little guilty himself. "Sorry, I know you wouldn't write something that personal on the blog. You're pretty good about keeping things nonspecific."

"I am. So please don't worry."

"I'm not worried. Not about myself."

No. He worries about her.

Until she got sick, she was okay with that—with letting him protect her, take care of her.

But cancer changed that. Made her stronger, more determined to take care of herself, and . . .

More aware that Rob can't protect her. He can want to, and he can try, but her big strong husband isn't in charge after all. He—and she, for all those years—only wanted to believe that he was.

Stronger, more independent and self-aware . . .

Sometimes she still bristles when Rob assumes the old role of protector, and she knows it bothers him when she won't let him.

She changes the subject, asking about his workday, his golf game, and who was at the club tonight. As he tells her, she manages to ask questions in all the right places, and to laugh at quips she knows are meant to make her laugh, though she doesn't really comprehend a word he's saying.

This is how it was back when she was sick, going through the motions of ordinary conversation.

Later—much later, long after the kids are home and the house is quiet, Landry lies awake in bed staring into the dark, still preoccupied with Meredith's death and wondering why Elena never called. She must have gotten home too late.

Uneasily remembering what Rob said, Landry wants to ask her whether she thinks there's any chance some online predator might have deliberately targeted Meredith.

Are the police also considering that angle?

Probably. They must be going through the blog word for word, looking for clues.

Meredith *was* really open, sharing information that Landry would never have put out there for just anyone to see.

But that doesn't mean you haven't let your guard down, too, from time to time.

Just today she handed out her phone number to a bunch of people she's never met—and she told Jaycee her first and last name.

But I didn't broadcast that stuff on the Web, she reminds herself. *I just told a couple of friends, privately, over e-mail and the telephone. Nothing wrong with that.*

No. But from now on she'll be extra careful not to provide any identifying details on her own blog. And tomorrow she should go through it and delete anything she wouldn't want to share with "opportunistic rapists and murderers," as Rob put it.

Heck—maybe she should just stop blogging altogether.

Maybe it's too dangerous.

Dangerous? Come on. You're just being paranoid.

The inner voice, blustering bravado, is the one that popped up often back when she was sick, reminding her never to let fear get the best of her.

You're going to keep blogging, because . . . because it's what you do. And you're going to stop worrying, because worry is a waste of energy. Get it? Got it? Good.

She rolls over, hoping to get some sleep at last.

The first-class cabin lights dimmed shortly after the flight took off from LAX.

Jaycee always gets a window seat on the red-eye so that she'll have something to lean a pillow on, keeping her face turned away from the rest of the passengers. But this was a last minute trip, and an aisle was all they had left.

"Unless you want to fly coach?" Cory asked over the phone when he made her reservation.

"You're kidding, right?"

"What do you think?"

"I haven't flown coach in years, and you know it. Too risky."

"Ah, but I so enjoy breaking your chops."

So here she is, in first class, yes, but stuck in an aisle seat at midnight, numb with exhaustion after racing all over Los Angeles on just the few hours' sleep she'd caught the night before. She would like nothing better than to close her eyes and wake up in New York, but knows from experience that she won't be able to get comfortable enough to sleep.

Certainly not without the prescription sleeping pills Cory gets for her, which she mistakenly packed in the bag she checked.

Oh, well. She lands at five-something, and if she goes straight home to bed until noon, she'll almost get a full night's worth of beauty sleep.

Left with five hours to kill, she can either try to read a magazine, or she can use the in-flight WiFi to get online and see if there are any updates about Meredith. She's had so little downtime today that she hasn't had a chance to see what's going on.

Jaycee takes her iPad out of her carry-on in the overhead bin and checks to see if anyone is paying any attention to her as she waits for it to power up.

The lucky businessman in the window seat beside her is huddled under a blanket, out cold, snoring softly, his head resting on a pillow wedged against the window. Across the aisle, a woman is similarly asleep against her own window, wearing a sleep mask—freebies here in first class on the red-eye. The woman's seatmate appears completely absorbed in whatever he's typing on his open laptop.

Good. The last thing she needs is some nosy fellow passenger snooping over her shoulder, trying to get a look at her screen.

She checks e-mail first.

She has several different accounts—a personal address, a business address, and one she uses for blogging. She usually doesn't open that as often as the others, but today, because of Meredith, she's been keeping an eye on it.

Since she last checked, Elena has responded to the e-mail BamaBelle sent this morning with her phone number and the link to the Cincinnati newspaper article about the murder. Elena sent a reply-all message expressing her sorrow over Meredith's death and saying she'd be working late but would call Bama tonight.

To Jaycee, it sounds as if she's trying to dodge having to make the phone call. She can certainly understand that—she herself had hesitated before making the call this morning. There were so many reasons not to cross that line from a strictly electronic relationship to more personal contact.

In the end, she concluded there were more reasons to call than to avoid it—primarily because the others might get suspicious if she didn't, especially at a time like this. As long as she was careful not to give anything away, she decided, it would be fine.

And it was—for the most part. She managed to keep the conversation focused on Meredith and evade any sticky questions she sensed Bama was about to ask.

Like her real name. After Bama volunteered her own, Jaycee quickly changed the subject.

Not that anyone was likely to recognize her *real* real name, the one she'd been born with nearly forty years ago, in a tiny Minnesota town pretty much no one has ever heard of, not far from the border with Manitoba, Canada.

But still . . . you just never know. Which is why she hasn't used it in ages.

Anyway—Landry Wells? With a name like that, no wonder she goes by a pseudonym. All anyone has to do is plug it into a search engine, along with Alabama . . .

Jaycee types it all in now, including her mother's maiden name—Quackenbush—presses Enter, and finds herself looking at BamaBelle's life story.

It's basically all there, if you have time to sift through the results—and right now she has nothing but time. She peruses a wedding announcement, a real estate sale for an address in Point Clear, birth announcements for two children—Addison Landry Wells, who would be seventeen now, and Robert Tucker Wells IV, fifteen. There's information about volunteer work and PTO posts, and there are pictures, too.

It's not as though Jaycee doesn't already know what BamaBelle looks like—she has a head shot on her blog. But it's interesting to see her as a young bride, as a PTO mom, and, in a photo taken just last week, in the Mobile society pages at a charity ball with her husband and another couple identified as Robert Wells's law partner John Sanderson and his wife Mercy.

She's also been tagged here and there in candid shots

on other people's social networking pages. Landry Wells doesn't have one of those herself; her Internet activity seems limited to her blog page—which, interestingly, does not come up on the search engine.

That means BamaBelle has done a good job of keeping her real self separate from her blogger identity. Not everyone is successful at that.

Meredith wasn't.

But I certainly am.

The man beside Jaycee stirs in his sleep. Skittish, out of habit, she quickly closes the screen she was reading.

It's just as well. Who cares who BamaBelle really is?

Who cares who I really am?

That's the beauty of the Internet. There, you can be anyone you want to be. You can escape your real life.

That's all Jaycee ever really wanted, from the time she was a little girl, abandoned by her unwed mother to be raised by grandparents who took her in out of duty, and nothing more.

She wanted to escape.

That's why she used to hide in the shed behind the house, until she got so cold or hungry that she had to drag herself back inside to face reality—usually, with punishment for not answering when they called her name.

It's why she looked forward to going to school every day, while her classmates complained and lived for the weekends.

And it's why she discovered that she liked being on stage when her freshman drama teacher convinced her to audition for the high school musical. She could step into the spotlight, leave behind her real life with all its problems, and for a few hours, at least, become someone else—anyone else.

At seventeen she fell in love with Steven Petersen onstage—and off. That was the year everything happened: the year her grandmother died, the year she got pregnant, the year Steve broke her heart, and the year she gave up her newborn for adoption.

Not that you wanted to keep her anyway. You didn't want anything tying you down, holding you back.

At eighteen she finally got to escape for real.

She left behind the name she'd been born with and the miserable house where she'd been raised, and the godforsaken northern town where few people ever really gave a damn about her. She changed everything she could: hair color, build, clothing style, the way she walked, the way she spoke . . .

She rests her chin in her hand, remembering. That was the first time she truly, officially, became someone else. But it wasn't the last. Not by any stretch.

As she muses, she realizes that the flight attendant, leaning against the galley counter reading a magazine, is glancing in her direction.

She averts her own gaze out of habit—all those years of trying not to make eye contact, afraid someone is going to recognize her, engage her in conversation.

Usually if you do that, people get the hint that you want to be left alone.

"Doesn't everyone?" Cory likes to ask her when she gets paranoid.

"I didn't always," she's reminded him—and herself. There was a time when she craved attention—from anyone. Even strangers.

Maybe there's a part of her that still does. That would explain it all, wouldn't it? Even why she couldn't leave well enough alone and simply lurk online; why she was compelled to engage by writing the blog, interacting with people online . . . people like BamaBelle, who have no idea who, or what, she really is . . . or isn't.

Yes, she wants to—*needs* to—interact with them at a safe distance. But face-to-face?

No, thank you.

Sneaking a peek at the front galley just in time to see the

flight attendant glance again in her direction, Jaycee casually reaches up to block her face under the pretext of finger-combing her bangs, careful not to knock her wig askew. Then she pulls a sleep mask out of her pocket, places it over a good portion of her face, and turns her head away.

Leave me alone. Please. Just leave me the hell alone.

Home at last, Detective Crystal Burns is greeted at the door of her West End Cincinnati town house by Ginger, her Chesapeake Bay retriever.

"What's up, Gingy?" She tosses her keys and badge onto the counter and bends over to pat the dog. "Did you miss me? Huh?"

Panting and obviously thrilled to see her, the dog follows her into the living room, where Crystal's husband, Jermaine, is snoring on the couch. Presumably, he'd also have been thrilled—if not panting—had she arrived home many hours earlier, in time for their planned candlelight anniversary dinner.

They were married two years ago today. Well, technically, two years ago yesterday, since midnight came and went a few hours ago.

Jermaine—fellow cop by trade, amazing chef in his spare time—finally had the day off on the heels of a grueling sting operation.

He went out and picked up a couple of steaks this morning, plus all the ingredients for Crystal's favorite garlic truffle mashed potatoes, asparagus with hollandaise, and fresh strawberry shortcake in homemade pastry shells.

That was before she got bogged down in the case she's working.

"It's okay," Jermaine said when she told him she wouldn't be home in time for dinner. "I get it, baby."

"I know you do."

That he gets it is the beauty of this second marriage.

Crystal's first husband worked in corporate insurance and not law enforcement, and thus failed to understand that when you're working a homicide, the case—and the endless paperwork that goes with the territory—has to take precedence over just about everything, including anniversary dinners.

Despite her many differences with her ex, she hung in there for almost twenty years of that first marriage. Long enough for their only child to graduate high school and join the military. Sometimes she wonders if she hadn't filed for divorce before her son was killed in Afghanistan two years later, would she ever have done it? Leaving that marriage had been hard enough as it was. The man wasn't just clingy and possessive; he was all but helpless when it came to running a household without her.

Jermaine is quite the opposite—efficient and self-sufficient enough to let her breathe. He doesn't work the homicide unit—he's vice—but they're both in law enforcement.

That's not all they have in common. Crystal met him at a bereaved parents' meeting. He, too, was divorced, but his marriage didn't falter until after his teenage daughter died.

It was a drug overdose. Tragic. Jermaine and his wife had their share of problems before that—what couple doesn't? But their marriage, like so many, couldn't withstand the trauma of losing a child.

Every day, Crystal gives thanks to the Lord that as they emerged simultaneously from the wreckage of their lives, she and Jermaine found each other. And she would have given anything to have been here with him tonight, celebrating the one reason she found the strength to go on living in this grim world where she hasn't just lost her only child, but spends each day confronting the rock bottom worst of humanity.

Leaning over the couch, she kisses the spot at the edge of her husband's receding, graying hairline.

Jermaine lets out a final loud, waking snore and opens his eyes.

"You're home."

"Nah . . . you're jus' dreamin'."

"Then how 'bout you make it a sweet dream, baby." He grins, pulling her down. "I haven't seen you in weeks."

"Feels that way, doesn't it?"

In the past couple of days, between his strip club sting and her homicide, they've only managed to connect on the phone.

But there are worse things. Far worse.

Crystal settles into his arms with a kiss and a deep yawn, resting her head against his barrel chest.

"Paperwork finished?"

"Finally."

"How was Cleveland?"

"Oh, you know . . . it rocks," she says dryly.

"Find what you needed?"

"No, we did not."

She and her partner, Frank Schneider, had driven up there two days ago to check out Hank Heywood's alibi for Saturday night, when his wife Meredith was murdered. He said he'd been home all night at his mother's house, cleaning out her closets and cabinets now that he'd moved the old lady into a home.

Crystal and Frank talked to the people who lived on either side of the mother's condo, hoping to find elderly busybody types who have nothing better to do than keep an eye on the neighbors.

Unfortunately, the single mom who lived on one side had gone away for the weekend with her kids. She'd seen Hank Friday afternoon as they were packing the car, but not since.

"For what it's worth," she told the detectives, "Mr. Heywood is such a nice guy. I can't imagine that he had anything to do with a murder."

It wasn't worth anything at all, thank you very much.

Crystal has met more than her share of cold, hardened criminals lurking behind Mr. Nice Guy facades.

She and Frank had better luck with Professor Malcolm, who lived next door on the other side.

He said he'd run into Heywood carrying a bunch of heavy-looking garbage bags down to the parking lot Dumpster at around seven o'clock Saturday evening, when he himself was on his way out to dinner. He returned to the building before eleven but didn't recall whether Heywood's truck was still parked out front.

That could mean that it wasn't there.

It could also mean that it was, and Professor Malcolm simply hadn't noticed it.

He did notice it when he left for church on Sunday morning, headed to an eleven o'clock service.

"Well?" Frank asked on the way back to Cincinnati. "If you were a betting woman—"

"Oh, you know I'm a betting woman, Frank."

He grinned, well aware that she and Jermaine like to sneak off to Vegas or Atlantic City every now and then.

"So if you were playing the odds," he went on, "would your money be on the husband?"

"It's not just about the odds. If you look at the victimology and possible motives—who stands to benefit most from the death?"

"Exactly." Frank started ticking off Hank Heywood's known stressors on his fingers. "The guy loses his job. His mother loses her marbles *and* her ability to live alone. He's going to lose his wife sooner or later . . .

"Looking at it strictly from a financial standpoint, sooner would be preferable, because his health insurance runs out soon, and if he doesn't find a new job with benefits, they're screwed. He's thinking it's better to collect on her life insurance policy now instead of later, right?"

Crystal shrugs. "At that point, if they've lost their health care for any amount of time, the payout might not even cover the debt they'll have racked up on her medical care."

"So we have motive. And opportunity. Yeah, we know he was seen in Cleveland Saturday night and again on Sunday morning, but it's a four hour drive, tops. He could've left after the neighbor saw him by the Dumpster, driven down to his house, killed the wife, and driven back before dawn."

Yeah. He could've.

Or, Hank Heywood could've been right where he said he was, sadly cleaning out his failing mother's condo in preparation to list it, completely unaware that his beloved wife of more than thirty years lay dying in the master bedroom they shared back home.

Still a tragic scenario, but that one would undoubtedly sit a hell of a lot easier with the three kids who lost their mother.

The rest of the family has fairly solid alibis for Saturday night. Both of the sons were home with their wives and kids. The daughter was at a party for a colleague. Her husband wasn't with her—he was with someone else, Keith Drover finally admitted after hemming and hawing when they interviewed him today.

"Another woman?" Frank had asked—probably recognizing a kindred philanderer, Crystal thought at the time.

Turned out that wasn't the case—exactly.

Drover begged them not to tell his wife the truth—especially after they said they'd need to talk to his lover to confirm his alibi.

Assured that they weren't going to turn around and tell Rebecca, on the heels of losing her mother, that her husband was in love with another man, the poor sap looked relieved. But only until Frank reminded him that this was an active homicide investigation.

"When you've got a high profile case, the dirty laundry

sometimes tends to come out before all is said and done," he warned Keith. "You might want to think about coming clean to your wife before she hears it from someone else."

Poor Rebecca. She's managed to hold it together so far—in fact, she was doing much better today than she was when Crystal first met her at the scene on that rainy Sunday afternoon. She can still hear the young woman's anguished screams; can still feel Rebecca clutching her sleeve, asking who had done this to her mother.

"We're going to find out," she promised her then, and again today, before she and Frank left the house after questioning the family members again. "Our job is to make sure justice is served."

That's what it's all about. You can't turn back the clock and bring the loved one back to the family, and Lord knows you can't take away the agony of loss.

All you can do is try to give them closure.

"So how's it going? What do you think?" Jermaine asks now, stroking Crystal's hair.

"Same thing I thought this morning, and yesterday, and the day before."

"Which is . . . ?"

"That Meredith Heywood wasn't killed by some stranger she'd surprised when he was robbing her house."

"You sure? There have been an awful lot of break-ins around here lately. That's nothing new."

She nods, well aware national statistics show that Ohio cities have a disproportionately high number of burglaries, with Cincinnati near the top of the list.

But—statistics again—stranger homicides are extremely rare. Victims—particularly female victims—usually know their killers.

She doesn't have to remind Jermaine of that.

But he's a cop; he's trying to remind her that sometimes, in an investigation, what you see really is what you get.

Not in this case, though.

She updates her husband about the rest of the evidence they've been gathering. It indicates that Meredith Heywood had been killed almost instantly with a blow to the head.

"What was the weapon?"

"Probably a household object. Could have been a baseball bat, a hammer, an andiron—not sure."

"From her household? Or did the perp bring it with him?"

"Again—not sure. We didn't find the weapon."

She goes on to tell him that the victim's body was found on the floor, which was clearly meant to indicate that she'd been hit while she was standing or moving.

But Crystal is fairly certain she'd been killed in her bed—maybe even while she was sound asleep—and then moved to the floor postmortem.

The bedding was spotless—too spotless. The spatter pattern surrounding the body on the floor indicated that it should have extended up onto the bedspread, but it didn't. The bedspread was pristine, and lab tests turned up no sign of blood.

Beneath the spotless sheets, the mattress gave off a faint bleach smell, and is still being tested for evidence of blood that may have been cleaned up by the perpetrator.

Nearby, the bedside table was overturned, a lamp broken, a water glass spilled.

"So it looked like there was a struggle," Jermaine says.

"Right. But there wasn't. It was staged, just like everything else."

The house appeared to have been ransacked. The family was able to pinpoint a few things that were missing—an envelope of cash kept in a desk drawer in the den, a small bureau-top chest filled with the victim's costume jewelry, the victim's laptop and cell phone that had probably been sitting out in the open.

But a professional burglar wouldn't have missed the coin

collection on the shelf of a basement closet whose door was left ajar as if it had been ransacked. Nor would he have overlooked the relatively valuable jewelry stashed in several padded cases tucked into the back of a drawer that was found open, its contents rumpled to look like someone had gone through it.

It was all for show, to cover up the real motive for the break-in: murder.

Whoever did it was a novice.

A more seasoned killer—or a pro, a hit man—would have made the fake burglary more convincing, and wouldn't have been so clumsy about moving and repositioning the body.

"So who did it? The husband?"

"I'm not sure."

"What's your gut telling you?"

She shrugs. "The guy is the picture-perfect image of a distraught, shell-shocked, bereaved widower."

"Which means absolutely nothing to you."

"Exactly."

Last year, she interrogated a twenty-year-old mother who'd drowned her own baby in a toilet. The girl—her name was Diaphanous Jones—never stopped crying while they talked, heaving sobs, gasping for air—the picture of maternal devastation. Yet, chillingly—she'd confessed her crime immediately after she committed it, and never once tried to retract.

Grief, regret—normal reactions to any loss. Visible emotions don't let you off the hook.

That Hank Heywood is, on some level, a bereaved husband is not in dispute. But there were a number of potent stressors in his life leading up to the murder. He was under a lot of pressure. Something might very well have happened between him and his wife that caused him to snap.

"Maybe he was seeing someone else," Jermaine speculates.

"Or maybe *she* was."

"You think?"

She shakes her head. "There's not a shred of evidence pointing in that direction, but . . ."

She and Frank haven't completely dismissed the idea that Meredith had a lover who might have been in the house with her in her husband's absence. Maybe the lover had killed her. Or maybe her husband had found out about him—or her— and acted out of vengeance.

Meredith's daughter had been adamant that her mother wasn't living a secret life—which Crystal is now inclined to take with a grain of salt, given Rebecca's husband's illicit affair.

Keith Drover seems certain his wife is clueless about it— but then that, too, could be open for debate.

In any case, Rebecca had insisted that no one close to her mother—no one she knew, anyway—would have been capable of hurting her.

"Everyone loved her," she said tearfully. Clutching a handful of sodden tissues, she answered all of Crystal and Frank's questions about friends and individual family members . . .

Something flickered in her eyes, though, when she was first asked about her father.

A hint of . . . *something*, and then it was gone.

Her parents had a great, loving marriage, she said.

Right.

Diaphanous Jones's family had told Crystal she'd been a great, loving mother.

She loved that baby more than anything . . .

"My mother and father worshiped each other," Rebecca said.

Most kids are going to believe that about their parents, if there are no overt signs of marital trouble in the household. Especially adult children who have moved on. Crystal's own son was stunned and bewildered when she called him at boot camp to tell him that she and his dad would be going their separate ways.

"But why?" he kept asking. "You guys never even fight."

Not true, exactly—but damn, she and her ex were good at hiding the tension. Practice makes perfect.

Maybe Meredith and Hank Heywood really were happily married.

Maybe not.

Hell, some days she wonders if any marriage—outside of her own, of course—is entirely happy.

"The other thing we're looking at," she muses aloud to Jermaine, "is the Internet."

"What about it?"

"The victim was a blogger. She put way too much of her personal life out there for anyone to read."

"Yeah, well, we've seen more and more of that sort of thing. People go blabbing on social networking Web sites, not just about birthdays and their mother's maiden names, but where they're going, and for how long, and who they're with. The next thing you know, they're reporting that someone's stalking them, or their identity's been stolen, or their empty home was burglarized . . ."

"Or worse," Crystal says with a nod.

She explains to her husband that Meredith Heywood was a breast cancer survivor who wrote a very public blog that had hundreds, maybe thousands, of followers.

"You think one of them killed her?"

"Could be. But if that was the case, it wasn't necessarily a complete stranger. Not in the usual sense of the word."

"What do you mean?"

She tells him about the last piece of evidence—the one that's been nagging her from the moment she first saw the body.

Jermaine shakes his head. "So you really do think it was the husband, don't you?"

She hesitates, remembering the raw pain in Hank Heywood's face.

Remembering the flicker of doubt in his daughter's eyes.

"I don't know," she says. "I honestly don't know."

This wasn't supposed to happen.

How on earth did this happen—again?

It's not like I'm someone who just goes around . . . killing people.

Meredith was the first, and she was supposed to be the last, the only.

But now look.

The crumpled figure lying on the ground moans, clenching and unclenching the hand that until moments ago held a puppy on a leash.

The puppy is running loose somewhere down the street, still dragging a length of leather and chain from its tagged collar.

The man's hand is covered in blood, reaching for the knife sticking out of his stomach, reaching . . . reaching . . .

He's too weak. He's not going to make it.

It was different with Meredith. She was likely unconscious before she grasped what was happening, unlike this poor soul who must know he's dying, an ugly, painful death at that.

With Meredith, it wasn't ugly and painful.

It wasn't impulsive, and it wasn't about anger. No, it was about—

Well, it was far more complicated than anyone could possibly understand. But it was the right thing to do.

This . . .

This was probably the wrong thing.

It was probably *the wrong thing? It was definitely the wrong thing!*

Look at him! Look what you did to him!

The man on the ground moans again.

Oh, dear.

"I'm sorry. Really. I didn't mean for this to happen, but . . . I only wanted to be left alone. Why did you have to stop me and ask for a light? Why couldn't you just walk on past me?"

Another moan, the low, terrible sound of an animal being tortured.

This is bad. This is wrong.

But I couldn't help myself.

He kept talking, and he said the wrong thing, and . . . and I've been under so much pressure these last few days with everything, that I just . . .

Snapped.

Yes, snapped, like a turtle, when someone gets too close.

Now someone is suffering.

Because of me.

No—that's wrong. This isn't my fault. It's his.

"You know, I told you I didn't have a light! Why didn't you let me walk away? Why did you have to try to make conversation? Who does that at this hour on a deserted street? Who are you? Who *are* you?"

Unlike Meredith, this person is a stranger in every sense of the word.

Unlike Meredith, he's suffering terribly.

All that's visible of his face in the predawn shadows is his mouth, surrounded by a stubbly growth of beard. Just a few minutes ago the mouth was smiling and forming questions, far too many questions. Now, it's contorted in agony, and blood is beginning to gush from it.

I can't stand to see him in pain, whoever the hell he is.

He's a human being.

I'm a human being, for Pete's sake. I have a heart. No matter what anyone thinks . . .

But who would think anything different?

No one in this world knows what really happened to Meredith, and no one is going to figure it out.

As for this stranger . . .

I have to do something to help him. Out of the goodness of my heart.

But . . . ugh. The lower part of the knife handle is covered with blood that's still gushing from the wound.

I wish I had gloves. From now on I should never go anywhere without gloves in my pocket.

Gloves were an integral part of Saturday night's plan.

But this, today, wasn't planned by any means. This was a spur of the moment impulse, an instinctive reaction.

Turtles only snap because they're trying to protect themselves.

That's the reason I snapped. It's the reason I was even carrying the knife in the first place.

This is a relatively safe part of town, but no neighborhood is immune to crime. At this hour, before the world has fully stirred to life, it would be foolhardy to walk the streets alone without some form of protection. You just never know what kind of lunatic might be lurking around the next corner.

That's why the knife was such a great find when it turned up in a secondhand store a while back.

"Now this here's a great tool," the shop owner said, demonstrating how the knife's four-inch blade opened and closed. "See how it folds up so that it'll fit right into your pocket?"

Yes. It was a great tool. But hardly worth the asking price.

The owner begged to differ. "That's a valuable antique, my friend. The handle is the real thing, not imitation. You can't buy something like this anymore. They outlawed using tortoiseshell a hundred years ago."

"Not a hundred years ago. Not even fifty. It's old, but technically it's not an antique. Tortoiseshell was banned in 1973 under the Convention of International Trade on Endangered Species."

The owner's eyes widened. "You know your stuff, don't you?"

A lot better than you know yours.

In the end, the man was willing to bargain the price down.

And he was right. The knife is a great tool.

A great tool that is now sticking out of a stranger's abdomen.

I need to get it back. I need to get out of here.

In the distance a dog is barking.

If it's the puppy, still running loose with a leash dangling from its collar, there's no telling what might happen. Someone might already have found the animal; might come looking for the owner right now.

Gloves or no gloves, it's time to act.

The knife handle is slick with blood. But with one firm tug the blade lifts right out of the man's bleeding torso.

The morning light seems to have shifted; his eyes are visible now, focused with surprising clarity, pleading, pleading . . .

"All right. I really am sorry about this, and . . . and I'll help you. Okay? I'll make it easier for you."

The man turns his head and closes his eyes as if he knows what's coming next—as if he can't bear to watch, or perhaps, as if making it easier for everyone, granting access by turning his neck at just the right angle for the blade to slice neatly through his jugular.

This time, blood spurts.

This time, mercifully, it's over. No more suffering.

The dog is still barking in the distance as the knife snaps closed.

What a mess. The blade and the tortoiseshell handle are covered in blood, but that's okay. It will wash off and be good as new.

One last thing . . .

"Here. I always carry one of these in my pocket for luck. Now . . . it's for you. I'm sorry. Really."

The tortoiseshell guitar pick goes into the front pocket of the man's jeans, the one where he keeps his wallet. In fact . . .

I'd better grab that.

If the man's wallet is missing, it will take a while for the police to identify him, and when they do, it'll look like he was mugged while out walking his dog.

It's time to get out of here, fighting the instinct to run every step of the way. It isn't far, just around the corner, but . . .

Slow and steady.

Always, always, slow and steady.

Part II

Saturday, June 8

Happily Ever After

When I was growing up in a landlocked antebellum home across the highway, I used to pedal my bike past the charming raised cottages and graceful southern homes along Mobile Bay, daydreaming about what it would be like to live in one of them.

Now I do.

This lovely home my husband and I bought as newlyweds isn't my only childhood dream come true.

As a girl, skirting sandy ruts and ducking low over my handlebars as I passed beneath low-hanging bows of massive live oaks, I liked to time my Saturday afternoon bike rides so there'd be a good chance I'd find a wedding in progress in the bayside garden at the Grand Hotel.

I'd park my bike in a secluded spot where I could spy on the beautiful brides in white lace with their dashing, tuxedo-clad grooms. Eavesdropping as they exchanged age-old vows, I made a vow of my own: "Someday, I'm going to meet Mr. Right and be married in that very spot."

A decade later—over twenty years ago now—I met Mr. Right at a Labor Day barbecue.

He was drastically different from the good time Charlies I'd found so captivating that summer after graduating from the University of Alabama. No longer a sorority girl, I was still drawn to frat boy types—until I met Rob. He was a few years older, quiet and ear-

nest, with strong southern roots and a law degree from one of the top universities in the Northeast. He'd just passed the bar and was newly employed by the Mobile law firm where he's long since been made a partner. He proposed a few months after our first date and we were married the following spring—right on the spot I'd picked out as a little girl, in the garden at the Grand Hotel amid blooming azaleas and magnolias.

We exchanged those same vows I'd eavesdropped upon and sighed over as a hopelessly romantic pre-teen. We promised to stay together for better or worse, for richer or poorer, in sickness and in health . . .

Sickness.

Health.

Those weighty words don't make much impact when you're a starry-eyed twelve-year-old dreaming of fairy-tale endings—or even when you're a lace-clad bride embarking on happily ever after.

Sometimes, dreams come true.

Sometimes, your worst nightmare becomes reality . . . then fades away, the way nightmares do the morning after.

My husband and I will celebrate our twentieth wedding anniversary tomorrow. Some years have been better than we expected, and a few of them have been much worse, but I choose to believe the best are yet to come.

—Excerpt from Landry's blog, *The Breast Cancer Diaries*

Chapter 6

Early Saturday morning—before the sun comes up—Rob drives Landry to the airport.

Sitting in the front seat beside him, clutching the full stainless steel coffee mug he handed her back in the kitchen, she gazes at the darkened landscape through the passenger's side window, resting her temple against the glass.

She wants to tell him to turn around and go home.

I've changed my mind.

I don't want to go to Cincinnati.

I never wanted to go.

I'm only doing it because I feel like I have to. Because it's the right thing, the brave thing—the hard thing. Because that's the role model I want to be for my children.

In this case, for her daughter. Addison is the one who's interested in what's going on with her right now. Tucker is in his own little adolescent world, caught up in video games, friends, his first job, and, most likely, summer girls. He knows Landry lost a friend, knows she's flying up North for the memorial service today, but asked no questions and has said very little about it, other than to look up from his iPhone long enough to offer an obligatory, "Sorry about your friend, Mom."

That's okay. He's a kid.

So is Addison, really. But Addie keeps asking if she's all right. She always does her chores without being asked, but the last couple of days she's gone out of her way to take care of things around the house, to make things easier.

It reminds Landry of the morning, years ago, when Addie made her breakfast in bed while she was in the midst of treatment. French toast. Landry's never been fond of sweets in the morning, and she'd woken up terribly nauseated that particular day. But she choked down the syrup-and-powdered-sugar-drenched French toast and asked for seconds.

Addison beamed. "I'm so glad you like it, Mommy. I knew a good breakfast would make you feel better."

My sweet, kind, caring girl, Landry thought then—and thought it again late last night, when she went into her daughter's room to kiss her good-night and good-bye for the weekend.

"I just got paid, so I bought you some magazines at work this afternoon," Addie said, handing over a bag from the hotel gift shop. "Good Hollywood gossipy ones, the kind you like, to keep you busy on the plane."

"You didn't have to do that, sweetie. Don't spend your money on me."

"I like to. You spend your money on me. Oh, and I made you this. Wear it with your black dress tomorrow."

Addison handed her an onyx bracelet featuring two silver beads etched with the initials MH.

She could barely thank her daughter over the lump in her throat, and gave her a long, hard hug.

"She loved jewelry," she told Addie. "Meredith did. She blogged about that. She said that's how she got into the habit of wearing earrings and necklaces to bed, because it made her head feel less naked after she lost all her hair."

"Oh, Mom . . . Poor Meredith. I wish I could have made that bracelet for her instead of . . . well, I was thinking of it as a memorial bracelet for you, but now . . ."

"I know. You're so sweet, Addie."

"So are you. You're being a good friend. Meredith would be glad you're going to be there for the service tomorrow."

"I'm sure she would be."

If the tables were turned, Landry knows, Meredith would be the first to get on a plane. That knowledge has been a motivating factor.

"Who all is going for sure?"

Landry told her the two she's certain about: A-Okay and Elena. Jaycee has a business commitment in New York and can't possibly get away.

"I know it's going to be a sad weekend for y'all, but it'll be nice to meet your friends in person, Mom—don't you think?"

"I'm sure it will be," she said, because that was the easiest answer.

In truth—she's not so sure.

Everyone's ambivalent about meeting under these circumstances. All this time, whenever they've talked about arranging an in-person get-together, Meredith was at the heart of the discussion. It's impossible to imagine meeting at last without her there.

Landry spoke to A-Okay again on Thursday, and to Elena as well, after Meredith's daughter posted the weekend funeral arrangements on her mother's blog.

Elena, with her thick New England accent, was a pleasant surprise when she called that afternoon. They don't have much in common—Elena is a decade younger, never-married schoolteacher—yet they chatted for over an hour, not just about Meredith, but about Landry's kids and Elena's first grade class, about travel and food and clothes and books and the sad state of Elena's love life.

"When you live in a small town and work in a small town elementary school, it's not easy to find a decent, eligible guy without baggage—especially when you have more than your share of it."

"Of . . . ?" She was having a hard time following Elena's rapid-fire speech and thick New England accent.

"Baggage. It's hard for a guy to deal with the fact that I'm scarred—in more ways than one." She pronounced *hard* and *scarred* as "hahd" and "scahd."

"Everyone has baggage," she said. "And the right guy will be able to deal with it."

"I guess. But I haven't found him yet." Elena sighed, then changed the subject back to the memorial service. "If you go, I'll go."

"I'm going."

"Then I'll get a flight. There are some great fare sales out of Boston right now. I just can't go until Saturday morning. I have a staff banquet Friday night."

Landry assured her that was fine, then hung up and called A-Okay, who picked up this time on the first ring.

That conversation was more stilted, but only because Kay isn't as outgoing a person as Elena. She's friendly in her own reserved way, though, and before they hung up, she said she'd drive down to Cincinnati on Saturday.

"Drive? Really?"

"It's only a couple of hours from here."

"Wow. I guess I don't know my midwestern geography very well."

"It's okay. I don't know my southern geography either. I've never even been south of Indiana."

"Really? You'll have to come down and visit sometime," Landry heard herself offering.

Kay was noncommittal. "That would be nice. I'll have to do that sometime."

All they have to do is get through this weekend in Cincinnati. If the three of them hit it off, great. If they don't, they can go back to being online acquaintances, as long as the lack of anonymity doesn't change things going forward.

"Jittery about flying?" Rob asks, glancing over at Landry as he flicks the turn signal for the airport exit.

"Me? No! I'm not afraid to fly."

She used to be, years ago, for a while. After September eleventh.

Before cancer.

Once you've had cancer, phobias over mundane things like commercial air travel tend to fall by the wayside. You no longer worry about being killed in a plane crash. In the grand scheme of things—when you're in the midst of fighting cancer, uncertain about what lies ahead—that might seem like the more merciful option.

Thank goodness those dark days are over.

As far as I'm concerned, remission is the same thing as cured, Meredith wrote once on her blog.

It isn't really. Not as far as most doctors are concerned. Cancer is a complicated disease; far too complex to be discussed in simplistic terms.

But Landry knew what she meant.

And now that she's been in remission for years, and her odds for a recurrence are low and shrinking by the day . . .

Yes. She's as cured as she's ever going to be. Her illness is behind her now. She's stronger than she's ever been.

She refuses to live the rest of her life looking over her shoulder as if a deadly predator is gaining on her. She'd rather focus optimistically on the future, with every reason to expect to live a long, healthy life just as her grandmother did.

Family history is in her favor. So are medical statistics for stage one cancer detected as early as hers was.

"Good," Rob is saying as he guides the SUV onto Airport Boulevard. "You shouldn't be afraid to fly. We've done enough of it over the years."

Yes. All those winter ski trips to the Rockies, spring beach breaks in the Caribbean, long weekends in Mexico, summer vacations in Europe . . .

They may not be jet-setters, but they've certainly done their share of traveling.

Together, that is.

"I'm just not used to going off alone," she tells him.

"I know you're not. But it will be good for you. All you ever do is stay home and take care of the kids and me and the house . . ."

"I like doing those things." Ordinary days. Ordinary nights. They're a blessing.

"I know you do," Rob says, "but everyone needs a change of scenery."

"It's not just that. It's not like this is a pleasure trip. It's something I need to do."

Every time she feels a hint of misgiving about what lies ahead, she remembers something she learned in Sunday school as a little girl, and later taught her own children as well.

When faced with a difficult decision or challenging situation, it can be helpful to ask yourself what Jesus would do if he were in your shoes. The answer might just guide you to the right path.

Now, for Landry, the question had become not just, *What would Jesus do?* but also, *What would Meredith do?*

Meredith was no saint—Landry knows she'd have been the first to laugh at that notion. But she was centered, and judicious.

Five minutes later she and Rob are out of the car in front of the terminal, the rear flashers blinking red in the darkness. Rob wanted to park and come in with her, but that seems silly.

She already checked in for the flight online. The printout containing her boarding pass is folded in her pocket, along with all the details of her car rental and the hotel reservation for Cincinnati. All she has to do inside is go through the TSA checkpoint to the gate. It's not as if Rob can accompany her down there and wait until she boards.

"I'd rather you get right back home to the kids," she tells him, as if the kids aren't going to sleep for at least another couple of hours, even Addison.

Now that she's leaving, she just wants to leave. A prolonged good-bye would make it even harder.

Rob takes her rolling bag out of the back, sets it on the ground, pulls up the handle. "There you go."

"Thanks." She removes her boarding pass from the packet of papers and shoves the rest back into her pocket. "Tell the kids I said good-bye, and I'll call y'all when I land."

"Call me when you get to the gate," he says. "Just so I know you got through security okay."

"I'll be okay. Don't worry."

"I'm not worried. Don't you worry."

"I'm not worried," she returns, but allows herself to lean on him, briefly, when he hugs her good-bye.

"I'll miss you," he says as she starts to lift her bag up over a puddle by the curb. "And Landry—be careful."

"It's okay. I've got it. It's not heavy."

"I don't mean with the bag."

For a moment their eyes connect. "I know," she tells him.

He's still worried that what happened to Meredith is no random crime. Yet there's been nothing in the news reports to suggest otherwise. The police are still investigating. No mention of questioning suspects or anything suggesting that an arrest might be imminent.

Whoever killed Meredith is still, presumably, out there somewhere.

Rob doesn't like that.

She doesn't like it either, but . . .

It has nothing to do with her. It doesn't make her less safe.

Chin up. Strength training.

"I'll be fine," she assures Rob, "and the next thing we know, you'll be picking me up right here. I'll only be gone for two days. Well, less than that. Really, it's just a matter of hours, when you think about it."

But a lot can happen in a matter of hours.

A lot can happen in a matter of minutes, in a matter of seconds.

Suddenly, it all seems so . . . precarious.

Why on earth is she leaving her husband and children to spend a weekend with a bunch of strangers in the wake of a murder?

Rob looks at his watch. "You'd better get going. I love you, Babe."

"I love you, too." Landry turns away quickly so that he won't see the uncertainty—or the tears—in her eyes.

Kay had left home early—much earlier than necessary—in the hope that there wouldn't be much traffic heading south out of Indianapolis on Interstate 74 at this hour on a Saturday morning.

She should have known better. This was a busy corridor at any hour on any day of the week. Headlights constantly bear down in her rearview mirror; taillights whiz past at dizzying velocity.

How do they all drive so fast?

Glancing at the dashboard, she's astonished to see the speedometer hovering at forty-two miles per hour.

Maybe the better question would be why are you driving so slowly?

It felt as though she was going the speed limit, if not above.

She presses the gas pedal.

The needle goes up, up, up . . .

Now it feels as though the car is careening dangerously.

Oops. She hits the brake.

Behind her a car honks. Its headlights swerve out around her, and even in the darkness she sees the silhouetted driver giving her the finger.

"What?" she shouts. "What do you want from me?"

Dammit, dammit, dammit.

She used to be such a competent driver, unfazed by darkness or traffic or weather. She drove to work in Terre Haute and regularly transported her mother to and from the specialist's office up in Chicago without batting an eye.

Now her eyesight is worse, thanks to advancing age. All these headaches . . . she probably needs glasses for distance, too, not just for reading.

Plus—because she didn't sleep a wink last night, thinking about Meredith and about the weekend ahead—her nerves are shot and her reflexes are slow.

But you'd better get your act together. Now is not a good time to fall apart.

In the rearview mirror Kay sees an unbroken string of headlights in the left lane and the glare of a semi bearing down behind her in the right.

Her hands tighten on the wheel. She holds her breath as the lights come closer, blinding her. The truck is about to barrel into her car . . .

But then the lights swoop away as the driver cuts off someone in the left lane to get out around her.

More angry horns, more rude gestures.

This is a mistake. She's much too exhausted, too frazzled, to be driving. She's risking her life to go to a funeral.

She'd told BamaBelle—Landry—that it was only a couple of hours away, as if it were no big deal to get behind the wheel and hit the highway.

It's not as if she's never done it before. She spent all those years commuting a full hour in each direction from the western suburbs to the prison, sometimes in harsh winter blizzards or tornado weather.

The drive to Ohio was the least of her worries—at that point, anyway, when she was on the phone with Landry.

She was far more concerned with the prospect of coming

face-to-face with BamaBelle and Elena, and whoever else might show up in Cincinnati. Concerned . . . but not enough to say no.

That sweet southern drawl was so convincing.

And Landry's right: they do owe it to Meredith.

Oh, Meredith . . .

Tears sting Kay's eyes, blurring the string of taillights through the windshield.

She wipes them away, and notices the first tints of pink sky, low above the flat horizon.

Okay. It's going to be okay. It's only one day. Twenty-four hours from now she'll be heading in the opposite direction. The nightmare of Meredith's funeral will be behind her.

She reserved a room at the same hotel where Landry and Elena are staying, about a mile away from the funeral home where Meredith's service is being held. She prepaid the reservation on her credit card, even, because the rate was considerably cheaper that way and frugality is a hard habit to break.

Mother always said not to waste dollars or even pennies today because you might need them tomorrow. She lived that rule to her dying day. Never treated herself, let alone her daughter, to a vacation or even dinner in a nice restaurant. Never spent money on anything but cigarettes. She didn't consider that a waste.

As for Kay . . .

God knows she can well afford to squander a couple hundred bucks if it turns out the others don't like her in person.

But she really hopes that they do. Desperately hopes so.

That's why you're going, isn't it? It's why you said yes when you meant no. Because the thought of friends—seeing friends, friends who care . . .

For the past few days the idea of coming face-to-face with her fellow bloggers seemed a lot less threatening than she'd imagined. Maybe because she misses Meredith so much, and needs to fill the aching void.

There's alone, and then there's lonely. One is safe and comfortable; the other . . .

Well, it never bothered her so much before. But the last few days haven't been easy. She keeps thinking of Meredith, remembering Meredith, knowing what Meredith would want—expect—her to do.

She was such a good person. So strong. So much stronger than she ever knew.

She was always making self-deprecating comments in her blog, masking her insecurities behind humor. She didn't allow herself to crawl into a hole and hide, not even in the face of the worst news imaginable.

If I could just be more like her . . .

But this is a start.

She has crawled out of her hole. It's the right thing to do, the smart thing to do, and what's the worst that can happen?

When the doorman calls up to tell her she has a visitor, Jaycee has just thrown on a pair of yoga pants, a tank top, and of course her blond wig. She doesn't wear it around the apartment when she's home alone, but Beatrice, her cleaning lady, comes on Saturday mornings.

Usually not until later, though. Jaycee was about to sit down with her first cup of coffee and her laptop to enjoy a few moments' peace.

"Who is it?" she asks Mike, the doorman.

"It's Mr. Wallace."

Cory. Of course. Always Cory.

She tells the doorman to let him up, then opens the laptop to quickly see if there were any overnight developments on Meredith's murder.

Nothing, other than a death notice in a small suburban Ohio newspaper, with mention of today's memorial service.

By now Jaycee knows that the others are either in Cincinnati or on their way: Landry, Elena, and A-Okay.

She got Landry's e-mail with all the arrangements—*I'm cc'ing you just in case you can join us last minute, Jaycee!*—and knows they're staying in a hotel out where Meredith lives.

Lived.

There's a knock on the apartment door. Jaycee quickly deletes the browser history, closes the laptop, and goes to answer.

Cory is standing there.

"What's going on?" she asks, stepping aside for the one person in this world who always knows exactly where to find her, even when she's hiding.

"I wasn't sure you'd be up."

"So you came anyway? Were you going to wake me up?"

"Absolutely."

He's clean-shaven, wearing jeans and a polo shirt beneath a rain jacket, his reddish hair spiking up over his forehead to make him look like a boy rather than a grown man. On a good day, he reminds her of Kevin Bacon—young Kevin Bacon, from the *Footloose* days—and she adores him. On a bad day . . .

On a bad day, she doesn't want to deal with him, period. Because she only wants to be left alone.

But most of the time Cory refuses to allow that. And once in a while she winds up grateful for his persistent presence in her solitary life.

"It's a crappy day out there," he announces. "Humid as hell, and it's supposed to rain."

Yeah, well, it's a crappy day in here, too—this being the anniversary and all. That fact won't have escaped Cory, she knows.

"Thanks for the weather report," she tells him. "Is that why you're here? Because I usually just check Accuweather online if I want—"

"I brought you a newspaper," he says, thrusting it at her, along with a white paper bag, "and a bagel."

"Thank you." She opens the bag, peers inside to see that it's sesame, toasted, plain, cut into four pieces. Just the way she likes it. "I'd say come in . . . but oh, look, you're already in. As usual."

"Love you, too," he says easily on his way to the kitchen.

She closes the door behind him, locks it, and follows him.

He helps himself to a cup of coffee from the pot she just brewed. "Did you use the Costa Rican beans Adam gave you the other day?"

Adam is Cory's longtime boyfriend. A travel agent, he's always jetting off to exotic places and bringing back gifts for his friends. Jaycee is touched that he considers her one of them—even now, after all these years, after . . . everything.

She wonders, sometimes, whether he knows . . . *everything*. But the past never comes up. Nor does the future. Usually, they just talk about his travels, and food, books, films . . .

Things normal people discuss.

Right. Because you like to pretend you're a normal person. It's a nice . . . escape.

"I haven't used the Costa Rican beans yet," she tells Cory. "This time, I used good old American beans I bought myself."

"Where, at Starbucks?"

"How did you guess?"

"You're a fan." He makes a face. "And it's so . . ."

"Ubiquitous?" she supplies. They've had this conversation before. Ad nauseam.

"Exactly."

"Some of us appreciate that."

"Some of us don't." He opens the fridge to look for milk. "So tell me . . . what's the point of this visit?"

"Open the paper," he says without turning around. "Page eight."

Uh-oh.

I should have known.

She puts the paper down on the counter.

Opens it to page eight.

Scans the page, then looks up at him, shaking her head. "I thought you said we were going to get past this. It's been—"

"I know how long it's been. What you need to do is—"

"I know what I need to do, Cory," she says grimly. "I've been trying to do it. It's impossible, okay?"

"Nothing is impossible."

He's wrong about that.

If only she could go back in time and erase not just the past seven years, but the past twenty—pick up where she left off in that dreaded, dismal little town she left behind years ago . . .

It would be easy, then, to change the course of her life, become someone else.

Someone whose name had never been heard beyond a five-mile perimeter; someone no one imagined was capable of becoming a success, or making a fortune, or . . .

Or committing a murder, even when you're only doing what has to be done . . .

The alarm goes off, jarring Elena from a sound sleep.

Lying in her bed in that split second before she opens her eyes, she knows that something is off, but what is it?

She forces her eyelids open. The room is dark—rainy day dark, though, not night dark. According to her digital alarm clock, the time is wrong. It's an hour later than she usually gets up, which is . . .

Wait a minute. This isn't a weekday, it's a Saturday.

She usually sleeps in on weekends, but this morning she only gets an extra hour because she has a flight to catch because she's going to—

Starting to roll over, Elena gasps.

That's it. That's what's off. Not the time or the dreary

light that's falling across her bed, but the fact that someone is sharing it with her.

Lying absolutely still so as not to wake whoever it is, she thinks back to last night. She was at the staff party, held at a banquet hall located about halfway between the school and the town where she lives. She remembers the speeches—she even delivered one, in honor of the retiring Betty Jamison— and she remembers the dinner, but not the dessert, and . . .

Wine . . . there was a lot of wine. Too much wine.

Again.

Dammit. When will she ever learn?

The waiter kept refilling my glass . . .

Yes, sure, it's the waiter's fault.

She remembers thinking that he was cute and wondering whether he was straight or not. She remembers that he was looking at her sympathetically, probably keeping the wine flowing because . . .

Oh, God.

She closes her eyes again, listening to her visitor's rhythmic snoring in time to the rain pattering on the roof.

She has a wicked headache; her mouth is dry, stomach queasy . . .

Queasy not just because of the wine, but because she just remembered the reason the waiter took pity on her.

She arrived late and got stuck at the end of the table next to the one person no one else wanted to sit near.

Now she forces herself to roll over, open her eyes, and confront the ugly truth snoozing away right here in her bed, covers thrown down to reveal his hairy chest.

Tony Kerwin.

Landry had been worried about making her relatively tight connection in Atlanta, but thanks to thunderstorms rolling across Georgia, the outbound flight is going to be delayed at least an hour.

Settled into a seat at the gate, facing a wall of plate glass so that she can watch the torrential rain, she calls home to let Rob know she made it this far.

"How was the flight?" he asks.

"Fine. Landing was a little bumpy because of the weather." She tells him about the delay, then asks to talk to the kids.

"Addison went out for a run, and Tucker's still in bed."

"Okay. Tell them to call me if they want. I have nothing to do but sit here and wait."

"I'll leave a note. I'm headed out golfing."

"Oh, right." He goes early to beat the afternoon thunderstorms that tend to roll in at this time of year.

"I was thinking that later, after I get out of work, I'll take them for crab claws and po'boys at Big Daddy's."

"Wish I could go."

"No claws and po'boys in Cincinnati?"

"I doubt it."

She can hear clattering plates and silverware in the background and knows he's emptying the dishwasher. For some reason, that makes her even more homesick than the sound of his voice . . . and she's only been gone a few hours.

After hanging up with Rob, she wonders briefly if she should text both Elena and Kay to let them know she might be arriving late, but decides against it. The memorial service doesn't start until three o'clock. Even with the delay, she'll be arriving with plenty of time to spare.

What now?

She has her laptop with her. She'd been thinking she might find time during the weekend to write a new blog post, something she hasn't done all week. She hasn't had the heart to write about the tragedy, or the interest in anything else.

I still don't. Maybe after the funeral. But not now.

The laptop stays in her bag. She's idly flipping through one of the celebrity gossip rags Addison gave her, trying to become absorbed in the latest tinsel town divorce scandal, when a shadow falls over the page.

She looks up, startled.

A man she recognizes as having been on her flight out from Mobile says, "Hi. Would you mind . . . I'm going to go grab a coffee and I'd rather not lug my bags." He points to a rolling suitcase and leather messenger bag a few seats away. "Can you keep an eye on them for a few minutes?"

He has a brisk demeanor and a northern accent. Remembering that the TSA is always making announcements about untended luggage, she hesitates, then nods. "Sure. No problem."

"Thank you. Can I bring you something? Do you drink coffee?"

"I do, but . . . no, thanks."

"Are you sure?"

"I'm sure."

She watches him stride away through the boarding area, then glances at his bags again, wondering whether he's on the same connecting flight or one that's delayed out of a nearby gate, then wondering why she's suddenly feeling vaguely guilty for wondering—not to mention for noticing that he's handsome.

Not as handsome as Rob, by any means. Different handsome. Dark handsome, versus Rob's golden boy good looks.

She's well out of her comfort zone now, not only traveling alone, but having a strange man offer to buy her a cup of coffee.

Although he probably didn't mean it like that . . .

Oh, please. Of course he didn't. He was just being polite.

Look at her. She's a middle-aged mom wearing jeans, a hoodie, and no makeup, her blond hair pulled back in a simple ponytail. She'd left too early to worry about what she looked like this morning and had been planning on having enough time at the hotel to pull herself together before she meets the others. Hopefully, she'll still have it, but if not . . .

What you see is what you get.

She licks her finger, turning a page of the magazine, scanning it—a photo montage of celebrity bikini beach shots with plenty of cleavage, only serving to remind her that her own bikini and cleavage days are long behind her. She turns another page, and then another . . .

Then, oops! Remembers she's supposed to be watching Mr. Coffee's luggage.

Restless, she tucks the magazine back into her carry-on, checks her watch, and takes out her phone again.

There's a text from Addison: *Dad said u called. Jumping into shower then have 2 leave 4 work. Talk 2 U later. ILY.*

She smiles and texts back ILY2: *I love you, too.*

Landry toys with her phone for a minute, remembering that she never did return her cousin's call from the other night. Barbie June left another message—a slightly pissed-off-sounding one—last night while she was out to dinner with Rob. She meant to call back, but when she got home she still had to pack, and by then she wasn't in the mood to talk to her cousin anyway, with the trip looming and the alarm set for 4:00 A.M.

She glances at the window again in time to see a large bolt of lightning zigzag the sky almost directly overhead. She has nothing but time on her hands for the immediate future, so she might as well call back now and face the wrath of Barbie June, who never takes kindly to being put off.

Her cousin answers the phone immediately, with a high-pitched, "Landry! I have been so worried about y'all!"

"Worried? Why?"

"It's not like you to ignore your messages, and I've been trying to track you down all week!"

"I'm sorry, it's been a rough week, and—"

"I heard what happened! Aunt Ardelle"—Landry's mother—"told Mama that you were flying away to a funeral up North!"

That gives Landry pause. She'd called her mother yesterday to let her know she was leaving for the weekend; that an old friend had died. When her mother asked who it was, she said, truthfully, "No one you know."

"A college friend?"

"Something like that." Then she successfully changed the subject, asking about her mom's roses. An avid gardener, Ardelle Quackenbush always welcomes the opportunity to talk horticulture.

Now, Landry tells her cousin the same thing about the funeral: "It's no one you know."

"Your mother told my mother it was someone from college."

"She did? Bless her heart. Her hearing is getting worse by the day. It wasn't someone from college."

"Oh, thank the Lord! I've been on the alumni Web sites all morning trying to figure out who it could have been and why I wouldn't have heard about it, too. Who was it?"

Landry sighs inwardly. "It was someone I met online."

There's a pause.

"One of those bloggers?" Barbie June asks. "The ones who are always writing notes to you like they know you?"

"How do you know that?"

"How do you think? I read your blog! I'm your cousin!"

Landry clears her throat. "I'm sorry. I didn't know you read it."

"Of course I do!"

Then why, she wants to ask, *haven't you ever said anything positive about it until now? Why are you always making disparaging remarks about anything having to do with social networking?*

"Which friend died?" Barbie June persists.

"Oh, I'm sure you wouldn't—"

"Landry! I just said I read your blog. I know who all the regulars are—the ones who always comment. I know you consider them friends. Who was it?"

Fair enough. If she's been reading, then Meredith's name will be familiar to her. Meredith was always one of the first to leave a comment whenever she posted a new entry.

"It was Meredith," she tells Barbie June.

"Really? I didn't even know she was sick again!"

Rather than inform her cousin that she wasn't, in fact, sick again, Landry asks, "How could you know?"

"I've read her blog, too. You can link to them through their names when they leave comments on your page. I've read most of— Oh. Well, there it is."

"There what is?"

"I'm on her blog now." Keyboard tapping. "There are all these comments about it being sudden . . . What in the world happened to her?"

This feels wrong to Landry—Barbie June asking about Meredith, almost as if she knows her. Until now her real life and online life have been as neatly compartmentalized as Addison's cases of beads. Now it's all been upended and jumbled together, leaving her oddly unsettled.

"Landry?"

"It was an accident," she says briefly, thinking that Meredith's—or maybe just her own—privacy seems to have somehow been violated. Maybe it shouldn't feel that way, but it does. She wishes she hadn't called back.

"What kind of accident? A car accident?" Barbie June is asking when a voice cuts in to distract Landry.

"Thank you."

She looks up to see that the owner of the luggage a few seats away has returned with his coffee.

Make that two cups of coffee. He gestures, offering one to her.

She pivots her phone away from her mouth to thank him.

"It's black," he says, "Do you take cream and sugar?"

"That's all right, I—"

"Landry? Who are you talking to?"

"No one," she murmurs into the phone. "I should go. I think we're about to board."

"But—"

"I'll call you when I . . ." About to say *land,* she amends quickly: " . . . get home."

"When will that be?"

"Monday."

"You're not coming home until *Monday*?" Barbie June sounds as though Landry just told her she'd boarded the *Queen Mary* on a one-way cruise to Europe.

"Sunday night. Late." *Too late to make phone calls.*

"Oh, well . . . have a good weekend, sweetie."

"You too."

Landry hangs up.

Sure. I'll have a great weekend—paying my respects to my dead friend.

She shakes her head, pocketing her phone, and the man hands her one of the cups of coffee. "I know you said no, but I figured you were just being polite."

"I was." *And I was thinking I shouldn't accept a cup of coffee from a strange man.*

"So . . . your mother?"

"Pardon?"

"Whoever you were talking to—that was your mother?"

"Oh—no. My cousin."

He flashes a grin and she notices his nice white teeth. "I figured it had to be family by the way you were trying to shake her."

"I wasn't really—"

"Oh, come on, sure you were."

"Sure I was," she finds herself agreeing, returning his grin.

"Yeah. Thought so. Been there, done that, a million times."

"I guess every family has one of those."

"Mine has many. And they're all in Cincinnati. I was thinking even twenty-four hours is a lot of time to spend with them, so . . . if there's anyone who doesn't particularly mind this flight delay, it's—"

"That guy?" she quips, pointing at a college-age kid stretched out on the floor nearby, peacefully asleep.

"Him, too, I guess. Seriously, I wouldn't mind if we sat here for hours. Oh, by the way, I almost forgot—" He pulls a couple of creamer and sugar packets out of his pocket, along with a plastic stirrer, and offers them to her.

"Thank you. Really." She peels the plastic lid off the cup. "I got up so early that I really do need this."

"Same here. And between being tired and what's waiting for me when we land, if we don't take off soon—not that I want to—I may have to switch over to something stronger."

"You know, that's not a bad idea." As soon as the words are out of her mouth, she wants to bite them back. Does it sound as if she wants him to buy her a drink now?

No—of course not.

She's just not good at this . . . solo travel.

Her phone rings. She jumps, almost spilling her coffee.

"Careful there. Here, let me hold that for you."

He takes the cup, and she pulls out her phone, sees Rob's cell phone number in the caller ID window.

"That's my husband," she says—maybe a little pointedly, and answers the phone. "Rob? Everything okay?"

"Everything is fine."

"Oh, good." She presses the phone to her ear with her shoulder as Mr. Coffee hands back the cup, gives a little salute and goes back to his seat.

"Tucker can't find any of the shirts he needs for work," Rob tells her, "and I looked everywhere—"

"Hanging up behind the door in the laundry room?"

"—except there."

"Go check. I'm pretty sure that's where they are."

She dumps a sugar packet into her coffee as he goes to look, resisting the urge to tell him that she reminded him where to find the shirts when they were on their way to the airport this morning. And, of course, she told Tucker last night. Twice. But neither of the men in her life can ever seem to find anything around the house.

"Got 'em," Rob says a few moments later. "Thanks. I've got to get him moving or he's going to be late. Do you know it took me fifteen minutes to get him out of bed?"

Welcome to my world, Rob.

"He's not really a morning kid," she points out unnecessarily, stirring her coffee.

"Yeah, no kidding. I'd better go give him his shirt. He's probably sleeping again."

"Probably. Love you."

"You too," he says—sincerely, if hurriedly.

Mr. Coffee is busy on his laptop when she hangs up. He doesn't even glance her way.

Relieved, she goes back to her magazine.

It's much too early to check in when Kay arrives at the hotel on the suburban outskirts of Cincinnati. She drives past it, making note of where to turn later, and then decides to head on down the road to familiarize herself with the place where Meredith's service is being held.

McGraw's Funeral Parlor is a squat yellow brick building set back from the two-lane highway. Next door on one side there's a bowling alley with a neon sign and a gigantic satellite dish that sits right on the property perimeter. On the other side sits a boxy duplex with an aboveground swimming pool in the small yard.

It bothers Kay, for some reason, to think of people swimming and bowling and watching TV in such close proximity to dead bodies and grieving families. She wishes the funeral—Meredith's funeral—were being held elsewhere.

Meredith's funeral . . .

Dear God.

She turns around in the empty parking lot and backtracks toward the hotel. For a moment she considers jumping right back onto the interstate and heading home.

No, don't do that. You're much too tired to drive, and hungry, too. You'll feel better if you get something to eat and relax for a bit.

There are a couple of restaurants near the Wal-Mart shopping plaza. It's too early in the day for Applebee's or Chili's, and she bypasses Starbucks as well. She entered one back home a few years ago, wanting a plain old cup of coffee, and was immediately intimidated by the sleek decor, unfamiliar beverages on the overly complicated menu, and the impatient girl at the register, who asked rapid-fire questions that might as well have been in a foreign language: "Tall, grande, or venti? . . . Blond, medium, or Bold Pick? . . . With or without room?"

Shuddering at the thought of repeating that experience—and in an unfamiliar city, besides—she opts instead for a Bob Evans restaurant, a familiar chain she's visited back home.

The parking lot is full. Inside, she finds herself surrounded by senior citizens, truck drivers, and families with small children.

"What are you doing up so early on a weekend, hon?" asks the friendly waitress, after taking her order.

"Me? Oh, I always get up early."

"Not me. If I weren't here, I'd be in bed until noon, believe me."

Kay smiles at her. She's the motherly type. Probably a grandma, too. Women like this always make her wistful—not just for what she, herself, is never going to be, but for what her own mother chose not to be. And now, for what she found, and lost, in Meredith.

"Can I bring you cream with that coffee, hon?"

"Yes, please. And real butter with the biscuits, please, instead of that spread, whatever it is."

"You got it."

Meredith was always blogging about eating natural foods, avoiding chemicals. She taught her so much about nutrition.

Some of the bloggers—like Elena—might argue that it doesn't matter much at this point. Not for them. As she put it . . .

Either you've already fought cancer and won . . . or you've lost, and at that point might as well throw caution to the wind.

Meredith's diplomatic response*: To each his own.*

Kay finds herself swallowing back the ache in her throat, thinking of her friend. It feels wrong to be here in Cincinnati, about to meet some of the others without Meredith.

She forces the sorrow away and notices a trio of white-haired women in the next booth. Two are smiling, chatting easily between bites of omelets and pancakes. The third is silently picking at a poached egg, wearing a dour expression.

Making eye contact with Kay, she scowls, and Kay quickly averts her eyes, wishing she'd thought to pick up a newspaper or something.

Dining out solo has never been very comfortable for her—though it's preferable to dining out with Mother, back when she was alive. That didn't happen very often, but on the few occasions when it did, Mother complained about the service, the prices, the food . . .

She was just like you, Kay silently tells the dour woman, though she doesn't dare sneak another peek. *A miserable human being.*

Why would anyone, blessed with the gift of longevity, waste all those years finding fault with everything around her—especially with her own daughter?

But then . . .

Why did I waste all those years trying to make her see past her resentment of me; trying to make her love me?

She had known damn well that it was futile from the time she was a kid. She should have walked out of that house the moment she turned eighteen and never looked back.

She thought of doing that. She did.

But where would she have gone? She had no plan, no college tuition, let alone money to live on campus. She'd always thought she might want to become a writer, but that was an impossible dream.

That's what her high school English teacher told her.

A frustrated novelist himself, he said, "Don't waste your time on anything frivolous when you have bills to pay. Get a real job and save your money, and when you're rich, you can write all you want . . . or win the lottery. Those are your choices."

On some level, Kay respected his blunt honesty.

On another, she hated him.

But she listened. And she stayed put.

Got a customer service job and worked her way through college at night, majoring in computer science. She was hired at the federal prison in Terre Haute right after she got her degree—hoping for an IT position, but offered one as a guard instead.

Her mother scoffed at that, scoffed at everything.

And still, Kay didn't leave.

What was I waiting for?

Sometimes she wonders.

Other times she knows: she was waiting for her mother to have a change of heart. To apologize, maybe. To realize that the only person who'd ever been loyal to her and deserving of her love had been right there under her nose all along.

Kay stayed, and she waited, and she nursed her mother through every stage of a brutal terminal illness. But on her deathbed, as Kay moistened those cracked lips with ice chips, they still refused to utter the words she longed to hear.

Mother's final words were for the man who had walked out on her when she found herself pregnant all those years ago.

It was his name she called with her very last breath; it was his face she saw, though Kay was right there in front of her.

She remembers the eerie sensation of her mother looking through her, as if at something—someone—over her shoulder.

"You're here!" she said, squeezing Kay's hand with more strength than she'd had in weeks.

"Yes, Mother, don't worry . . ."

"You left me! Why did you leave me?"

"I didn't leave you, Mother! I've been right here by your bed!"

"Why?" Tears were rolling down her mother's cheeks now. "Why? I needed you so, and you left . . ."

"But I didn't! I didn't, and I won't!" Kay was crying, too.

The hospice volunteer who had come to stand beside Kay rested a hand on her shoulder and whispered, "She's not talking to you, dear. It's all right."

"What do you mean?"

"It's common. I've seen this happen many times. At the end . . . sometimes, they see . . . loved ones."

"She's hallucinating?"

The woman hesitated, then shrugged and said again, "It's common."

Kay nodded, lips pressed together to keep them from trembling. She felt her mother holding her hand, squeezing it. Stared at her mother, who was looking right at her, but not seeing her. Saw her mother's eyes squint a little.

"You came back for me, Paul! I knew you would . . . yes, I'm ready. I'm ready. What is that light? . . . Oh . . . Oh, yes. Yes, let's go."

Those were her last words.

Kay held her hand until it grew cold.

"All right, here we are . . ." The waitress is back with her coffee and orange juice, plus biscuits.

With real butter.

Meredith would approve.

Kay's phone buzzes in her pocket as she breaks open a biscuit.

She pulls it out and sees that there's a text from Landry.

Boarding flight to Cincy now. Delayed. Will call when I get to hotel.

Kay quickly texts back, *OK, safe flight.*

Replacing her phone in her pocket, she feels relieved. That just bought her a little more time before they have to meet. Maybe by the time Landry arrives, she'll feel ready.

If she doesn't . . .

There's no turning back now.

Jaycee steps out of the elevator in the marble lobby of her building wearing a sleeveless black summer dress, large hat, and dark sunglasses, carrying the kind of oversized designer purse the women in this neighborhood use to carry as little as a cell phone and lipstick or as much as a change of clothes, a small dog, laptop, and umbrella.

Mike the doorman is at his post, leaning on the security desk with a newspaper open in front of him. Either it's not the *Post,* or he hasn't yet read his way to page eight, or he really doesn't know her true identity after all. The apartment isn't listed in her name—in any of her names. Discretion is the name of the game in a building like this. That's why she lives here.

Whatever the case, Mike doesn't bat an eye when he spots Jaycee.

"'Morning," he says, going to open the door for her. "Need a cab?"

"No, thanks." She steps out onto the sidewalk, noting that the sky is starting to cloud over.

But she leaves the hat and sunglasses on, as always.

"Have a nice day," Mike calls after her, and she gives a little wave as she walks toward Fifth.

She turns a corner, another corner, and another, leaving her neighborhood behind. Despite the threat of rain, the streets are crowded as always: dog walkers, tourists headed for the Metropolitan museum, young families bound for the park with strollers, trikes, and training wheels. No one gives her a second glance.

Fellow New Yorkers rarely do; too caught up in the daily tribulations of maneuvering through their own daily lives in this challenging city. Naturally, she stays away from tourist haunts where gawkers might be more prevalent; stays away from public places in general. For years she rarely even left her apartment. But that's become harder and harder to do lately, thanks to Cory.

He insists that he has her best interests in mind, and she supposes that's true. She can't stay hidden away forever. It's why, for the past eighteen months or so, she's been laying the groundwork for—

In her bag, her phone buzzes, vibrates. She ignores it.

Probably Cory. He left half an hour ago, on his way to the gym.

"Just lay low. I'll check in this afternoon," he told her.

"No need. I'll be fine."

"You," he said, "are never really fine when it comes to this stuff. And I know you well enough to know that is especially true today."

She didn't argue with that. It is true, but even if it wasn't . . .

It's just easier, she's discovered, to let Cory think he knows her better than anyone.

"Better than you know yourself," he once had the audacity to claim.

Not true at all.

If he really knew her, he'd realized she wasn't about to lay low, trapped in her high rise for a day, a weekend, or God knows how long until the latest storm blows over.

If he really knew her, he'd expect her to escape.

Yes. When the going gets tough, the tough get going . . . literally. She's been doing it all her life.

On Lexington Avenue in the Sixties, Jaycee steps to the curb, turns to face oncoming traffic, and raises her arm to hail a cab.

A yellow taxi promptly pulls over.

She opens the door and climbs in.

"Where to?" the cabbie asks as he starts the meter.

"JFK." She leans back in the seat, clutching her bag on her lap.

Reaching Out

The first time my blog went live, I remember feeling totally alone, envisioning the void beyond my laptop. I was writing extremely personal stuff, things I might never mention to anyone in real life, face-to-face, yet there it was, heading out to . . . where?

Somewhere.

I guess deep down I was hoping someone might find it. But I doubted it, and knowing no one was reading made it easier to keep going. It was very liberating, writing about the day cancer changed my life or how exposed I felt at the hands (literally) of my surgeons or the difficulties keeping my job at the prison a priority.

Then one day it happened: a stranger—a reader— commented on my blog. And then another one did. And another. Each comment that said I was understood, justified, and among friends lifted my load bit by bit until somewhere along the way I got my brain back. It was no longer jam-packed with thoughts of cancer, but slowly, the real things that make up my life filtered back in.

Would that have happened simply with the passage of time? Would that have happened without all of you? I don't think so. Sharing freed me from cancer's hold. Discovering and connecting with an amazingly supportive and caring online community did that and more in ways I never thought possible.

—Excerpt from Kay's blog, *I'm A-Okay*

Chapter 7

"Need a hand with your bag?"

Landry turns to see her handsome friend from the gate area standing right behind her in the narrow aisle of the plane, gesturing at her rolling bag.

"Oh . . . that's okay, I . . ."

"Which seat are you in?"

"Right there, 12C. Aisle."

He's already picking up her bag, lifting it into the overhead bin above her seat.

"Thank you," she says, sitting down.

"No problem." He turns to lift his own bag into the bin just opposite, then settles into seat 12D, directly opposite. What a coincidence.

As the rest of the passengers board, obscuring her view across the aisle, she texts Rob to let him know that she's on the plane at last. The flight delay was extended—twice—meaning they're now going to land almost three hours late. She'll be lucky if she has time to drop her bag at the hotel before the memorial service starts.

Okay, call me when you land. Love you, Rob texts back immediately, probably still out on the golf course.

She sends back a little sideways text heart the way Addison showed her, using the < and the 3 key. Then she texts Kay and Elena to let them know what time she lands.

She'd already texted them both earlier, after the second delay was announced. Neither has responded so far, but maybe—

"Ladies and gentlemen, the cockpit door is now closed," the flight attendant announces. "Please turn off and put away all electronic devices."

So much for hearing from her friends before she gets to Cincinnati.

The plane jerks as it begins to roll away from the gate. Landry puts her phone into her pocket and leans back. The two people beside her—a young couple occupying the window and middle seat—are whispering to each other.

Unfortunately, she already finished all the magazines Addison gave her, along with the newspaper she picked up back in the airport. Her only other reading material is digital—meaning she can't access it until they're in the air and the flight attendants green-light electronic devices again. She looks in the seat pocket for the airline magazine—does this airline even publish a magazine?—and finds just a barf bag and safety card.

Nothing to do but stare at the illuminated FASTEN SEAT BELT sign in the row in front of her.

Until her friend across the aisle asks, "So what's in Cincinnati? Family? Friends?"

"Friends," she says simply. "You have family there?"

He nods. "It's my hometown. I lived there until I retired last year."

"*Retired?* You're *retired*?"

"I'm youthful for being in my late sixties, don't you think?"

"I . . . um . . ." She could have sworn he was in his midforties or so.

He laughs. "I'm just kidding."

"You're not retired?"

"Oh, I'm retired. But I'm not in my sixties—or even my fifties. Yet. I retired at forty-eight. That's the upside of being a cop."

So he's still older than he looks—but not that much older.

"How about you?" he asks.

"Me? I'm not a cop. Or retired. Or in my fifties. Yet."

He grins at the quip and points a finger at her. "Quick. Very quick. I like that."

She can't help but smile. This isn't flirting, though. Absolutely not.

"So what do you do?"

"I'm . . . a writer."

Really? Where did that come from?

"What do you write?"

"A blog. I'm a blogger, really."

"A blogger is a writer. So you're a writer."

Gratified, she smiles. "Right. And I'm a mom. Mostly a mom. And a wife," she adds hastily.

"Wife . . . mom . . . blogger . . . writer. Got it." He nods. "What do you blog about?"

She hesitates. "You know . . . my family . . . my husband, my kids, I have two kids . . ."

Cancer, I have cancer . . .

Had. Had cancer.

The intercom clicks on and the flight attendant launches into the safety demonstration.

Saved by the bell.

Thrusting her feet into a pair of black flats, Elena holds the bedpost with one hand to keep her balance, while fumbling through the clutter on the adjacent dresser top with the other hand. Her cell phone is here, thank God—imagine if she'd lost that? Although the battery is run way down. Ordinarily, she charges it overnight; clearly, last night she wasn't in any condition to—

The toilet flushes in the bathroom.

Reminded that she's not alone, Elena closes her eyes, bracing herself.

She hears the water run just long enough for hand-splashing, not hand-washing—and then the bathroom door opens and Tony reappears in her bedroom.

At least now he's clothed from the waist down—unlike when he got out of her bed ten minutes ago. Rather, when she kicked him out.

"What are you looking for?" he asks.

"My keys."

"I have them."

She looks up. Seeing him standing there, in her bedroom, half naked—there are so many things she wants to say. But she has a flight to catch, and there's no time for anything other than a strained, "Why do you have them?"

"Did you really think I let you drive home last night?"

That gives her pause. Dammit.

"So you drove my car?"

"You don't remember?"

Clenched, she shakes her head. *Dammit, dammit dammit . . .*

In a way, she's grateful to have forgotten pretty much everything that happened last night after the toasts. That's probably a blessing.

On the other hand, it's dangerous, she knows, in more ways than she can count, to have drunk herself into oblivion—again.

"I didn't drive your car," Tony tells her, sounding almost smug. "I drove *my* car. With you in it. You honestly don't remem—"

"Where's my car, Tony?"

"At the restaurant, where you left it. Where do you think it would—"

"At the *restaurant*? Are you kidding me?"

"Relax. I can drive you to—"

"I don't have time for this! I have to get to the airport!"

"Well, whose fault is that?"

She closes her eyes, seething.

Mine. It's my fault.

But I hate him even more than I hate myself.

Elbow on the arm of her seat, chin in hand, Landry focuses on the flight attendant standing in the aisle. She listens—well, pretends to listen, because it would be impolite not to—as though she's never heard the safety spiel before in her life.

" . . . keep in mind the nearest exit may be behind you . . . in the event of a water landing . . . loss of cabin pressure . . ."

She remembers the first flight she took after her cancer diagnosis, to Saint Thomas for her sister-in-law Mary Leigh's Christmas wedding in the Virgin Islands. She recalls thinking, as the crew was going through the safety drill, that at least when you're on a plane and a life-threatening situation pops up, you've been told exactly what to do.

But if you have the misfortune, as you're going about your daily business, to be struck out of the clear blue sky with a life-threatening illness . . .

Well, then you're completely on your own. There is no plan. No escape chute, no flotation device.

She blogged about that later; wrote about cancer as if it were an airline journey, with mock in-case-of-emergency instructions. It was a clever post, one of her first that generated lots of appreciative comments.

The safety presentation concludes, and the flight attendants go back to preparing for takeoff as the plane joins the endless line of other delayed aircraft inching toward the runway. The worst weather has passed—for now—but a stormy day is forecast here.

Actually, there was unsettled weather along the entire

East Coast. She overheard other passengers talking back in the gate area. One was trying to connect to Philadelphia, another to Hartford.

Wondering whether Elena will be able to fly out as planned, Landry gazes past her row mates, noting the still-gray sky beyond the portal. Then the man in the window seat abruptly pulls the shutter down, obliterating her view.

She looks around for another portal and once again makes eye contact with the man across the aisle.

"So where do you live in Alabama?" he asks.

She keeps the answer vague: "Baldwin County."

"Me too. Gulf Shores. Right on the beach."

"Nice."

"Yeah. Alabama is the best place in the world to retire, did you know that?"

"Is that a statistic?"

"No. Opinion. Mine. My wife wanted to go to Florida, but I won that battle. I don't win many, believe me. But that was the important one."

Wife—so he has a wife. She relaxes at last. He's just a nice, friendly guy making conversation to pass the time. Nothing more.

"You're not that far from Florida," she points out. "The panhandle, anyway."

"Yeah, well, my wife was thinking Boca. She has family there. Too fancy for my blood. Hers too—but she wouldn't admit it."

"How does she like Alabama?"

"Loves it. What's not to love? Can't beat the weather, or the friendly people, or the tax breaks."

"So you're both retired?"

"Not exactly. The wife's in real estate, so she got licensed down there, and I'm licensed down there, too."

"To do what?"

"Pack a pistol," he says with a grin. "What else?"

"What do you mean?"

"I'm just kidding around. Well, not about the gun license. But it's just for my job." He reaches into his pocket, takes out his wallet, passes her a white business card. "Here. In case you ever need me. You never know."

She looks down.

BRUCE MANGIONE, PRIVATE INVESTIGATOR AND
PERSONAL SECURITY

"No, you never know," she agrees, and tucks the card into her bag.

"I can't believe you're spending all this time and money to go to a funeral for a perfect stranger," Tony tells Elena as they barrel along interstate 93 toward Logan Airport.

"She's not a stranger. She's a friend. One of the closest friends I—"

"You never even met her!"

"So? I have plenty of friends I've never met."

"Yeah, well, that's just . . ."

He doesn't bother to complete the comment, and Elena isn't about to ask him to.

Jaw set, she keeps her head turned toward the passenger's window, eyes fixated on the suburban landscape flashing past against an overcast sky.

Anything is better than looking at Tony.

Whenever she thinks about last night, she cringes. Of all the one night stands she's ever had—and there have been plenty, more than she remembers—this is by far the worst. She doesn't even like the man. How the hell did she end up bringing him home?

Oh, come on. You can guess, can't you?

After a few too many glasses of wine, the usual loneliness and bad judgment set in . . .

That's how it usually happens—more and more often, it seems.

You try to fill the gaping void left by your mother's death, or your father's neglect, or your own illness, or . . .

Who knows what really lies at the root of her problems? The only thing that's certain is that she feels empty inside; has felt empty for a long time now. Most of her life, but the real problem started when she got sick.

So she tries to fill the emptiness with booze, and empty talk, and meaningless sex . . .

Tony Kerwin. For God's sake.

When are you going to learn?

Sometimes, the morning-after haze is frustrating, and she struggles to piece together the events of the evening before. But in this case, she realizes, amnesia might actually be a blessing.

"So you said this woman is someone you got to know online?" Tony asks.

"Did I?"

"Last night."

"Oh."

Maybe amnesia isn't a blessing.

What else did I say to him last night? she wonders nervously. *How much does he know about Meredith—and the others? About me?*

"Did you ever even talk to her on the phone?" Tony asks.

"What does that have to do with anything?"

"I don't get it."

She shrugs and gestures at the car in front of them. "You might want to back off that guy's bumper."

"I thought you were in a hurry."

"I'd like to get there alive. Back off, okay? Please?"

He ignores her.

Damn him.

Thank goodness the school year is almost over. Another

few weeks and she won't have to see him again until fall. By then this will have blown over.

That she was forced to accept a ride to the airport from him is beyond maddening, but what choice did she have? There wasn't time to collect her own car from the restaurant parking lot, nor even time to arrange for a car service. Her only option was to let Tony drive her—or miss the flight.

Even now that might happen. She steals a quick glance at the dashboard clock. They're cutting it really close. Maybe the tailgating is okay after all.

"What time does your flight get back into Logan tomorrow?" he asks.

"Why?"

"So that I can pick you up."

Pick her up? Does he think . . . does he think this is—that they are . . . a *thing*?

"Oh—that's okay. I'll get a cab."

"To Northmeadow? I don't think so."

"I meant a car service. I'll get a car service."

"That'll cost a fortune. I'll pick you up."

"I don't get back until late." She's trying to remember what time the flight is. Six? Seven? She can always pull the reservation out of her bag and check it, but . . .

It doesn't matter. He's not picking her up.

"I think . . . not until eleven, maybe midnight," she tells Tony. "Too late."

"That's fine. I don't mind."

"No, don't pick me up. Really. Please."

"Please?" he echoes. "I'm trying to do you a favor and you're begging me not to? Okay. Whatever."

Great. Now he's hurt. Or pissed off. Both, apparently.

Do you really care how he feels?

"Listen," he says after a long pause, "about this Cincinnati thing—"

"Did I tell you it was Cincinnati?" She could have sworn

she'd just said Ohio earlier, when she was rushing around trying to get ready to leave.

"Yeah. You did. You don't remember?"

She sighs inwardly.

"Anyway . . ." he goes on after realizing she's chosen to ignore the question, "do you want me to come along?"

"Come *along*? To a *funeral* in *Cincinnati*?"

"Why not? I got nothing better to do this weekend."

That, she believes.

He goes on, uncharacteristically earnest, "You might need a friend there to support you."

You're not my friend, Tony.

"No, thanks," she says.

"Okay. Just thought I'd offer."

"That's very sweet, but I'll be fine."

"Is someone picking you up there when you land?"

"Yes. A *friend*."

The word spills from her tongue with deliberate emphasis.

So what if it's a lie?

"Who? Another 'friend' you've never met?"

She doesn't bother to answer that.

"You know, you should be more careful, Elena," Tony tells her. "All these strangers . . . it's not a good idea to be so trusting. I mean . . . you said your friend was murdered . . ."

Oh, crap. Did I tell him that, *too?*

"How do you know that whoever killed Meredith isn't going to come after you next?"

Meredith. She apparently even told him the name. What else did she tell him? Next thing she knows, he'll be rattling off her e-mail password and bank account PIN number.

"Hey, look—" Tony flips on the turn signal. "We made it."

She looks up. They've reached the airport exit at last.

*   *   *

This has been the most horrific week of Beck's entire life. But as she stands in front of the mirror in her cheerful blue and yellow childhood bedroom wearing a somber black dress, she knows the worst is yet to come.

She hasn't been to many funerals—she barely remembers her paternal grandfather and maternal grandmother's. Her maternal grandfather died just a few years ago, though that was hardly a heart-wrenching tragedy, as he was in his nineties.

But this . . . today . . . Mom . . .

This is going to be brutal.

How is she going to make it through the next several hours? How is she going to stand up and read a poem at the service?

One thing is for damned certain: it won't be by leaning on Keith.

Yes, he's been dutifully at her side these past few days. Physically, anyway.

But emotionally? He's completely checked out. Not just checked out of the situation, but out of their marriage. If she wasn't a hundred percent sure of it last week at this time, it's since become abundantly clear.

And not just to her.

Her brother Neal pulled her aside last night to ask if everything is okay between her and Keith.

"What do you mean?"

He looked her in the eye. "You know what I mean, Beck."

She shrugged. It was no wonder Neal had noticed.

Ever since Keith drove back here to talk to the cops the other day, he's been quieter than usual, almost standoffish with visitors—and there have been many. Everyone loved Mom. The house has been full of people.

For Beck, that's meant an endless round of hostess duties. That, in and of itself, has been a challenge.

This is her mother's house, not hers. Mom's kitchen,

Mom's friends. Mom was always the one who decided what to serve, which platters to use, whether to make coffee or serve cold drinks, which glassware went into the dishwasher and which had to be washed by hand . . .

Beck and her sisters-in-law always helped, of course. But Mom called the shots.

Now it's just her. Her brothers' wives have had their hands full looking after their little ones, who are overwhelmed just being in the house with all these people—and without Grandma.

Both Teddy and Neal have been busy talking to people, tending to details. Teddy, the numbers guy, has been handling the bills and the paperwork; hands-on Neal dealt with the logistics of cars clogging the driveway and the street, the funeral service arrangements, where to seat all the visitors . . .

Poor Dad is too shell-shocked to do anything but sit and stare as people pat him on the shoulder.

But Keith . . .

Keith has spent the last few days either hiding away upstairs or on his phone incessantly checking his e-mail or texts. That didn't escape Neal, the more intuitive of Beck's brothers.

Touched by the concern in his eyes when he asked her about it, Beck said, "Now isn't a great time to get into what's going on with me and Keith."

"I know it isn't," he agreed, putting an arm around her. "But when you need to talk . . . I'm here. Okay?"

She nodded her thanks, unable to speak.

Her brother—both her brothers—have solid marriages. Teddy rekindled the flame with his high school prom date a few years after graduation and walked down the aisle with her at twenty-three; Neil wed his college sweetheart. They've both always made it look so easy.

Maybe that's why she said yes when Keith proposed,

though he seemed halfhearted about it and she had her reservations even then, mostly based on his mercurial moods.

She didn't share that with anyone, though, not even her friends, or her mother. She figured everyone must have doubts but also assumed it was normal for relationships to run hot and cold. Anyway, that was the logical sequence of events, right? *Graduate high school, graduate college, get a job, get married, buy a house . . .*

Have babies is supposed to be the next step, but it looks like for her it will be *Hammer Out Separation Agreement*.

"Rebecca?" Keith pokes his head into the room as she reaches up to fasten a string of pearls around her neck. "Your father wants to know if you're ready to go."

"Almost."

The funeral director asked the family to be there a couple of hours ahead of everyone else. That was the case when her grandfather died, too—but it was so they could have a private viewing of the body.

Today, with Mom, that's not going to happen. Her body was cremated. That was Dad's decision. He said it was what she would have wanted.

Beck isn't so sure about that, but she wasn't about to argue.

Her hands tremble; she struggles with the clasp on her necklace.

Keith, still standing behind her in the doorway of her room, doesn't move to help her. Not surprising.

She wonders if he remembers that she wore these pearls on their wedding day. Mom gave them to her. Beck stumbled across them last night in a velvet case in a dresser drawer here in her bedroom, still right where she stowed them before she and Keith left on their honeymoon.

Whoever broke into the house—whoever murdered her mother—didn't find them.

He didn't find a lot of things you'd have expected to be stolen.

Maybe that's why the detectives don't seem convinced it was a just a simple robbery gone bad. They didn't come right out and say that the other day, but Beck could read between the lines.

They suspect her father.

That they didn't arrest him doesn't mean they've ruled him out—but it doesn't mean they haven't.

She can only hope that after interviewing everyone in the family, including Dad himself, they realize it's ludicrous to think he could be behind this.

But if it goes any further and the police want to talk to Dad again . . .

Beck and her brothers have been quietly discussing whether they should hire an attorney. It's not something anyone wants to bring up to their father, but they've agreed that if the questioning persists after today, they should all stop talking to the detectives and get in touch with a lawyer.

Maybe they should have done it before now, but they don't want to raise any red flags or be labeled as uncooperative. That would only complicate matters or, God forbid, seem to implicate Dad in some wrongdoing.

Finally, Beck's shaky hands manage to fit the hook into the clasp on the pearl necklace.

"How long do you think the service will last?" Keith asks.

"I have no idea. An hour? Two?" She picks up a hairbrush.

She doesn't turn to look at him, but she can see him reflected in the mirror. He's wearing a dark suit, and he trimmed his beard for the occasion, but he didn't shave the damned thing off.

She's been asking him to do that for months, ever since he grew it. She's never been a fan of facial hair. He knows that. So why, she wondered at first, would he grow the beard in the first place?

Because someone else in his life—someone who matters more than I do—is a fan of facial hair.

That's the answer that makes the most sense.

"Okay. So I'll be waiting downstairs," Keith tells her, starting to go.

"Wait."

"What?"

"You can leave," she says. "After the service. If you want. You can go back to Lexington."

She waits for him to tell her that it's okay—that he'll stay here another night, at least. That he won't leave her yet.

Ever.

He doesn't say that.

He doesn't say anything at all, just nods and leaves the room.

Okay. So . . .

She inhales deeply, puffs it out slowly, ruffling her bangs with her own gust of breath.

Jackass. He really is a jackass.

Beck brushes her bangs back into place, studying her own reflection in the mirror.

You look so much like your mother . . .

How many times has she heard that in her life?

But she's never really seen it until lately. Mom had short blond hair; she has long brunette hair. Mom had dark brown eyes; hers are hazel. Mom was short and kind of round; she is tall and lanky.

And yet . . .

We do look alike.

She can finally note the resemblance in the curve of her eyebrows, the slope of her nose, the fullness of her lower lip as opposed to the slash of an upper . . .

Her image blurs with tears.

She feels around on the dresser for a tissue, keeping her eyes wide-open, not wanting her mascara to run. She's gotten pretty good at that over the past week. As soon as you blink, it's raccoon city.

So you don't blink. You blot.

She finds a tissue. Dabs at her eyes. Stares at herself.

Oh, Mom.

Is this the way it's going to be? Every time she looks into the mirror, is she going to miss her mother even more desperately?

Remember me when I am gone away . . .

That's the first line of the Christina Georgina Rossetti poem she will be reading at the funeral. Her mother had been an English major during her fleeting college semesters before she met Dad, and she kept all her texts on the bookshelves in the den. Beck found the poem among them, one of many with the corner of the page folded down and notes scribbled in the margins. It seemed fitting.

"I wish I could talk to you, Mom," she whispers. "I wish you could tell me . . ."

So many things.

What to do about the mess she's made—no, Keith has made—of their marriage.

How to help Dad, not just today, but every day, going forward.

And . . .

Most importantly . . .

"Who did this to you, Mommy?"

The words escape her on a sob, just as she sees a shadow come up in the doorway.

Keith again.

"What?" she asks, high-pitched, sounding strangled.

He just looks at her.

"What?" This time she almost screams it.

"Nothing."

He walks away without saying another word.

* * *

No first-class ticket for Jaycee this time. Not on this no-frills airline.

But at least there were plenty of seats available on the last minute flight to Cincinnati, and she has an entire row to herself.

As the plane taxis out to the runway, she pushes her sunglasses up to her hair and presses her forehead against the window, staring at the gray mist shrouding the New York skyline to the northwest.

She probably shouldn't be doing this—flying to Cincinnati on a whim.

But when Cory showed her that newspaper, her first instinct was to escape; catch the first flight out of town. She didn't even care where she went, as long as it was someplace between the coasts, someplace off the beaten path like . . .

Ohio?

I'm cc'ing you just in case you can join us last minute, Jaycee . . .

Browsing the last minute travel Web site, she impulsively entered Cincinnati into the search engine.

Before she could rethink the idea, she had booked a ticket on the next flight out. In the cab on the way to the airport, she used her phone to call a luxury hotel downtown as opposed to the one BamaBelle had mentioned in her e-mail—she doesn't want to run into the others.

No? Then why are you going at all?

The truth is, she's not sure. She just knows that she can't stay here, and she feels as though she should be there. For now, that's enough.

"Hi, I'm just wondering whether you have rooms available for this evening?" she said to the desk clerk at the Cincinnatian.

"Yes, we do. Would you like to make a reservation?"

"I'll call back. Thanks."

But no thanks. Hotel reservations need credit cards, and

credit cards leave tracks. Much safer to walk in and pay cash, like she did in L.A. last week.

Maybe, when she lands, she'll simply hole up in a suite, order room service, and spend the weekend in seclusion.

Or maybe she'll decide to attend the memorial service for Meredith.

Maybe I owe it to her. And to myself. For everything I did wrong when it came to my connection with Meredith, in the end, I cared about her. We were friends.

One thing is certain: if she does go to the service, she'll keep to herself. The others will never even have to know she's there.

It'll be just like on the Internet, where she can be shrouded in anonymity until when or if she does decide to make her presence known—or she can simply lurk, silently watching.

Bruce Mangione is quite the conversationalist. Throughout the endless wait on the runway, he keeps Landry engaged—mostly with talk of movies they both happen to have seen and books they both happen to have read.

Then, after a lull during taxi and takeoff, he asks again about her plans in Cincinnati for the weekend.

"You said you're visiting a friend?"

"Yes."

"So . . . doing some sightseeing?"

"Actually . . ." She takes a deep breath. "It's a funeral for a friend. I'm going with other friends."

"I'm sorry."

She nods, uncomfortable.

"Was it sudden?"

Again she nods, and finds herself wanting to tell him the whole story. He is, after all, a former cop. Maybe he has some insight into how this could have happened to Meredith.

But that's silly, isn't it? It's not as though he works in Cincinnati law enforcement anymore. And even if he did—

or if he had a direct pipeline into the investigation—it's not as if he'd share details of the case with a perfect stranger on a plane.

Anyway, she doesn't necessarily want to get into how well she knows—or rather, doesn't know—Meredith. Why complicate what should really remain pleasant small talk between two people who are never going to see each other again?

She changes the subject, asking him if there's a magazine in his seat-back pocket.

He looks. "No magazine."

"I was wondering if maybe I just didn't have one, or if the airline doesn't publish one."

He shrugs. "I'm not sure."

They both fall silent again as the plane gains altitude. Hint taken. He's no longer asking for the details about Meredith's death.

But maybe she wishes he would. Maybe she wants to tell him what happened. After all, he's a private investigator. Maybe he can—

Her thoughts are interrupted by a bell signal.

"Ladies and gentlemen," the flight attendant announces, "the fasten seat-belt light is still on and we ask that you please remain seated. However, it's now safe to turn on electronic devices . . ."

Landry bends over to take her electronic reader from the bag under the seat in front of her. When she straightens, she sees that Bruce Mangione is already opening his laptop.

The moment has passed.

It's probably just as well.

"So what's Jermaine doing today?" Frank asks, in the passenger seat beside Crystal as she pulls onto the interstate, heading toward the western suburbs.

"Same thing he does every Saturday, working. What's Marcy doing?"

"Same thing she does every Saturday: taking the kids to activities. Swim lessons, ballet, Little League . . ."

Three kids. Three different directions. God bless Marcy.

Frank's wife is a bubbly, energetic woman adored by everyone, including her husband. But that doesn't stop him from straying.

"You're missing it all," Crystal observes, merging into traffic. "Their ball games, their dance recitals . . ."

"Yeah, well . . ." Frank shrugs. "Sometimes, that's not such a bad thing. Have you ever sat through seven innings of T-ball in the rain?"

Crystal takes her eyes off the road long enough to send him a look that says, *You don't want to miss a thing. Trust me.*

Frank shifts uncomfortably. "Sorry."

Of course he's aware of her son's death. They weren't partners then, but he knows a lot about what unfolded in her life before they met. Knows everything, really. You work long, hard hours with a person, you become privy to their deepest, darkest secrets.

She's no angel, but she's got nothing to hide these days.

Unlike Frank.

She tries not to judge. She really does. What goes on in other people's marriages is their business.

Still, whenever Frank talks, she doesn't just listen . . . she offers advice. Unsolicited, of course, because no cheating man is going to ask a woman—especially one who knows and likes his wife—what she thinks about his extramarital affair.

Her advice to Frank is always the same: end it.

End the affair. Go home to your wife every night and be grateful for what you have. A loving spouse. Three beautiful healthy kids. A roof over your head and a job that will keep it there . . .

Sometimes, she thinks she's getting through to Frank—but then he'll slip and say something, or she'll see something, and she'll know he's still involved with the other woman he's been seeing for a while now.

A fellow cop.

Someone who understands . . .

Like Jermaine understands Crystal.

So, yeah. Who is she to judge?

She thinks about Hank Heywood. He's still riding high on their short list of suspects, but they haven't turned up a scrap of evidence against the guy. If he has anything to hide, it's well-buried.

He did tell them about his wife's secret—that her cancer had spread—but he asked them not to share that information with the rest of the family.

Unfortunately, Hank Heywood's request was not as simple to honor as Keith Drover's appeal that they not mention his affair to his wife. Drover's illicit relationship has no direct impact on the investigation—not at this stage, anyway. His alibi seems to have checked out—unless, of course, his lover is an accomplice who's covering for him.

Anything is possible. But—at this point, anyway—they have no reason to suspect Drover, and he has no apparent motive for wanting his mother-in-law dead.

The man's lover, Jonathan Randall, is an adjunct at the University of Kentucky. He seemed a bit rattled to be questioned in connection with a homicide investigation, though he said he already knew about the murder. He confirmed that he and Keith were together at his apartment until the wee hours on Saturday night—and volunteered that they were together again on Tuesday night, while Rebecca Drover was in Cincinnati with her family.

Crystal wonders whether he'll show up today for the memorial service. Probably not—but stranger things have happened.

She and Frank will be there partly to pay their respects, partly to observe the family, and partly to keep an eye out for anything—or anyone—unusual in the anticipated crowd of mourners.

Before leaving home this morning, she'd discussed the case again with Jermaine as they shared a bathroom mirror.

"I'm telling you, babe," Crystal said, running a brush through her shower-damp hair, "the killer was someone close to Meredith Heywood—or someone who felt as if he knew her. It might have been someone who was acquainted with her only through her blog, but whoever it was still cared about her on some level."

"And you're basing that on . . ."

"Instinct, and the way the body was positioned."

"That's right. I remember." Jermaine squirted a fat cloud of shaving cream into his hand. "You said that was one of the first things that struck you when you arrived at the scene."

She nodded, closing her eyes and envisioning the way Meredith Heywood's nightgown was arranged neatly and demurely down to her ankles, as if to preserve her dignity.

"It wouldn't—couldn't—have settled that way if she'd fallen dead in a scuffle," she told Jermaine.

"So whoever killed her had some remorse."

"Exactly."

"You know there's a thin line between love and hate," her husband reminded her. "Remember that article I showed you, back when you were working on the case involving that mother who drowned her baby?"

"Diaphanous Jones. I do remember."

The article was from one of the scientific journals Jermaine likes to read. It discussed a recent neurological study that had found that contrary to popular thinking, intense love and intense hate aren't opposite emotions at all—they're strikingly similar, biologically and behaviorally speaking. Both can arouse passionate behavior; both can trigger irrational action; both involve the same circuitry in the brain.

"Okay," she'd said. "So did Meredith Heywood's killer act because he loved her? Was it some kind of twisted angel of mercy scenario? Or was it because he hated her?"

"Maybe both," Jermaine said with a shrug, and put his arms around her from behind. "But since you're always saying I have a one-track mind, you can rest easy, because my brain circuits are only wired for one thing when I think of you."

She'd laughed as he pressed up against her. "I don't think we're talking about your brain, here."

That was a pleasant, if fleeting, distraction.

Now, her own mind is right back on track, constantly working, working, working the case from every angle.

As she and Frank near the exit for McGraw's Funeral Home, she's confident that if Meredith Heywood really was killed by someone who knew her well enough to love her or hate her—even just via the Internet—then there's a good chance that person will be drawn to show up today.

They often are.

And if that happens . . . we'll be watching.

Sheri Lorton has been on autopilot ever since her husband, Roger, was senselessly murdered while out walking their puppy early Thursday morning. It's amazing, when you think about it—and she has scarcely allowed herself to think about it—that she's managed to propel herself through forty-eight hours that have involved walking, talking, breathing . . .

Forget sleeping and eating. Even on autopilot, she's incapable of accomplishing either of those.

But the rest of it—somehow, she's still upright, functioning in the aftermath of the worst thing that's ever happened to her.

She had no inkling of the looming tragedy when she awakened Thursday morning to barking beneath the bedroom window. She tried to sleep through it at first, then finally peered out to see Maggie at the back door, dragging her leash from her collar. Roger was nowhere in sight.

At the time, unaware that the world can end in an instant, Sheri assumed the puppy must have gotten away from him and found her way home. They'd only had Maggie for a few weeks, and she was pretty feisty.

She let the dog into the house and set out a bowl of water, wondering if Maggie was too much of a handful after all. They'd decided against having children—Roger has three from his first marriage—and it had taken him almost a decade to agree with her notion that a dog might make their house feel more like a home. Maybe he'd been right about adopting a more mature dog, though.

"I think you might just have too much energy for us, huh, Mags?" she'd said, watching Maggie lap up the water eagerly, wondering how she could possibly bear swapping the puppy for a better-behaved dog.

She called her husband's cell phone to tell him Maggie had found her way home, but heard it ring in the next room. He'd left it behind again, plugged into the charger—not unusual for the quintessential absent-minded professor.

She figured he must be out combing the streets for the dog. But when minutes turned into a half hour with no sign of him, Sheri began to get nervous.

Hearing sirens in the distance, she called the police station. By that time, runaway puppy or not, her conscientious husband should have been at home showering and getting ready to leave for work. He was teaching an early class this session on Advanced Abstract Algebra, and with summer construction between their neighborhood and campus, the commute had been longer than usual.

The police officer on the other end of the line seemed to take the call in stride, as if people went missing every morning around there. Sheri couldn't imagine that was the case, though. The surrounding blocks had changed over the past decade since they moved in, but this was hardly a sketchy inner-city neighborhood.

The cop asked a few questions—including what Roger was wearing.

Sheri hadn't seen him since she dozed off beside him the night before, but she knew him well enough to guess at the clothing he'd had on. Jeans, a T-shirt, and, because the morning was cool, a front-zip hooded sweatshirt jacket.

When a pair of uniformed officers turned up at her door an hour later, she assumed they were coming to gather more information, having convinced herself that the sirens she'd heard screaming through the neighborhood earlier were probably responding to a fire or something . . . something . . .

Something, anything, else.

Please, God, not Roger . . .

Oldest, most comforting rule ever: when you hear sirens and worry, they never turn out to be wailing for the person you're worrying about.

Rules: made to be broken.

A body had been found matching her husband's description.

Catapulted into grief and disbelief, Sheri remembers thinking, in the back of her mind, that he must have had a heart attack. He was fifteen years older, in his mid-fifties, a small man—short in stature with a slight build, though not as fit as he should have been. And he was a smoker.

Whenever the dreadful truth managed to hit her— *murder*—it trampolined away again.

Only now, two days later, has it really begun to sink in.

Now that her husband's body has been released to the funeral director for burial, a somber detective is standing on the doorstep offering Sheri condolences and a small bag filled with the "final effects."

In other words, the contents of Roger's pockets and his gold wedding ring.

His wallet, of course, is missing. And the officer tells her they're hanging onto the clothing he was wearing—jeans, a T-shirt, and a hooded sweatshirt, just as she'd guessed. Evidence, he explains.

Of course. The case is unsolved.

All they know is that someone mugged Roger as he walked the dog Thursday morning, viciously stabbing him and leaving him to bleed to death on the street where a passerby found his body. Too late.

"Again, I'm so sorry for your loss," the officer tells Sheri as she stands numbly clutching the bag.

"Thank you."

Over the policeman's shoulder, out on the sidewalk, a couple of neighborhood kids roll by on skateboards. Across the street, toddlers in bathing suits jump through a front yard sprinkler as their mothers keep a watchful eye from the porch steps. Out there in the world beyond Sheri's doorstep, it's a gloriously sunny Saturday morning: birds chirping, lawn mowers buzzing, kids playing . . .

Incredulous, Sheri tries to focus on what the officer is saying.

"We're doing everything we can to find the person responsible, Mrs. Lorton."

"Thank you."

"Here's my card. Call me if you need anything at all. I'll be in touch."

"Thank you," Sheri says yet again, pocketing the card.

She closes the door, tosses the bag aside, and collapses on the floor, sobbing.

Cancerversaries = Bullshit

I don't commemorate Suspicious Ultrasound Day, Biopsy Day, Diagnosis Day, Mastectomy Day. No offense to those of you who do. But for me, those dates are just uncomfortable to remember and always will be. It's certainly easier to look back with some perspective years later, but I'm not sure anything is gained by marking those days as an anniversary. To me, it's more the whole journey that matters and how far I've come overall.

However, there is one milestone I'd like to mention. The Boobless Wonder turned one last week. As my first grade students like to say, "That's cool, right?"

When I started this blog, I never considered how long I'd keep it up. I went in thinking "One day at a time," because honestly, sharing intimate details with the cyber world seemed batshit crazy. Looking back now, I see that it was never the world I was reaching for, but one person that might relate to my experiences. Maybe I'd find someone else going through the same crap and we could support each other.

In the aftermath of my diagnosis, my brain was still so cluttered with all things cancer, I'd lost the ability to go about my days. It was one thing to have a calendar full of appointments, a million never-ending questions, pain from expanders, then implants, but it was quite another to talk about it all the time to my fellow teachers, my friends, even the jerk I was dating at the time. I mean, who wants to listen to it?

Even those closest to me needed a respite once in a while. Which I totally got, but that didn't change the fact I was on overload, my emotions consistently raw.

I realized I needed an outlet. A way out of my own head, some breathing room from those oppressive walls of cancer.

This is where I found it. And so, Happy Blogaversary to me! Sharing personal crap on the Internet turned out better than I ever hoped.

PS That doesn't mean I think cancer is a gift! I don't!

PPS No offense to those of you who do!

—Excerpt from Elena's blog, *The Boobless Wonder*

Chapter 8

Bright sunshine and clear blue skies in Northern Kentucky—where the Cincinnati airport is located—catch Landry off guard.

The weather had been so gloomy at takeoff after a non-existent sunrise in Mobile, and it poured nonstop in Atlanta. Somehow, she didn't expect to be greeted by a dazzling summer day upon reaching her destination, but there it is, beyond the wall of plate glass in the terminal. Somehow, it makes her feel slightly reassured about whatever lies ahead.

As she makes her way to the ladies' room, she finds herself scanning the faces of passing strangers, and of the women waiting on the long line to use the stalls. Among them she might just find Elena, whom she knows should also be landing here right around now.

Landry knows what she looks like, having seen the photos posted on Elena's blog. Dark hair, round, pleasant face, in her early thirties . . .

Which describes many of the women she's encountered so far in the airport.

Stepping out of the stall, she makes eye contact with one. "Elena?"

The woman looks at her.

"Are you Elena?"

She shakes her head, shrugs. *"No habla ingles."*

Landry apologizes, conscious of the curious stares of other women in the line. She wonders what they're thinking, then decides not to care, tired of fretting about . . .

Well, just about everything.

What would Meredith do? She'd move on without a backward glance.

Landry dries her hands and does just that.

It's probably better that she hasn't run into Elena here at the airport, she decides, having caught a glimpse of her reflection in the mirror. She's definitely looking travel weary. The sooner she can get to the hotel and pull herself together, the better.

At the car rental counter, she finds another long line and busies herself calling Rob from her cell phone while she waits.

"So you made it."

His familiar drawl makes her aware of just how far from home she really is.

"Yep—I made it."

"You doing okay?"

She hesitates. "Sure."

"Good. Listen, I was just talking to John, and he used to have a client up there. He said that if you get a chance, you should try the chili at Skyline."

"Did you tell him this isn't a pleasure trip? I mean, I'm walking into a funeral for a friend who was murdered . . ."

And they haven't caught whoever did it.

"I know you are," Rob says quickly. "I'm sorry. I didn't mean to—"

"No, it's okay. I know."

He's back there at home, where everything is nice and normal, instead of here in a strange place worrying that whoever killed Meredith might turn around and come after her.

Because of course there's no reason to think that.

Is there?

She stares at the blond hair of the woman standing directly in front of her and idly speculates about whether it's a wig. It looks like one. Fashion choice by a brunette who thinks blondes really do have more fun, Landry wonders, or is she just yet another woman who's lost her hair to cancer treatment?

"Next!" calls the counter agent, and the woman steps forward.

"I'm going to have to hang up in a minute," Landry tells Rob. "It's almost my turn."

"Okay, wait—do you have any idea where the new car insurance cards are? Because I need to put them into the glove compartments and I can't find them anywhere."

Of course he can't.

She reminds him—again—that she thumb-tacked them to the bulletin board in the kitchen.

"I looked there."

"Look again."

"But I didn't—"

"Next!" calls the rental counter agent, finished with the woman ahead of Landry.

"Trust me," she tells Rob, "they're on the bulletin board. I've got to go."

She hurriedly hangs up, steps forward, and pulls out the folded papers containing printouts of her reservations.

"Thank you, Mrs. Wells. Are you a member of our frequent renter program?"

"No, I'm not."

"Would you like to join?"

"No, thanks." *I'd like to get into a hotel room with a hot shower, that's all I'd like right about now.*

"Are you familiar with Cincinnati?"

Feeling more impatient by the second, she admits, "No, I've never been here before."

"You'll want a GPS system in the car, then. And I'll get you some maps." The agent briskly steps away from the counter.

"I can tell you how to get where you're going," says a familiar voice behind Landry.

She turns to see Bruce Mangione, Private Investigator and Personal Security.

They hadn't done much more talking for the duration of the flight. He'd gotten busy on his laptop after takeoff, and she'd finally managed to lose herself in the celebrity biography she'd downloaded to her e-reader the other night. The other passengers seemed equally subdued, probably thanks to having risen in the wee hours to make an early flight, then spending several mind-numbing hours at the gate. No one—not even the flight attendants—seemed to be in a conversational mood anymore.

After they landed, Bruce Mangione lifted Landry's bag down from the overhead bin, she thanked him, and that was that. She lost track of him amid the mass exodus that began when the door opened onto the jetway.

"Hi," he says. "I've been standing behind you but you seemed busy and I didn't want to interrupt."

"Oh . . . thanks . . . I just—that was my husband."

"I just called my wife, too. She gets nervous when I fly. Sounds like your husband is worried about you, too."

"He . . . not really. I mean . . ." She wonders how much he heard. "He just likes to make sure I'm okay."

"I don't blame him. Crazy things can happen. Trust me—in my line of work, I've seen it all. So where do you have to go now that you're here?"

"I think it's a Residence Inn . . . or maybe a Fairfield Inn. One of those Marriott chains . . ." She starts to reach for the reservation paper she left on the counter.

"You're going to the hotel before the funeral?"

Caught off guard by his mention of the funeral, she turns

back to him in surprise—then remembers that she told him about it on the plane. Still, she wonders again how much he overheard of her conversation with Rob just now. She wasn't exactly whispering.

Not that it matters . . .

Does it?

"The hotel is right down the road from the funeral home," she tells him with a shrug, "so—"

"All right, Ms. Wells, here you go . . ." The counter attendant is back, handing over a couple of maps and a contract. "The shuttle driver will wait for you if you hurry, right through those doors, if you'll just sign here, here, here, initial here and here . . ."

"Thank you." She scans the contract, signs, signs, signs again, initials and initials, and turns quickly to Bruce. "I've got to run. It was nice—"

"Are you sure you don't need directions?"

"I don't think—"

"Next!"

"Go ahead," Landry tells him, gesturing at the rental counter and grabbing the handle of her bag. "I'll be fine, thanks. Nice meeting you."

"You too," he calls as he steps up to the counter.

It isn't until Landry has stepped out of the shuttle at the rental lot that she realizes she left the paper containing her hotel reservation back on the counter. And she isn't sure of the name of the hotel chain, let alone the address.

Dammit. She'll have to go back.

Wait a minute. She received an e-mail confirmation when she made the reservations. She should be able to find that in her phone . . .

She turns toward the shuttle as the doors close, but at the last second the driver sees her and opens the door. Two minutes later she's behind the wheel of a rental car, typing the hotel's address into the GPS.

There. See that? I can take care of myself just fine, she silently tells herself. *No reason to worry. Not at all.*

A man raps gently on the driver's side window, and Jaycee jumps.

She hadn't even seen him approach the car. She'd been too busy watching BamaBelle drive off in her mid-sized rental, which had—as luck would have it—been parked in the spot adjacent to hers.

Then again, perhaps that's not as big a coincidence as it seems. Bama had, after all, been standing directly behind her in the line back at the counter.

Jaycee was so caught up in her own problems that she wouldn't have even noticed her there had she not overheard that distinct southern drawl talking on the cell phone. Even then, she wasn't positive it was Bama—or rather, Landry, as she'd introduced herself a few days ago when Jaycee spoke to her from Los Angeles.

But when Landry mentioned Meredith's name, Jaycee knew for certain.

Sure enough, she snuck a glance over her shoulder and recognized a slightly older, more worn-out-looking version of BamaBelle's official blog site photo.

Bama didn't even notice, caught up in whatever she was saying to her husband—it had to be her husband—on the phone. Mostly, she seemed to be trying to convince him not to worry about her.

Even if Landry had given her a second glance, she'd of course still have no clue who she was, because she doesn't use a head shot on her blog.

From time to time she's toyed with the idea of posting a photo—though not her own image, of course. It would be easy enough to steal a stranger's digital snapshot and claim it as her own.

But there would be a certain level of risk involved with that, and why tempt fate?

After handing over the ID Cory had arranged for her years ago, the one that bears her real name and a drab, barely recognizable photo of her—Jaycee finished her own rental papers and headed out to the shuttle as Landry took her spot at the counter. The bus was almost full. Jaycee sat in one of two empty seats up front and willed the driver to pull away before Bama could get on.

It almost seemed like that was going to happen—he waited a few more minutes, then pulled the doors shut. But before he could pull away, he spotted Landry coming out of the terminal and opened the doors again.

Landry sat down right next to her, of course—it was the only empty spot on the bus. Jaycee held her breath on the ride over, but Landry didn't give her a second glance; not then, when they were shoulder-to-shoulder, and not when they found their way off the bus to cars parked right next to each other.

"Excuse me? Ma'am?" The man knocks again on Jaycee's window and gestures for her to roll it down.

She hesitates—courtesy of a decade's worth of New York street smarts—then obliges. Clearly, he works here—he's wearing a jacket and name tag emblazoned with the rental car company's name. Besides, nothing terrible is going to happen to her in broad daylight in a public place, right?

"Yes?" She regards him from behind her sunglasses.

"I just wanted to ask . . . and you probably get this all the time . . ."

She sighs inwardly as he talks on, fighting the urge to roll up the window and drive away.

Few things irk her more than strangers without boundaries.

"Ladies and gentlemen, we have begun our initial descent into the Cincinnati area. Please turn off and put away any electronic devices you've been using. If you'd like to use your cell phone right after we land, please make sure you keep it handy, because you will not have access to the overhead bins until we reach the gate."

Hearing the flight attendant's advice, Elena remembers her cell phone. The battery was almost drained when she turned it off back at Logan. No need to turn it on now; she'll charge it as soon as she gets to the hotel.

She forces her eyes open and lifts the shade covering the window beside her seat. Brilliant sunshine spills into the cabin. Leaning into the glass, she sees a network of roads, waterways, houses, and forests far below. Almost there.

After guzzling her beverage service Bloody Mary, she spent the duration of her flight either dozing or pretending to be asleep—anything to avoid conversation with the chatty elderly man in the aisle seat. He was perfectly friendly, but she wasn't in the mood for conversation. Not after what happened with Tony.

She couldn't get out of his car fast enough back at the airport, still insisting that he needn't meet her flight tomorrow night. She didn't give him the correct information, but for all she knows, he saw it posted beneath a magnet on her refrigerator and will show up.

Of all the men she could have chosen for a one night stand . . .

She still can't quite grasp that it really happened—and now, of all times, on the heels of the week from hell, leading into what promises to be one of the most heart-wrenching funerals ever?

But then again, is it any surprise? She's never dealt very well with this kind of pressure. Her response to stress has always been to run away or self-medicate—preferably both, simultaneously. Which is why she ordered a double Bloody Mary as soon as the plane took off, much to the amusement of the man in the aisle seat.

"Nervous flier?" he asked.

"No—tough day," she said, only to be met with one of those *You think you've got problems? Listen to mine* spiels.

She tuned him out while pretending to listen, inserting comments in all the right places. You get very good at that, being a first grade teacher. Her students like nothing better than to give her blow-by-blow recaps of their favorite cartoons, and self-editing is hardly their forte.

Right now she keeps her forehead fastened to the window, not wanting to engage in another round of Good Listener. Her head is still pounding and she might be tempted, this time, to tell the old guy to keep his problems to himself. She's got enough of her own—Tony being the most recent, but hardly the least troubling.

Again, she thinks back to last night. Her skin crawls when she thinks of it.

So don't think of it!

That's what Meredith would say—and famously did, in the blog post where she asked, *Why dwell on the past when you can focus on the future?*

Some followers slammed her for being insensitive.

Not Elena. She couldn't agree more. Her own past was no picnic.

The plane banks and she loses sight of the ground. They're getting ready to land.

Forcing her thoughts to what lies ahead, she feels her pulse quicken.

I can't believe we're really going to meet each other in person at this time tomorrow, Landry had e-mailed yesterday afternoon. *I just wish it were under better circumstances.*

Meredith would be glad we're going to do this, Elena responded, and Kay wrote,

I know she'll be there in spirit.

Elena didn't respond to that particular comment. What could she do—argue?

She's done it before, against her better judgment, both with online friends and in real life. That never ends well.

It's surprising how many people out there disagree with her personal belief that when you're dead, you're gone. Period.

None of this afterlife mumbo jumbo for her.

Her argument: if that were possible, then her own mother—who had loved her dearly—would have been with her in spirit for all these years, instead of abandoning her to a miserable, lonely childhood and a life-threatening disease.

Believers have all kinds of responses to that theory. Usually, spirituality comes into it. They're never particularly pleased to learn that she is almost as fond of religion—of God, really—as she is of cancer.

"Ma'am?" Someone touches her shoulder, and she turns to see the flight attendant, reaching past the man in the aisle seat, who is now wide-awake. "Please return your seat to its upright and locked position."

She does.

"Did you have a nice nap?" asks the chatty passenger, then proceeds to tell her about all his health problems that make it impossible for him to get a good night's sleep anymore.

As he talks, Elena tries once again to push her thoughts to what lies ahead, but this time she can only think of what happened earlier, right before she got out of the car at the airport.

First, Tony asked her again whether she wanted him to come to Cincinnati with her.

"Thanks," she said, "but no thanks."

"I'm serious."

"So am I."

Then, his last words to her, right before she slammed the car door, were chilling: "Have it your way. And listen, don't worry, Elena—your secret is safe with me."

He waved and pulled away, leaving her to wonder just what he meant by that.

The turtle that started it all had meandered—as turtles have a way of doing—out of a pond on a hot summer's day.

It looked like a scum-slicked rock, lying there in the sun in the mucky high grass at the edge of the green water. Like a rock that just begged a romping kid to pick it up and throw it into the water, providing a welcome disruption to the late afternoon torpor and making a nice big splash that would cool things off.

That was the plan, anyway.

When you're five or maybe six years old and you pick up a rock, and a reptile head pokes out at you, hissing like a snake and gnashing teeth strong enough to sever bone and tendon . . .

The power wielded by that snapping turtle was somehow simultaneously terrible and wonderful.

I thought it was some kind of monster.

In a way, it was. The most frightening monsters of childhood imagination lurk in places you'd never expect: beneath the bed, behind the door, inside the closet . . .

It was an important lesson learned, early on: monsters really can cross the threshold of your safe haven and jump out at you when you least expect it, so you'd better keep your guard up and develop some coping mechanisms.

I was lucky that day.

Lucky I didn't lose a finger . . .

Lucky for a lot of reasons.

Turtles, as it turned out, are viewed in many cultures as harbingers of good fortune.

The incident spurred a lifelong fascination with the fabled creatures, which led, eventually, to *Terrapin Times.*

That was the name of the first blog, the one launched years ago, before many people even knew what a blog was.

Terrapin Terry was the perfect screen name to use for that one. Terry—or T2, as online followers like to say—is an expert on all things turtle-related, comfortably ensconced in a world populated by people who are equally fascinated by the creatures, some to the point of being addicts.

It was positively intoxicating to find so many kindred spirits. But the best was yet to come.

Other blogs.

Other screen names.

Other identities, really, if one chooses to look at it that way. Each a fully formed character with a separate circle of friends.

Online, you can be anyone you want to be.

I have been so many different people . . .

Eventually, it became too exhausting, too complicated, to keep up with them all. Now, the only blogs that are still active are the turtle one and the breast cancer one . . .

And never the twain shall meet.

It's safe to imagine that the circle of breast cancer bloggers have never heard of Terrapin Terry, and that the turtle fans have never heard of—

Then again, you never know.

Maybe somewhere out there a fellow cancer blogger is following the turtle blog, posting comments under another screen name, with no idea that Terrapin Terry is really—

Probably not. But anything is possible on the Internet. That's the beauty of it.

The beauty . . . and the danger.

I Get By with a Little Help . . .

After I was diagnosed, my oncologist's nurse told me that it wasn't a good idea to keep my feelings bottled up inside. She said it might help to talk to others who were going through the same thing, and that she could put me in touch with a local network through the cancer center.

I said thanks, but no thanks. I was sure I'd be just fine dealing with it on my own.

But I wasn't. As my treatment progressed—surgery, radiation, medication, reconstruction—I felt more and more isolated.

My family was there for me, of course. They were willing to listen, and I tried, in the beginning, to express my fears and frustrations. But I couldn't bear seeing uncertainty and dread reflected back at me on their faces.

My father was still alive then. I'm an only child, and I was always Daddy's girl. Now he was so worried about me that I usually wound up trying to reassure him instead of the other way around. The same was true with my mother, and with my husband. It was hard enough to be strong enough for myself, let alone for everyone else.

Plus, I felt guilty dwelling on my cancer as a constant and depressing conversational topic—not that I had the heart or the energy to discuss anything else.

Finally, I gave in and attended a support group meeting up in Mobile. The other women in the room were in various stages of breast cancer treatment— some, it was obvious, in the final stages. At the first meeting, I listened in silence as the others talked about their own situations, and ranted, and cried.

At last I was surrounded by people who understood what I was going through because they had dealt with—or were dealing with—the same thing. Or worse.

For some, much worse.

At the third meeting, a particularly vocal woman I'd met at the first group session and noticed was conspicuously missing at the second announced that she'd just been given months, maybe just weeks, to live. She was a perfect stranger, but there I was sobbing along with her and the group members who took turns comforting her and each other.

I decided I was never going back there. It was too sad. I couldn't take it. It made me feel worse, not better.

And so I returned to shouldering the burden in solitary silence. I told myself that I could get through on inner strength, a positive attitude, and faith alone, as my grandmother had forty years ago. Again, I thought I was going to be just fine on my own.

Again, I was wrong. I needed someone. I needed all of you. This is my virtual support group, blessedly free of eye contact and tears. I can show up on my own time and I don't have to speak if I'm not in the mood, or make excuses if I feel like fleeing abruptly. This is my haven, my home. I thank God every day that I eventually found my way here, and I thank you for being my friends.

—Excerpt from Landry's blog, *The Breast Cancer Diaries*

Chapter 9

Riding the elevator down two floors to the hotel lobby, Landry smooths the skirt of her black dress. It wrinkled pretty badly in her suitcase, and she didn't dare use the iron in the room. As soon as she plugged it in, she smelled something burning and noticed scorched fabric stuck to the bottom.

She called down for another iron, but it didn't arrive by the time she had to leave for the funeral, so here she is, rumpled and running a few minutes late to meet Kay and Elena. She feels better, though, every time she looks down at the onyx bracelet Addison made for her. And no matter what happens today—this weekend—she'll be back home tomorrow night, and everything will be back to blessed normal.

With a ding, the elevator arrives in the lobby and she takes a deep breath as the doors slide open. She's jittery—in a good way—about the prospect of coming face-to-face at last with friends who've been lifesavers in the most literal sense of the word, if positive energy really does have healing powers, as Meredith believed.

Stepping into the lobby, she glances around. It's not a true budget hotel, but not fancy, either. This is the kind of place frequented by traveling salespeople, families with kids, senior citizens . . .

Bloggers coming face-to-face for the first time . . .

Landry passes the front desk, manned by a young woman reading a paperback romance, and the computer station occupied by a teenage boy, and the darkened dining alcove blocked off by a sign advertising the hours for the free breakfast. Just beyond is a large seating area where she, Elena, and Kay agreed to find each other.

Well, she and Kay agreed, anyway, in text messages exchanged after she checked into the hotel. Elena hasn't been in touch since before she left Boston, saying her phone battery was almost dead but she would check in with them when she got to the hotel and could plug it into her charger.

The seating area is empty, other than a frazzled-looking young mom sitting on a couch. She's trying to feed a fussy baby a bottle and scolding a toddler for noisily pushing a luggage cart across the tile floor. In the far corner, a man—probably her husband—has a cell phone clasped against one ear and a palm covering the other ear, as if to tune out the commotion behind him.

Realizing she's the first to arrive in the lobby, even though she's late, Landry perches on the arm of a chair perpendicular to the couch and exchanges curious glances with the young mother, wondering if it's possible . . .

No. No way. The woman is a blonde, and anyway, neither Elena nor Kay has children.

Unless one of them does and didn't mention it.

But if this woman happens to be one of the bloggers, wouldn't she be expecting Landry? Wouldn't she speak up and introduce herself?

What if she doesn't recognize me? After all, I was younger in my picture, and not nearly as weary, or frumpy, as I am now . . .

And what if . . .

Suddenly, Landry's situation seems to have gone from promising to precarious. Rob's warnings—months, years of warnings—fill her head.

You never know who you're dealing with online. It could be anyone . . . People can make up whatever they want . . . Men can pass themselves off as teenage girls—predators do it all the time . . .

Elena and Kay are her friends, just as Meredith was her friend, and yet . . .

There's no getting around the fact that they're strangers. All of them. Strangers, lifesavers . . .

They know her deepest, darkest secrets. They know where she is, and that she's all alone in a strange city, and what if . . .

What if none of it was real?

She nervously toys with the bracelet, rolling the two silver beads etched with Meredith's initials between her thumb and forefingers.

What if none of her friends even exists in real life? What if all those personalities were made up; figments of some twisted imagination? Even Meredith?

No—Meredith was real. She has to be real. She was in the newspaper.

But what if—

Behind her the elevator doors ding open.

A woman steps out.

Middle-aged, tall and heavyset, she has plain features and graying shoulder-length hair parted on the side. She's wearing a black pantsuit that's a little on the dowdy side for a woman who's at least a decade shy of her retirement years. With a tentative expression, she looks toward the seating area.

Kay.

It's her; it has to be her.

Paranoia evaporating, Landry utters the name impulsively, punctuated by an exclamation rather than a question mark.

The woman breaks into a relieved smile and walks

toward her in sensible shoes most likely bought on sale at Kohl's, plus an additional thirty percent off with a coupon, knowing Kay, Landry thinks affectionately.

Getting to her feet, she realizes belatedly she doesn't know how to greet her friend for the first time.

Handshake? Hug?

Hug, she decides in the last moment.

Kay's stocky frame seems to stiffen for a moment, and Landry thinks she's made the wrong choice.

Kay has intimacy issues. Anyone who's read her blog knows about that. All those years spent with a cold, unfeeling parent, and working in a federal prison, hardly a cozy environment . . .

But then Kay relaxes and she hugs back. Hard. And when they pull away to regard each other at arm's length, Landry sees tears in Kay's eyes and can feel them in her own.

She hastily wipes them away with her sleeve, as does Kay.

"Sorry—I didn't mean to jump on you with a big ol' hug like a long lost friend without even introducing myself."

"It's all right." Kay smiles, shyly, but warmly. "Landry, right? BamaBelle?"

"That's me. I was beginning to think no one was going to show up!"

"I thought the same thing! I had to force myself to come down here. I've been up there in my room for hours, pacing and trying to convince myself not to turn around and drive back home."

"I'm glad you didn't."

"Me too."

They smile at each other, and Landry is suddenly conscious of the young mother watching them, listening with interest, oblivious to her toddler rolling the luggage cart away again, this time toward a corridor lined with first floor rooms.

"Have you seen Elena?"

Kay shakes her head. "I just saw the texts she sent before she took off, saying that her phone was dying."

"Hopefully she made it here."

"Hopefully she did."

There's a crash down the hall. "Mommy!"

The woman on the couch jumps up, thrusts the baby and its bottle on the man with the cell phone and heads in the direction of the noise.

A split second later a woman in a black dress—Elena, is it Elena?—appears in the hallway, shaking her head as she strides toward the lobby.

Spotting Landry and Kay, she breaks into a smile and calls out, "Is that you, guys?" Without waiting for a reply, she adds, "I just had a close call! I nearly just got run over by a luggage cart."

Cart is pronounced "caht," New England style. Landry grins. Definitely Elena.

This time a hug feels right from the start.

As she and Elena embrace, Landry catches a whiff of alcohol on her breath. She must have had a drink on the plane, or maybe after she landed. Probably nerves. Who can blame her?

Elena steps back to take a better look at them. "You're both just the way I pictured you."

"I was thinking the same thing," Landry agrees. "I'd know y'all anywhere."

"Me too. I just wish . . ." Kay trails off, shaking her head.

Remembering Meredith, Landry touches Kay's hand. Her fingers are icy. "I know. It's hard."

Kay moves her hand away to look at her watch. "We should go. It's late. Can one of you drive? I . . . I forgot to fill up the gas tank after we got here."

"I will," Elena offers, but Landry is already pulling her own rental car keys out of her pocket.

"That's okay. I'll drive."

"I don't mind. I'm parked right out front."

"I've already got the address plugged into the GPS," Landry tells Elena firmly. "Really. I want to drive."

"That's fine if you're sure you really want to. Just so you know you don't *need* to," Elena says, and for a moment Landry is taken aback.

Then she sees Elena's smile.

"Remember that blog Meredith wrote?" Elena asks them. "The one about the difference between wanting something and needing something?"

"I remember it," Kay says as Landry nods. "It was one of her better blogs. But there were so many good ones. A lot of the things she wrote keep coming back to me now. It's kind of comforting. Almost like she's still talking to me, you know?"

"Sometimes I feel the same way," Landry says, and Elena agrees that she does as well.

As they head out into the bright June sunshine and across the parking lot, Landry can't help but think that she really doesn't just *want* to drive—she *needs* to. After all she's been through—and all the lectures she's given her teenagers—there's absolutely no way she's getting into a car with a driver she suspects has been drinking. Elena doesn't seem the least bit inebriated—for all Landry knows, that was just mouthwash she sniffed on her breath—but there's no need to take chances.

As the rental car comes into view, Landry aims the electronic key and presses the button to unlock the doors. If she were back home with her kids, this is the point where they'd both yell, "I call shotgun!" and race each other for the front passenger seat.

She turns to Kay and Elena to joke about it, but quickly changes her mind. Elena has stopped in her tracks behind them, frowning as she looks at her cell phone. Her energy is completely different now, Landry notices; not a hint of the bubbly, upbeat woman who burst into the lobby a few minutes ago.

"Everything okay?" Landry asks her.

"Hmmm? Oh . . . yes. It's fine. I was just getting a call from a friend back home that I'd rather not answer right now. Some people will drive you crazy if you let them, you know?"

Landry thinks of Barbie June. "I know."

"I'm just going to turn off the phone." Elena holds down the power button. "I didn't have time to fully charge it back up anyway, so I might as well conserve battery power for now." She shoves it back into her purse and looks up.

"Okay—I'm good to go," she says brightly, and resumes walking toward the car at a jaunty pace.

Noticing that Elena seems to have bounced back just as quickly as she'd faltered, Landry can't help but wonder about the friend who'd tried to call her just now.

The drive to McGraw's Funeral Home takes less than five minutes, though there's more traffic now than when Kay did her morning drive-by.

She's glad to see that although the bowling alley parking lot looks busy, no one is using the swimming pool at the duplex next door, as she'd feared. It would be disrespectful to Meredith if people were splashing around and having a good old time in their bathing suits just a stone's throw from her remains.

"Oh my goodness, the parking lot is completely full," Landry murmurs, slowly driving past rows of occupied spots. "Do y'all see anything?"

"I think you'd better follow those signs for the overflow lot," Elena advises, pointing.

"Wait—is that a space?" Landry hits the brakes.

It isn't.

"Let's just go to the overflow," Elena urges again, checking her watch.

There's no denying she's a bit of a backseat driver. If she were at the wheel, Kay thought, she'd be intimidated by Elena's control freak tendencies, but she notices they don't seem to bother Landry. The two of them have kept up a steady stream of conversation on the way over. Kay couldn't get a word in edgewise—not that she's tried.

Most of the chatter was about kids—Landry's two teenagers and Elena's first grade students.

Having never had children—or, really, even known them in the course of her adult life—Kay has nothing to contribute in that regard. But lack of conversational connection isn't her sole reason for keeping quiet. Mostly, she's preoccupied with what lies ahead.

In her opinion, Landry and Elena aren't quite mindful enough of the reason they're all here: to say good-bye to Meredith.

The solemn nature of the occasion does seem to sink in as they walk toward the funeral home, though, as the other women fall silent at last.

That Meredith left behind dozens—no, *hundreds*—of people who loved her is obvious the moment they cross the threshold into the large chapel adjacent to the foyer. An endless line snakes through the hushed room, weaving up and down rows of folding chairs.

She, Elena, and Landry join the mourners gradually making their way up to the bereaved family standing beside the large urn that holds Meredith's remains.

As they await their turn, Kay studies the Heywoods.

She's heard so much about them over the years that it's easy for her to tell them apart. Gray-haired Hank, of course, is obviously Meredith's husband. But Kay can easily see which of the three young women is her daughter—Beck looks a lot like her mother.

She can tell the two daughters-in-law apart, too: Teddy's wife, Sue, is pregnant; Neal's wife, Kelly, is the redhead.

As for the brothers, they look quite a bit like each other and their father, but Kay remembers that Neal, the middle son, is the tallest one in the family, much to his older brother's frustration when they were growing up. Meredith blogged about that once.

By default, the fourth man in the family—the serious-looking bearded fellow—would have to be Meredith's son-in-law, Keith.

Only the grandchildren—her beloved "stinkerdoodles"—are missing.

So these are the people Meredith lived for, the people she couldn't bear the thought of "abandoning," as she put it.

It's not that I don't think they'll survive without me, Meredith wrote to her on the day they both confessed that their illnesses had progressed. *In fact, financially, they'll be better off, that's for sure. I'm like George Bailey.*

Kay didn't understand that reference, not even after she quickly Googled the name and found that George Bailey was a character in the old movie *It's a Wonderful Life.* She's never seen it. She isn't big on movies; hasn't caught a film or even turned on the television in years.

When she asked Meredith what she meant by the comment, Meredith explained that the plot revolves around a character, George Bailey, who winds up destitute, other than a life insurance policy.

"But he's the richest man in town in the end, of course," Meredith said, "because he had friends, so many friends who loved him."

As did Meredith.

The room is warm and crowded, the air thickly scented with the perfume of hundreds of women and all those funeral flowers. They're everywhere, in vases and baskets and wreaths surrounding the urn and spilling over into the seating area—further testimony to just how much Meredith meant to so many.

Kay thinks of her own solitary life.

Mother's raspy voice echoes in her head: *It's not better to have loved and lost . . . If you don't love, you can't lose.*

No. That isn't the case at all, Kay thinks, inching forward with the line of mourners waiting to connect with the Heywood family.

You were wrong, Mother. As wrong about that as you were about everything else.

When it's her turn to meet the Heywoods, she moves robotically down the line with Landry and Elena, introducing herself as one of Meredith's blogger friends.

"You all meant so much to Mom." Meredith's daughter clasps her hand. "She was always telling us about you."

"She talked about all of you, too," Kay tells her. "She was so proud of you. She told me all about the beautiful Mother's Day party you all had a few weeks ago. She even e-mailed me pictures, and she said you made her favorite cheesecake . . ."

"Actually, I wound up buying it," Rebecca Heywood replies with a sad smile. "I wish I'd had a chance to make it for her that day."

"I'm sure it didn't matter. What mattered to her was that you were all there with her. That's what she remembered."

And then the person behind her is reaching for Rebecca's hand and it's time for Kay to move on.

The rest of it—everything else she'd wanted to tell Meredith's family—will have to be left unsaid.

Jaycee's cell phone buzzes in her oversized bag on the passenger's seat of the rental car as she pulls into the parking lot behind McGraw's Funeral Home. She reaches inside without looking at it and turns it off. Whoever it is—probably Cory—can wait. The service was scheduled to start ten minutes ago. She wanted to be late—but not any later than this.

Clearly, Meredith was as popular with her real-life

friends as she was with the online group. Every spot in the lot is taken.

Jaycee can't help but flash back to another funeral in another time, another place. Empty parking lot, with only herself and the pastor to stand beside her grandmother's simple pinewood casket.

She sobbed through that ceremony. Not because her grandmother was dead—she'd hated her. Not because she was pregnant, either. But because Steven Petersen—her one true friend, the love of her life—hadn't had the decency to show up. He could have come for her sake, not for her grandmother's; Steve had hated her, too.

That was the last time she allowed herself to shed tears in public. It was the last time she ever lost someone who truly mattered.

Steve.

After all they'd been through together . . .

No. Don't think about that now.

Thoughts of Steve always lead to thoughts of *her* . . .

Pushing the blood-drenched memories from her mind, Jaycee follows the signs and drives around the ugly yellow brick building to the overflow lot. The gravel patch there is nearly full of cars. On the far end, across from the last couple of empty spaces, she spots the sedan Landry rented at the airport.

Obviously, she, too, arrived late—despite her flight having landed with plenty of time to spare. Did Landry also dawdle in her hotel room, having second thoughts about showing her face here today?

In the end, Jaycee opted to come. The funeral, after all, is why she flew to Ohio in the first place this morning—aside from needing a convenient escape hatch.

She wasn't going to allow herself to come all this way without paying her last respects to one of the few friends she had left in this world.

She pulls into a spot across from Landry's rental, turns off the engine, and glances into the rearview mirror. Between her broad-brimmed black hat and oversized sunglasses, only her mouth, nose, and jaw are visible. No one is going to recognize her if she slips quietly into the back and then leaves early.

Her heels poke into the gravel as she steps out of the car. It's slow going until she reaches the pavement. Now her pace is steadier, heels tapping along briskly. As she makes her way toward the entrance, she spots a black Crown Victoria—an unmarked cop car?

Of course.

Meredith was murdered. It would make sense that there would be a police presence at the service today. They'll be watching the crowd carefully, looking for suspicious behavior, perhaps pulling people aside for questioning—a thought that's almost enough to send Jaycee straight back to her car.

Before she can turn around, the door opens and a man in a dark suit beckons to her. The funeral director, she realizes. He's been watching her approach through the glass panel. There's nothing she can do but walk up the steps and cross the threshold.

"In there," the man whispers, gesturing at a pair of closed doors.

She nods her thanks and crosses the foyer, conscious of his eyes on her. Reaching for the knob on the right, she gives it a gentle tug. Both doors swing open, but the one on the left quickly closes again with a loud sound before she can catch it.

Jaycee keeps her head down. There's a rustling commotion; several people in the crowded room turn to look at her as she carefully closes the other door.

A robed reverend is speaking beside the gleaming urn—no plain pine box for Meredith Heywood's remains—and every folding chair and inch of perimeter wall is occupied.

No one else is wearing a hat or sunglasses. Realizing this getup makes her even more conspicuous, Jaycee removes both and wedges herself into a narrow slot beside the door, staring at the carpet, reminding herself why she's here.

Not just because she wanted to escape New York on what would have been a difficult day, thanks to Cory's early delivery of the morning paper with its disturbing news item.

No, she's here for Meredith.

Meredith, who lived her life in such a way that her funeral is standing room only. When all is said and done, that's all that really matters, although . . .

When her time comes, she thinks, her own funeral might be just as crowded—or more so. But not with friends and relatives who loved her for who she was and will truly miss her when she's gone.

No—they'd be drawn to her funeral for very different reasons . . .

Unless something changes very drastically.

You can do that. You can change, even now. It's not too late.

Meredith's voice seems to fill her head.

Of course, even when she gave that little pep talk, Meredith never knew the truth about her . . .

But she does now, Jaycee realizes. Wherever she is.

Maybe her spirit really is here, offering support, and . . . forgiveness.

Jaycee closes her eyes, head bowed.

If you're here, Meredith, I'm so sorry. I hope you know that I only did what I had to do.

What I thought I had to do.

As she reflects on the choices she made, a feeling creeps over her—not peaceful comfort, but a familiar wariness that has become second nature after all these years: the distinct sensation that she's being watched.

She lifts her head slightly, half expecting to see Meredith's ghost—or perhaps one of the bloggers, having somehow spotted her and figured out who she is.

That's impossible, though. Even if they're here, they can't possibly know that you're . . . you. Her. Whoever— whoever you've convinced them you are. Jaycee.

When she looks up, she finds herself making immediate eye contact with a woman who's standing along the wall toward the front of the room, staring right at her.

She's African-American, so she can't be Landry, Kay, or Elena. She's just some random person who for some reason seems to be paying more attention to the mourners than to the service itself.

She's the cop, Jaycee realizes. God knows she's had more than her share of contact with them. She can sniff out law enforcement even from this distance.

Now, as the woman gets a good look at her face, her eyes narrow with recognition.

Jaycee quickly looks down again, heart pounding. So much for blessed anonymity. The lady cop's gaze remains as palpable as the searing glare of a heat lamp.

Damn it, damn it, damn it.

She shouldn't have come. She should have fought the familiar old instinct to run away. Anniversary or not, newspaper article or not, she should have spent the weekend locked safely into her apartment in the sky, away from prying eyes.

As the service draws to a close with Meredith Heywood's daughter reading a poem, there isn't a dry eye in the house— except, perhaps, for Crystal's and Frank's.

It isn't that they're immune to emotion in a tragic case such as this, but when you're a homicide detective, you have to compartmentalize.

Crystal sweeps yet another shrewd gaze over the crowd of mourners. Most of them are surreptitiously dabbing their eyes with tissues or sobbing openly.

Hank Heywood sits on the aisle seat in the front row with his head buried in his hands. Across the space vacated by Rebecca, her duplicitous husband Keith seems detached from her brothers, who sit beside him with their wives between them, all four of them clasping hands.

Keith is fixated on his wife as she reads the poem, not daring to sneak a peek at his secret boyfriend.

Jonathan Randall slipped into the service right after it started, standing in the back.

Crystal noticed him immediately—and noticed Keith turning his head to look for him moments later, as if sensing his presence. He offered a glassy smile when he spotted Jonathan, and Jonathan returned it.

Crystal watched them closely as the service progressed. They barely glanced at each other, but she could feel the vibe between them and knew they were as aware of each other as middle schoolers deliberately *not* noticing members of the opposite sex at a dance.

She also kept a steady eye on Hank Heywood. The man appears utterly shattered. His daughter kept her arm around him throughout the service, letting go only to walk shakily to the podium to read her poem.

Her voice wavers as she speaks, and she stops several times, too choked up to go on. Now the poem is winding down.

"And afterward, remember, do not grieve . . ."

As Rebecca reads the line, Crystal sees, out of the corner of her eye, movement near the exit at the back of the room.

She looks up just in time to see Jenna Coeur disappear through the double doors.

Crystal hadn't immediately recognized her when she first arrived—late, and wearing an oversized black hat and sunglasses in a room almost entirely populated by sturdy, well-scrubbed midwesterners in department store suits and dresses.

She must have realized she stuck out like a cupcake on a plate of toast, because she skittishly removed the hat and glasses, further attracting Crystal's attention. There was something furtive about her movements, the way she kept her head down . . .

Crystal's instincts told her that she was looking at a woman who had something to hide.

The moment they made eye contact, Crystal realized that her instincts were dead on. She had something to hide, all right: she'd been at the center of one of the most notorious murder cases in recent years.

Jenna Coeur's dark hair might be dyed blond or concealed beneath a wig now, but her natural beauty and famously distinct resemblance to the actress Ingrid Bergman was immediately recognizable. She looked like Bergman in *Casablanca* at the height of her career: the large eyes beneath arched brows, the strong nose, the high cheekbones.

What, Crystal wondered with interest—and yes, with suspicion—was *she* doing here?

After that fleeting eye contact, Jenna never lifted her head again, just stood staring at her clasped hands for the remainder of the service, as if praying.

Praying, no doubt, that she hadn't been recognized.

But she had.

And now she's made her escape, getting a head start before the mass exodus begins.

Crystal reminds herself that it may mean absolutely nothing, in the grand scheme of things.

Coeur was, after all, acquitted.

That may very well mean she didn't commit murder.

It may also mean that she did—and got away with it.

Once, anyway.

Crystal weaves through the crowd as quickly as she can without disrupting the service.

At last she reaches the door and steps outside—just in

time to hear a car spitting gravel as it pulls out of the parking lot onto the highway, just beyond her range of view.

Jenna Coeur, driving away.

But I won't forget that you were here, Crystal promises silently. *And believe me, I'm going to find out why.*

A Cause Worth Fighting For

Last weekend, while I was tied up with a prior commitment, many of my fellow bloggers gathered for the National Breast Cancer Coalition Advocacy Training Conference. Here were women I've never met, but spend time with everyday. Whose words and work I admire. Whose thoughts I connect with. They gathered in Washington to fight for NBCC's goal to end breast cancer by 2020.

At last, an exciting mission, empowering when embraced. For too long it seems we were stuck in a sea of pink, hearing of changes, wanting to believe advancements were being made. Needing to believe optimistic statistics when in actuality approximately 40,000 people still die from this disease every year.

About as many as two decades ago.

That's not advancement. That's not change. That's a number hidden so far down in a sea of pink we barely see it, but deep within ourselves, where the scary thoughts thrive, we know it's the truth. Pink awareness is not enough.

The people attending this event heard the conversation shift. They refocused on facts, and with a concrete goal in sight discussed how research, combined with action and dedication, could have the 2020 eradication deadline within our grasps.

Social media was at its finest as bloggers tweeted

from their workshops. I couldn't absorb the information fast enough and want to thank them for taking time to spread the inspiration around.

If I had to choose a place to be that weekend, it would have been there in Washington, beside this group of incredibly motivated women. Dragging cancer to the center of the room for all to see. Believing it was now possible to kick out the unwanted guest . . . never to be seen again.

—Excerpt from Jaycee's blog, *PC BC*

Chapter 10

Jaycee had spotted a Starbucks along the mile of suburban highway between the interstate exit and the funeral home. Now, making her way back, she keeps an eye out for it, desperate to grab a cup of coffee for the road. Good, strong, familiar coffee, as opposed to the watered-down stuff they served her on the flight.

Cory might tease her about her affinity for Starbucks, but there's something to be said for consistency and availability. Especially when you've traveled all over the world, or been trapped in a prison cell—neither of which guarantee you a decent cup of coffee on a daily basis.

She should know, unlike Cory, who spent his life luxuriating in the concrete canyons of Manhattan and the rugged canyons of L.A., taking creature comforts for granted.

Zeroing in on the familiar green and white logo on a signpost up ahead, Jaycee checks the rearview mirror out of habit, to make sure she isn't being followed. She half expects to spot the Crown Victoria from the funeral home parking lot on her tail.

But all she sees is a red pickup truck, a couple of SUVs, and a little white car, and they all fly right on past as she turns into the parking lot.

Good.

She's pretty sure that the woman back at the funeral home recognized her—and that she happened to be law enforcement. But even if that was the case, the woman would have no reason to come chasing after her, right? Attending a funeral isn't a crime.

Hell, some *crimes* aren't even a crime.

No one knows that better than you do.

Not that she wants to think about all that now. She came here to escape.

Right. Brilliant move.

Most people needing a reprieve would hop a plane to some remote Caribbean island. But not you. Nope. You fly away to a funeral.

Yes, but a friend's funeral—a friend who meant a lot to her. A friend she hasn't fully allowed herself to grieve, even now.

But when you get right down to it, is she really here in Ohio solely because of Meredith? Ever since the others began making plans to come for the service this weekend, there was a part of her that wistfully longed to join them even though she knew it was impossible.

She isn't one of them. Not really.

As usual, she tried to push the uncomfortable truth to the back of her mind. But it's pretty telling that the moment trouble popped up and she needed to flee, this is where she wound up.

I guess I was meant to be here all along, watching from the sidelines.

So what else is new?

Jaycee parks the car, grabs her wallet from the oversized bag on the seat, and goes into Starbucks wearing just the sunglasses and of course her blond wig, but not the hat. Aside from baseball caps, no one around here wears hats, not even to a funeral. She should have known better than to choose a disguise that would make her even more conspicuous. She won't make that mistake again.

Stepping across the threshold, she takes a deep breath of java-laced air and is instantly soothed by the familiar, manufactured-to-be-inviting setting: mood lighting, intimate tables and chairs suitable for one, hipster baristas, vintage crooners on the audio system. The people sitting and sipping are either caught up in quiet conversations, absorbed in their laptops, or plugged into headphones. No one gives her a second glance as she joins the line of people waiting to order.

When it's her turn, she steps forward and asks for the usual: a venti latte with a triple shot of espresso.

"Name?" asks the girl behind the register.

"Annie," Jaycee tells her, and watches her write it in marker on a venti-sized cup.

Annie was her first cellmate, a crackhead prostitute with three little kids and the proverbial heart of gold. She'd killed her dealer—or was it her pimp? Jaycee doesn't remember the exact details of the case now; it was a long time ago and they weren't cellmates for very long. She only knows that while Annie might have been a murderer—though she said she'd done it in self-defense—her odd blend of streetwise sass and protective maternal attitude helped Jaycee survive some rough days, and rougher nights.

"Don'chu forget me now," Annie said before she was transferred to another jail, closer to where her kids were. "When I get out, I'm go'an come look you up."

"I'll probably still be here."

Annie was already shaking her head. "You go'an get off, girlfriend. You mark my words."

She was right.

Annie never did come find her. Chances are she's probably serving a long prison sentence, or back on the streets, or dead.

But Annie didn't want to be forgotten, and she hasn't

been. Jaycee uses the name now as her random default identity for Starbucks and anywhere else she has to place an order with a name attached. She used to choose something different every time, but that became confusing. She'd forget who she was supposed to be.

Even now, there are days when she forgets: Jaycee, or Jenna Coeur, or her real name . . . or any number of identities she's used and discarded over the years.

She pays for her beverage and pockets the change. Back home in New York she'd have left it in the tips cup on the counter. Here, hardly anyone does that. She's been watching.

When in Rome . . .

That's the key to keeping a low profile. You fit in with the locals. Don't provide reason for them to give you a second glance. Throwing tip money into the cup would necessitate an extra thank you from the cashier or might arouse resentment in the customers behind her; not tipping makes her just like everybody else.

Less than a minute later the barista is calling, "Ann?"

Jaycee thanks her and takes a sip. The hot, pleasantly strong liquid slides down her throat.

Ah. Finally, a moment of peace.

She eyes the seating area, spotting an empty table for one beside the big picture window facing the road.

Maybe she won't take her coffee to go after all. It would be a relief just to settle down for a few minutes and check her e-mails and text messages. By now Cory must have figured out she's gone. He's probably worried.

He doesn't know about Meredith, of course—and she has no intention of telling him.

As Meredith's daughter finishes reading the last few lines of her poem, Landry wipes tears from her eyes with a soggy tissue. She can't help but marvel at the young woman's strength; can't help but compare her to Addison.

If it were my funeral, she'd do the same thing, Landry finds herself thinking. *She's so strong. Stronger than I could ever be*.

Meredith would have been proud.

The minister steps back to the podium with a few final words, and at last it's over. The crowd begins to move.

Someone touches Landry on the arm.

She looks up to see an attractive African-American woman flashing a badge.

"I'm Detective Crystal Burns," she says, addressing all three of them. "I'm assuming you're friends of Meredith's?"

Caught off guard, Landry nods.

"Mind if I ask how you knew her?"

It's Elena who answers promptly, "Only through the Internet."

The detective pulls out a little notebook, and Landry grasps that this is not going to be a quick, simple conversation.

"Ladies," she says, "I know this is not the best time or place to talk. I'd like to take down your names and ask you a few quick questions, and then maybe, if the three of you are staying in town, we can meet a little later to talk further?"

Landry quickly speaks for all of them: "Anything we can do to help, Detective."

The bag containing Roger Lorton's final effects has been lying on the floor beside the front door ever since the detective delivered it this morning.

It isn't until later in the day—much later—that Sheri finally musters the strength to pick it up and carry it to the living room, trailed by the puppy's jingling dog tags. She sits in a chair and Maggie settles at her feet. She's been sticking close to Sheri's side these past few days, since Roger's murder. Every once in a while she looks up as if there's something she wants Sheri to know.

You saw the person who killed him, didn't you, girl?

But you can't talk, and whoever did it is going to get away with it.

Sheri dully looks down at the bag on her lap, fighting back tears.

Finally, she opens it and looks inside.

The first thing she sees is the wedding ring, catching the sunlight that falls through the window. She pulls it out, swallowing hard, and slides it over her fingers one by one. It's much too big for all but her thumb. She leaves it there for now. Maybe she can wear it on a chain around her neck.

The bag's remaining contents are meager. One by one she removes a house key, a small plastic bottle of hand sanitizer Roger always carried, a pack of cigarettes, and a couple of folded bills. Roger never keeps cash in his wallet, always places it in a separate pocket. Years ago, when they first met, Sheri asked him why. He said it was so that if a pickpocket robbed him, he wouldn't be left without both cash and credit cards.

Whoever stole his wallet was probably looking for quick cash, probably drug money. Why else would you mug someone?

Sheri finds scant satisfaction in knowing that the murderer came away with nothing but credit cards, none of which have been used since the wallet went missing and aren't likely to be now. Oh, and Roger's silver lighter, the one he always carried. It's missing as well.

About to set the empty bag aside, she frowns and peers into the bottom. Something else is there, a small, dark triangular object.

Pulling it out, she sees that it's a guitar pick.

Certainly not Roger's.

How did it end up with his belongings?

It must have gotten mixed in with this stuff back at the morgue, maybe fallen out of someone's pocket . . .

You'd think the authorities would be more careful when dealing with someone's final effects.

Final . . .

Final.

With a sob, Sheri crumples the bag and tosses it onto the floor. The wedding ring goes with it, sliding off her thumb and rolling across the hardwoods.

With a whimper, Maggie lifts her nose from her paws and looks up at Sheri wearing a morose expression, as if she, too, is mourning.

Remember me when I am gone away . . .

Beck still can't believe her mother is gone.

The funeral had been as torturous as she'd expected; struggling to maintain her composure, she'd been relieved the moment it ended.

But now she's crying all over again as departing mourners take turns embracing her. No one seems to know quite what to say, other than to tell her how sorry they are, or how much they're going to miss her mother, or how fitting the poem was, or how aptly the eulogy captured Mom.

The minister hadn't known her very well, but he'd asked the family to help him prepare, taking notes as they shared anecdotes that had them laughing and crying, often simultaneously.

"Thank you," Beck says, over and over, in response to the compliments about the service and the expressions of sympathy.

Some comments and questions are unexpectedly awkward: a few people want to know whether the police have a suspect yet.

She just shakes her head.

"Do you have any idea who might have done it?" a woman—a total stranger—asks her.

Beck just shakes her head as her uneasy gaze seeks and then settles on Detectives Burns and Schneider, across the room. She wasn't at all surprised to see them here today and knows it's not simply because they want to pay their respects to her mother.

They're thinking the killer might be in the crowd.

Beck is thinking the same thing. When she allows the thought into her head, it's all she can do not to flee for the nearest exit. The rest of the family appears to be feeling the same way.

And Dad . . . poor Dad.

Every time she glances at his face, she feels his pain.

She just hopes the detectives can, too; hopes they know he couldn't possibly be responsible for what happened to Mom. No matter what statistics say . . .

No matter what I saw that day last month . . .

He didn't do it. It's that simple.

"Oh, Rebecca . . ." A childhood neighbor grabs onto her, hugging her hard. "I'm so sorry for all of you. Your poor father is going to be lost without your mother. Just make sure you take care of him."

"Don't worry," she says grimly. "I will."

Climbing into the backseat of the rental car after a long, silent walk from the funeral parlor to the back lot, Elena is still rattled by the brief encounter with the detective.

The woman took down basic information—their names, home addresses, ages—and arranged to meet them at their hotel later.

"I wonder if she's doing that with everyone," she says as Landry and Kay settle into their seats.

Neither of them asks who—or what—she's talking about.

"I'm sure she is," Landry says.

"Probably," Kay agrees, pulling on her seat belt.

"We should stop off someplace on the way back to the hotel," Elena suggests as Landry shifts the car into reverse, "and get something to eat."

Something to drink is what she means. Her nerves are shot.

"Now?" Landry asks. "I thought we were planning to go out to dinner later."

"We are, but we should get something now. Just, you know, something light. Especially since we have the detective coming to talk to us."

"That might take a while. I could go for a cup of tea myself," Kay agrees.

"I guess I wouldn't mind some coffee," Landry decides, and so it's settled.

Coffee. Tea. Terrific.

Elena had been thinking along the lines of cocktails—a little more hair of the dog for her pounding head. The Bloody Mary on the plane had done nothing to take off the edge. And now they have to face a meeting with the detective investigating Meredith's death . . .

I want a drink.

No. I need *a drink.*

"There were a couple of restaurants back toward the hotel," Landry says. "I'll head back that way."

Elena settles back in the seat, resigned to a low-key coffee break—for now—and wishing she'd insisted on driving, or at least that she'd taken her own car. The parking lot has become crowded with moving people and cars, and Landry is taking her sweet old time maneuvering toward the exit.

To be fair, it's not as though she can just barrel out of here. Still, she's as slow and deliberate about driving as she is about everything else.

When they first met back at the hotel, Elena had to fight the urge to hustle her friend along—even conversationally. Everything about the self-proclaimed Alabama belle strikes her as languid. Not a bad thing, necessarily. Just . . . different.

Kay is different as well. Different from Landry, and from

her, too. Practical and perfunctory, she reminds Elena of someone's maiden aunt.

Not of her own aunt—maiden, or otherwise. Thanks to her father, she'd lost touch with her extended family after her mother died. But her dim memories of her parents' sisters and sisters-in-law are of vibrant women very much like her mother.

Had she initially met these two women, Kay and Landry, in person, rather than online, Elena is pretty sure they wouldn't have clicked at all.

There's a lesson in there somewhere, she decides. But what is it?

She's always telling her students to look beyond the obvious.

"Dig deeper," she urges her first graders. "Don't accept anything at face value."

Good advice.

Okay. So look at Tony. If she'd first gotten to know him online, might she possibly have clicked with him in a way that she doesn't in person?

Just the thought of him sets her nerves on edge now. He'd called her cell phone and left her a message while she was on the plane, asking her to give him a call back when she landed.

She didn't—and not just because her battery was drained. He called again while she and the others were leaving the hotel, and that time she ignored it. He didn't leave a message, and she turned off the phone immediately afterward.

Now, reluctantly turning it back on, she sees that she missed a couple of calls.

The first one is from Tony.

Really? *Really?*

Scrolling through the missed calls log, she sees that his number is attached to all of them—and there are half a dozen. He left her a message the first time he tried her, then just kept dialing and hanging up on her voice mail.

Reluctantly, Elena puts the phone to her ear. She might as well hear what he had to say. Maybe he wanted to apologize for being . . .

Well, for being Tony.

"Elena, I need you to give me a call right away . . ."

Even in a recording, he annoys her. He urgently needs her to do something now? When she's halfway across the country, at a funeral?

" . . . I've been thinking about it and I don't think you should be alone right now, and . . . you know what? Just give me a call the minute you get this. Okay. 'Bye."

Jaw clenched, Elena presses Delete. Then she turns off her phone, in case he decides to call back yet again.

I'm not alone, Tony. I'm with my friends. Although . . .

In the front seat, Kay is pointing. "There's a McDonald's."

Elena doesn't acknowledge her. *McDonalds? I'd rather be anyplace else right now—including alone.*

Yes, preferably alone at a bar somewhere, drowning her sorrows. That's what you do after a funeral. It's what her father did after her mother's . . .

For thirty years.

"I don't think McDonald's is exactly what we're looking for," Landry tells Kay.

Relieved, Elena looks toward the opposite side of the road. "There's a Chili's. And an Applebee's."

Landry makes her face. "I'm not crazy about— Oh, wait, I see Starbucks!"

She flicks on the turn signal and pulls into the left turning lane toward Starbucks as if it's all decided.

Elena opens her mouth to put in her vote for going back to the hotel, or to someplace that has a bar, then thinks better of it.

If she goes back and sits in her room, she's only going to stress about Tony and . . . everything.

And if she goes to a bar . . .

Look what happened to her after all that wine last night.

Look what happens every time she drinks too much.

With the detective meeting them soon, it's probably best to stick with her friends and drown her sorrows in a cup of coffee. At least that'll keep her out of trouble—for now.

Several cars in front of them make the left turn into the parking lot, and Landry creeps forward with each one. When it's her turn, the light turns yellow. There's only one oncoming car and it's far enough away . . .

"You can make it," Elena advises.

But Landry is braking. Stopping. So is the oncoming car.

Elena can't help herself: "You could have made it."

"Like I always tell my kids when they're at the wheel, yellow means slow down, not speed up."

"Not where I'm from."

Landry shrugs. "Where I'm from, slow and steady wins the race."

Finally, the light is green, the coast is clear, and they're pulling into the busy parking lot. Starbucks is hopping at this hour on a sunny Saturday afternoon.

Reaching for the back door handle, Elena flashes back to what Tony said to her as she got out of his car at the airport this morning.

"Your secret is safe with me . . ."

What was he talking about?

What did I tell him?

She rubs her temples with her fingertips as they step from the parking lot glare into the dimly lit interior—then stops short, spotting Tony at the far end of the counter, waiting for a beverage.

Landry promptly crashes into her from behind. "Oops, I'm sorry!"

"It's okay," Elena murmurs.

It's not him. As he turns, she's almost positive the man is a total stranger who has on the kind of sleeveless muscle T-shirt Tony sometimes wears.

Or is it?

It has to be a stranger. This is Ohio. Tony's back in Massachusetts.

Still, Elena keeps a wary eye on him as he walks out without a backward glance, half expecting him to come back.

He doesn't.

Of course not, because he isn't Tony.

Waiting anxiously for her turn to order coffee, she stares blankly at the menu board she's seen a thousand times at Starbucks back home, frustrated with herself.

After connecting with the others back at the hotel, she'd finally managed to banish unpleasant thoughts of Tony and last night. But now that she's heard his message and seen evidence of all those missed calls, toxic tendrils are once again unfurling in her mind, choking out all other thoughts.

Tony knows "her secret."

Tony wants to talk to her.

He wants to see her, be here with her . . .

Back at home, she had a printout of the hotel reservation right next to the flight information, under a magnet on the refrigerator. Did he wander around her apartment while she was sleeping?

What if he really did follow her here?

What if he pops out any second now? *Surprise!*

The thought is enough to make her queasy.

"Elena?"

She blinks, and realizes Landry is talking to her, gesturing at the waiting cashier. "Your turn to order."

"Oh, sorry, I'm just feeling a little . . . out of it," she murmurs, and asks for a venti black coffee.

"Are you okay?" Landry asks.

She'd never understand. Aside from Meredith's death and the cancer diagnosis they all share, Landry Wells has her life together. Elena came here thinking she was finding kindred spirits: women who know what it's like to walk in her shoes.

But they don't. When this weekend is over, Landry is going to go back to her handsome lawyer husband and her two beautiful kids and her big house on the water. And Kay is going to go back to . . .

Well, who knows what Kay's life is really like?

For better or worse, cancer or not, it's a world away from hers, which means . . .

Which means I have never been more alone in my life.

"So did you see her?" Crystal demands of Frank, the moment they're safely back in the car.

He's driving this time, headed back to the station house. She has some information to look up on the Internet—the sooner, the better.

"Did I see who?"

"Jenna Coeur."

His eyes widen. "Did I see her where?"

"At the memorial service," Crystal says impatiently, pulling her iPad out of her bag.

"*Jenna Coeur* was there? Are you sure?"

"Positive. I recognized her but I don't know if anyone else did, and I could tell she was trying to keep a low profile. She was disguised as a blonde—or maybe she is a blonde now— and she came in late and then snuck out right before the end of the service."

"Why was she there?"

"Good question." Crystal rapidly types the name Jenna Coeur into the search engine. "There's obviously some connection between her and Meredith Heywood. We need to figure out what it is."

"Maybe they're old friends or something, from when they were kids."

"I doubt it. Meredith lived in Ohio all her life and I'm pretty sure Jenna Coeur was from someplace in the northern Midwest—Minnesota, North Dakota . . . something like that. Her real name was Johanna Hart."

"Coeur means heart in French."

"You speak French?"

"I took it in high school. That's one of the only words I remember. That's because on Valentine's Day junior year there was this Parisian exchange student who—"

"Frank."

"Yeah."

"As much as I love to hear about your teenage Casanova years, we're talking about Jenna Coeur right now."

"Right. I'll tell you the other thing later," Frank says as he pulls out onto the highway. "Her name was Mimi. It's a good story."

"Aren't they always?"

"Named Mimi? French girls?"

"No, I meant aren't they always good stories. Anyway—" Crystal breaks off as the search results appear. She scans the links, then clicks the top one and quickly reads the news item that pops up.

"Looks like our friend is back in the headlines today, Frank."

"Yeah? What did she do?"

"Today? She went to a funeral and left early. But ask me what she did seven years ago today."

"What did she—" Frank breaks off. "Oh. That was seven years ago already?"

Crystal nods, scanning the retrospective news item about Jenna Coeur—also known as the notorious Cold-Hearted Killer.

"She was acquitted, you know," Frank comments.

"Yeah. I know."

"Just like O. J. Simpson at his criminal trial." He shakes his head. "If you ask me, they both got away with—"

"But O. J. Simpson wasn't at Meredith's funeral. Jenna Coeur was. Why?" Crystal types in Jenna Coeur's name along with Meredith's, looking in vain for a connection.

The two women's lives must have intersected at some point in the past, even though they're nowhere near the same age, haven't ever lived in the same state, and God knows they've probably never traveled in the same social circles . . .

It doesn't make sense. Jenna Coeur has been a recluse for the past few years. Why would she show up in Ohio today?

"I'm having a hard time coming up with any scenario where these two might cross paths," she muses aloud. "Not in the real world, anyway . . ."

But what about online?

That's a strong possibility—and one she fully intends to bring up when she interviews Meredith's blogger friends later.

As Landry pours sugar into her steaming latte, still thinking about her conversation with Detective Burns, she finds herself wondering about Bruce Mangione, the man who'd brought her coffee back in the Atlanta airport.

Chances are, he'll be on her flight home tomorrow. He'd said something about just being in Cincinnati for twenty-four hours, and there are only a couple of Sunday options for connecting flights back to Alabama.

If he is there, she'll have to thank him again. They'd parted ways so quickly at the rental car counter . . .

And maybe she can ask him what he thinks about Meredith's murder.

Landry assumes the detectives haven't made much progress on the case, and she wonders what, exactly, Detective Burns is going to ask when they meet at the hotel later.

I wish I felt like I might have answers for her, but I probably have more questions than she does.

What if the case is never solved?

What if whoever killed Meredith gets away with it?

No. That can't happen. They need some kind of closure. *They*, as in her family; *they*, as in the blogging community; *they*, as in . . .

Me.

I need closure.

I need to know that Meredith was the victim of a random crime, not stalked and killed because she shared too much online.

I need to know that what happened to her can't possibly happen to me.

"Are we staying, or going?" Elena asks, interrupting her thoughts.

"It's up to you guys," Landry says with a shrug.

About to press her lips to the white plastic lid of her cup, Kay glances up and shrugs. "I don't care. I'll stay or go. It's up to you, Landry. You're driving."

Landry isn't used to being the driver or the decision maker. At home she often defers to Rob's judgment, or to the kids'.

But today she's discovered that she kind of enjoys being in charge. "Let's stay."

No sooner do the words escape her mouth than she sees the skittish expression on Elena's face. "Or we can go," she adds quickly. "I really don't care."

"I wouldn't mind sitting down." Kay is holding a cup of tea and a blueberry muffin.

"Good. We'll sit."

Landry allows Kay to lead the way to the only empty round table, over by the plate-glass window facing the road. They settle into three chairs, sandwiched between a high school girl reading a magazine and listening to music that's audible from her earbuds and a woman who has her back to the room and is busily thumb-typing on her cell phone.

Watching Kay sip her tea as Elena gulps her coffee like it's water, Landry can't help but note their differences again—from each other, and from her. Elena is a little younger and brasher than the women she's used to, Kay a bit older and more reserved.

If Landry had crossed paths with either of them in real life rather than on the Internet, they probably wouldn't even be friends.

Making eye contact, Elena smiles with her eyes, her mouth hidden behind the cup.

Our differences don't matter, Landry thinks. *These women were there for me when I needed them. That's all that counts.*

Elena yawns deeply, then says, "It'll be so nice to sleep in tomorrow morning. Too bad it's back to the early morning grind on Monday."

"I can't believe y'all are still in session up there. My kids have been out for weeks."

"That would be great. I always think June would be the nicest time to travel to all the places I want to go. By the time we're out of school, it's almost July, and then August—prime season at all the nice hotels within driving distance, and airfares are up, too. I can't afford to fly *and* pay for a place to stay plus meals. So I always wind up spending most of my summer sitting around at home."

"Sounds like my summer," Kay says. "My life, actually, ever since I got laid off."

She used to be a guard at a federal prison—the one where the Oklahoma City bomber Timothy McVeigh was executed back in 2001, she mentioned once in a blog comment, wryly calling it her one brush with celebrity.

"Wouldn't it be great if we could all just go on a real vacation together?" Elena muses. "Spend a few days at some lakeside cottage or on a beach, just relaxing in the sun . . ."

"We can!" Landry doesn't stop to reconsider the idea that just popped into her head. "My house is right on the water, and my husband is going away on a Father's Day golf trip next weekend. If you guys buy your plane tickets—you said there were cheap fares out of Boston right now, Elena . . ."

"There are, especially last minute. I got here for less than two hundred bucks round-trip."

"You'd have to connect through Atlanta, most likely, or maybe Charlotte, coming from the Northeast. You can stay with me and you won't even have to pay for food," Landry goes on. "I have plenty of room."

"I thought you only had a three bedroom house."

"I do," she tells Elena, taken aback, "but how do you know that?"

"You wrote it, once. That you wished you had a guest room for when your in-laws come to stay, and then Meredith told you not to worry because you'd have an empty nest with plenty of room before you knew it."

Landry plays back the vague memory of that online conversation, remembering, with a pang, that Meredith warned her not to wish away a moment of these precious years with her children under her roof.

Next thing you know, BamaBelle, you'll be rocking a little baby who looks so familiar you'll think it's your own . . . and then you'll remember that it's your son or daughter's child, and you're the grandma.

Hey! I'm too young to be a grandma!

I thought I was, too, and the next thing I knew, I had a whole new batch of stinkerdoodles running around my house. Just you wait. It'll happen so fast you won't know what hit you!

Landry swallows a lump in her throat and tries to tune back into what Elena is saying.

"We can always stay in a hotel if we come visit. Are there any nearby?"

"There's the Grand."

"The one where you and Rob were married?" Kay asks, and adds, seeing the surprised look on Landry's face, "You blogged about that once."

"I did? Your memory is a lot better than mine. Yes, that's the place. But it's a resort, and it's expensive at this time of year. Listen, I might not have *plenty* of room but I do have *enough*. Stay with me. This can be our girls' getaway."

"Don't tempt me," Elena says with a grin.

"I'm *trying* to tempt you. Have you ever been to Alabama? We have it all: beautiful beaches, history, great food . . ."

"I've never been anywhere down South except Disney World, and believe me, the last thing I want on vacation is to be surrounded by a gazillion little kids."

"Well, I only have two, and they're quiet, and hardly ever home anyway. So if you come see me, I won't have to be lonely while Rob's away."

Not to mention scared. She wouldn't admit it to Rob, because he'd promptly cancel his trip, but she's not particularly anxious at the thought of being alone overnight in the house after what happened to Meredith. Well, alone with the kids.

Good old strength training aside, she can't help worrying that she might have slipped online about Rob's golf weekend after all. If not this year, then maybe in the past—it's an annual Father's Day event.

Combing her archives using search terms didn't turn up any evidence that she'd ever mentioned it, and she knows paranoia is probably getting the better of her, but still . . .

She forgot she'd ever posted about having only three bedrooms, and about the Grand Hotel . . . who knows what else she's written and forgotten?

"If you're serious about that," Elena says thoughtfully, "I might be into it. When would it be, exactly?"

Landry notices that Kay sits quietly listening as they discuss the details.

"So you'll come?"

"I'll come," Elena says. "What do you say, Kay?"

"You said you've never been south of the Mason-Dixon line," Landry reminds her. "It would be nice to have some fun together after this sad weekend, wouldn't it?"

She smiles. "It would. It would be great."

"Great. And we can invite Jaycee, too," Elena decides, as Landry is distracted by several new customers walking in, all wearing dark, formal clothing. Are they coming from the funeral service, too? It seems as though the whole town turned out for Meredith.

"So what did you think of Meredith's family?" she asks the others.

Kay clears her throat. "They were just like she described them, don't you think? The daughter, and the sons . . ."

"That poem her daughter read was beautiful." That comes from Elena.

"It was," Landry agrees. "It had to be really hard for her to get up there and do that."

"She was amazing. Meredith would have been so proud." After a moment's reflection, Elena adds, "But I didn't like her husband at all."

"Why not?" Kay asks in surprise. "The poor man just lost his wife. I'm sure under other circumstances he would have been—"

"No, not Meredith's husband. The daughter's husband."

"Oh! What was his name again? Keith?"

"Right. Keith. That was it."

"What didn't you like about him?" Landry asks. Her own contact with the man was limited to a brief handshake after being introduced.

But now that the subject has come up, she decides there really was something off-putting about him.

"He just seemed aloof," Elena says with a shrug.

"You shouldn't judge people under those circumstances, though," Kay speaks up again. "They were all hurting. Can you imagine what they've been through?"

"I can," Elena says, "but everyone goes through rough times. That doesn't change the fact that some guys are jackasses under any circumstances."

Her words land like a brick tossed onto the table.

Kay's bushy eyebrows rise above the rims of her glasses.

"Something tells me we're not just talking about Meredith's son-in-law anymore," Landry tells Elena. "Who's the jackass in your life?"

"Harsh language for a sweet southern belle like you," Elena fake-chides her.

"I'm just quoting you, my dear."

"The jackass's name is Tony, and I can't believe I'm even bringing it up . . ."

"Why?"

"Because I promised myself that I wasn't going to think about him at all while I was here. And I definitely wasn't planning to talk about him."

"It might make you feel better."

Elena shakes her head. "Probably worse."

"What happened?" Kay asks her.

"With Tony? One night stand. Last night. Ever have one?" Elena's expression makes it clear she already knows the answer to what she just asked Kay: no one night stands there. Certainly not recently; probably not ever.

Kay shakes her head and looks down at her teacup.

Elena looks at Landry. "You?"

"A million years ago," she confesses, remembering. It isn't pleasant. "I was in college."

"Really? That was the last time?"

"I've been married forever, Elena."

"Oh. Right. I forgot."

"So what happened?" Landry asks. "Last night, I mean."

"Basically—wine. Wine happened. Does that explain it?"

It might have, years ago. In college. Wine, beer, potent spiked punch at a fraternity party . . .

But Elena is a grown woman. Does she have a drinking problem?

Reminding herself not to jump to conclusions, Landry asks, "So you had too much wine, and you didn't know what you were doing? Is that it?"

"Pretty much. It's been such a stressful week, between issues with the kids in my class, and Meredith, and . . . well, you know. Bad week. Crazy time of year. We had this school function last night, and we were both there—"

"You and the jackass?" Landry cuts in with a wry smile that is returned.

"Right. He teaches P.E. at my school, and—well, I did go out with him once, last year. It's funny—I told Meredith about it because I was psyched about the date before it happened. And I promised to let her know how it went, and she was waiting and expecting to hear that he was the love of my life, but . . ."

"No?"

"No way. One date was enough to convince me that I can't stand him—and it took him forever to get the message even though I felt like it was loud and clear. But apparently I somehow forgot all that last night, and . . . now he's kind of . . . stalking me."

"*Stalking* you?"

Seeing the alarmed look on Landry's face, Elena backtracks quickly: "I probably shouldn't say 'stalking.' That's a little extreme. But he's just . . . this is how it was after we went out. He's really persistent and oblivious that I'm . . ."

"Just not that into him?" Landry supplies.

"Not into him at all! But somehow he must think I want to hear from him, and he's been trying to get ahold of me ever since I got here. Before I left this morning he said he wanted to pick me up from the airport tomorrow and I said no, and then he wanted to come here with me, and of course I said no to that, too. I don't want him here. I don't want him *there*. He makes my skin crawl. Did you ever have someone who just—" She breaks off with a shudder.

"Is he dangerous, do you think?" Kay's fleshy face is etched in concern.

"Who knows? He's a creep." Elena shakes her head.

Landry persists, "But do you feel threatened?"

Elena tilts her head as if contemplating the question, then shrugs. "I don't know. But, I mean, look what happened to Meredith. You never know what people are capable of doing."

There's a long silence.

"Do y'all think—" Landry cuts herself off, realizing now might not be the time to bring this up.

"What?" Elena prompts.

"I've just been wondering—what if Meredith's blog was responsible for . . . I mean, what if some crazy person was following her online—you know, even stalking her, like this Tony guy is with you, Elena—"

"No, I said he's not really stalking me."

"I know, but . . . you said yourself that there's something you don't like about him and he's scaring you."

"No, I didn't say 'scaring.' "

"I'm sorry, I guess I'm just jittery because of what happened to Meredith, and—anyway, what I'm trying to say is, what if she attracted some crazy follower on her blog? And what if whoever it was went after her because he knew she was alone in the house, and he knew where to find her . . ."

"I've thought of that." Elena nods. "She really put it all out there, you know? More so than some of us."

"I know. I hate to think that someone evil could have been reading all of her innocent posts, watching her, waiting to—" Seeing the horrified look on Kay's face, Landry breaks off abruptly. "Kay, are you all right?"

"I am, I just . . . I thought it was random. A burglary. I didn't think . . ." She shakes her head. "Oh my God."

"It's definitely made me think twice about what I'm willing to share online," Elena tells them. "I mean, anyone out there can be reading our blogs."

"Including your friend Tony."

"Don't think I haven't thought about that, Landry. Maybe it's time to stop."

"Stop blogging?"

"Stop spending so much time with the online group. The public one, anyway. It's one thing to spend so much time networking online when you're first diagnosed, dealing with the shock and the treatments and feeling alone. But lately I just do it out of habit. I mean, the three of us can still stay close. Now that we've met, I can't imagine losing touch with you guys. But the others—not that I don't appreciate all the friends I've made online, but with Meredith gone . . . I don't know. Maybe it's time to take a step back. Especially if . . . do you really think something happened to Meredith because of what she wrote?"

"Do *you*?" Kay looks up at last.

"Maybe. How about you, Landry?"

She nods slowly. "I do. In my gut . . . I really do."

Finding herself within arm's reach of Landry Wells for the second time today, Jaycee doesn't dare turn her head as she listens to the conversation unfolding behind her.

She couldn't believe her eyes when she saw the familiar rental car pull into the parking lot as she sat at the table by the window, sipping the last of her coffee.

For a split second she wondered if the three of them had spotted her at the funeral and followed her here.

She had to remind herself, once again, that they don't

know what she looks like. She's just jittery because she's fairly certain the lady cop recognized her. But not, of course, as Jaycee the breast cancer blogger.

As Jenna Coeur.

And Jenna Coeur has nothing to do with Landry, Kay, or Elena.

They're here, she realized, for the same reason she herself is here; for the same reason most people go to Starbucks. The coffee is good and the chain is popular. Plus, it's near the funeral home—not to mention their hotel.

She should have considered that before she stopped. Or if she had to stop, she should have jumped back on the highway and gotten out of here with her coffee.

When she saw them coming, it was too late. She knew she was trapped. Leaving now would mean walking right past them. She sat hoping they'd take their coffee to go, but of course they didn't. And as fate would have it, for the second time today the only vacant spot in the place is right next to her.

It's almost as though somebody up there is trying to tell her something.

Meredith?

If so, she'd better cut it out, because her nerves were edgy enough before all this.

Then again . . . now that the three of them are settled into the next table, she finds herself almost glad for the encounter. After spending so much time wondering what it would be like if things were different and she actually could have met them in person, it's almost as if she's a part of things after all. She's heard every word they've said since they sat down, and almost choked on her own saliva when Landry mentioned her blogger name.

But right now they're discussing Meredith. More specifically, her murder.

"I still can't believe anyone who read her blog could have been evil enough to come after someone like her."

That's Landry talking. Jaycee finds it easy to distinguish her drawl from Elena's rapid-fire Boston accent and Kay's flat midwestern one.

"What do you think the detective is going to ask us when we talk to her?" Kay asks, and Jaycee realizes she wasn't the only one at the funeral who captured the attention of law enforcement in their midst.

"She probably thinks we might know something. Which we don't." Elena pauses, then amends, "At least, *I* don't."

"Maybe there's something we didn't realize at the time," Landry tells her.

"I can't think of a thing."

"I can't either. I'm just glad for the opportunity to feel like I'm doing something constructive after feeling helpless about it."

"Me too," Elena replies. "And I hope they're going to do whatever it takes to make sure this guy doesn't get away with it, whoever he is. Did you see how that detective was looking at everyone leaving the service? Like she thought maybe the killer was right there with us?"

"But it's been a week since . . ." Kay again, hesitating. "I mean, don't you think he's long gone by now? Why would he show up at the funeral today?"

"Maybe it's not someone online. Maybe it was some local thug, and for all we know, they already have a suspect." Landry again.

Elena gives a short laugh. "I didn't see anyone there who looked like a thug, did you?"

"Sometimes thugs don't look particularly thuggish."

"True. But even if it was an unthuggish thug—and someone local who knew her—he still could have been reading her blog."

"I know. I bet that detective has been combing through every word Meredith ever wrote, and everything anyone ever wrote to her."

"I've been doing the same thing," Kay tells Landry. "I keep looking back over her old posts, trying to see if there's any clue that she might have run into some kind of trouble, or . . . you know, if she made someone angry."

"Meredith was pretty outspoken. She made plenty of people angry," Elena points out. "But angry enough to track her down and hurt her? I don't think so. I really think it had to be some random person who was just plain crazy."

"All I know," Landry says, "is that the world already feels emptier without her in it."

Jaycee listens to them chatter on, moving back to the topic of what Elena should do about Tony.

"I don't even want to turn my phone on again," she says. "I'm afraid I'll have more hang-up calls from him."

"Just keep it turned off, then," Kay advises, but Landry has the opposite advice.

"I think you should deal with it now, or you'll be dwelling on it all weekend—and so will he. If he's truly obsessed, he might . . . I don't know . . ."

"Snap and kill me?" Elena asks, then groans. "I'm so sorry. I forgot, for a second, about Meredith. I was kidding."

"We know you were," Landry tells her. "It's okay."

"Let me see if he's called again."

Jaycee hears a rustling behind her. After a few moments Elena says, "Two more hang-ups just since we've been sitting here, and a third call with a message."

"Listen to it."

"Okay. You know, I hate myself for wasting all this time and energy on him. And I hate him for making me . . ." Another long pause. "Oh, God. You have to hear this message. I'll put it on speaker, here, listen."

Despite the coffeehouse background buzz, the call is clearly audible to Jaycee.

"Babe, it's Tony. Where the hell are you? Why aren't you calling me back? I told you I just want to talk to you. Are

you ignoring me, or did something happen to you? Call me
as soon as you get this. I mean it."

Everything about the call—the harsh words, the menac-
ing tone—sends chills down Jaycee's back.

Where the hell are you . . . ?

How many times has she heard it before? Sickened, it's
all she can do to stay seated, back turned to the three of
them, pretending to sip from a cup that's long since been
empty.

"Why is he calling you 'Babe,' as if he's your boyfriend
or something?" Landry asks.

"Because he's creepy and crazy and he probably thinks
he is. He's delusional."

"Delusional?" That's Kay, worried.

"Definitely. That's what my friend Sidney is always
saying, and I'm starting to think she's right."

"Well, I definitely think he sounds like a jerk," Landry
says. "If I were you, I'd call him back and tell him off.
Maybe that's what he needs to hear."

"Maybe. But I don't feel like dealing with him. Maybe
I'll just call the cops instead."

"Seriously?"

"No. I guess I can always block his number from getting
through to my phone. There's a way to do that. I really don't
need this kind of stress in my life. It's dangerous, like Meredith was always saying, remember?"

"What?" Landry sounds shocked. "Meredith talked
about being stalked by someone crazy and delusional?"

"No! God, no! I meant *stress!*" Elena says. "She blogged a
few times about those studies showing that breast cancer patients who have daily stress have much shorter survival times."

"Oh—I misunderstood."

"Geez, Landry, a few minutes ago we were talking about
Meredith's murder. Do you really think I wouldn't have
brought it up then if I knew she had a crazy stalker?"

Elena's tone is sharp, Jaycee notices. She seems to have a quick temper. Or maybe she's just aggravated by the situation, and who—having overheard that phone message from crazy Tony—can blame her?

Landry—good for her—changes the subject, announcing that it's getting late. They decide they should get back to the hotel. From the sounds of it, the detective is meeting them there.

Behind Jaycee, chairs scrape. She takes another pretend-sip, distracting herself from panic with the amusing notion that if the cup weren't empty, she'd have downed a gallon of coffee by now. She focuses on her phone, thumb-scrolling through her in-box as if she's absolutely absorbed by her e-mail.

Then it happens.

She hears a clatter on the floor, and something skitters under her chair. Glancing down, she sees a cell phone coming to a stop between the pointy toes of her two black pumps.

Elena's cell phone, judging by which of the three voices utters a curse.

"Sorry about that," Elena says—to her? Is she talking to her?

Not daring to turn around, she holds her breath.

"Ma'am?"

She's talking to me! Oh, no!

Jaycee's mind runs wildly through her options.

She can continue to sit frozen, completely ignoring Elena and forcing her to crawl under the table to retrieve her own phone—which will certainly attract attention not only from the three women behind her, but from everyone around her, increasing the likelihood that they'll scrutinize her and perhaps recognize her.

Or, she can remind herself—again—that there's no way Elena or the others would possibly realize she's Jaycee the blogger, and she can do what any normal person would do in this situation, which is pick up the phone and hand it back to its owner with a polite smile.

That is precisely what she does, facing Elena head-on with a pleasant, "Here you go."

"Thanks. Sorry about that," she repeats.

"No problem."

They nod politely at each other, and then Elena walks away with Landry and Kay.

Heart beating as if she really did drink a gallon of coffee, Jaycee watches them go, feeling as though she's just had a close call, when really it wasn't.

To them, she was just a stranger.

Then she sees Landry turn back over her shoulder. She levels a long, searching look at her, frowning, almost as if . . .

She knows!

No, wait—how can she know?

It's impossible. She can't recognize her as Jaycee.

She can, however, recognize Jenna Coeur, just as the lady detective did.

And Landry, like the detective, has Meredith's murder on her mind. What if she starts to wonder how Jenna Coeur could possibly have known Meredith Heywood?

I shouldn't have come. This was stupid.

Stupid, stupid, stupid . . .

Sweet Dreams

When I first found my way here, I was exhausted. Not just from the physical and emotional burden of illness, but from sheer lack of sleep. I had always been a person who could climb into bed, close my eyes, fall asleep, and not wake up until morning.

Now I spent night after night lying awake, tossing and turning.

Oh, how I wanted to escape. But there was no escape, not really. Sleep—whenever I finally managed to find it—might have brought a few blessed hours' respite, but then I'd jerk my eyes open, panicked by the vague sense that something terrible had happened, and the realization—Bam!—that it had. It was the exact opposite of waking from a terrible nightmare to the broad daylight relief that it was just a dream. The nightmare greeted me with the dawn and haunted my every waking moment. In the end, that was worse than not sleeping at all.

It was on one of those sleepless nights that I stumbled across a cancer blog for the first time. And on another, I worked up the nerve to make a comment. Not long after that, I remember, I began to chat privately with some of you, and those sleepless nights became a little less lonely, and less scary.

I remember one online exchange I had with Meredith when she wrote, Some morning—not soon, but someday—you're going to wake up and not have that awful feeling that something is terribly wrong.

Wake up? *I wrote back.* You're implying I'm actually going to sleep again.

You will, *Meredith told me.* I promise.

She was right.

Eventually, I started sleeping again. Eventually, I started waking up the old way—slowly stirring to consciousness. Eventually, things were back to the way they used to be. Back to normal.

And now, if you'll excuse me, it's getting late. I'm going to climb into bed, close my eyes, fall asleep, and not wake up until morning.

—Excerpt from Landry's blog, *The Breast Cancer Diaries*

Chapter 11

Back at the hotel, Landry returns to her room under the pretext of freshening up before Detective Burns arrives.

But the moment she closes the door behind her, she dials
Rob's cell phone. He picks up on the first ring: "How was it?"

"The funeral? It was . . . you know. Hard. Sad. Awful."

"I'm sorry."

She changes the subject. "Did you find the insurance
cards?"

"Yeah, you were right. They were on the bulletin board. I
don't know how I missed them when I looked."

She closes her eyes for a second, smiling. Then it's back
to the business at hand: "Listen—I just wanted to run something by you quickly." She tells him about the conversation
with the detective at the funeral home, and that the detective
asked to meet them there at the hotel to discuss the case
further.

"The first thing to remember," Rob says, "is that this is
routine. An interview, not an interrogation. They're looking
for information."

"I know. It's not like I'm a suspect."

"No. I don't know about your friends, though."

"They're not suspects, either."

"Did the detective tell you that?"

"No, but—"

"Just remember that they're *strangers*, Landry. For all we know—"

"Please don't say it, Rob."

"I won't. Just be careful up there, okay? They obviously haven't made an arrest yet."

"Right. I'll be careful."

"And twenty-four hours from now you'll be on your way home."

Home. Where nothing bad can happen to her?

Doesn't she know better than anyone that staying safely at home doesn't guarantee that the bad things won't touch you?

"I should go."

"Okay. I love you," Rob tells her. "I know they're your friends and you want to trust them, but I can't get past wanting to protect you. You're the most precious thing in my world."

She swallows hard, and can't seem to find her voice.

He's right to be worried. She's worried, too. Didn't she just admit to Elena and Kay that she believes Meredith was killed by someone who read her blog and knew she'd be alone in the house that night?

A lurker, most likely, but . . .

It could have been one of us. That's what the police are thinking. That's what Rob is thinking. It could have been someone posing as a blogger, someone we trusted, someone with a screen name . . .

Just because Elena and Kay turned out to be the real deal—and Meredith, too, of course—doesn't mean the others are. Landry thinks back to all those comments she exchanged with other bloggers; all the private chats and e-mails that let them into her life, into her family's lives . . .

Not to the extent that Meredith did, and yet . . .

Maybe Elena is right. Maybe it's time to take a step back from blogging.

"I really wish I could be there with you when you talk to the detective," Rob tells her.

"Because I need a lawyer present?"

"Just . . . be careful what you say and how you say it."

"I don't have anything to hide. You know that. And I want to do whatever I can to help them find Meredith's killer. We all do."

"You and the other bloggers? Who are they? Elena and Kay?"

"Right. They're the only ones who came to Cincinnati."

"That you know of."

"Well, I'd know if there were others."

"How?"

"Because I'm sure they would have mentioned it."

"Don't be so sure of anything right now, Landry. Okay? Don't trust anyone."

"What about you?" she asks, mostly just teasing. Mostly.

"You can always trust me. I love you."

"I love you, too, and . . ." She looks at her watch. "I have to go. It's time to meet the detective."

It hadn't occurred to Beck that people—everyone, it seems, with the exception of her own husband—would drift back to the house after the funeral.

Keith is on his way back to Lexington. To be fair, he'd asked her, as they left McGraw's, if she'd really meant it when she told him he was free to leave.

"Yes, I meant it," she said, and was surprised to realize that she really did. The marriage might not be over officially—legally, or financially—but emotionally she's finished. It's only a matter of time; she knows now that she'll extract herself as soon as this trauma is behind her.

Mom would have been so upset had she lived to see her daughter's marriage end in divorce . . .

Or would she? Maybe she'd have been happy to see her

find her way out of a bad situation. Maybe she'd have invited her to come live at home while she gets back on her feet . . .

Maybe I can still do that, Beck found herself thinking for a split second before she remembered that home isn't home anymore. Not without her mother.

The house that was once filled with love and laughter now represents only sorrow. Beck can't imagine ever laughing again—here, or anywhere else. Can't imagine ever loving again, ever being married again or having children . . .

"I'm so sorry," Keith whispered in her ear before he drove off in the wrong direction as Beck climbed into the black limo with her family.

Sorry. So sorry . . .

Sorry for what?

For leaving? For her loss? For his extramarital indiscretions?

She still doesn't know what he was apologizing about. She supposes she will, soon enough . . . if she even cares to.

Back at the house, she'd had every intention of going straight to her room to have a good cry, alone at last. Instead she's been on kitchen duty ever since she walked in the door, trailed by half the neighborhood. People are bringing platters of food, and the doorbell keeps ringing with deliveries: flowers and fruit baskets, trays of pastries, hot meals ordered from local restaurants by well-meaning faraway friends and colleagues . . .

"You just go ahead and let us take care of serving and cleaning up," one of the neighbor ladies told her when they first arrived.

But every few minutes, it seems, someone wants to know how to find the coffee filters, or whether there are more plastic cups, or where the garbage goes.

Or, if she manages to escape the kitchen and start making her way toward the stairs, someone inevitably waylays her to ask about a framed family photo on the wall, or show her some memento of her mother, or to tell her how sorry they all are . . .

Sorry. So sorry . . .

Everyone is sorry—but no one is sorrier than she is. Exhausted, all she can do is move from one task to another, from one well-meaning visitor to another, longing to be left alone.

"You look worn out," her former first-grade teacher—an old friend of her mother's—comments, after informing Beck that the powder room under the stairs is running low on toilet paper.

"It's been a long day."

"One of the longest days of the year, unfortunately," the woman mentions before drifting back to the crowded dining room as Beck heads up the steps to grab a spare roll of toilet paper from the hall bathroom.

Glancing out the window on the landing, she sees that the sun is, indeed, still riding high in the sky. It won't be setting for at least a few more hours. By then, she can't imagine having the stamina to climb these stairs again and get ready for bed.

Maybe she should just lie down now for a quick nap. No one will miss her if she's gone for half an hour.

She slips past the bathroom and the closed door to the master bedroom, unable to imagine ever opening it again.

She just can't stop picturing her mother here alone at night; an intruder in the house; a violent attack . . .

We need to get rid of this house—the sooner, the better.

In her own room, she takes a moment to swap her high-heeled black pumps for a pair of loafers, not caring what they look like with her dress. Her feet ache. Her *heart* aches.

Oh, Mom . . .

She sinks onto the bedspread she and Mom picked out so long ago in Macy's—they both fell in love with the splashy pattern.

"The colors remind me of the bright blue sky and yellow sunshine," Mom said. "It'll always be a beautiful summer day in here!"

Today doesn't feel like a beautiful summer day inside or out. Beck massages her forehead with her fingertips and finds herself staring at her laptop on the desk across the room.

Does it hold the key to her mother's murder? If she could just figure out the password and get into the e-mail account . . .

But what are the odds that she'll find a clue to the killer's identity somewhere in the files? Does she actually believe Mom was exchanging e-mails with him in advance? That it was someone Mom knew?

If it was—if it was someone I know, too, like . . . like . . .

She can't even bring herself to entertain the thought.

Maybe she's better off never uncovering the truth.

What does it even matter now? Mom is gone. Nothing is going to bring her back. The worst has happened; it's in the past.

"Beck? Beck! Are you in there?" Teddy's wife, Sue, is knocking on her bedroom door.

She hurriedly wipes tears from her eyes. "Yes, I'm in here."

Sue opens the door. Roundly pregnant, with Beck's sleepy-looking nephew Jordan on her hip, she asks, "Are you okay?"

Then, catching a look at Beck's face, Sue shakes her head and answers her own question. "Of course you're not okay. Sorry."

"No, I'm okay. I am. Well . . ."

"You are but you're not. No one is. I'm sorry to bother you. The minister's wife is stuck in the powder room without toilet paper, and I can't find any under the sink in the hall bathroom, so—"

"Are you serious?"

"No, there were just some cleaning supplies, and—"

"No, I mean about Mrs. Alpert stuck without toilet paper?" Beck finds herself grinning through her tears.

"Totally serious. She was calling through the door for help and Jordan heard her. She said there are no tissues in there or anything, so . . ."

"She can't wipe her keister," Jordan reports solemnly.

That does it. Beck bursts out laughing. Sue joins in, and so, after a moment, does Jordan.

Beck laughs until her sides ache—a good kind of ache— then heads back downstairs with Sue and Jordan, the e-mail account forgotten for the time being.

Lying on the bed in her hotel room, head propped against the pillows and laptop open on her lap, Kay tries to focus on the screen. She'd been hoping to catch up on some blogs, but her energy is zapped from the drive, the funeral, the anxiety over meeting Landry and Elena . . .

And now a meeting with the detective investigating Meredith's murder?

It's all too much. I can't handle this. I can't.

She'd give anything if she could throw her belongings back into the seldom-used, slightly musty-smelling suitcase she pulled last night from her mother's attic; if she could just walk out of this hotel and go home and hide, make it all go away.

But she can't leave Landry and Elena. They're her friends—her *family*—and they need her, just as Meredith needed her. As long as the three of them stick together, everything will be okay.

A tone from her laptop's speaker indicates that a new e-mail has arrived in her in-box.

She opens it and finds that it's from Elena—a note to Jaycee, with both Kay and Landry on the cc list.

I'm here in Cincinnati with Landry and Kay. Meredith's

funeral was moving and very much a tearjerker, as I'm sure you would guess. The rest of us need each other now more than ever. We've already made plans to get together again for a girls' weekend at Landry's house in Alabama next weekend. Is there any way you can join us? Details to follow. I just wanted you to know that we're thinking of you and wish you were here with us.

Kay nods with approval, glad Elena thought to include Jaycee and extend the invitation despite wrestling with some pretty serious problems of her own. Remembering what she shared about her stalker—Tony—Kay feels worried all over again, and she knows Landry does as well.

I really don't need this kind of stress in my life. It's dangerous . . . breast cancer patients who have daily stress have much shorter survival times . . .

What if something happens to Elena now?

What if, one by one . . .

No.

Nothing is going to happen to anyone else. It can't.

They're my friends. My family.

At last, after all these years, she finally knows where—and to whom—she belongs. She only prays that cruel fate won't rip them from her life as it did Meredith.

"They're late." Sitting beside Crystal in the hotel lobby, Frank lifts his wrist and taps his Timex.

"One minute late."

"Late is late."

Crystal shrugs, considering the possibilities.

That the bloggers might have lied about where they're staying doesn't rank very high on the list. Nor does the prospect that they skipped town.

Either of those scenarios would mean that there's some kind of conspiracy involved here, and Crystal doesn't buy that for a second.

Far more likely: they lost track of time, or they dozed off, or they're reluctant to sit down and discuss their friend's murder . . .

Perhaps all of the above.

"They'll be here soon, I'm sure," she tells him.

He shrugs and continues tapping his foot. Patience is not Frank's strong suit.

Glad the lobby is almost deserted, Crystal keeps an eye on the grouchy-looking, pockmarked teenage boy parked at the computer kiosk, who is oblivious to their presence, and on the desk clerk, who is not. She's been casting curious glances their way ever since they arrived and arranged with the on-duty manager to conduct their questioning in a conference room down the hall.

They didn't mention that it involves a homicide. But maybe the desk clerk has put two and two together. It's a small town, after all; the guests might have asked her for directions to the funeral home earlier.

Or maybe the desk clerk is just being vigilant, as she should in her position.

Hell, if everyone were a little more vigilant—or nosy, as it were—her own job would be much easier.

Hearing the elevator bell ring at last, Crystal and Frank look over expectantly. The doors slide open and Landry Wells—aka BamaBelle—steps out.

Standing to greet her, Crystal notes that she's changed out of her black dress, now wearing a pair of trim off-white linen pants with a sea-foam-colored summer cardigan. Her blond hair is caught in a neat ponytail and she's got on a fresh coat of pink lipstick that matches her manicure and pedicure polish.

How is it that certain women—often, southern women—always manage to look so pulled together, even under duress?

Crystal—who rarely looks in a mirror after she leaves the bathroom in the morning and would never think to reapply lipstick in the middle of the day—is not one of those women.

"I'm sorry I'm late." Landry walks quickly toward them, heeled sandals tapping on the tile floor. "I had to call home and check on my husband and kids and it took longer than I thought."

"Do you know where the others are?" Crystal asks.

"They should be here any second. We all went to our rooms when we got back."

"Okay. Why don't you and I go have a quiet talk in the conference room while Detective Schneider waits here for your friends?"

"Sure."

Crystal escorts Landry down the hall behind the front desk as the clerk pretends not to watch them over the open romance novel in her hands.

With a view of the side parking lot and part of the pool's chain-link fence, the conference room is a no-frills rectangle that contains little more than a long table with eight chairs and a blue plastic water bottle cooler.

Crystal closes the door behind them. "Have a seat, Ms. Wells. Or do you go by Mrs.?"

"Either, but you can call me Landry." She perches on the chair nearest the door, giving off the expectant, anxious vibe of a mom sitting in the Little League stands as her child comes up at bat, or in the audience as her kid takes a turn in a spelling bee.

She doesn't belong here, in the middle of a murder investigation, Crystal finds herself thinking as she takes the adjacent seat at the head of the table. She should be back at home, with her family.

"All right, Landry. Let's get started." Crystal sets her bag on the floor, taking out her laptop and a notebook and pen, but leaving the recording equipment inside.

No need to make Landry Wells needlessly skittish. She always records witnesses she has a hunch might later become suspects, but she's certain that won't happen in this case.

Her Internet search on Landry's name had resulted—among other things—in a photograph from an Alabama newspaper's society page. Snapped Saturday night at a charity ball, it depicted an elegantly dressed Landry accompanied by her husband and another couple identified as the husband's law partner and his wife.

So there we have it—an alibi, she thought, when she noted the date.

Crystal opens the laptop and it instantly buzzes to life, already bookmarked on Landry's most recent blog post—written several days ago, presumably before she found out about Meredith.

She flips her notebook to a clean page, picks up a pen, and clears her throat. "I just want to talk to you a little bit about your relationship with Meredith, and about her blog, and yours, and . . . I'd like your take on how the whole thing works."

"You mean blogging?"

"The dynamic you have with other bloggers, that kind of thing."

"Oh. Okay. Well . . ." Landry looks as though she has no idea where to begin.

"Why don't you tell me first what made you decide to write your own blog?"

"Have you read it?"

Crystal nods. She'd first stumbled across it a few days ago, having noticed that someone named BamaBelle commented often on Meredith's page, and tracing the comments back to the blog. She did the same with a number of others.

Today at the funeral home, after asking the three women about their online identities, she'd finally been able to connect the blog titles and screen names with real women behind them.

Afterward, when she wasn't fruitlessly searching for a link between Jenna Coeur and Meredith Heywood, she'd spent the better part of the last hour reading—and in some cases, rereading—Landry's, Kay's, and Elena's blogs, noting their interaction with Meredith, each other, and fellow bloggers.

It came as no surprise to her that the attractive, genteel southern stay-at-home-mom was behind the homey, conversational *Breast Cancer Diaries*, or that the reserved midwesterner wrote the staid *I'm A-Okay*.

The shocker was that the saucy *Boobless Wonder* blog was penned by a first grade teacher. But a few minutes in Elena Ferreira's presence revealed an engaging, if somewhat frenetic, personality that seems convincingly reminiscent of the voice she uses in her blog.

Nothing unusual jumped out at Crystal in any of the blogs, other than a remarkably casual level of intimacy among a collection of strangers who had ostensibly never met in person. But then, she's seen that phenomenon within other online communities. When people come together on the Internet, the usual social constraints fall away with the promise of anonymity.

"If you've read my blog," Landry says, "then you know that I was diagnosed with breast cancer. That's why I blog."

Crystal shoots straight, as always. "But lots of people have breast cancer and don't blog. Why do you?"

Perhaps taken aback, Landry tilts her head.

Crystal is about to rephrase the question, but then Landry answers it in a soft voice, as if she's conveying a secret. Maybe she is.

In a lilting drawl that sometimes takes Crystal a moment to translate, Landry talks about the fear and shock and—more importantly—the loneliness that set in after her diagnosis. She describes the support group she visited early in her treatment, and the horror of coming face-to-face with doomed patients. She smiles faintly when she mentions her first foray onto the Internet in search of information, finding not just that, but also companionship—ultimately, friendship.

"I wasn't isolated anymore," she tells Crystal. "I realized these women were talking about things I could relate to. And that maybe I had something to say, too. Something I couldn't say to the people I saw every day."

"Because . . ."

"Because they just wouldn't get it."

Crystal asks her a few more questions about the evolution of Landry's own blog before leading into how she got to know Meredith.

"She was kind of like the older sorority sister who takes a new pledge under her wing, you know?"

Crystal nods, though she doesn't know. Not from experience. But she bets Landry does.

Sure enough, the question is met with a nod and a faint smile. "I was Alpha Gamma Delta at University of Alabama."

"Roll Tide."

Landry's smile widens to a full-blown grin. "That's right!"

"So Meredith was . . . what, like a big sister? A mentor?"

The smile fades promptly at the mention of the dead woman's name.

She forgot, for a moment there, Crystal realizes. *Forgot why we're here; forgot her friend was murdered.*

Now that Landry remembers, renewed sorrow taints her pretty face as she contemplates the question. "Maybe she was more motherly than sisterly . . . is sisterly a word?"

"You're the writer. You tell me."

"You know . . . it's funny, I don't really consider myself a writer, but . . . I guess that's what blogging is, right? I kind of like thinking of it that way, and I know Meredith did, too. It's what she always wanted to be."

"A writer?" Crystal knows this—some of Meredith's

blog posts referred to the literary road not taken—but she waits for Landry to elaborate.

"We talked a lot, privately, about stuff like that. She said she'd always dreamed of writing a book, and she recently told me she'd been toying with the idea of compiling some of her blogs into a collection and trying to get it published."

"You talked on the phone?"

"No, usually e-mail."

"Is that how you all communicate privately?"

"That, or instant-messaging."

"No phone."

"Well, I can't speak for the others—maybe some of them call each other—but we don't. At least, we didn't, until this week, after Meredith . . ."

Crystal nods. "And by 'we,' you mean . . ."

"The bloggers I'm closest to. There's a little group of us—Meredith was a part of it."

"And the other two women who came with you to the funeral?"

"Elena and Kay—yes, them, too."

"Who else?"

"The others aren't here. I've never met them. And one is—Nellie passed away."

Crystal raises an eyebrow. Another one? "When? What happened?"

"Oh, it wasn't . . . she wasn't . . . killed. It was cancer."

Right. Of course it was. Crystal even vaguely remembers reading about the death in past entries on several of the blogs, including Meredith's.

But for a moment there her mind jumped to the possibility of an opportunistic serial killer preying on this vulnerable group of women, perhaps even posing as one of them . . .

Again she thinks of Jenna Coeur.

But she wasn't a serial killer, she reminds herself. *She just killed one other person . . .*

Just?

Crystal wants to ask Landry if Meredith ever mentioned her, but she's getting ahead of herself. First things first.

"So there was . . . Nellie, did you say?"

Landry nods. "She was from England. Whoa Nellie was her screen name."

"Hang on a second." Crystal turns to the laptop, searches, and finds herself looking at Whoa Nellie's blog. The photo shows a thin middle-aged woman sporting a crew cut—no postchemo head scarves for Whoa Nellie—and the top entry was written by her husband, reporting her death and linking to her obituary.

Crystal clicks it, reads it silently, then turns back to Landry.

"Okay. So there's Nellie, Meredith," she counts off on her fingers, "and then there's you, and Elena, and Kay . . . Who are the others in your clique?" The word slips out, and Landry reacts with a wrinkled nose.

"Clique? We're not a clique. That makes it sound like we're being exclusive."

"And you're not?"

"No. We're just a group of women who gravitated together, like any other friends, except . . ."

Except they all have cancer, and most of them have never met.

Crystal nods. She gets it. "So are there any others in the group, besides the five of you?"

"Just one more."

Pen poised, Crystal asks, "Who is it?"

"Jaycee. She writes *PC BC*. She lives in New York."

"Is that with a G or a J?" Crystal asks, once again trying to translate the drawl.

"With a J. You spell it J-A-Y-C-E-E."

Crystal begins to write it down. Midway, her pen goes still.

Jaycee.

PC . . . BC . . .

J C

Jenna Coeur.

It was probably random; an accident.

But for some reason, Sheri Lorton can't seem to let it go. The guitar pick.

Why would Roger have had one in his pocket? He doesn't—*didn't*—play.

He's the last person in the world anyone would ever imagine picking up a guitar.

He's not—he *wasn't*—into music at all. He wouldn't know Jimi Hendrix from Jimmy Page from Jimmy Buffet. Hell, he wouldn't know any of them from Jimmy Fallon. He didn't watch television either.

A dedicated academic, all he really cared about was his work—specifically, higher math—and his family. Not in that order.

At first she had been convinced it had gotten mixed in with his belongings by accident.

But the more she thought about it, the less likely it seemed. The bag was sealed, and inventoried, and the guitar pick was listed on the contents log.

She's considered—and dismissed—the likelihood that Roger might have found it on the sidewalk and picked it up. He's a germaphobe; he never left home without his hand sanitizer. He scolded her whenever she stumbled across and reached for a faceup penny in a public place.

"But it's good luck," she'd tell him, putting it into her pocket.

"Not if you contract a disgusting disease from it."

"I'll take my chances. And since you worry about disgusting diseases, you might want to quit smoking."

But of course, he wouldn't. Couldn't. Not even for her.

"It's my one vice, Sheri."

"It can kill you. Don't you want to stick around and grow old with me?"

"I'll grow old with you. Don't worry."

Wandering around the empty house they'd shared, remembering that conversation—rather, those conversations, because they'd had it more than once—she wipes tears from her eyes.

Mingling with her intense grief is a growing sense of uneasiness about the damned guitar pick.

What if it's a clue?

What if the killer accidentally dropped it . . .

Into Roger's pocket?

Not very likely, but not impossible.

"Maybe I should tell the police," she speculates aloud.

Maggie, ever on her heels, seems to agree with a jangling of dog tags. Sheri reaches down to pet the puppy's head.

"I wish you could talk, Mags. I wish you could tell me who did this to him."

Maggie wags her tail, but she, too, seems wistful.

Crying again, Sheri goes into the bathroom for tissues. Then Maggie is at the door, needing to be let out into the yard. Then the phone rings: one of Roger's colleagues checking in to see how she is.

By the time she hangs up, lets the puppy back into the house, and feeds her, Sheri is utterly spent. Maybe even exhausted enough to finally get some sleep.

It's not time for bed yet, by any stretch of the imagination. The late afternoon sun still beams through the screened windows, and the chirping birds beyond won't give way to crickets for at least another four or five hours.

But sleep would bring a sorely needed reprieve from this living hell, and so she climbs the stairs to the bedroom.

Closing the windows to quiet the birdsongs and drawing the blinds to block out the sun, Sheri pushes away nagging thoughts of the guitar pick.

I'll deal with it later, she tells herself as a mighty yawn escapes her. *Or maybe I'll just forget about it.*

What does it matter? Roger is gone. Finding out who killed him won't bring him back.

She slips into the bed they shared and rolls over onto Roger's side.

There, on the bedside table, pushed up against the base of the lamp, she sees his silver lighter.

It hadn't been stolen after all. He must have forgotten it that morning as he tucked the cigarettes and wallet into his pocket.

He must have been frustrated, reaching into his pocket for that first morning cigarette he always enjoyed so thoroughly and realizing he couldn't even light it.

Landry resists the urge to check her watch, not wanting Detective Burns to get the impression that she's anxious to leave this conference room—though that is, indeed, the case.

It's not easy to sit here and reveal personal details to a total stranger . . .

Which is, ironically, precisely why she became involved with the Internet—and, by association, with Meredith and the others—in the first place. Now Detective Burns is pumping her for information not just about herself, but about her fellow bloggers.

Is it because she suspects that one of them killed Meredith?

Do I suspect that, too?

It's not the first time Landry has speculated about it, but until now she's been able to talk herself out of it.

They're strangers, Landry . . .

With Rob's comment echoing in her ears, and now this, suddenly, it seems not only possible, but plausible . . .

Still, maybe she's just paranoid.

Who wouldn't be, sitting here being interrogated by a homicide detective?

Okay, this isn't an interrogation; it's an interview. She knows there's a distinct difference between the two, and Detective Burns made it very clear up front that she was interested in conducting the latter.

But now that the woman has abruptly stopped taking notes and is sitting there as if she's just been handed an incriminating piece of evidence, Landry backtracks through the conversation, wondering what she could possibly have said to inspire the reaction.

She was merely spelling Jaycee's name, and Detective Burns was in the midst of writing it down. Before that . . .

Shifting her weight in the chair as if snapping out of a trance, the woman resumes writing, then looks up again at Landry.

"Jaycee. You say she lives in New York? As in New York City?"

"That's right."

Detective Burns types something into her laptop, focused on the screen as she asks, "What else do you know about her?"

"She has some kind of corporate job—"

"Where?"

"I don't know."

Now the detective is looking at her. "But she told you this?"

Landry considers the question. Did Jaycee actually tell her, or did she simply infer it based on the fact that Jaycee was frequently traveling and talking about meetings?

"I'm not sure."

The follow-up questions come fast and furious, punctuated by the tapping keys of Detective Burns's keyboard: How long has Jaycee been blogging? Has Landry ever met her in person? Ever spoken to her on the phone? What does Jaycee sound like? What does she look like?

"I've never seen her," is Landry's response to the last question. "She doesn't post personal pictures."

Seeing the expression on the detective's face as she utters those words, Landry realizes that they do, indeed, seem incriminating.

"But lots of people don't post photos of themselves," she finds herself hastily adding, struck by the instinct to protect Jaycee.

Why?

Because I'm sure she's innocent?

Or just because she's one of us?

That, she realizes, is the reason, pure and simple. It was the same back in her sorority days. She didn't know some of her sisters nearly as well as others, and while she loved many of them, there were a few she didn't even like very much. Still, they were bound by sisterhood and had each other's backs, always.

Looking thoughtful, Detective Burns returns her gaze to the screen and rhythmically taps the same key on her laptop—as if she's scrolling down a page, Landry thinks. Probably Jaycee's blog.

She asks a few other questions about Jaycee—questions Landry can't answer, like whether she's married or has children; where she grew up; exactly when she was diagnosed; where she might be today, at this very minute.

"All right," the detective says, in a shifting gears tone, "let's take a look at something."

Relieved to be moving on to a new topic, Landry watches her type something on her keyboard, wait and then peer at the screen.

After a moment Detective Burns turns the laptop around so it's facing Landry. "Do you recognize this woman?"

Landry leans in to look. There's a glare, and she can't see anything until she reaches out and tilts the screen at a different angle.

Now the image on the screen is plainly visible—and instantly recognizable. Landry immediately says, "That's

Jenna Coeur. I actually just read an article about her in the newspaper this morning, on the plane."

"How much do you know about her?"

"Quite a bit," she admits. "I've seen all her movies—I mean who hasn't? But I also read a lot of celebrity magazines and books, and I read that true crime best seller a few years ago. *Coldhearted*, I think was the title, and it was . . ."

She trails off as a terrible, preposterous thought occurs to her.

"You don't think Jenna Coeur had something to do with Meredith's death?"

"Do you?" the detective returns.

"No! Why would she? It's not like she and Meredith knew each other . . ."

"You're sure about that?"

"I'm positive."

"Because Jenna Coeur was at the funeral today. So obviously, there was a connection."

Speechless, Landry can only shake her head, her mind reeling.

Surely Meredith would have mentioned a personal connection with a woman who went overnight from being one of the most beloved movie stars of the twenty-first century to one of the most notorious murderesses of all time. That's not the kind of thing you keep to yourself. Not if you're Meredith, who not only appreciated, but seemed to share, her own interest in all things Hollywood.

One of Meredith's many off-topic-of-breast-cancer blogs was about her random brushes with celebrity, like spotting Nicolas Cage in a New Orleans restaurant and seeing one of the Real Housewives at an airport. That was a popular post: most of the other bloggers shared their own celebrity run-ins in the comments section. Kay mentioned Timothy McVeigh's execution at the prison where she worked. You'd think that alone would have inspired Meredith to mention her own connection to another notorious criminal.

When Jenna Coeur's televised high-profile trial was unfolding, it seemed like the entire world was tuned into *Court TV*—including Rob, who was far more interested in the legal posturing than the movie star aspect of the case.

Jenna wasn't convicted, but only because she had the best defense team her millions could buy. She reportedly wanted to take the stand, but her lawyers refused to allow her to testify. Later, she never issued a statement other than to say— through her attorneys—that she was relieved the ordeal was over, was grateful to her legal team, and would appreciate privacy as she tried to rebuild her life.

That didn't seem likely. Every journalist in the country sought the big interview with her. But she never stepped back into the spotlight to proclaim her own innocence. She simply faded into obscurity . . .

Only to pop up today at Meredith Heywood's funeral in Ohio?

It made no sense. None whatsoever.

"If Meredith knew Jenna Coeur, she probably would have mentioned it at some point. So I honestly don't think she did," Landry tells the detective again. *It's either that, or I didn't know Meredith.*

"Unless," Detective Burns says, "Meredith *wasn't aware* that she knew Jenna Coeur."

Momentarily confused, Landry digests the comment and her eyes widen. "You think they were connected online?"

"It's feasible, isn't it?"

Landry nods slowly as her mind hurtles through various scenarios. Plucking the most logical one, she asks, "So you think she was lurking on Meredith's blog?"

"Maybe lurking. Or maybe interacting, but disguised."

"I didn't even know she had cancer." You'd think something like that would get out.

"Maybe she doesn't. Maybe she's just pretending she does."

Landry's jaw drops. "Why would anyone in their right mind—" She cuts herself off. No one in her right mind would fake cancer. Just as no one in her right mind would slaughter her own daughter in cold blood.

Cold-blooded . . . coldhearted . . .

That's Jenna Coeur.

Detective Burns rests her elbow on her table and her chin in her hand. "Tell me again," she says with quiet deliberation, "what you know about your blogger friend Jaycee."

Wondering why she's abruptly shifting gears, Landry tries to tear her thoughts away from Jenna Coeur and focus on the question at hand. Belatedly, she realizes that the detective is pronouncing Jaycee's name oddly, without the emphasis on the first syllable and with a distinct pause before the second.

Then it hits her: Detective Burns hasn't shifted gears at all.

"You think . . ." Landry shakes her head in disbelief, even as a forgotten thought tries to barge back into her head. "You think Jaycee is really Jenna Coeur?"

She pauses for the inevitable response—*"Do you?"*—but receives only a shrug.

Jaycee . . .

J.C. . . .

Jenna Coeur . . .

An elusive thought flits at the edge of her consciousness. There's something she should remember . . .

"Can I take a quick look at her blog page?" she asks the detective, gesturing at the laptop. "I just want to see . . . maybe there's something there that will give her away if it's her."

"Be my guest. I don't think there is, though."

Landry clicks over to Jaycee's blog, noting that there have

been no new entries all week. That's not unusual—none of them have been posting. She'd assumed everyone is, like her, too shell-shocked by Meredith's death—not wanting to put the loss into words yet, but not able to write about anything else, either.

"She usually writes about general topics related to breast cancer—usually political stuff, criticizing spending, encouraging lobbying . . . that sort of thing."

"Jenna Coeur was one of Hollywood's most vocal political activists."

"That's right. I remember." Truly, she knows her movie stars. Reads about them, follows them online, watches those gossipy infotainment shows on television . . .

And there's something . . .

Something else . . .

"It's not a stretch to think that if she wanted to pose as a blogger," Detective Burns is saying, "she'd cover topics that might actually mean something to her."

"No, that does make sense."

Landry scrolls down the page, tap, tap, tapping the down arrow key, knowing there's something she should be remembering.

Frustrated, she flips over to her own blog and clicks to the archived entry about brushes with celebrity, wondering whether Jaycee contributed to the barrage of comments. As she scans them, finding nothing, the detective continues to question her.

"When you spoke to her on the phone this week, did she—"

"Oh my God! That's it! That's the thing I was trying to—when she called me, it was from a California area code. She said she was at a hotel in L.A."

"Do you still have the number? Was it on your home phone, or—"

"No, it was on my cell . . ." Landry is already pulling

it out of her pocket. "And at the time, I thought there was something familiar about her voice . . . I kept thinking she reminded me of someone. No wonder."

She quickly scrolls through the call log, hoping the number is still there.

It is.

She reads it off to Detective Burns, who jots it down, then grabs the laptop and enters it in a search engine. "She wasn't lying about where she was. The number belongs to a hotel off the Sunset Strip. Do you have a phone number for her in New York, or her cell?"

"No—yes!" Landry remembers. "She gave me her cell, then hung up before I could get the home number."

"Do you have it in your phone contacts?"

"No, I wrote it down somewhere at home."

"Do you think you can get it?"

"I can try."

Detective Crystal nods and gestures at the phone in Landry's hand.

"Oh—you mean right now?"

"If you don't mind."

"No, it's fine. I'll just call home and . . ." She dials the house, trying to remember where the number might be. For all she knows she scribbled it on a napkin and then mistakenly threw it away.

Rob answers. "What's up? Everything okay? How'd it go with the detective?"

"I'm still . . . listen, can you do me a quick favor? I need you to find a phone number I wrote down a few days ago. I might have put it on the bulletin board like I did the insurance cards."

"I'll check."

He does, and reports that it's not there. Hearing voices in the background, Landry asks, "Is that the kids? Can you put Addison on the phone?"

"Sure. Tucker's here, too. You can talk to them both. But don't you want that phone number first?"

"I do want it—that's why I need Addison. She's a lot better at finding things than y'all are."

"Ouch," he says mildly, and hands the phone over to their daughter.

"Mom?"

A new wave of homesickness washes over her with the sound of her daughter's voice. "Hi, sweetie. I need your help. I wrote down a phone number the other day, probably on scrap paper, and it's around there somewhere. Can you look for it? I was in my bedroom, I think, when I talked to her, so you might want to start there."

"Sure. Hang on a second."

Landry nods at Detective Burns. "My daughter's looking."

"Gotcha. For what it's worth, my husband can never find anything either. Men, right?"

Caught up in the unexpected moment of female bonding, and forgetting all about why they're here, Landry shakes her head with a smile. "Right. My son is the same way. Do you have kids?"

"I had a son."

Had means she lost him—and Landry can see it in the sorrow in her dark brown eyes.

Before she can figure out what to say—what else is there, besides *I'm so sorry*?—Addison is back on the line. "I think I found it. Is it written in blue Sharpie on the back of a supermarket receipt?"

"That's it. Can you read it off for me?"

Addison does, repeating it twice to make sure Landry gets it right as she relays it to Detective Burns, who immediately Googles it.

"Thanks, sweetie. I'll call back a little later to talk to you and to Tucker, too."

"Okay. I miss you. I love you."

"I miss you and love you, too. I'll be home tomorrow."

Hanging up, she's pretty sure she glimpses a fleeting bittersweet expression on Detective Burns's face, and she wonders again about the child she lost.

But the moment is gone; the detective is frowning at the computer. "That's the phone number for a sushi place in New York. Unless your daughter got it wrong."

"She wouldn't. But I'll make sure." She quickly texts Addison, asking her to double-check the number.

The response is, predictably, prompt and efficient. The number was right—as in *wrong*. As in, it looks like Jaycee deliberately withheld her real number.

"I'll call it"—Detective Burns is already dialing— "just to be sure."

Landry is sure even before she hears the detective say into the phone, "I'm sorry, I dialed the wrong number," and hang up.

She looks at Landry. "That was Wasabi Express asking me for my take-out order. Looks like your friend Jaycee had no intention of letting you find her."

Diagnosis: Trypanophobia

That's the official name for this crippling lifelong affliction of mine. Trypanophobia, otherwise known as fear of needles.

Not just needles prodding into me, but into anyone at all. I'm ashamed to admit it, but when my kids were little, I used to have my mother—and then, after she passed away, a friend or neighbor—come with me to the pediatrician's office on days they needed shots or to have blood drawn. I'd sit in the waiting room while someone else held my children's hands as needles poked into their arms. I've always felt guilty about that. But I couldn't help it.

I have thin veins; it's never been easy for a nurse or doctor to tap into one without a whole lot of painful poking around. And if my phobia didn't ease up with pregnancy or motherhood, then it sure as hell didn't happen after my cancer diagnosis. If anything, it became worse than ever.

That was why I ultimately opted to have a port implanted to deliver chemo medication—not that I could avoid the needles even then. There were plenty of other reasons for doctors and nurses to jab me, sometimes repeatedly, with every office visit.

But I remind myself that the needles I've always dreaded have become my lifeline now. And that's reason enough to put up with them and to wear every bandage that covers a bloody cotton ball like a badge of honor.

—Excerpt from Meredith's blog, *Pink Stinks*

Chapter 12

Crossing the threshold to her Manhattan apartment at one o'clock Sunday morning, Jaycee locks the door behind her and peels off the blond wig at last. She throws it on the nearest surface—a table where she usually tosses what little incoming mail she receives here.

Mostly it's just catalogues, fliers, takeout menus, and envelopes filled with coupons, addressed to Resident. The real stuff—bills, bank statements, correspondence, most of which is funneled through a mail drop—goes to Cory.

He's been handling it all for her ever since the old days, when she was being hunted for drastically different reasons.

In some ways there's quite a contrast in being sought-after because you're a movie star and being sought-after because you're a cold-blooded killer.

In other ways there's no difference at all.

Back then she was often alone, and not by choice. Everyone wanted something from her. Everyone, it seemed, except Cory, and . . .

Her.

She'd thought Olivia was different. That was why she'd let her in. Trusted her, just as she'd trusted Steve all those years ago.

That time, it led to heartbreak. This time, it proved to be a fatal mistake . . .

Fatal for Olivia.

She closes her eyes, trying to forget, listening to the sound of her own breathing, and then . . .

Forty-odd stories below, sirens race down the avenue.

Sirens . . .

There were sirens that night. She's the one who called 911 when it was over, hands sticky-slick with Olivia's blood.

She doesn't remember it, or what she said to the dispatcher.

But everything was admitted as evidence at the trial: the bloody fingerprints on the telephone, even—despite her lawyers' protests, which were overruled—the recorded conversation that opened with her own voice—robotic, not frantic—reporting, "She's dead."

"Who's dead?" the operator asked.

"Olivia. She's—my daughter. I killed her."

By the time the sensational headlines hit the morning papers—JENNA COEUR MURDERS TEEN DAUGHTER—she was under arrest, sitting in jail while Cory, ever the efficient manager, assembled the stellar defense team that would coach her through the trial and eventually get her off the hook.

Reasonable doubt was the key. Her lawyers moved heaven and earth to produce it.

She initially thought building a self-defense case would be a much safer bet, but they wouldn't hear of it.

"In a parent's murder of a child? No jury would buy it. Not with all the evidence against you."

"But—"

"Look, Jenna, the prosecution is going to bring in a bunch of experts who are going to testify that you're guilty as hell. And the jury is going to believe them. Unless—*until*—we blast holes into every one of those experts' testimonies. Got it?"

She did get it—once she realized that her lawyers didn't actually give a damn whether she was innocent or guilty. She'd hired them to get her acquitted, and they did.

Five years ago she walked out of jail a free woman. She spent the first two years contentedly hidden away at a Caribbean island home owned by her lead attorney. The only people who ever laid eyes on her were the household help, and they either didn't recognize her or were paid well enough not to care who she was.

But she couldn't stay there forever. With Cory's help, she made her way back to New York. But it took months before she even dared emerge from her apartment.

She never would have dreamed she'd eventually agree to take part in Cory's crazy plan, the one that led her to Meredith and the others . . .

And to being recognized by that detective at the funeral.

She has no doubt that at this very moment the homicide investigators are trying to figure out why Jenna Coeur would have been there.

Sooner or later they're bound to make the connection, if they haven't already.

But she sure as hell wasn't going to stick around Cincinnati worrying about it.

No, much better to stick around here and worry about it, helpless as a bird with clipped wings in a treetop nest.

She opens her eyes and sighs.

The street sirens have faded into the distance.

Just one more week of this, she promises herself, kicking off her shoes and padding into the bathroom to scrub off her makeup. Next week at this time it will all be over and she can move on at last.

Wide-awake, too disturbed—and too cold—to sleep, Kay lies stiffly in the unfamiliar bed listening to the strange night sounds: thumps and footsteps from the other side of

the wall, voices and closing doors in the hall, the on-off
clunking and hum of the air-conditioning unit whose tem-
perature she can't seem to regulate.

If she could only get some rest . . .

Sometimes she lies awake at night worrying that cancer
cells are growing again inside her body. Imagining how
they will spread and destroy it, section by section, a stealthy
predator bent on eventually robbing her of her senses, of her
ability to reason, to move, to breathe . . .

Tonight she trades troubling thoughts of disease for spec-
ulation about the strange twist in the murder case.

Jenna Coeur . . .

When Detective Burns showed her the photo, she didn't
immediately recognize the woman.

"Should I?" she'd asked.

"Most people do."

She shook her head. "Who is she?"

The moment Detective Burns said the name, the light
dawned.

It would be hard to find a living soul who hadn't heard
of Jenna Coeur. Kay isn't a movie fan and she doesn't watch
much TV, but you couldn't really escape her altogether. The
famed award-winning method actress was on the cover of
every magazine and supermarket tabloid long before her notorious murder trial.

Detective Burns refreshed Kay's memory a bit, and so
did Landry and Elena, after they'd all been interviewed by
the detectives—one of the most nerve-racking experiences
of Kay's entire life.

"This is my cell phone number," Detective Burns said
at the end, handing over a card. "If you think of anything
else—anything at all—that might help us find out who did
this to your friend, promise that you'll call me right away.
Any time of the day or night."

Kay promised.

When it was over, she felt better that both Landry and Elena confessed that they, too, had been anxious—even more so now that they knew about the Jenna Coeur connection.

By then it was late. No one was in the mood to go out to dinner as they'd planned. The three of them just sprawled together on the bed in Elena's room, sipping cocktails they mixed from the minibar and discussing the bizarre turn of events.

It was almost like an old-fashioned slumber party. Kay felt closer than ever to her new friends. Only, instead of telling scary, made-up stories, the three of them discussed the terrifying notion that Jaycee—their Jaycee—is really Jenna Coeur.

Detective Burns seems to think so, and both Elena and Landry believe it as well. Kay pretended to agree, because it was easier than arguing with two strong-willed women like that—particularly Elena. But deep down inside she isn't convinced.

Maybe you just don't want to be convinced.

Maybe it terrifies you to think that somebody in your little circle is not who she's pretending to be.

"How much did you share with Jaycee?" the three of them took turns asking each other, worriedly.

They tried to remember how many details they'd revealed. For Kay, not a whole lot. Later, alone in her room, she went back over her e-mails and private messages just to be sure, although . . .

Does it really matter now?

Jaycee—or Jenna—whoever she is . . .

"She's not going to come after us anyway," Elena said firmly. "We don't have to worry."

"I'm sure you're right," Landry agreed. "I just wish you hadn't told her about next weekend."

"She didn't even respond. Don't worry."

Kay reluctantly suggested they cancel the girls' getaway plans, but neither of them wanted to.

"We're doing it, and you're coming, too, Kay," Elena said firmly, pulling out her phone. "Here, let's get online and find you a plane ticket."

"I don't know. I'm not crazy about flying. I haven't even been on a plane in years," she confessed.

"I used to be a nervous flier," Landry said. "Before cancer. But now I always think that if the plane crashes, well . . ." She shrugged. "It's out of my hands."

"And there are worse ways to go," Elena added. "In a plane crash, you're there one minute, gone the next. It's not death that scares me. It's dying."

Kay told her that she feels exactly the same way.

Then she found herself remembering her mother's final tortured weeks on this earth—not to mention the agonizing final blog posts from Whoa Nellie and others who had gone down that terminal road. And Meredith's trepidation as she faced the final stages of her disease.

Meredith was terrified over the prospect of what might lie ahead. She didn't want to go through that; didn't want to put her family through it.

I've always been the kind of person, she wrote to Kay, *who likes to get the first flight out the morning a vacation ends. Once I know it's over and I have to go, I just want to go. Get it over with. It was like that when we left our kids off at college, too. No long, drawn-out good-byes for me. I couldn't stand it. Years later the kids told me they were surprised I didn't leave skid marks getting out of there, while all the other parents were lingering. Of course, they didn't understand that it was because I loved them too much—not that I didn't love them enough.*

Thinking of her own mother, Kay wanted to tell Meredith that she knew all about not loving someone enough, both on the receiving end and on the giving end. But she didn't say it.

She didn't like to talk about her mother ever, not even with Meredith.

Despite her earlier exhaustion—when she didn't know how she was going to keep her eyes open until sundown—Beck has yet to fall asleep. Now the sun is coming up again, casting rosy shadows through the crack in the sunshine-and-sky-colored curtains her mother hung at her bedroom windows the spring before she left for college. Cheerful curtains, Mom called them.

"I feel so bad we couldn't afford to buy them until now," she said. "You can take them with you, and the new bedspread, too, for your dorm room when you leave."

"No," Beck said. "They belong here, for when I come home."

Home . . .

She'd never considered the concept before—never realized that *home* was less about the place than it was about people in it. Without Mom here, home has become just a house.

Now just she and her father are left to rattle around in it. Her brothers and their families left even before some of the postfuneral crowd did, but she, of course, is stuck here. She can't leave Dad alone, and even if someone else were willing to stay with him—

Where would I go?

The house she shares with Keith is no longer home either.

I have no home.

What now?

Dad will sell the house. He'll need a place to live. So will she. But not here, in Cincinnati. It would be too far a commute to her job in Lexington.

Anyway, there's nothing really keeping Dad here now that Mom is gone. He doesn't even have a job.

Maybe he'll want to make a fresh start someplace new . . .

But . . .

All alone?

Will he be alone?

Thoughts of what might possibly happen next for him—for all of them—continue to spiral in Beck's head until at last she gets out of bed, too depleted to lie here for another moment listening to the morning birds and the patio wind chimes tinkling gently below, stirred by a warm morning breeze that tickles the cheerful drapes.

Opening her bedroom door, she half expects to smell coffee brewing and hear pots and pans clattering in the kitchen. Mom always liked to make pancakes for breakfast on Sunday mornings. Even later, especially when the grandkids slept over. She liked to play restaurant with them the way she did with Beck and her brothers when they were little.

They got such a kick out of the way she'd pretend to be a waitress taking their orders, and would dream up all kinds of crazy things—beef-'n'-booger surprise was one of Beck's brothers' favorites, and now it's her nephews', too.

No matter what the kids would try to order, though, Mom would say, "One stinkerdoodle special, coming right up!"

Then she'd bring them a plate filled with pancakes that had smiley faces made out of chocolate chips or raisins.

On this Sunday morning, there are no pancakes on the griddle and there's no coffee wafting in the air.

The house creeps with silent shadows as Beck descends to the first floor, on tiptoe in the hope that her father is still asleep on his recliner in the den.

He isn't, though.

The door is ajar and the lamp is on; when she peeks in to check on him, she sees him sitting at his desk in front of the computer.

"Dad?"

He jumps, cries out.

"Sorry. I didn't mean to scare you. What are you doing?"

"Nothing, just . . . nothing." He pushes his reading glasses up onto his forehead and rubs his eyes.

"Did you sleep at all?" she asks him, and he shakes his head. "I didn't either. I was going to make some coffee."

He makes a face. "I drank enough coffee yesterday to kill someone."

The words hang uncomfortably in the air for a moment.

"So did I," Beck says, "but I need more anyway, if I'm going to make it through this day."

"I'd better have some, too. Be there in a few minutes. I just want to finish something."

He's back to typing on the keyboard as she leaves the den.

In the kitchen, she starts the coffee, then busies herself reorganizing the kitchen cabinets, moving around all the serving bowls and platters well-meaning neighbors and friends insisted on washing last night before they left. At that point she was so tired of people she'd have been more appreciative if everyone had just cleared out of here and left the mess to her.

Now, as she puts things back where they belong, she finds that every piece invokes a memory. Mom always served Christmas cookies and Valentine's Day brownies on the red oval platter. The big cut-glass bowl had held fruit salad at every Easter brunch. And she'd just seen the white ceramic pedestal plate a few weeks ago, holding the cheesecake she'd picked up at a bakery on her way into town. She'd been planning on baking one from scratch, using Mom's own recipe, but she and Keith had gotten into a monster argument the night before and she didn't have the time—or the heart—to putter in the kitchen.

She remembers wistfully watching her parents that day, thinking their marriage seemed idyllic compared to her own.

Well, whose wouldn't?

Is it possible her perspective was skewed because of her own miserable life with Keith? Was she just imagining that her parents were happily married? Was there something brewing beneath the surface, something she should have noticed; something she could have stopped in time, had she only known?

No. Dad had nothing to do with what happened to her. He loved her. That was that.

And yet, another memory nibbles away at the edge of Beck's consciousness; one she's been trying to keep at bay.

Too worn-out to fight it this time, she lets it in.

About a month ago she'd called in sick to work and driven into town on a weekday to have lunch with an old high school friend, now a lawyer, about the possibility of a separation agreement. She wasn't going to tell her parents she was coming; the last thing she wanted was for them to worry about her—and her marriage—on top of their financial mess, now that Dad had lost his job.

Miranda, Beck's lawyer friend, said she had to stay fairly local because she had a meeting right before lunch and another right after. Beck chose a chain restaurant she knew her mother hated, figuring there was no way in hell she'd run into her parents there. She didn't.

She ran into her father.

He was walking out just as Beck was hurrying in—late—to meet Miranda.

She was so flustered seeing him that she started stammering—but so, she remembers now, did he.

"What are you doing here?" they asked each other.

Beck told a semi truth—that she'd taken the day off to have lunch with an old friend—and was planning to pop into the house afterward to surprise him and Mom if she had time.

"But I was afraid I wouldn't," she said, "so I didn't want to disappoint anyone."

"I won't tell Mom. If you have time, stop over. If you don't, your secret is safe with me."

That was when the woman came out of the ladies' room and walked right up to her father—almost as if he'd been waiting for her.

Maybe he had, Beck realized, when the woman said to him, "All set?"

"Louise," he said, "this is my daughter, Rebecca. Beck, this is Louise Falk. She's been helping me with . . . some financial paperwork."

Beck and Louise shook hands, and then Dad said, right in front of Louise, "I'd appreciate it if you didn't mention this to Mom. I don't want her to worry. You know how she is."

Beck knew.

At the time, she was so thrown off by having run into her father that she didn't think to question whether he'd been telling the truth about Louise.

No, it hadn't occurred to her to question it until her mother lay dead and the police were asking her whether her father might be capable of terrible things.

She's sworn to them—and herself—that he wasn't.

Because he isn't.

He—

"Is the coffee ready?"

She jumps, almost dropping the big white platter, as her father comes up behind her.

"Oh—it's ready," she realizes. "Sit down, Dad. I'll pour you a cup."

"Thanks."

Watching him go over to the table and pull out a chair—his chair, the one he's been sitting in at family dinners for as long as she can remember—she wonders what he'd say if she asked him, now, about Louise.

About whether she really was a . . . financial consultant, or whatever he'd implied.

But if she asks, then he'll think she has doubts . . .

Do you have doubts? she asked herself.

Yes. Maybe she does.

But even if Louise wasn't—even if she was his—

Mistress? Dad with a mistress?

The thought seems ludicrous. But even if that were the case, it still doesn't mean he had anything to do with Mom's death.

So she can't ask him. She just can't. Somebody has to be on his side.

I'm all he has right now, she thinks as she sets the cup of hot coffee in front of him. *And he's all I have.*

"We should have just teamed up and rented one car yesterday," Elena tells Landry on Sunday afternoon as they meet up inside the airport terminal after returning their respective rental cars. "That way, we could have come and gone together."

"I know! Why didn't we do that?"

"Because we were both secretly afraid the other one might be a lunatic psycho in person."

"Oh. Right. I forgot that part." Landry smiles at her, marveling at how quickly she grew to feel comfortable with Elena in the past twenty-four hours. "I'm really glad you're not crazy after all."

"There are so many people in my life," Elena tells her as they pull their bags along toward the security area, "who would find that comment amusing."

"Like . . . ?"

"My brother, for one."

"Why is that?"

"He thinks I'm crazy," she replies with a wry smile.

Elena, Landry realizes, never really writes much about her family, and she's barely talked about them at all this weekend.

*Meanwhile, I've talked about nothing but. She must be
sick of hearing about Rob and the kids . . .*

But I can't help it. I miss them.

"The thing is," Elena says, "I kind of had a hand in raising him."

"Your brother?"

"Right. And our childhood wasn't exactly—well, you
know we lost our mom when we were pretty young."

It was a terrible train accident. That, Landry remembers.
Elena had mentioned something about it last night, when
they were talking about Meredith, how they hoped she
hadn't suffered.

"I bet she never knew what hit her," Elena had said. "Like
my mother."

"That would be a blessing," Kay agreed. "It's what she
would have wanted. It was dying that she dreaded. Not death
itself. Dying."

"Don't we all?" Elena had asked.

Landry didn't say that she dreaded all of it. Dying. Death.

Because of her family. Rob, and the kids . . . she couldn't
bear to think of them left here to muddle through without her.

Meredith would have understood that. But Kay and Elena
don't have husbands or children; Kay doesn't have any
family at all, and Elena isn't close to hers. They don't have
to worry about leaving behind people who still need them
desperately.

Maybe I'd feel different if I were completely on my own.

"After our mother died," Elena is saying, "our father kind
of . . . checked out. He was a good dad before she died, but
afterward, he . . . well, he couldn't cope with losing her."

Landry nods as if she understands, and she's trying to.
If something were to happen to her, there's no telling how
Rob—also a good dad—might react.

Nothing can happen to me. He needs me. The kids need me.

Back when she was first diagnosed, that thought ran

through Landry's mind all day, every day. She used to pray that she could at least see her kids through childhood. Now that it's nearly over—Addison is on the brink of eighteen!—she knows that's not nearly enough time.

I want to be here for all of it: their high school and college graduations, their wedding days . . . I want to be a grandma; I want to grow old with Rob, I want—

She wants what anyone wants. What Meredith wanted.

To be needed.

Those were the wants and needs she'd written about in that blog, the one they were talking about yesterday.

The TSA agent standing by the roped-off security checkpoint interrupts Landry's thought process and the conversation. "I need to see your boarding passes and IDs, please, ladies."

They show their paperwork.

As they roll their luggage into the long line snaking toward the body scan machines, Elena resumes talking about her family. "My dad drank. A lot. And when he did—which was all the time, basically—he kind of left us to our own devices. Sometimes I tried to mother my brother; other times, I was a wild child who should have been reined in. Only nobody did that for me."

"Are you close to your brother now?"

"I might be if he weren't overseas. He's in the military. The nice regimented lifestyle he always craved, poor kid."

"And your dad?"

"He doesn't live far from me."

"Do you see him?"

"Not really," is the answer, delivered in a case closed tone. "So listen, about next weekend . . ."

Right. Next weekend.

Elena and Kay are coming to Alabama: they've already bought their tickets online.

Elena stops pulling her bag to consult her boarding pass,

then an overhead sign. "I have to go that way. I'm boarding in a few minutes."

"I'm going that way." Landry points in the opposite direction. She's not boarding for well over another hour, but there seemed to be no reason to hang around the hotel alone—and there's no reason to follow Elena to her gate.

"I guess this is good-bye then, for now." Elena throws her arms around her. "I don't really want to go back."

"Hang in there, with the Tony thing," Landry says, remembering.

Last night Elena told her and Kay that she'd blocked his number on her cell phone, so at least he can't call her anymore.

"Ugh, don't remind me," she says now. "I dread seeing him at school tomorrow morning. I really hope this week flies by. Not just because of Tony, or because it's my last week of work before the summer, but because I can't wait to see you and Kay again."

"Same here," Landry says hollowly, hoping that by then there will have been an arrest and they can all put this nightmare behind them.

Long distance driving, for whatever reason, is somehow easier for Kay today.

Maybe because she's once again accustomed to being at the wheel after yesterday's long journey.

Maybe because the funeral—and all the accompanying dread—is behind her now, just as the outskirts of Cincinnati have fallen away in a rearview mirror, showing nothing but the road she's already traveled.

Or maybe it's simply because she's surprisingly well-rested.

After wrestling with her thoughts—and uncooperative, unfamiliar bedding—into the wee hours, she'd managed to finally fall asleep, and stay asleep, for a full eight hours, and then some.

She was still sound asleep in her room when Landry called to tell her they were going to breakfast.

"Come on down and join us," she said.

"I'm not even dressed yet."

"We'll wait."

"I don't want to hold you up."

"You're not. We don't even have to leave for the airport for a few hours. Come on. Breakfast for three."

Over pancakes and coffee, they again discussed Meredith, and the Jenna Coeur business. But they managed to laugh a lot, too, and made plans for next weekend. Decadent desserts, Netflix movies, a beach day.

"I can't wait," Kay told them. "I've never even seen the ocean."

"And here I was afraid you were going to back out," Elena said.

"Why would I?"

"You're afraid to fly."

"I know, but you're my friends. Who knows how many more opportunities we'll have to see each other?"

"Lots more opportunities," Elena said firmly.

Kay allows her hands to tighten on the steering wheel. Again she wonders, *What if . . . ?*

No. Nothing can happen to the others, to any of them. It's going to be fine, from now on. Forget cancer. Forget Jenna Coeur, whoever, wherever, she is. Forget Tony, crazy Tony, Elena's so-called stalker. Nothing bad is going to happen, not to any of them. Not ever again.

"Whatever you do," Landry told them before they parted ways, "please don't mention next weekend to any of the other bloggers and don't post anything about it online. Just in case . . . you know."

Yes. They know.

They promised her they wouldn't say anything.

"I just wish I hadn't told Jaycee," Elena mentioned yet again.

"If Jaycee is just Jaycee, we have nothing to worry about," Kay pointed out.

"And if she's not . . ."

"We still have nothing to worry about. It's not like she has any reason to hurt any of us. And it's not like Elena gave her your address."

"It wouldn't be hard to find."

"But why would she want to?" Kay asked. She shook her head. "I really don't feel like she's a threat to any of us. Even if she is Jenna Coeur. That might be a bizarre coincidence, but it's not like it puts us in danger."

By the time they parted ways, the others seemed reassured.

Seeing a blue rest stop sign looming through the windshield, Kay puts on her right turn signal. She's feeling pretty good, but she's got a long trip ahead and it's probably a good idea to stop and stretch for a bit.

What a difference a day makes. Now, anything seems possible. Anything at all, as long as she has her friends.

When Landry arrives at the gate for her flight, she sees that there are only a few passengers waiting in the boarding area—and Bruce Mangione is one of them.

He's sitting reading a newspaper, with empty seats on either side of him. It would be awfully bold of her to walk right over there and take one of them. What if he gets the wrong idea?

He won't if you tell him about the case.

Her feet are already propelling her toward him, but guilt dogs her when she thinks about Rob. He doesn't know about the Jenna Coeur twist yet. She was going to tell him when she called home this morning, but the kids were right there, wanting to talk to her, too, and they were all headed for church. By the time they got back, she was having breakfast with Elena and Kay.

She probably could have snuck in a quick call home, but it

wasn't really something she wanted to get into on the phone with limited time. She'll tell him as soon as she lands, of course.

For now . . .

Maybe she shouldn't tell this total stranger about it. Even if he is a detective. Even if she did Google his name last night, just to see what came up.

Retired cop, just like he said.

Private investigator and personal security, just like he said. He even has a Web site that lists his credentials, along with his specialties: Missing Persons, Infidelity, Surveillance, Background Checks, Criminal Investigation . . .

Okay. He's certainly qualified. But it's not like she's planning to hire him.

Am I?

Maybe I am.

To do what, exactly, though?

Solve the case?

It's not as if there isn't an entire homicide squad working it. But their main concern is solving the murder, and her concern is . . .

Well, she does want the murder solved, of course. But it's safe to assume that her own personal safety—and thus, that of her family—is probably more consequential to her than it is to Detective Burns.

Plus, she's seen enough police procedural dramas and read enough thrillers—fiction and non—to know that private investigators don't have to deal with the tremendous amount of red tape and bureaucracy police detectives face.

Bruce might be able to find out more information about Jenna Coeur and Jaycee; whether there's a connection between them—and between Jenna and Meredith.

Landry's bag, rolling around behind her, gets caught on a chair leg. It thumps, and Bruce glances up.

He starts to look down again, then double-takes and recognition dawns. "Writer mom," he says, pointing a finger at her. "Landry, right?"

"That's right. How was your family weekend? Are you on the next flight, too?"

"I am. You're early."

"So are you."

"That," he says, "should be your first clue to just how much I enjoyed my family visit."

"I'm sorry."

"It was to be expected. Hope your weekend was better."

"I was at a funeral, so . . ."

"I'm so sorry. I forgot. Your friend." He shakes his head. "That must have been rough."

She nods and tells him, briefly, about the funeral, but that there were other complications.

He raises a dark eyebrow. "What kind of complications?"

Here goes, she thinks, and gestures at the empty seat beside him. "Do you mind if I . . . ?"

"Not at all." He tucks his newspaper into the bag at his feet. "Sit down."

"I just want to ask you a couple of questions. Maybe you can help. You said you're a detective . . ."

"That's right."

"My friend—the one whose funeral this was—she was murdered."

"I'm sorry. What happened?"

She explains, trying to make the tale as uncomplicated as possible and realizing there's no way to boil it down to a simple story. But he listens intently, nodding, leaning closer as the seats around them begin to fill up. She keeps her voice down, particularly when she utters the name anyone would recognize.

"Jenna Coeur?" Bruce echoes, frowning. "The actress? The one who—"

"Right."

"What was she doing there?"

"Nobody seems to know." She takes a deep breath. "I was hoping you might be able to find out."

Chin in hand, he simply waits for her to continue.

She tells him the rest—about the possible connection to Jaycee, about Elena having invited her to the reunion next weekend.

"I'm afraid that I might have inadvertently put my family at risk."

"You can always just cancel this reunion until some other time."

"But they've got plane tickets, and . . . look, I love the two women I met this weekend. There are very few people in this world I can talk to face-to-face about . . . what I've been through, with cancer. And now, about Meredith. We're all facing the same loss. We're all in the same boat. I really want to see them again. But . . ." She takes a deep breath. "I want to hire you. I'd just feel better if you could check out Elena and Kay and confirm that there are no surprises in their backgrounds. They're going to be staying under my roof, with my children in the house. And if you could tell me more about Jaycee, and maybe track down Jenna Coeur in the process—that would be even better."

"Is that it? Find Jenna Coeur? You don't want me to, I don't know, maybe find some long lost relatives while I'm at it? Or, I don't know, find Jimmy Hoffa and Amelia Earhart and maybe Elvis?"

She can't help but smile. "No, that'll do. For now."

He pulls out a notebook and a pen. "I'll do what I can. Tell me everything you know."

She nods, feeling relieved. "It might be better if you took out your laptop. I can show you."

Meredith was supposed to be the first, the last, the only.

Then came that stranger—Roger Lorton, his name turned

out to be. The man who popped up in the wrong place at the wrong time, asking for a light.

They wrote about his murder in the newspaper. Said he was mugged, apparently, while out walking his dog.

No one will ever connect that to Meredith's death . . . or to me.

And this next one . . .

No one is going to connect it, either, because they're not going to be looking for a murderer at all.

No one will ever suspect it didn't just happen.

It's how it should have been, with Meredith.

If only she hadn't been so afraid of needles.

But I respected that; I had to spare her that final ordeal. I tried to make her death as painless—and as quick—as I possibly could.

Maybe it was the wrong choice. There's no way of knowing.

You can't second-guess the past; you can only keep moving ahead.

The same thing will happen with this next target.

It's a simple process of elimination; a step that might be unpleasant to anticipate and carry out, but is absolutely necessary for the greater good.

The thing that really infuriates Tony Kerwin is that all along he was just trying to do Elena a favor—make that *favors*— and how did she turn around and treat him?

Yeah. Like crap.

As he scrubs himself in the shower after his early morning gym workout, he runs through the mental list of everything he's done for her.

She owes him, man. Owes him big-time.

Driving her home on Friday night when she was skunk-drunk—favor number one.

Seeing her safely inside—favor number two.

Granted, maybe he shouldn't have moved in for a kiss, but he just couldn't help himself. The chick is hot. He's been thinking about her ever since he took her out last fall, trying to figure out a way to get her interested in him again. Playing hard to get didn't do the trick, but he was hoping a good hard kiss might.

It did, which led to her bedroom—and favor number three, he thinks with a smirk.

And then favor number four—not commenting after he found the prosthesis in her bra and the angry scar where her breasts should have been. Who knew she was hiding such a deep, dark secret?

"Cancer?" he'd asked when he found it.

Either she pretended not to hear him or she really didn't. She was pretty wasted.

He dropped the subject—for the moment, anyway—and got back down to business—favor number five.

That was followed, the next morning, by favor number six—driving her to the airport up in Boston, and by offering favor number seven—picking her up from the airport last night.

First she flatly—and rudely—refused him, then she avoided his calls all day Saturday. To top things off, by Sunday she had apparently blocked his number on her phone, because every time he tried to call her, he got a recording: "The number you are trying to reach has calling restrictions that have prevented the completion of this call."

It took him a few calls to realize what she'd done, and every time he heard the message—which gave way to an immediate dial tone—he was increasingly infuriated. Not just with her, but with himself. He'd gone out of his way, and for what?

Ungrateful bitch.

Although—he does feel a little better now that he at least knows why she made up that story about having a boyfriend last fall, after he took her out on their one and only date—unless you count Friday night's hookup.

He doesn't.

He's an old-fashioned romantic. He can't help it. He wants to wine and dine her—well, he *wanted* to. Not anymore. Not after the way she treated him.

And here he'd been willing to give her the benefit of the doubt, even after she lied to him back in the beginning.

He'd known all along that she wasn't really seeing someone else. He'd followed her around long enough to know that she was home alone most nights, or out with her friend Sidney.

He'd actually thought she made up having a boyfriend because she was trying to get him to stop asking her out. Now he knows it was obviously because she'd been ill with breast cancer. She probably thought he'd be turned off by that; by her scars.

I wouldn't have been. I would have made her feel beautiful. She didn't give me a chance.

Damn her, anyway.

Now it's Monday morning. He has to go to work and see her there.

Is he looking forward to that?

Hell, no. Good thing this is the last week of school.

He steps out of the shower, rigorously towel dries himself, throws on a pair of shorts, and heads for the kitchen. He'll get dressed for work later. Plenty of time for breakfast in front of the TV, where he'll catch up on the latest Red Sox trade.

Standing at the counter, he peels a couple of bananas and tosses them into the blender for his daily smoothie. Then he adds four raw eggs. Plenty of protein—that's what you need to start the day.

Too bad Elena chose to keep her breast cancer a secret from him. If he had known, he could have been giving her healthy tips like that. He could have had her on a solid fitness regimen and—

Feeling a rush of movement behind him, he starts to turn around, only to feel a piercing jab, like a bee sting, in his neck.

What the hell?

By the time the gloved hand pulls the syringe out of his body and tucks a tortoiseshell comb into the back pocket of his shorts, Tony Kerwin is lying on the floor dying an agonizing death.

Part III

Saturday, June 15

The Day That Changed My Life Forever

I was thirty years old when I got my diagnosis. I had to go see my doctor for test results while I was on my lunch hour at school—his office was right around the corner. I remember wishing it were a hell of a lot farther than that, because I had about a minute to transition from "You have the big C" to "the letter of the day is C."

It was. Can you freaking believe it? The letter of the day was a C.

That's just the way it worked out.

And the whole time I was standing in front of my first-graders that afternoon teaching them that C is for Cat and Car and Cup, I was thinking that C is also for Cancer and also for a whole lot of Curse words that I wanted to scream.

—Excerpt from Elena's blog, *The Boobless Wonder*

Chapter 13

Bright sunshine glints on the tranquil waters of Mobile Bay, beaming hot on Landry's bare arms as she cuts roses in her garden. Saturday morning sounds fill the air: the pleasant buzz of hedge clippers, lawn mowers, motorboats; the neighbor kids; laughter as they romp in the yard; the occasional barking of dogs being walked along the water.

Filling a second large plastic bucket with fragrant pink blooms, Landry needs enough flowers not just for the usual vases in the living and dining room, but also for the kids' rooms where her guests will be staying. Addison can sleep in the master bedroom with her, Tucker on the couch downstairs. They weren't thrilled about the prospect of giving up their rooms, but they'll live.

Right now they're at work. Landry will be leaving for the airport—again—in forty-five minutes.

The first outing was at 5:00 A.M., when she dropped off Rob and his golf clubs for his early flight to North Carolina.

Even after he got out of the car and was hugging her good-bye, he was talking about canceling the trip, worried about leaving her.

"We'll be fine," she kept saying. "I'll have plenty of company all weekend."

"I know. I'd just feel better if—"

"If they weren't 'strangers'?"

"I didn't say it."

"You didn't have to. Look, you've spent every Father's Day with your dad your entire life. He's getting up there in years. You never know how much longer you'll have with him."

With anyone.

"I know," Rob said. "I keep thinking of that. I want to go—I need to go, but—"

"You're going. *Get it-got-it-good.*"

He laughed. "Bossy."

"So are you. I'll see you Monday. Go."

He went.

And her friends are on their way.

Bruce Mangione delved into both Kay and Elena's backgrounds and is ninety-nine-point-nine percent certain that they are who they claim to be. Not a threat to her family's safety.

"Ninety-nine-point-nine?" Landry echoed when he reported that verdict a few days ago. "Not a hundred percent certain?"

"Nothing in this world," he told her, "is a hundred percent certain. Anyone who tells you that it is full of—"

"Okay," she said. "It's okay. I never was worried about the two of them anyway. It's Jaycee who scares me."

"But she isn't coming this weekend, right?"

"No. She never even responded to Elena's invitation."

She took the folder Bruce handed her, filled with documentation showing that Elena and Kay are just Elena and Kay, and she handed him a check.

If she opts not to tell Rob about it, he'll never notice it's missing. She's the one who handles all the finances. Ironic, because he's the one who makes all the money.

But she will tell Rob. Just . . . not yet. Not until this is all behind them.

She may never tell her friends, though—Kay and Elena—
that she hired a private investigator to check out their backgrounds along with Jaycee's. Neither of them has children.
They don't know what it's like to imagine someone under
your roof creeping around the house in the wee hours, capable of . . .

God only knows what.

Jenna Coeur's daughter Olivia was Addison's age when
Jenna presumably stabbed her to death, in her bed, in the
middle of the night.

Jenna is still out there somewhere.

Bruce is still looking for her; looking, too, for solid evidence that Jenna Coeur and Jaycee the blogger are the same
person.

The fact that Jaycee has completely dropped out of sight
since last week would seem to back that theory. She has
yet to resurface in the blogosphere—though as Landry told
Bruce, that's not necessarily unusual. She's never been as
vocal, or as regular, a presence as most of the others.

Still, you'd think she'd want to at least respond to Elena's
update about Meredith's funeral . . .

Unless she was there herself.

Every time she allows her thoughts to go there, Landry
is tempted to cancel the weekend after all. But she won't let
herself do that. The three of them need to be together this
weekend—in person. Now, more than ever.

For Elena, the week held yet another unexpected loss.

On Tuesday night she called Landry to report that Tony
Kerwin, the guy who had been harassing her last weekend,
had dropped dead of a massive heart attack.

"A heart attack? How old was he? I thought he was your
age." Landry's father died the same way, but he was in his
late seventies, overweight, and had been battling heart disease for years, thanks to a fondness for anything deep-fried
and smothered in southern gravy.

"Tony *was* my age," Elena told her. "It was one of those fluke things. He never showed up for work on Monday—which I'll admit made me very happy because I was dreading seeing him, and of course I had no idea anything was wrong. But then today when he didn't come in and didn't call in, I guess someone reported it and the police got the landlord to let them into his apartment. They found him dead on the kitchen floor."

"Oh my God, Elena, I'm so sorry. You must be . . ."

Sad? Guilty? Relieved?

"I don't know how I feel," Elena admitted. "Right now I can't seem to get past the irony that I couldn't stand the guy, and he got to take the easy way out."

"Out of the problems you were having with him?" Landry was incredulous.

"That too, but I meant he took the easy way out of life in general."

"He didn't exactly *choose* to take it, Elena."

"No, I know, but still . . . he didn't have to suffer. One minute he was alive, the next—bam. Never even knew what hit him. Easy way out," she repeated yet again.

Uttered by anyone else, under any other circumstances, the candid comment might have seemed inappropriate. And maybe it was, in a sense. But Landry understood exactly where Elena was coming from.

In the grand scheme of things—particularly in their cancer-riddled, murder-tainted corner of the world—dropping dead of a massive heart attack, while tragic, might be seen as a blessing. There are worse ways to go. Two years ago the doctors assured Landry and her mother that Daddy never suffered a moment's pain, most likely death was instantaneous.

"It's the way he'd have wanted it." Mom literally wept on Landry's shoulder, tears of grief and of gratitude. "He never could have endured knowing that he'd have to leave us. He wouldn't have wanted to know that the last time we saw each other was good-bye forever."

No. That would have been torturous for him.

"Are you *sure* it was a heart attack?" Landry asked Elena—not doubting it, yet not quite able to grasp that something like that could strike someone so young.

"Well, I'm no coroner, but that's what I heard—that it was natural causes. Crazy at his age but he was a fitness freak, so who knows? He probably worked out too hard that morning, or maybe he had an undiagnosed heart condition or something."

Landry suggested that they postpone the weekend get-together in light of Tony's death, but Elena wouldn't hear of it.

"No way. No reason to do that. It's not like he and I were— Look, you know how I felt about him. I couldn't stand the guy. Do I feel bad about the way I talked about him? Kind of, but it's not like he didn't deserve it."

Again, she had a point. Still, it seemed a little cold-hearted . . .

No. Coldhearted—that's Jenna Coeur.

Not Elena.

Elena was tormented by Tony; she considered him a stalker, and maybe that wasn't far off the mark. Landry herself had heard his obnoxious telephone message.

It's tragic whenever someone dies before his—or her—time, but that doesn't erase earthly transgressions or inspire instant forgiveness in those who were wronged by the dearly departed.

"I need this now more than ever," Elena went on, chattering a mile a minute as always, "and I know Kay does, too. We've already got plane tickets—which are nonrefundable, by the way. There's no reason to cancel. The wake is on Thursday. I'll go pay my respects to Tony, teach my last class on Friday, and fly down there on Saturday morning."

So it was settled.

And right now, Landry thought, she only wants—*needs*—to reconnect with the only people in the world who understand what she's going through.

As long as Meredith's murderer doesn't pop up as a surprise guest, everything will be fine.

Which, she's convinced herself—mostly—would be all but impossible.

Then again . . .

Anyone could probably find out where I live, if they really wanted to.

Point Clear is a small town populated by friendly southerners. In order to find Landry, an outsider would only have to mention her first name to anyone here, or even up the road in Fairhope. The well-meaning locals would direct her right to the Wells doorstep, where . . .

Well, what would he—or perhaps more likely *she*—do?

Ring the bell? Ask to come in?

Try to break in? The house has a sophisticated alarm system. There's no way she'd get past it. If she tried, the police would be summoned and be there in a flash.

Or Bruce. She could call him. He has a pistol permit, as he reminded her when she hired him.

"If you need me," he said, "I can come this weekend."

Yeah, it would be fun to explain to her houseguests—and her kids—why the strange man with the gun is lurking around the house.

Everything is going to be fine, just like she assured Rob when she left him at the airport.

And now it's time to turn around and go back to pick up the others. Elena and Kay are connecting from Boston and Indianapolis on the same flight from Atlanta.

Landry puts the clippers into the back pocket of her shorts, picks up the two buckets of roses, and heads inside. She has a little over half an hour to arrange the flowers in vases and finish making the house—and herself—presentable for her guests.

Elena is sitting in a middle seat toward the back of the plane when she sees Kay board at last.

Good. She had expected Kay to miss the connection. The inbound flight from Indianapolis to Atlanta was late, and Kay is cutting it close. The flight attendant closes the door right behind her.

Elena watches her walk down the aisle, looking nervous. Kay keeps glancing over her shoulder, as if someone is going to chase her down and order her off the plane or something.

It's probably because she's not used to flying. She'd confessed earlier that she's only been on planes a couple of times in her life, and not in many years.

Elena tried to prepare her, sending her an e-mail with instructions about how to get through airport security without incident: wear shoes that are easy to take off, have nothing in her pockets, make sure her laptop went through the scanners in its own bin, no liquids in her carry-on but instead placed inside a quart-sized clear plastic bag in containers that are three ounces or less . . .

There are so many rules now, Kay wrote back anxiously.
Don't worry. You'll be fine.

If only they could sit together, Elena thought, but there were only single seats left by the time they booked their tickets.

Too bad Kay didn't get into Atlanta soon enough to join her at the airport bar. After a couple of Bloody Marys, she'd be feeling no pain.

"Kay!" Elena calls as she walks right past without spotting her. "Kay!"

The man next to her, on the aisle, rattles his open newspaper and makes a grouchy sound. Elena ignores him.

Kay stops, glances back, spots her and looks relieved. "Elena! Hi."

"I thought you might miss the flight."

"So did I." Again, she looks over her shoulder.

"Don't worry," Elena tells her. "You made it. They're not going to kick you off now."

"No, I know, it's just . . ."

"Your luggage!" she exclaims, realizing Kay has only a purse over her shoulder. "You didn't do carry-on like I told you?"

"I thought it would be easier to check it."

No doubt because she made Kay fret about all the security procedures.

"It's not a good idea to check bags when you have a connection," she says. "It's really tight because you were late—I bet your bag didn't make it on."

Kay looks even more distressed.

Elena backpedals: "Don't worry. I'm sure they'll get it on the next flight. No big deal. You need to relax. You look like you're going to keel over again. Your luggage will be—"

"No, it's not that. I just thought I saw . . . never mind."

"What?"

The man beside Elena clears his throat and turns a page of his newspaper.

Yeah, yeah. I get it. We're pissing you off, sir. I don't really care.

"What did you think you saw?" Elena persists.

"Ma'am, please take your seat so that we can make an on time departure!" the flight attendant calls from up front.

In response, Kay moves toward the only open seat on the plane: a middle seat against the back wall of the passenger's cabin, across from the bathroom. Elena is well aware that the passengers in her own row—either the grouchy man on the aisle or the morbidly obese woman by the window—will not make a last minute switch and sit in Kay's seat instead, so that she can sit up here. And chances are, the people sharing Kay's row would prefer their window and aisle seats to a middle seat a few rows ahead. Particularly with an open newspaper taking up a good portion of Elena's seat on one side, and the oversized woman's flesh spilling into it on the other.

Unable to wait until they land for Kay to explain, Elena says to her retreating back, "What did you think you saw?"

Kay turns just briefly, allowing Elena to connect with the disturbed look in her eyes. "You know. *Her*. In the airport. Just now."

"Her . . . who?"

"J . . . C," is the chilling reply, before Kay hurries back to take her seat.

Hollywood, Crystal Burns has come to realize, is more efficient at keeping secrets than the FBI and CIA combined.

All week, she and Frank have been trying to track down Jenna Coeur; all week, they've been coming up with dead ends.

An online search revealed that plenty of people have reported sighting her since her acquittal—mainly in New York City and Los Angeles, as you'd expect. Most seem legitimate. Other sightings, as you'd expect, are clearly bogus.

One nut job believes that she was an alien queen who has since shape-shifted herself into the secretary of state. Another—some loser on a porn message board—claims that Jenna Coeur has resurfaced in a film called *Schlong Island Getaway*.

Naturally, Frank volunteered to check out that one, just to be sure.

"It's not her," he reported, "but you wouldn't believe what she does in the final scene. She—"

"I don't want to hear it, thank you very much. And I can't believe you watched the whole thing."

"I fast-forwarded most of it."

"Terrific, Frank."

Now, on a sunny Saturday morning, Frank is busy attending his youngest's kindergarten graduation ceremony, with Crystal's wholehearted blessing.

And here she sits, sifting and resifting her way through the mountain of information she's collected about Jenna Coeur and Jaycee the blogger—one and the same person, as far as she's concerned.

That theory was cemented by the fact that Jaycee is clearly no ordinary blogger. The cyber crimes unit is involved in the investigation now, backtracking through every trace she left online, but so far they've turned up no hard evidence. A lot of people are careful, trying to preserve their online anonymity, but she's taken great pains to cover her tracks on the Internet.

Crystal checked out of the Los Angeles hotel where Jaycee placed last Wednesday's call to Landry Wells. No one recalls having seen Jenna Coeur there; the room connected to the outgoing call to Landry's number was occupied by a walk-in guest who registered as Jane Johnson and paid in cash. Naturally, in Hollywood, that kind of thing doesn't raise an eyebrow. The hotel's lobby security camera footage shows a slender woman in a large hat and sunglasses who seemed to keep her face deliberately turned away from the cameras. She could very well be Jenna Coeur—or any white-hot starlet seeking to be incognito.

Then there's Wasabi Express on the Upper East Side of Manhattan. The fact that Jaycee rattled off the number, according to Landry Wells, would seem to indicate that it's one she knows by heart. But no one who works at the restaurant recalls ever having seen, let alone ever even having heard of, Jenna Coeur. Not surprising. It's a busy counter place; all of their business is either takeout or delivery to various high rises. She could have used any alias and left the money for her order with her doorman; chances are the delivery kid never had any contact with her, not unusual in that well-heeled neighborhood.

There are hundreds, thousands, of residential buildings

on the Upper East Side. Canvassing all those doormen is a daunting task that looms high on Crystal's agenda, along with countless others. It's conceivable that Jenna Coeur has been living in one of them, safely tucked away in a tower and unnoticed, for years now. After all, she had money. Tens of millions, even after paying for her legal defense team.

And there you have it: the core difference between Jenna Coeur and Diaphanous Jones, now serving life in prison for the murder of her own child.

Money.

It can't buy everything, but the acquitted actress seems to have proven that it can sure as hell buy freedom—and a safe place to hide, where no one would ever find you.

No one but me.

Staring at the frozen image on her computer screen, showing a beautiful woman with huge, haunted eyes, Crystal shakes her head.

Look out, because I swear to God that I will track you down before you hurt anyone else. This time, you'll get away with murder over my dead body.

"And what would you like to order, sir?" Beck asks her nephew Jordan, seated at the kitchen table with his legs dangling from the chair.

"I'll have the bugs with a side order of . . . um . . . more bugs!"

"Yes, sir." She scribbles on the pad in her hand, the same one her mother used when she pretended to be a waitress. She located it in a kitchen drawer after Jordan asked her if they were going to play restaurant like Grammy always did.

"Of course we are," she assured him, and found the pad, along with a box of pancake mix and half a bag of mini chocolate chips in the cupboard.

She gladly said yes last night when her brother Teddy called to ask if she'd keep an eye on Jordan for a while this morning. He was driving down to help Dad deal with some insurance paperwork, and wanted to leave his pregnant wife alone at home to get some rest.

Beck had been planning to drive home this morning to deal with her life and was glad for an excuse to put that off until tomorrow. When she called Keith to tell him she wouldn't be back until Sunday, he, too, seemed relieved. Their daily conversations have been perfunctory, cementing her realization that the marriage has run its course.

"All right, sir," she looks at her nephew over the pad of paper, pencil poised, "you say you'd like the bugs with a side of bugs. Would you like the bug sauce on that?"

Jordan screams with laughter. "Yes, please!"

Smiling, Beck puts the pad aside and hands over a coloring book and crayons to keep him busy while she cooks.

At the stove, she drops a few pats of butter onto the hot griddle.

Watching it ooze to liquid, she thinks about Keith.

The thought of ending their marriage—and the inevitable mess that will entail—is overwhelming right now.

Maybe they can keep going through the motions for another couple of months—or even just weeks—until she finds the strength to do what has to be done.

She pours pancake batter onto the griddle and carefully dots each pool with chocolate chips to create eyes, a nose, a smiling mouth.

There. Just like Mom used to do.

So many happy memories . . .

So many difficult moments over the past two weeks, and many more ahead.

For all she knows, Keith is going to hit her with separation papers when she walks in the door. Well, at least she won't be doing that today.

She still hasn't figured out how she's supposed to leave her father here alone.

Both her brothers have offered to take turns staying here with him in the weeks ahead. But they both have kids at home, and Neal has to work, and Teddy has to look for work . . .

She also has a job to get back to. She told her boss she'd be back Monday morning. But she could ostensibly commute to Lexington for a while. Or . . . forever.

Sooner or later her father is going to have to learn to live alone.

So, for that matter, is she.

"I'll be fine. Go home to your husband," Dad told her last night, picking the carrots out of the stew she'd made him. She'd forgotten that Mom always left them out; Dad can't stand cooked carrots.

Does Louise know that?

The errant thought popped into Beck's head out of nowhere. She hated herself for it. All week, she'd been trying to banish the idea that her father might have had an affair, an affair that might have led him to—

It's preposterous.

But . . .

I'd appreciate it if you didn't mention this to Mom. I don't want her to worry. You know how she is.

At the time, it hadn't even occurred to Beck that there might have been reasons other than the one he gave.

Even now, knowing that Mom was sick again, that her cancer had spread . . .

It makes even more sense that Dad would be trying to protect Mom from any kind of stress.

And it would be right in character for him to meet with a financial advisor without her knowledge.

Their marriage was always kind of old-fashioned in that way. Dad handled money matters, driving, lawn care, household repairs. Mom covered the cooking and laundry and decorating, the kids and school . . .

"Aunt Beck?"

"Hmm?" She looks up to see Jordan watching her.

"I miss Grammy."

Sodden grief crashes in, barely allowing her to push out the words, "Me too."

"I wish she didn't get sick and die."

That's what Teddy and Sue opted to tell him, wanting to shield their innocent child from the terrible truth.

Keith disapproved of the lie, but who is he to judge? He's not Jordan's parent. Not a parent at all.

To think that she had assumed he'd be the father of her children one day . . .

Mom had assumed the same thing, having told her, on Mother's Day, as Keith gave a long, scientific answer to some question Jordan had asked, "He's going to be a good daddy someday."

No, he isn't, Beck wanted to say. *All Jordan needed to hear was a simple yes or a no, not this complicated lecture.*

Now, as her nephew watches her with big, sad eyes, she blinks back tears, hoping he doesn't start asking her questions that can't be answered with a simple yes or no.

"Aunt Beck?"

"Hmm?"

"I think the bugs are burning."

"What?"

He points at the skillet behind her, and she turns to see it smoking.

With a silent curse, she scrapes the charred pancakes into the garbage and starts over as Jordan goes back to his coloring book.

This time she watches the griddle carefully, keeping thoughts of Keith and her mother and her father—and Louise—from distracting her.

A few minutes later she's delivering a plate of perfectly cooked smiley-faced pancakes, doused in maple syrup, to the table. "Your bugs, sir, with a side of more bugs and bug sauce on the top."

"Aunt Beck! That's not how it goes! You're s'posed to call it the stinkerdoodle special!"

"I'm sorry, sir," she says with a grin. "Enjoy your . . ."

Stinkerdoodle.

That's it!

"Aunt Beck! Where are you going?" he protests as she sets the plate in front of him and bolts from the room.

"I'll be right back, sweetie. I just have to grab my laptop."

"Ladies and gentlemen, we're expecting a few bumps on the ascent and there's some stormy weather along the panhandle, but we'll do our best to find as smooth a ride as possible. We're next for takeoff. Flight attendants, please be seated."

As the plane hurtles down the runway, Kay grips the arms of her seat and squeezes her eyes closed.

She should have driven. Highway driving—once she got used to it again during all those hours on the road last weekend—had turned out to be soothing.

Flying is the opposite.

Her heart is pounding; her head is pounding, too. Her entire body aches, further evidence that stress—sheer terror—can take a drastic physical toll on a person.

The plane lifts into the air, and she holds her breath.

A bell dings in the cabin.

Kay's eyes fly open.

Does it mean they're going down?

No one else seems to be agitated—except Elena, who is jumping to her feet a few rows ahead. The man in the outer seat doesn't look pleased as he rises to let her out into the aisle, but Elena doesn't seem to care. She hurries back toward Key, gesturing for her, too, to stand up.

Kay glances up at the FASTEN SEAT BELT sign, still lit on the panel above the seats.

"It's okay," Elena tells her.

The woman seated to Kay's left, blocking her access to the aisle, stays put, shaking her head in disapproval.

"She has to go to the bathroom," Elena tells the woman.

"How would you know?"

Elena rolls her eyes impatiently. "Would you mind letting her up, please?"

"It's okay," Kay tries to tell her. "I don't need to—"

"Yes, you do. Come on, Kay."

A flight attendant steps out of the galley behind them just as Kay's seatmate stands to let her out. "Ladies," he says, "the seat belt light is still on. It's not safe for you to move around the cabin right now. Please be seated."

Kay expects Elena to argue, but to her credit, she doesn't.

"I'm sorry," Kay tells the woman beside her as they settle back into their seats.

No reply.

Jaw set, Kay leans back stiffly to endure the flight, hands clenched in her lap in an effort to stop the trembling.

The woman in the window seat to her right—young, wearing an engagement ring and reading a bridal magazine, a whole rosy future ahead of her—glances at her. "Nervous flier?" she asks sympathetically.

Kay nods. "Afraid so."

"Me too."

"You don't seem nervous."

"I took a Xanax. You want one?"

"Oh . . . no, thanks."

"I'm going to visit my fiancé. He's in the Coast Guard down there, and as much as I hate flying, I'd do anything for him. How about you?"

"I'm going to spend the weekend with friends, and actually . . . I'd do anything for them, too."

They smile at each other. Then the bride-to-be goes back to her magazine, and Kay breathes a little easier. Just a little.

* * *

Cory picks up on the first ring. "Where are you?"

"Where do you think?"

"Airport, I hope."

"Yes. Where else would I be?" Jaycee keeps her voice low and her back turned to the other passengers milling around near the Starbucks. As soon as she finishes this call, she's going to get a strong cup of coffee. Between her sleepless night, the flight, and what lies ahead, she's going to need it.

"Just making sure you made it. I was afraid you were going to back out."

So was I, she thinks, but she doesn't tell Cory that. No reason to get him all worried for nothing. She's going ahead with it, like she promised. She's been resigned to doing what she has to do—well, to what Cory's been telling her she has to do—for a while now.

Funny—the lyrics to the old "Going on a Lion Hunt" role play game she learned years ago in Girl Scouts are going through her head again lately.

Can't go over it . . . can't go under it . . . can't go around it . . . gotta go through it.

The same refrain was endlessly on her mind when she was pregnant twenty-odd years ago, knowing there was no escaping the looming horror of childbirth, the trauma of adoption.

Gotta go through it.

She was going to have to deliver that baby, and she was going to have to give it up.

Funny, too . . . She'd initially resisted when Steven tried to talk her into terminating.

Years later, when the screaming, bloody human mess she'd delivered into this world left it in the same state, she wished she'd listened to him in the first place.

"Go ahead!" Olivia shrieked. "Do it! I dare you! I dare you!"

Jaycee squeezes her eyes shut for a moment to block out the memory.

Then she assures Cory, "I'm not backing out. Don't worry."

"Good. This is all in your best interest. You know that, right?"

"I'm not so sure I agree, but it's too late to back out now anyway."

"Call me when you get there so that I can give you a pep talk if you feel—"

"I said I'll do it."

"Good," he says. "Because a big, bold move is your only way out of this. You know that, right?"

Of course she does. She's known it for a while now. Eighteen months, to be exact. That was when he first approached her with this crazy idea.

Since then, the idea has morphed into an actual plan. Laying the groundwork has been a painstaking two-steps-forward, three-steps-back endeavor. But at last it's time for full-blown execution.

It's now or never, as they say.

"I've got to go," she tells Cory. "I'm desperate for coffee."

She glances again toward the Starbucks and locks eyes with a stranger at the end of the line. He doesn't look away. Casual interest? Or did he somehow, despite her sunglasses and wig—this time an auburn one—recognize her?

Not taking any chances, she walks away, phone still pressed to her ear as Cory signs off with a benign— considering what she's facing, "Good luck."

"Good luck?" she echoes. "Gee, thanks." She hangs up, shaking her head.

Good luck . . .

Hasn't luck always been on her side? Ever since she left Minnesota and Johanna Hart behind, anyway. Even after she became Jenna Coeur . . . especially after she became Jenna Coeur.

By a stroke of luck, she became one of the biggest movie stars in the world; by a stroke of luck . . .

You basically got away with murder.

There's no reason to think her luck is going to change now.

It's going to be okay, Jaycee tells herself, turning off her phone and tucking it back into her pocket. *You've got this. You can do it. Whatever it takes.*

Sheri Lorton is jerked to consciousness by something wet swiping at her face. Startled, she opens her eyes to see that the puppy, Maggie, is licking her cheek.

She starts to laugh and call out to Roger, then remembers, and the laugh ends in a sob.

He's gone.

She's alone.

Alone, except for this crazy dog.

"I'm sorry, girl. You need to go out, don't you? And I slept late."

Ironic that she went from not sleeping at all last week, in the immediate aftermath of her husband's death, to feeling as though all she's wanted to do this week is sleep.

Probably because she forced herself to go back to work on Monday morning. It's not as though they can't get along without her at the campus admissions office where she works. They told her to take as much time off as she needed.

But what else was there for her to do? Sit around the house and cry?

It was the right decision. Back on campus, she was busy when she wanted to be, and when emotions overwhelmed her—which they did, frequently—she could cry on the shoulders of colleagues who had known Roger. It got a little easier later in the week, until she went on an errand that took her past the Academic quadrangle where his office was located. She lost it, and vowed to take the long way around from now on. Probably forever.

Every day after work she came home, walked and fed the dog, and then fell into bed and into a deep, dreamless sleep until the alarm went off at six.

Today, of course, it didn't go off.

Poor Maggie.

Sheri pets the dog, then hurriedly follows her down the stairs and opens the back door to let her out into the sun-dappled yard.

If only Roger had done that on the fateful morning that shouldn't have been his last. But he didn't think it was fair for a puppy to be limited to the confines of a small fenced yard.

"She needs the exercise," he'd told her, "and so do I. You're always telling me I need to get into shape, build up some muscle . . ."

She didn't point out that walking wasn't going to turn her scrawny husband into a he-man anytime soon. Any physical activity at all was probably a good thing, she thought at the time. Even strolling while smoking.

Standing at the sink, filling the glass coffeepot with water, Sheri finds herself thinking, again, of the tortoiseshell guitar pick found among her husband's belongings.

It's been in the back of her mind ever since she decided it would probably be a good idea to at least mention it to the police. But the week got away from her; she's been too caught up in mourning, working, and sleeping to do anything about it.

Today, she decides, turning off the tap and dumping the water into the coffeemaker. *I'll do it today.*

Thanksgiving Gratitude

Today most of us will gather around tables with loved ones, stuff ourselves with heaps of home-cooked food, and give thanks for our blessings.

Me? I'll be sitting alone in my kitchen eating a turkey sandwich, most likely, same as I do every year. But don't feel sorry for me. I have plenty to be grateful for. My health, with continued remission, tops the list. All of you, my good friends, are right up there, too—along with the incredible, unexpected education I've gained late in life.

Since my diagnosis, it sometimes seems that I've learned everything there is to know about breast cancer—about the disease itself. But there have been other lessons along the way: lessons I learned once I started blogging, precious lessons you have taught me.

I learned how similar we all are, despite having different backgrounds. And how very different we all are, despite sharing similar postdiagnosis experiences.

Thanks to you, I've had my eyes opened to the shameful inequity in fund-raising.

I've come to know very little progress has been made in finding a cure for metastatic breast cancer, and that early detection is by no means a cure.

I've learned that although I live by myself, and

spend most of my days and nights in solitude, I'm far from alone. I've learned that I can care deeply—and yes, even love—people I've never met. With that, I've gained not just friendship, but also something I never imagined: the return of a childlike wonder for the world around me, so foreign to my own midwestern city. Beyond my house in Indianapolis are places I now want to explore because someone in our cyber community has brought it to life.

I want to watch a marching band do formations on the football field at a huge southern college and peek inside the graceful old houses of sorority row.

I want to sit on a rocky beach beside a lighthouse and watch the sun rise over the Atlantic ocean, and I want to eat lobster pulled out of the sea just minutes ago.

I want to buy a hot dog from a street cart in New York City and check out the view of Central Park from the top of a skyscraper.

I want to cheer for the home team in the stands at the Great American Ballpark and taste Skyline chili.

I want to fly across the ocean to England and see a real castle and Big Ben and London Bridge.

And so today, and every day, I'm grateful for the blogging friends that have stopped along the way, read my words, shared their own and broadened my small world. Who would have thought writing about cancer could do that?

—Excerpt from Kay's blog, *I'm A-Okay*

Chapter 14

Something's wrong, Landry realizes, watching Kay and Elena walking out into the airport terminal, clearly in the midst of a weighty discussion.

Well—a one-sided discussion: Elena, pulling a wheeled carry-on bag, seems to be doing all the talking. And whatever she's talking about has them both so absorbed that they don't even remember to look around for her.

"Guys," she calls, "over here."

Distracted, they glance over, wave, and head toward her—Elena in such a hurry that she nearly bowls over several leisurely southerners on the way. Landry senses that her rush has nothing to do with being glad to see her again, and everything to do with whatever they were talking about.

"Kay just saw her in the airport," Elena blurts, then catches herself and leans in for a hug. "Sorry. Hi. Thank you so much for coming to get us, for having us . . . I'm sorry, I didn't mean to be—"

"What is going on?"

Still hugging her, Elena whispers in her ear, "Jenna Coeur. Kay saw her."

"What?" Landry's heart skips a beat. "Where?"

"At the airport."

She jerks back, looking around.

"Not this airport. In Atlanta."

Catching up to them, Kay asks, "Did she tell you?"

Landry nods numbly. "You saw her at the airport?"

"I *thought* I saw her. I'm not a hundred percent sure."

Of course not. Nothing, according to Bruce, is a hundred percent certain. But . . .

"What was she doing? Was she on your flight?"

"No!"

"Are you sure?"

"Yes. That, I'm sure about. The woman I saw—if it was her—she was still sitting in the gate area when I got on the plane, and I was the last one to board."

"They closed the door right after Kay," Elena confirms. "Did she see you see her?" she asks Kay.

"I don't think so."

"What made you think it was Jenna Coeur?" Landry asks.

"She looked like the woman in the picture Detective Burns showed me on Saturday."

"But she didn't get on this flight," Landry can't help saying—again—as her gaze flicks uneasily at the other passengers coming from the gate area.

"No, she didn't," Kay assures her. "Don't worry about that."

"Every seat was taken," Elena tells Landry. "I'm thinking she must have been on standby. She's probably on the next flight from Atlanta."

"There are a few more, this afternoon and tonight." Landry knows the schedule. She took one of those flights herself, on Sunday. With Bruce Mangione.

I have to call Bruce.

Right now.

I have to tell him—

"Kay, I think you should let Detective Burns know." Elena says interrupting Landry's thoughts. "She gave me her personal cell phone number. I plugged it into my phone."

"I have it, too," Kay says, "but I'm not even positive it *was* Jenna Coeur, so—"

"You're trying to talk yourself out of it."

"Maybe I am," Kay tells Elena, "but . . . I mean, I *thought* it was her. It probably wasn't."

But if it was . . .

If Jenna Coeur is on her way to Alabama . . .

Then what? Do you honestly believe she's coming here to kill you all?

The thought is preposterous.

Still . . .

"Detective Burns needs to know anyway," Landry says. "Do you want *me* to call her?" She, too, has the detective's personal cell phone number.

"No. I can make the call."

"Then I'm going to go to the ladies' room," Elena announces. "I've had to go since we left Atlanta, but they left the seat belt sign on the whole way and the flight attendant wouldn't let me get up."

"I thought you just wanted to talk to me," Kay tells her.

"I did, but I also had to pee. I drank a couple of . . . cups of coffee during the layover. I'll meet you guys by the baggage claim. Kay checked a bag," she adds, to Landry.

"Sorry." Kay shakes her head. "I should have done carry-on like Elena said, but I haven't flown in a long time and there are so many rules now . . . I was a little intimidated."

"I just hope your bag made the connection," Elena tells her, "and I'm really glad Jenna Coeur didn't."

Apparently overhearing the familiar name, a nearby middle-aged couple turns their heads as they walk past, shooting Elena a curious look.

At Landry's belated "Shhh!" Elena whispers, "Sorry. I'm used to speaking loudly and enunciating for my first graders. I'll be down at baggage in a few minutes."

She disappears into the ladies' room, leaving Landry and Kay to regard each other anxiously.

"What do you think is going on?" Kay asks.

"You're the one who saw her. I don't know what to think."

"I thought it was her, in that moment. I really did. But now I keep wondering if I was just imagining things."

"Deep down . . . do you think that's all it was? Just your imagination?"

Kay hesitates, then shakes her head, eyes wide. "She's coming here, isn't she?"

"I hope not. I really do. Call Detective Burns. I'm going to call my husband."

"To tell him about this?"

"What? No! I just want to . . . make sure he landed. I'll meet you over at the baggage claim in a few minutes."

"Okay. Where is it?"

Landry points in the right direction, then hurries away, already reaching for her own cell phone.

She doesn't dial until she's slipped into a distant, shadowy, relatively private corner of the terminal.

He picks up on the first ring.

Not Rob. Rob can't help her right now; he's seven hundred miles away.

"Bruce Mangione."

She takes a deep breath. "I think I'm in trouble. Big trouble. I need your help."

Use a made-up word you wouldn't find in the dictionary, not a name or initials . . .

When Beck remembers the advice she gave to her mother—and realizes Mom took it—she wonders how she possibly could have missed the password until now.

Then again, when the worst tragedy imaginable has struck the person you love more than almost anyone—no, more than *anyone*—in the world, is it any wonder that your mind is too grief-clouded for logic?

But now all that matters is that she's guessed it correctly at last.

It took her a while, even after she figured out that *stinkerdoodle* was the password, because the word was only part of it. She had to remember the rest of the advice she'd given her mother.

Substitute a digit for a letter—a zero for an O—or replace it with a symbol, like the at symbol for an A, or a dollar sign for an S . . .

If you use the phone number, put the digits in reverse . . .

Mom had done all of the above. The password is *$tinkerd00dle5697.*

Open Sesame . . .

At last granted access to her mother's e-mail account, she begins scrolling through the mail folders, hoping to find everything intact: old mail, sent mail . . .

"Aunt Beck?"

"Mmm-hmm?" She looks up to see Jordan tearing a page out of his coloring book.

"I made this for you."

"Oh, Jordan . . ." She swallows hard and gathers him close, examining the picture and complimenting him on the beautiful colors and the way he'd tried to stay inside the lines. "Great job, sweetie."

"You can hang it on the fridge like Grammy used to."

"I will." She stands and crosses over to the refrigerator, looking for a magnet that isn't already holding up a grandchild's artwork.

"No, I meant your fridge at your house."

"Oh. I will. I'll do that." *Just as soon as I figure out where my house is going to be.*

"Aunt Beck? Can I watch TV now? Please?"

Well aware that his parents limit his screen time, Beck is

pretty sure she should say no. Instead she says "Absolutely," her thoughts consumed by her mother's e-mail account— and what she might find there.

Standing at the baggage claim with Kay and the other passengers from their flight, Elena looks at her watch. "Why is this taking so long?"

"You're in the South now. Everything probably takes a little longer," Kay tells her. "Just be patient."

"Patience isn't exactly my thing."

"Really?" Kay asks dryly, watching Elena pace until at last there's a buzzing noise and the conveyer jerks into motion.

Bags—none belonging to Kay—begin to topple down the chute.

"I think the connection was too tight," Elena tells her as one passenger after another grabs luggage and rolls it away. "I bet your bag didn't make it."

"Don't say that! I need it!"

"You should have carried on, like I told—"

"There it is!"

Looking triumphant, Kay hurries forward to grab a small black carry-on that could have easily been stowed above—or even beneath—an airplane seat.

Elena fights the urge to chide her again. The bag made it. That's all that matters, right?

"Now all we need is Landry," she mutters. Then, seeing the look on Kay's face, she adds, "Patience. I know, I know. I need patience."

That, and a nice big, strong drink to relax my nerves.

She paces again.

At last Landry hurries around the corner, phone in hand. "Oh, good! You got your bag, Kay! Are y'all set to go?"

"More than set," Elena can't help saying pointedly.

"Sorry my phone call took so long," Landry tells her.

"He's at work, so it took a few minutes for them to track him down."

"I thought he was in North Carolina."

"No, my husband is in North Carolina."

"Isn't that who you went to call?"

"Is that what I said? I meant my son." Landry gives a flustered little laugh.

"I bet it's easy to get them mixed up, now that Tucker is growing up," Kay tells her.

Elena says nothing at all, regarding Landry through narrowed eyes.

What if something strange is going on here?

What if I just walked into some kind of trap?

Landry is the one who, last weekend, had so much to say about the potential for Internet imposters. What if she, herself, is one of them?

Elena studies her now as they walk out to the parking lot. She's fiddling with her car keys, checking her cell phone every couple of seconds.

"Are you waiting for a call back or something?" she asks.

"What? Oh, no . . . just checking the time."

Right. She's wearing a wristwatch.

An expensive one, Elena noticed earlier. She certainly looks like the wife of a fancy lawyer.

But what if she's not?

"Do you want to try to reach Detective Burns again?" Landry asks Kay.

"We should probably just wait for her to get back to us."

"I can't believe it's taking this long. Are you sure you called the right number? She said she always picks up."

"I know, but she didn't. I left a message for her to call as soon as she can. I'm sure she will."

Landry nods, clearly on edge.

They exit the airport into the glare of heat so humid that

Elena feels as though she's trying to breathe through a sop-
ping towel pressed against her mouth and nose.

"Wow. It's hot here," Kay observes, and the needless
comment gets on Elena's nerves. Everything is getting on
her nerves right now. Her friends' languid pace as they cross
the blacktop, the trickling tickle of sweat on her hairline,
the weight of the bag she's pulling along, the fact that she's
here at all.

At last they reach a black BMW. Landry aims the key
chain to unlock the doors, then opens all four of them and
starts the engine with the air-conditioning blasting. She
loads their bags into the trunk but tells them not to get into
the car yet. "Let's wait a minute for it to cool off. It's an oven
in there."

It's an oven out here, too. They wait in silence.

Then Elena asks, "Do you really think Jenna Coeur is
planning to blindside us?"

She wants them both to say it's ridiculous.

Neither does.

"Why else would she come down here?" Landry is grim.

"If it really was her . . . then maybe it's a coincidence,"
Kay says.

"You believe in coincidences?"

Kay hesitates. "No."

"Me neither." Landry bites her lip and shakes her head,
looking down at her phone yet again.

"I do," Elena tells them with a shrug. "I'm not saying this
is one of them, but I believe in—"

She breaks off as Landry's cell phone rings.

"There's a coincidence now," Kay says. "You were looking at your phone, and it rang."

Not really a coincidence, Elena thinks, since Landry has
done nothing but look at her phone, clearly expecting a call.

"I've got to take this." She hurriedly motions them to get
into the car. "Go ahead. Get in. It's cooled off."

It hasn't.

But Elena and Kay climb in and Landry closes their doors after them, sealing them into the oven. Still outside, she answers her phone as she closes the driver's side door.

Elena hears her say, "Addie? Listen, I need you to do something for me . . ."

In the front seat, Elena turns to look at Kay in the back.

"Addie," Kay observes. "That's her daughter. Addison."

Yeah. No kidding.

Biting back the sarcasm, swallowing her craving for a calming drink, Elena says only, "She's really freaked out that you saw Jenna Coeur in the airport."

"Maybe I just thought it was her."

"What, are you thinking you're delusional or something?"

"No! I just—I didn't get a close enough look to be sure. Maybe . . ." Kay shrugs and rubs her forehead, as though it's hurting her. "I don't know. I could have been wrong."

"I hope you were."

A minute later Landry is back, climbing into the driver's seat with a strained smile. "Ready to go?"

They paste on their own smiles and tell her that they are.

The Day My Life Changed Forever

Back when I was an English major in college and planning to become a writer one day, I read a lot of poems. One of my favorites was Robert Frost's "The Road Not Taken." It begins:

Two roads diverged in a yellow wood, And sorry I could not travel both . . .

I went many years without remembering that poem—decades spent being a wife and mother and day care provider, but not a writer. Not yet. I figured there would be plenty of time to reclaim that childhood dream and make it a reality when I retired, when my children were grown and out of the house . . .

Then came the day I found myself sitting in a doctor's office as he delivered the bombshell I never expected to hear.

I had breast cancer? Me?

Two roads diverged . . .

The old poem barged back into my brain and hasn't left since. The road not taken has new meaning when you're faced with a life-threatening illness and you realize you might never have time to do all the things you once wanted to accomplish.

Chances are, you wouldn't have done them anyway. Chances are, you stopped wanting to do them years ago. But until you got sick, they were still out there, floating randomly in the realm of pos-

sibility. Now they'd been snatched out of reach, but somehow you knew your life had been purposeful and well-lived even if you never become a Pulitzer prize winning author or even a college poetry professor. Just living—that was meaningful enough.

As I sat that day listening to my doctor describe the journey that lay before me and the decisions I would have to make, I wanted nothing more than to backtrack to the happy, simple days I'd left behind. But that, unfortunately, wasn't one of my choices. Neither was stopping in my tracks and doing nothing at all. There was only one option: choose a path, keep forging ahead, and do my best to never, ever second-guess the road not taken.

—Excerpt from Meredith's blog, *Pink Stinks*

Chapter 15

Landry was planning to serve lunch—tea sandwiches and fruit salad—in the air-conditioned dining room. Behind locked doors.

The others overruled her, though. They'd prefer to be outside—in the "fresh air," as Kay calls it, apparently having missed the memo that no such thing exists at high noon on a Deep South summer's day. Not even here on the porch, where the ceiling fan does its best to diffuse the afternoon heat that swaddles like a wet towel, allowing not even a breath of breeze off the water to stir the live oak boughs that shade the yard.

Torpor has fallen over the world beyond the porch railing. In the rose garden, fat bumblebees barely seem capable of moving from blossom to blossom. Out on the water, a mere smattering of this morning's fishing boats remain and there isn't a kayaker in sight. It's too hot for paddling. Or pedaling, though occasionally a pair of flushed-looking tourists will pass on bicycles that seem to move more languidly, even, than the bumblebees.

Sweat rolls down the back of Landry's neck as she fills tall green glasses of sweet tea and decorates each with a sprig of fresh green mint. She sets the coordinating green pitcher down beside the vase of pale pink roses she carried out on a tray from the kitchen with a stack of china plates, linen place mats, and napkins.

"You don't have to go to all this fuss," Elena protested as Landry set the outside table as nicely as she'd have set the one in the dining room.

"I want to. Y'all are my guests."

The well-bred belle in her won't forget that, even now.

But that's fine. All she has to do is get through one moment at a time. Not so difficult, really, now that she knows her kids will be safely out of the house—and harm's way—for the remainder of the weekend.

That was her first instinct all along. She should have gone with it, instead of having to put a contingency plan into place when she found out that Jenna Coeur might be on her way here.

Her first phone call—after Bruce—was to Everly. She knew her friend would take both kids overnight, no questions asked.

But Everly didn't pick up at home, and when she answered her cell sounding too groggy for eleven o'clock even on a Saturday morning, Landry belatedly remembered her friend had gone away for Father's Day weekend, visiting her widowed dad who retired to Hawaii years ago.

"Is everything all right?" she asked Landry, reading the tension in her voice.

"Everything's fine."

"I don't believe you."

"I just needed a quick favor, but it's not a problem, I can ask someone else."

Her mother, or Barbie June. Neither fell into the no-questions-asked category, though.

She had lunch with her mother two days ago, feeling as though she'd been neglecting her, and was grateful when Mom mentioned her busy weekend ahead, taking a senior bus trip to Mobile to see the Saturday matinee of a touring musical, with dinner afterward.

Ardelle Quackenbush is the kind of woman who would drop everything in a heartbeat to be there for her family; Landry knows she'd insist on missing the show just to be on standby for teenagers with weekend plans of their own. Nor does she want to inflict upon the kids her mother's early bedtime and house cluttered with fragile antiques that must not be touched.

She correctly guessed that her cousin—also a well-bred belle—would graciously accept overnight guests in a heartbeat despite feeling neglected lately, as long as Landry framed the favor properly: "Sweetie, how would you like to put those two beautiful guest rooms of yours to good use tonight? We have company this weekend and the kids have to give up their beds, and of course they'd much rather sleep at Aunt Barbie June's than share the pullout here at home."

Next she texted the kids at work and told them both to call her during their breaks. Neither was thrilled to be shuttled off to Aunt Barbie June's for the night but they grudgingly agreed.

Now only she is here to face whatever is going to happen next.

Hopefully nothing at all. Bruce is at the airport, waiting for the next flight from Atlanta. Waiting for Jenna Coeur.

If she's on it.

Landry passes the platter of sandwiches, the bowl of fruit salad, and keeps the conversation going. She asks Elena about the last few days of school. Wants to—but doesn't— ask Kay again about the woman she saw in the airport.

Wants to tell her to try calling Detective Burns yet again, even though she's overheard Elena encouraging Kay to do that as well—twice—since they got back from the airport. The first time, as they headed upstairs to settle into their rooms, Kay replied that she'd wait another half hour before calling again; the second time, as they took their places at the lunch table, Kay told Elena she'd just left another message.

If she hadn't spoken to Bruce already, Landry thought, she'd probably be leaving messages of her own for Detective Burns.

"Look, it's not as urgent as you think," he told her when she brought it up in a whispered phone call from the laundry room before lunch. "There's not much she can do with the information except follow up on it the way she would any other potential Jenna Coeur sighting. She needs to know, but I can pretty much guarantee you that she's not going to jump on the next flight to Alabama—especially since you said your friend isn't even positive it was her."

He's right. They're all preoccupied and jumpy.

"Hang in there. I'm at the airport and I'm not budging until that flight arrives from Atlanta. She won't get past me. You can all relax."

"I haven't told them about you yet."

"You might want to."

"I will," she promised, but has yet to do it. Maybe because a part of her still clings to a shred of suspicion about the others.

She forces herself to nibble a cucumber sandwich and tries to focus on what Elena is saying.

" . . . and I don't know, all I could think was, thank God he isn't here. I'll never have to see him again. Maybe it makes me an evil person, but . . ." She shrugs, stabs a grape with her fork, and pops it into her mouth.

Tony Kerwin, Landry realizes. That's what she's talking about: her relief that she didn't have to face him at school this week.

It doesn't make her an evil person.

But then a terrible thought occurs to Landry, and the tiny bite of sandwich lodges in her throat.

What if it hadn't been a heart attack, after all?

What if Tony Kerwin had been murdered?

Thoughts racing, she excuses herself to go inside and get dessert ready. The others offer to help, but she waves them away. "I've got it. Just relax. I'll be back in a few minutes."

She hurries up the stairs, past the closed bedroom doors. She put Elena in Tucker's room and Kay in Addison's.

"I thought your kids were going to be home tonight," Elena protested when she showed them upstairs.

"Change of plans."

"That's too bad. I was hoping to meet them."

What if Elena—and not Jaycee, or Jenna Coeur—is the person she should have been worried about all along?

In the master bedroom, she closes and then—after a moment's hesitation—locks the door. She grabs her laptop from the desk and sits on the edge of the bed, opening a Google search.

Déjà vu.

She did this when Meredith died, trying to figure out what had happened to her— though not as frantically.

She types *Tony*—then corrects it to *Anthony*—*Kerwin*, taking a guess on the spelling.

She got it right; an obituary pops up.

She scans it.

. . . died suddenly at his residence on Monday, June 10 . . .

But of course the cause of death isn't listed. It never is.

If he'd been murdered, though, there would be online newspaper coverage, as there was after Meredith's death.

There is none for Tony.

Going back to his obituary, she rereads it, then the funeral notice.

In lieu of flowers, the family would appreciate donations in Tony's memory to the American Heart Association.

That, Landry thinks, would certainly indicate a heart attack.

He died at home. There would have been an autopsy. If

it had shown anything unusual, that would have come up by now. Because you can't disguise murder as a heart attack . . . or can you?

She returns to the search engine.

Two minutes later she has her answer—and the implications rock her to the core.

Beck has gone through every e-mail exchange in her mother's files, going back a couple of years.

Nothing in her sent or received folders indicate that anyone was out to get her; not a shred of evidence to incriminate anyone.

Least of all her father.

Is that really what you were expecting to find?

There are only a few e-mails between her parents—mostly references to job hunting and household paperwork. But there were plenty of e-mails Mom sent to friends that seem to indicate the marriage was as solid as ever.

I miss Hank, she wrote to Jaycee, one of her blogger friends, just a few days before she died. *I can't wait until he's back home and things are back to normal. I hate being alone at night.*

I do, too, Jaycee wrote back. *I wish I had a Hank!*

There was another e-mail, further back, sent to a neighbor asking for the recipe for the potato side dish she'd made for a dinner party the night before. *Hank devoured it, in case you didn't notice,* Mom had written. *I want to make it for dinner some night.*

Recipe . . .

That reminds Beck.

One of the bloggers she met at the funeral had mentioned that Mom e-mailed her about the cheesecake Beck had brought over on Mother's Day.

She doesn't recall seeing anything about that in the files.

She goes back to May 12, Mother's Day, and begins

working her way forward through the sent mail, looking for the exchange.

That's strange. It isn't there.

She checks the received e-mails.

Not there, either.

It's nothing earth-shattering, and yet . . .

It's bothering her.

She can't remember which of the bloggers even said it. So much of last Saturday's service is a blur. There were so many people . . .

She sighs, rising from the kitchen table.

Maybe the e-mail was there, and she's so delirious she just missed it. She needs a break, and it's time to go back to the living room to check on Jordan again. He's been asleep on the couch for over an hour now. She turned off the television and covered him with a blanket when she first found him like that.

Looking down at her sleeping nephew's sweet face, she's swept by an overwhelming sadness.

He may not remember Mom. Beck lost her maternal grandmother when she was his age; she doesn't remember her at all. Mom used to try to jog her memory, showing her photos of her sitting on her grandmother's lap as a little girl or holding hands with her at the zoo . . .

"Remember that day?" she'd ask.

Beck wanted to remember so badly . . .

But she just didn't.

That bothered her mother.

"You loved her so much," she told Beck, "and she was crazy about you and your brothers."

Maybe so. But she died, and every trace of her disappeared from Beck's mind.

That's going to happen to Jordan, too. Everything Mom did for him, and with him . . .

He'll only know about it because they'll tell him stories

and show him pictures. He won't *know*, in his heart. He won't *remember*.

He opens his eyes abruptly, as if sensing that she's there. "Hi, Aunt Beck."

"Hi, sweetie. Did you have a nice nap?"

He nods sleepily. "I dreamed about Grammy."

"Really? What happened in your dream?"

"She was just laughing and laughing, and Grampy was giving me horsey rides on his back like he used to."

She smiles, eyes suddenly swimming in tears. "That sounds like a really nice dream."

"Yeah. It was happy. Do you think Grampy will play horsey again when he gets back?"

"Maybe not today," she says. "But someday. Someday, I'm betting he will."

In the past hour the sky above the bay has gone from deep blue to pale blue with patchy clouds to completely overcast. The air hangs heavy with humidity and the incessant rattling hum of locusts in the coastal grasses that sound to Elena like a perpetually shaking tambourine, further rattling her nerves.

Forcing down a final bite of the pecan pie Landry served for dessert, she fights the urge to jump up and excuse herself from the table . . .

Just as Landry did a short time ago, when she left to get the dessert and didn't come back for so long that Elena finally went into the kitchen to see if she needed help. She wasn't there, and a pair of pecan pies sat at the ready beside a stack of plates.

What, Elena wondered, was she up to?

It could have been innocent—maybe she was on the phone with her husband, or tending to some household chore . . .

But when Landry reappeared with a dessert tray, she neglected to make eye contact with anyone, and her hands were shaking so badly the stack of plates rattled.

Now Elena sips the sickeningly sweet tea, wishing it were laced with vodka, and wipes her soaked hairline with a napkin. The drenching heat is nearly as oppressive as the paranoia that's fallen over the group like a storm cloud.

Why aren't Landry's kids going to be here tonight, as planned? Does she even have kids? A husband? Or did she stage this picture perfect bayside house right out of *Southern Living*? Is it filled with mere props, everything from the gallery of framed photographs in the dining room to the teenage bedrooms to the sneakers in the mudroom cubbies carefully positioned to make herself appear to be an ordinary mom, when in fact she's . . .

"I hope y'all are going to have more of this pie, because I've got plenty," she tells them, and Elena wonders if she might even be faking the accent.

Nobody wants more pie.

Or, when she offers, more sweet tea.

Nobody wants anything but to be someplace, anyplace, other than here.

Kay is quiet by nature but paler than the cloth napkin she's twisting in her hands, and her pie has gone untouched.

Does she realize it's a trap? Elena wonders. *Or is she in on it? Is it a conspiracy?*

Playing the role of charming hostess, Landry chatters brightly—too brightly—about the restaurant where she's made a dinner reservation.

"And I hope y'all like seafood, because—" She breaks off to look out over the water as thunder rumbles in the distance. The sky has gone from milky to ominous black layers mounting along the horizon.

"It's going to rain," Kay says unnecessarily.

"It is." Landry is on her feet. "We should go inside."

Reluctant to go into the house with them, Elena points to the ceiling overhead, where the fan still rotates in a futile attempt to cool things down. "We won't get wet here."

"We will if it rains sideways. It's blowing in across the water. Let's go in."

She doesn't want to go in, dammit. That's why they're out there in the first place. Inside, she can't escape quickly if she needs to.

But Kay, too, is already standing. "I'm going to lie down for a little while, if no one minds."

"Are you feeling all right?" Elena asks her, and she shakes her head.

"The trip wore me out. I'm sorry."

Poor Kay. She's not here to blindside her. She's here because she needs their friendship. She has no one else in the world.

Kay starts helping Landry gather up the plates and glasses, but Landry stops her.

"I'll get that. You can relax in the living room, if you'd like—we have lots of books, if you feel like reading. Or maybe everyone needs a nap. I know y'all were up early."

"I wouldn't mind some downtime," Kay says with a yawn.

"Same here." Elena stands. "I'm wicked tired."

Landry's smile is stiff. "Sweet dreams, then!"

With narrowed eyes, Elena watches her scrape the crumbs off the plates.

Then she follows the others inside and up the stairs.

As Kay closes the bedroom door behind her, she can hear the rain already starting to fall, pattering on the low-pitched roof directly above her head.

Thunder rumbles, this time much closer.

She sits on the edge of the bed, looking around the pretty bedroom—Landry's daughter's bedroom.

What would it be like, she wonders, to grow up living in a room like this, with a mom like Landry?

She hopes Addison knows how lucky she is. And Tucker,

too—Landry's son. She hopes they know they're blessed with everything—the only thing—that really matters.

Not beautiful bedrooms in a lovely house in a charming southern town, but parents who are together, and love them.

Kay was hoping she'd have a chance to meet the kids, but they're not home this weekend.

"It's better this way," Landry said, and Kay has to agree.

It wouldn't be right, the kids being here. There's too much tension in the house, and now—

A ringing phone interrupts the thought. Her cell, she realizes. It has to be Detective Burns, returning her call at last.

She checks caller ID and recognizes the 513 area code. Yes, she was right.

But of course she was. Her phone never rings. She doesn't have a circle of friends and family, not like Meredith. Not like Landry.

There's no one back in Indianapolis wondering how her Alabama weekend is going.

There will be no one to miss her when she's gone for good—not there, anyway.

But these women—her online friends—will notice she's gone. And of course, Meredith's family will as well, when they receive their unexpected inheritance.

They're all I have.

But all I ever wanted was a family, and now I finally have it. Someone will care that I lived. Someone will care when I die, like they cared when Meredith did. Someone will cry for me, will remember me.

She presses the Talk button, swallowing a lump in her throat.

"Hello?"

"Kay, this is Detective Burns calling from Cincinnati. I just got a message that you were trying to reach me earlier. You should have called the number I gave you. That's my direct line. I don't check this one very—"

"I'm sorry." She presses a hand to her aching head. "I forgot about that. I'm traveling, and I don't even know if I have it with me . . ."

"Where are you?"

"Alabama. At Landry Wells's house. A bunch of us are here for the weekend. The reason I called was because I thought I spotted Jenna Coeur in the airport when I was catching my connecting flight back in Atlanta . . ."

"You thought you spotted her?"

"I was pretty sure, but now . . ."

"Kay," Detective Burns says, "listen to me. It wasn't her. You don't have to worry about her. Not today, anyway."

Six of One Is Not Always Half a Dozen of the Other

Today is September 22. The date looms large in my brain. It's the anniversary of my preventative bilateral mastectomy.

Did I change my fate on that day?

I tried to. The decision to have the surgery was mine. The idea . . . mine. It was not the first suggestion of any surgeon, since the only evidence of cancer was small and contained. Lumpectomy was the preferred procedure.

Breast Preservation was a term I learned then and heard quite often in those early diagnosis days. As if saving breasts were the point here, the ultimate goal. As if just cutting out the cancer as carefully, neatly, and least intrusively as possible was the mission, and perhaps for some it is. I remember sitting with the first surgeon I consulted, thinking I was missing something because although saving breasts is intrinsically tied to saving a life for some, it wasn't for me.

Even though my own grandmother had beaten the odds, I had heard plenty of horror stories about women who hadn't. Women who were declared fine for many years, only to have the cancer come back with a vengeance. So in my mind, as I was told survival rates for those with mastectomy versus lumpectomy were basically the same, I knew I couldn't do it. I had a husband and children who needed me.

Every person, every diagnosis of breast cancer, is unique. No two circumstances are ever the same and neither are the ways of approaching, dealing, and living with this disease. No one is right or wrong. Each moment is personal, and for me . . . I knew I couldn't walk away after a lumpectomy and weeks of radiation feeling positive about my outcome, in spite of comparable statistics. I knew I'd question my choice everyday, worry I hadn't done enough, harbor regret.

Ultimately, I guess it mattered more for the peace of mind it granted me, rather than better odds. I believe I had done all I could to stave off recurrence, knowing full well neither method was guaranteed, but now I wouldn't second-guess myself, and that . . . was everything.

Did I change my fate that day? Who knows?

Do I miss my old, unaltered, presurgery physical self? Sometimes. But not the tiniest fraction as much as I'd miss seeing my kids from childhood through adulthood to parenthood, or growing old with the man I love. And in the end . . . what is more important than that?

— Excerpt from Landry's blog, *The Breast Cancer Diaries*

Chapter 16

Landry's cell phone rings as she loads the plates into the dishwasher. Startled, she drops one. It shatters on the stone floor.

"Dammit!" She looks up at the ceiling, wondering if the others heard it and are going to come down to investigate.

Hopefully the rain and thunder masked the sound.

Pulling out her phone, she sees that the caller is Bruce and hurriedly answers it.

"The flight came in," he reports. "She wasn't on it."

"Okay." Landry paces, keeping an eye on the stairs. There's been no movement from above.

"I'm going to stay here and wait for the next flight from Atlanta."

"Okay," she says again, staring at the sheet of rain beyond the glass.

She's probably supposed to feel relieved. But it would have been so much simpler—it would be over—if Jenna Coeur had just walked off the damned plane.

Now they're trapped here in limbo, waiting, waiting . . .

"How about what I told you?" she whispers to Bruce, wandering into the living room with the phone. "About Tony Kerwin?"

"Look, there are definitely drugs, like succinylcholine

or potassium chloride, that can simulate a heart attack and would be metabolized in the bloodstream to appear as chemicals that would normally appear in a human body. They wouldn't show up in an autopsy."

"So they could have been used on Tony, to make a murder look like accidental death."

"Theoretically, yes. You'd have to be looking for an injection site on the body in order to catch something like that, and unless the medical examiner had reason to look for it . . ."

"He'd never see it."

"That's right. But don't jump to conclusions, Landry. It wouldn't be easy for the average person to pull off something like this."

"Why not?"

"For one thing, you can't use over-the-counter potassium chloride pills from a drugstore. You'd have to have a liquid form and inject it. But again . . ."

"You don't think that's what happened."

"I really don't."

"Why not?"

"Because there are very few places where those drugs would even be found. Succinylcholine alone—SUX—is used in anesthesiology and it's used along with liquid potassium chloride for—"

Hearing a creaking on the stairs, Landry freezes, and the rest of Bruce's sentence is lost on her.

She holds her breath, poised, watching the steps, waiting for whomever it is to descend.

But nobody does.

"Landry?" Bruce is saying. "Are you there?"

"I'll call you right back," she blurts, and hangs up, eyes still on the vacant stairway.

Maybe it was her imagination.

Or maybe someone is up there spying, eavesdropping.

Who is it? Kay, or Elena, or . . . someone else?

* * *

Walking into the police station, Sheri keeps a tight hold on the guitar pick in her hand. She'd wrapped it in plastic, just in case.

You never know.

There might be fingerprints.

Pen in hand, the desk sergeant looks up from whatever he's working on. Official business, she hopes. Better not be a goddamned Sudoku puzzle when her husband's murder remains unsolved . . .

"Can I help you?"

She clears her throat. "I'm Sheri Lorton . . ."

He nods.

"Roger Lorton's wife."

She waits for recognition.

He waits, utterly clueless.

Okay. He doesn't know her.

This is a big city. People die—are killed—every day. Cases go unsolved forever.

She shouldn't take it personally.

But how do you not?

Sheri rests her hands on the desk and leans in. "My husband was murdered last week. Walking our dog. Stabbed in cold blood on the sidewalk. I think I've found something that might be relevant to the detectives working on his case."

He nods, picks up the phone on the desk. "I'll get someone to help you, Mrs. Lorton. And . . . I'm sorry for your loss."

Just days ago, shrouded in an opaque veil of anguish, she'd thought it didn't matter to her—the investigation. Because nothing can bring him back.

Now, though her widowed heart will ache for the rest of her life, she knows that the healing will only begin when the person who stole her husband is found—and punished.

* * *

Slow and steady . . .

   Slow and steady . . .

   That's the key, though impulse decrees the polar opposite approach.

   Hurry!

   Do it quickly!

   Just get it over with!

   No.

   No, that would be dangerous. Now is not the time to make a mistake.

   Slow . . .

   Take out the knife, the one with the tortoiseshell handle.

   Think about that long ago day by the pond, when a plain old rock turned out to be a ferocious snapping turtle.

   Steady . . .

   Open the blade.

   Slow . . .

   Think about where it has to go.

   Steady . . .

   Think about cause and effect.

   Slow . . .

   But it's time. Now. It's time.

   Steady . . .

   Raise the knife . . .

   Do it.

   Do it!

   At last . . . it's done.

"You really believe that Elena killed Tony?" Bruce asks as Landry clutches the phone to her ear. She's sitting inside her car in the garage, suffocatingly hot with the doors closed and the windows rolled up. But it's the only place she could think to continue this conversation without possibly being overheard.

She did briefly consider opening the garage door so she can turn on the engine and the air-conditioning without asphyxiating herself—but her guests would hear the door go up and come to investigate.

She even considered driving away but couldn't bring herself to leave Kay alone here with a murderer.

Elena.

Elena?

One moment the idea seems preposterous to Landry; the next it makes perfect, chilling sense.

"You said yourself that it's possible Tony was murdered with poison that made his death look like a heart attack," she reminds Bruce. "Who else could possibly have had such a strong motive? She wanted him out of her life."

"There could be other people who felt the same way."

"Other people who just came from the funeral of a friend whose murder is unsolved?"

"It could be a coincidence."

"It could be, but . . ."

Landry keeps playing and replaying her last conversation with Elena at the airport on Sunday. She said she couldn't stand the thought of going back home to face him, and the next day he was dead.

Coincidence?

Really?

"I checked her out," Bruce tells her, "and there's nothing in her past to suggest that she's capable of cold-blooded murder."

Cold-blooded.

Coldhearted.

Jenna Coeur in the airport . . .

What does that even matter if Elena was the one who killed Meredith?

Anyway, Bruce said Jenna didn't get off the plane. She *isn't* here.

Is she really trying to get here?

Was Kay mistaken about seeing her in Atlanta?

Can first grade teacher and party girl Elena really be hiding a sinister self?

Nothing makes sense.

Bruce . . .

How do I even know he's for real? He was just a stranger on a plane, handing me a business card . . .

He might not be an investigator at all. That could have been a dummy Web site.

Her thoughts are spinning, spinning, spinning . . .

"Does Kay know?" Bruce is asking.

"No."

"You might want to go tell her what you're thinking. If you're right about this, then the two of you need to get out of there before . . ."

Bruce doesn't finish his sentence.

He doesn't have to.

Landry disconnects the call, opens the car door and steps out into the garage.

It's quiet. Deserted . . . or so it seems.

But there are shadowy corners where someone could be concealed, watching her.

Someone . . . even Bruce.

He told her he's at the airport waiting for Jaycee to get off a plane, but what if he's making her think he's her protector when really . . .

The call is coming from inside the house.

The line from an old slasher movie barges into her brain.

Her legs wobble as she starts moving across the floor, expecting someone to jump out at her with every step she takes.

Bruce . . . Elena . . . Jaycee . . . or Jenna . . . whoever the hell killed Meredith.

*   *   *

Heart racing, Elena slips through the back door, crosses the porch where they all ate lunch just a short time ago, and begins running through the yard.

It's pouring out. Jagged yellow lightning slices the gray-black sky.

Get away, get away . . .

She slips on the wet grass as she runs. She throws her arms in front of her to break the fall and her hands land in the mud at the edge of the garden.

Heart racing, she gets to her feet and starts running again, looking back over her shoulder to make sure no one is coming after her.

Get away, get away . . .

She turns right when she reaches the waterside path, heading north.

There's no one out here now.

No one behind her. No one to see her stop, at last, to rest for a moment and let the rain wash the mud—and the blood, not her own—from her hands.

Addison's bedroom door is ajar.

Landry hesitates, wondering if she should push it open and walk right in. Tucker's closed door is just down the hall; behind it, Elena might be able to hear her if she called out to Kay or knocked.

Then again, the rain is falling hard on the roof, and the thunder might be loud enough to drown out noises from the hall. She waits until the next clap and knocks, calling softly, "Kay? Kay?"

No reply.

She's probably sleeping. She looked exhausted, poor thing. Exhausted, and sick.

I've got to get her out of here.

Under ordinary circumstances Landry wouldn't dream of walking uninvited into a room occupied by a houseguest. But in this case it's for Kay's own good.

She pushes the door open, crosses the threshold . . . and screams.

Kay is lying on the floor in a pool of blood, a knife protruding from her abdomen.

The Los Angeles press conference is airing live on the cable entertainment network.

Sitting in front of the television, waiting for it to start, Crystal is focused on her computer. In the past hour the search engine has exploded with fresh hits in response to the name Jenna Coeur.

In about ten minutes she's going to be stepping in front of the cameras with Wesley Baumann, the avant-garde movie director.

"This is bound to be the comeback of the decade," a blond reporter is excitedly telling the television audience. "Maybe even the comeback of the century!"

According to online rumors, Baumann will be announcing that he's just cast Jenna Coeur in the lead role of his next film.

"The whole world is waiting to get a look at Jenna. She hasn't been seen in public since she left the courtroom after being acquitted for the murder of the illegitimate teenage daughter she'd given up for adoption when she was just a teen herself."

The scene cuts from the milling crowd of press and lineup of microphones to a montage of flashback photos and film clips: scenes from Jenna Coeur's films, the stunning actress on the red carpet and smiling on the arms of A-list actors, then an ambulance pulling away from her Hollywood Hills mansion, the mansion cordoned off by yellow crime scene tape, Jenna Coeur being escorted into and out of the courthouse amid a hail of flashbulbs, driving away in a black limousine, never to be seen again until . . .

Well, not yet. But according to the press, she landed at LAX about an hour ago and is at this moment behind the scenes with Wesley Baumann, getting ready to step into the spotlight again at long last.

Obviously, Kay Collier was wrong about having spotted her in Atlanta.

Maybe she was wrong, too, about having seen her at Meredith's funeral.

Maybe that was someone else.

Someone who bolted the moment she saw me looking at her?

And what about Jaycee the blogger?

Frustrated, Crystal gets up to pace again, keeping an eye on the television screen.

Maybe Jaycee's someone else, too. Some ordinary blogger trying to protect her anonymity on the Internet.

Someone who had absolutely nothing to do with Meredith Heywood's fate at the hands of someone who either loved her—or hated her—enough to kill her.

Which—and who—was it?

"Nine-one-one, what is your—"

"My friend! She's been stabbed! Please—"

"All right, ma'am, calm down. You say your friend has been stabbed?"

"Yes! Oh, Kay . . . No . . ."

"Is your friend breathing?"

"I think so . . ." Landry reaches out and touches Kay's neck, feeling for a pulse below her ear. It's there, but faint.

"Ma'am—"

"She's breathing," she tells the operator. "Hurry. Please hurry."

"They've already been dispatched, ma'am. Who stabbed your friend?"

"I don't know," she says helplessly, staring down at the tortoiseshell knife handle protruding from Kay's abdomen. "I honestly don't."

As the flamboyant movie director Wesley Baumann, clad in what appears to be a brocade smoking jacket and an ascot, steps up to the televised podium, Crystal shakes her head. Crazy Hollywood people. Can't the guy just wear a regular old suit and tie like a normal businessman?

"Thank you very much for being here, and good afternoon," Baumann says to the array of microphones and cameras in an affected accent that's far closer to Britain than the Bronx, where he was born. "It gives me great pleasure to announce my newest project, which has been many years in the making. Part of the reason for this is that I could envision only one actress in the lead role—but first, I had to track her down, and then, I had to convince her. Neither proved to be an easy task."

Dramatic pause.

Rolling her eyes, Crystal half expects him to thrust a lit pipe between his lips.

He refrains, going on to talk a bit about the film, and it turns out to be a biopic about the life of Ingrid Bergman.

Okay, now it makes more sense. Jenna Coeur is a dead ringer for the late Hollywood legend. Casting someone so notorious in such a high profile project is bound to be controversial: added appeal for an unconventional, media-courting director like Baumann.

"The script calls for a versatile actress with the range to depict Bergman from her early years in Stockholm through Hollywood's golden era to middle age and her valiant seven-year battle with breast cancer."

Those two words hit Crystal like a punch in the gut.

Coincidence? Or . . .

"And now," Baumann continues, with a sweeping gesture as he looks stage left, "I'd like to introduce the extraordinarily versatile, extraordinarily lovely . . . Miss Jenna Coeur."

As she steps up to the podium, her head is bowed. Her shoulders rise with one deep breath, as if to steel her nerves, and then she looks up, directly into the cameras.

It's her.

Not just Jenna Coeur, but *her*—the woman she saw at Meredith's funeral.

"Hang on, Kay . . . just hang on . . . help is coming . . ."

Kay can't see Landry and she can't answer her but she hears her voice loud and clear.

The hearing is the last sense to go, she recalls the hospice nurse saying years ago, when Mother lay dying. *Go ahead and talk to her. She'll hear you.*

Perhaps. But Mother was listening to someone else.

You came back for me, Paul! I knew you would. . . . yes, I'm ready. I'm ready. Let's go.

That was when Kay realized that death would not be the dark, lonely moment she'd feared ever since that long-ago day her doctor's receptionist, Janine, had called to tell her the test results were back.

Life—it was *life* that had been dark and lonely.

Not death.

When you die, there's light—bright, beautiful light. Mother talked about that. And there are people there, waiting; people you love, and they'll never leave you. You'll never have to say good-bye again.

Kay's parents found each other again on the other side, this time forever, and Meredith . . .

She knows Meredith's beloved mother had to be waiting for her when she crossed over.

And now it's my turn, and Meredith is already there.
She'll be waiting for me.
She'll be coming to find me, any second now . . .

"And you're sure your husband wouldn't have picked this up somewhere else—" The homicide detective studies the plastic-wrapped guitar pick. "—maybe not from the sidewalk that morning, but the day before? Maybe he bought it, or someone gave it to him, or—"

"No." Sheri shakes her head firmly. "That's impossible."

"Impossible is a strong word, Mrs.—"

"But it is impossible. Trust me." She'd already told him about Roger's germaphobia; how he would never in a million years pick up a filthy guitar pick from the sidewalk.

Now she explains, "He would have taken those jeans, clean, out of his drawer that morning. He never wore something two days in a row. That's just how he was. Everything went into the hamper at night when he took it off."

Sitting back in his chair, the detective—in his quintessential rumpled shirt—nods thoughtfully.

"I do all the laundry," she goes on, "and I always check the pockets, so it wasn't there when I washed the jeans. It got there that morning. Someone else put it there. Not Richard."

"Okay." The detective leans forward, looking again at the guitar pick. "I don't know what this means, but for starters, we're going to look for prints, and I'm going to see if I can use it to link any other recent murders here in Indianapolis."

Stumbling along the waterfront path as it winds past the outbuildings of the Grand Hotel property, Elena spots a long wooden fishing pier ahead. Two men are there despite the thunderstorm, standing side by side along the railing holding bamboo rods above the water.

Elena stops running, clutching her side, panting hard.

"Help!" she calls. "Please, please . . . someone is trying to kill me . . ."

They don't turn their heads toward her, can't hear her voice above the hard summer rain.

She looks over her shoulder, still expecting to see . . .

Landry, Jenna . . . whoever slaughtered Kay in the picture-perfect teenage girl's bedroom decorated in seaside colors.

She tries to catch her breath, shouts again, "Help! My friend . . ."

My friend is dead.

I went to tell her that I thought we should get out of that house before something terrible happened, and . . .

And it already had.

I found her, and . . .

And I panicked, and . . .

And I didn't stop to help; I didn't even stop to grab my cell phone to call for help.

I just ran. Ran away, ran for my life.

Again she looks over her shoulder.

No one is chasing her.

But I know what I saw. I had her blood on my hands. Dear God . . .

Kay. Poor Kay.

Blinded by the glare of flashbulbs, Jenna is transported back to that day at the courthouse, the day the verdict was read.

"We, the jury, find the defendant not guilty . . ."

Not guilty.

Stunned, she turned to her legal team, certain she must have heard wrong. She hadn't. Her attorneys had never let on to her that they anticipated any other outcome, but relief was evident in their faces and posture. As for her . . .

Not guilty?

She clearly remembers what happened that night at her mansion in the Hollywood Hills.

Olivia, the daughter she'd given up for adoption, had found her way back into her life—

Just as Steven once had, about seven, maybe eight years after she left Minnesota and transformed herself into Hollywood royalty. Of course, she saw him for what he really was, and had been all along: a dirt bag nobody. The irony: he didn't even want her back. He wanted money. He'd gotten himself into trouble. Loan sharks, drug dealers . . . something like that.

She didn't give it to him.

Later, Jenna heard, he'd disappeared.

She didn't care.

Olivia did.

Olivia had maneuvered her way into her life as a personal assistant, never letting on who she really was.

It wasn't until later—when Olivia was dead and she was sitting in a jail cell—that Jenna uncovered the whole sad story about what had happened to her daughter back in Minnesota. Olivia had been adopted as an infant by parents who abused her, then bounced from foster home to foster home, fantasizing about her birth parents coming to the rescue. They never did.

She eventually found Steven, not long after Jenna refused to bail him out of trouble. He blamed her for that. And when her newfound father figure vanished, Olivia, too—neglected, mentally ill, delusional Olivia—blamed her. Fantasy festered.

One night, she snapped.

Crept into Jenna's bedroom with a butcher knife.

It was my life, or hers. I did what I had to do . . . Or did I?

Was there a part of her that knew all along who Olivia really was, and what was coming, and did nothing to deter it? A part of her—a spurned, furious part of her—that wanted to punish Olivia for the sins of her father?

No one will ever know the whole truth.

No one but me. And I'll never tell.

It doesn't matter now anyway.

Wesley Baumann touches Jenna's hand, resting on the podium.

She looks up at him.

He gives a little nod.

She can hear Cory's voice in her head. *You can do this.*

Okay.

Thanks to him—thanks to Wesley—the nightmare is over. Jenna Coeur is coming back at last.

"Thank you." Her voice seems to echo in hundreds, thousands, of microphones. Flashbulbs are still exploding before her eyes. The room is silent, waiting. Someone coughs.

You can do this.

"Seven years ago last week marked the beginning of a nightmare I never thought would end. What happened that night is a very long and complicated story. Maybe someday I'll decide to tell it. But right now the only story I'm interested in telling is Ingrid Bergman's. I've been preparing for this role for eighteen months, learning everything I could about this fascinating woman . . . this courageous woman. About the way she lived . . . the way she died."

A lump rises in her throat. She's thinking not about Ingrid Bergman, but about Meredith Heywood. And the others.

Eighteen months ago she set out to learn everything she could about breast cancer. She stumbled across a vibrant online community of women who were living with—and dying from—the disease. Ever the method actress, she was drawn into their world, essentially becoming one of them. She celebrated their triumphs, mourned their losses, and took up their battle cry, immersing herself not just in the emotions, but in the politics.

For eighteen months their world was her world.

Now it's time now for her to move on.

She takes a deep breath. "I'm grateful to Wesley Baumann for giving me this opportunity, and to my manager, Cory, for believing in me, and to the friends who saw me through the last seven years . . . I couldn't have done it without you."

I only wish you could know how much you meant to me—or why I left without saying good-bye.

"Kay . . . who did this to you, Kay?"

Landry's voice, farther away now.

Was it like this for Meredith? Kay wonders. *Could she hear me moving around her bedroom that night as she lay there on the floor? I should have talked to her. I should have told her why I did what I did. That it was out of love for her. I couldn't bear the thought of her suffering the way Mother had. I knew she couldn't bear it either . . .*

Sick . . . bald . . . dying . . .

When Meredith told her she was terminally ill, something shifted inside Kay.

All those years at the prison, watching criminals march off to the lethal injection chamber, had taken their toll. Killers who had tortured innocent victims to death were allowed to escape their hellish prison existence by the most merciful means imaginable. They were the ones who deserved to suffer. Not their victims.

Not Meredith.

She knew what she had to do. She had to help her friend escape.

Maybe I had selfish reasons, too. Maybe I couldn't bear the thought of being the first to go. Maybe I needed Meredith to be there, waiting for me, so that I wouldn't be alone when the time came.

Was it so wrong, really?

When she first came up with the plan, Kay didn't think so. It made a bizarre kind of sense, and after all, it was going to happen anyway. She even did some reading about euthanasia.

Mother used to talk about that a lot. Dr. Kevorkian had been tried and convicted around the time her own illness began to progress.

"They do lethal injection executions at the prison where you work," she'd say. "You can get your hands on those drugs, can't you?"

"No, Mother," Kay would tell her. "I can't."

Yes, she could.

She did.

She kept the deadly liquid in the drawer of her nightstand, just in case Mother's pain became unbearable.

Kay found herself imagining the heartfelt deathbed apology her mother would make, for withholding her love all those years.

I do love you, Kay, Mother would manage to say. *I've always loved you, more than anything in the world.*

Sick . . . bald . . . dying . . .

And then her mother would beg her to help her, and she would gently inject her with the drugs that would stop her heart and end the suffering at last.

That wasn't how it happened.

The apology never came, and so . . .

Kay allowed the torture to go on.

She didn't *cause* it. She wasn't *evil*.

She just didn't put a stop to it. She let it happen.

Sick . . . bald . . . dying . . .

Dead.

The potassium chloride and SUX didn't go to waste, though. Kay planned to use the lethal cocktail on herself someday, when the time was right. She even packed it into her bag the day she drove to Cincinnati for Meredith's funeral, along with a syringe. Just in case . . .

Most of the time, she was at peace with how she'd helped Meredith, but there were moments—moments when her head ached and her thoughts churned and she wasn't so sure.

Then last weekend, when she met the others in person—Landry and Elena—she realized she wasn't alone in this world after all. She needed them, yes—but more importantly, they needed her.

From Cincinnati, she drove to Massachusetts. It wasn't easy—that long drive on busy highways though the Northeast corridor—but she did it. For Elena.

The way Tony Kerwin was tormenting her . . .

All that stress was toxic. She had to do whatever she could to save Elena from a recurrence.

I'll do anything for my friends, she told the woman on the plane this morning, the one with the rosy future. She meant it.

Roger Lorton—she hadn't done that for her friends, though. She'd done it for herself. That was a bad morning. She'd gone out for an early walk to try to clear her aching head and tangled thoughts, thinking about Meredith, thinking about Mother . . .

When he asked her for a light—and she saw that cigarette—she couldn't help it. He got too close, and in her mind's eye he wasn't a stranger with a cigarette between his lips, he was Mother. She snapped.

Like a turtle.

He was small, much smaller than her. It was easy to overpower him.

She left him with the guitar pick, just as she left Tony Kerwin with the comb and Meredith with the pendant. Good luck tortoiseshell for all, wishing them Godspeed on their final journey.

When remorse struck, later—only occasionally—she reminded herself that it was all for good reason. Even Roger Lorton, a perfect stranger who had nothing to do with anything, really.

But he was a smoker, like Mother. Polluting his lungs, polluting the air for the rest of the world, not caring if he got cancer or if anyone else did.

Selfish, reckless . . .

Just like Mother.

The doctor had assured Kay, years ago, when questioned, that her own cancer had originated in her breast and not her lung, meaning that it hadn't come from second-hand smoke exposure. But Kay didn't buy it.

It doesn't matter now. Mother is long gone.

She won't be waiting for Ray. Nor will Paul Collier, the man who impregnated his wife and then left. Never a father, certainly never "Daddy."

But that doesn't matter, either. Not anymore.

Kay purchased a round-trip ticket to Alabama so that no one would guess the truth later, but she never had any intention of using the return trip. She came knowing she was going to die in this place, surrounded by friends. Here, where she wouldn't lie alone and rotting away, undiscovered, in a lonely house for days, weeks, maybe months.

But she couldn't let them know she'd taken her own life, because then they might figure out that she'd taken Meredith's.

No one must ever find out about that.

Her friends, and Meredith's family—they'd never understand. They'd hate her, and she couldn't bear that. When she's gone, she wants to be remembered with love, wants her life to have meant something to someone. Until now, there was no chance of that.

No harm, she realized, in letting the others go on believing what they already do: that Meredith was killed in a random break-in, or that a notorious murderess had infiltrated their little circle. How fortuitous the Jenna Coeur connection had turned out to be, popping up to provide an easy answer to all her problems.

That's why she planted the idea that she'd seen Jenna

Coeur in Atlanta that morning; why she hadn't tried very hard to track down Detective Burns afterward. She was going to let them think the notorious Coldhearted Killer had made it here and killed her. It was going to happen in the middle of the night.

Then the detective called back and told her Jenna Coeur had surfaced in L.A.

Her plan muddled, she wondered whether she should hold off.

But, no—it was time.

She owed it to Meredith—to her family. And it had to look like a murder. No one could ever suspect suicide. Not with her life insurance policy hanging in the balance, along with a hefty estate.

The Heywoods are the beneficiaries in her will.

Thanks to her shrewd lifestyle, some wise investments, and owning a modest house that's drastically appreciated in value over the years, she is worth quite a bit of money . . . rather, she will be, when the house is sold and the estate is liquidated.

Worth more dead than alive, as Meredith put it. Just as Meredith was—except, as she explained to Kay, her own policy was so modest it wouldn't go very far anyway.

But her money will.

The Heywoods' financial troubles will soon be over.

Of course, they don't know that yet. The windfall will be a pleasant surprise.

Meredith would have been pleased.

Yes, she has worked hard to lay the groundwork for this final, necessary step. Her affairs are in order. Meredith's family will get their inheritance, along with a sealed letter she left with her lawyer. In it, she simply tells the family how much Meredith meant to her, and how, lacking a family of her own, she chose to help theirs. That was it. No other explanation, nothing that would ever arouse suspicion. She couldn't bear that.

Earlier in the week she'd discontinued her other blog. Terrapin Terry was going on a yearlong sabbatical to the Galapagos Islands to study the turtles there.

Her laptop, too, is gone. She'd erased the hard drive, then thrown the whole thing into a Dumpster before driving to the airport this morning, covering her tracks.

The knife was packed in her suitcase—the real reason she had to disregard Elena's advice and check it.

What if it hadn't made the tight connection?

Then this wouldn't have happened after all.

She'd have had to wait.

The last thing she ever touched was the tortoiseshell handle . . . for good luck.

Yes. She'd thought of everything.

It was time. She was ready to go, regardless of where Jenna Coeur was—or wasn't.

Let them think that Jaycee had done it. Or that there had been another random break-in. Let them think anything other than the truth.

I just want them to love me.

I need them to love me.

And this way . . . they do.

They'll never know.

"Kay . . ." Landry's voice is fading. Landry is holding her hand, squeezing it. "I'm here with you, Kay. Come on. Hang on . . ."

No. She can't. It's time to let go.

She's ready to find the light, and Meredith . . .

Meredith is somewhere, waiting.

We'll get together someday, Meredith promised her. *One way or another. I just know it.*

Kay whirls through time and space, flying backward through the years.

I know it's difficult to hear news like this, the doctor tells her, *but the important thing is that we caught it early.*

We're going to discuss your treatment options, and there are many . . .

It's not better to have loved and lost, Mother rasps in her cigarette voice. *If you don't love, you can't lose . . .*

Kay is a little girl again, all alone, always alone, standing by the edge of a pond on a hot summer's day, reaching for a rock . . .

Reaching . . .
Slowly . . .
Reaching . . .
Steadily . . .

Kay draws her last breath and spirals into the darkness.

Sitting on the couch with Jordan on her lap, reading him a story, Beck has managed to put the remaining questions surrounding her mother's e-mail out of her mind for the time being. Losing herself in the silly rhyme and rhythm of Dr. Seuss is just what the doctor ordered—particularly on the heels of several failed attempts to get through Jordan's first book choice—Robert Munsch's *Love You Forever*—without breaking down sobbing.

Mom bought that book for him when he was born, her first grandchild. She used to read it for him sitting in this very spot, cradling him in her lap, even as an infant. He doesn't remember that, of course, any more than he'll eventually remember more recent times with her.

We should have taken pictures, Beck thinks, turning a page and pausing the story so that Jordan can absorb the picture first, as he likes to do, tracing the colorful figures with a chubby index finger.

We shouldn't have just posed for photos on big occasions like Christmas morning and birthdays.

Yes, they should have captured the little things, the everyday moments that feel like a dime a dozen when they're happening but are priceless when they're gone.

"Anybody home?" Teddy calls from the kitchen.

Beck breaks off reading long enough to call, "In here!"

Teddy comes in, looking instantly relieved to see them. He must have told Beck half a dozen times to be sure to lock the doors after he and dad left . . .

Even though whoever killed Mom came in through a window.

A random stranger?

The thought is no less chilling two weeks after the fact, and yet . . .

She wants to think that her mother died secure in the love of her family and friends; can't bear to think that she drew her last breath thinking she'd been betrayed.

That e-mail exchange . . . the one her friend had mentioned . . . doesn't seem to exist. Either she'd lied about it— why?—or it's been deleted.

Why? And by whom? By Mom, before she died? By whoever stole her cell phone and laptop?

"Aunt Beck is reading to me, Daddy. Hop . . . Hop . . . Hop on Pop . . ."

"Why don't you hop right up here on Pop, big guy." Teddy holds out his arms and his son stands up on the couch and leaps into them.

Watching them hug, Beck smiles wistfully.

Maybe someday she'll have a child of her own.

After this business with Keith is settled, and she's had time to regroup, rebuild . . .

Maybe.

"How did everything go?" she asks Teddy, standing up and setting the Dr. Seuss book aside. "With Dad and the paperwork?"

He shrugs. "It could have been better. Louise did her best, but—"

"Louise?"

"From the insurance company."

Beck stares.

"She doesn't know what happened, Ted," Dad says from the doorway. "I didn't want her to worry. I didn't want any of you to worry, but . . ." He shrugs. "Too late now."

I didn't want her to worry . . .

It's almost exactly what he'd said about Mom the day Beck ran into him having lunch with Louise.

Louise . . . from the insurance company?

"I had to let Mom's life insurance policy lapse. I couldn't afford the premium. I was trying to figure out a payment plan, a way to keep it going—that's why I met with Louise the day I ran into you in that restaurant. It threw me off, seeing you there, knowing you didn't know that Mom was sick again . . ."

No wonder. No wonder he'd been so edgy. No wonder she'd thought he was hiding something. To think she assumed the worst about him . . .

"We were in the tail end of the policy's grace period when she died. It ran out at midnight, but the coroner—" Her father breaks off, takes a deep breath. "The coroner pinpointed her death after twelve. Too late, according to Louise."

"Oh, Dad." Beck walks across the room and puts her arms around him. "It's okay."

"We're out of money. I can't pay the mortgage."

She shrugs. "Sell the house."

"I'm going to have to. But even then . . ."

"It's okay, Dad."

Money . . . a house . . . even people, and memories . . .

Things you have. Things you lose, no matter how hard you try to hold on.

"It's not okay." He shakes his head. "She wouldn't have wanted this. I let her down."

"No, you didn't. You didn't let her down. Dad, you loved her. She knew that. We all knew that."

In the end, that's the thing, the only thing, that matters.

The only thing that lasts forever, if you're lucky enough to find it. The love.

Jordan might not remember Mom, but her love is his legacy, and Beck knows it will live on forever, through him, through all of them.

Kay is gone.

Holding her hand, Landry felt her go; felt the muscles unclench, felt the life evaporate from her flesh.

Shaken, she stands and backs away, toward the doorway, then remembers . . .

Whoever did this is lurking somewhere out there.

She's better off in here, locked in, until help gets here. The 911 operator assured her they're on the way.

She presses the button in the doorknob and moves back across the room to the bed. Sinking onto the edge of the mattress, she thinks of Elena.

If she did it, then she's not vulnerable.

But what if it was someone else? Jenna, or Jaycee, or Bruce . . .

Then I need to warn Elena.

Her gaze falls on a cell phone—Kay's cell phone—sitting on the bedside table.

Kay used it to call Detective Burns, to let her know about Jenna Coeur in the airport, and now . . .

Now it's too late.

The detective needs to know what's going on, Landry realizes.

She hits Redial.

The phone rings . . . rings . . . rings . . . rings . . .

And goes into voice mail. "You've reached Detective Crystal Burns. Please leave me a message and I'll get back to you as soon as possible. If this is an urgent matter, please call my cell phone at—"

Wait a minute.

This is supposed to *be* her cell phone.

Landry lowers the phone and looks at the screen to see which number she just dialed.

It's not the one Detective Burns gave her on that card, the one she'd committed to memory. The one Kay swore she'd called.

Why would she lie?

Does it matter? She's dead. It's not as if she killed herself, much less Meredith, or Tony Kerwin . . .

There's no evidence, even, that Tony was murdered.

She replays everything Bruce told her about that. He said it would be possible, that certain drugs mimic a heart attack and wouldn't be detected in an autopsy if—

"Oh my God."

Stunned, she remembers exactly what he was saying when she was on the phone with him earlier, right before she thought she heard someone on the stairs.

"There are very few places where those drugs would even be found. Succinylcholine alone—SUX—is used in anesthesiology and it's used along with liquid potassium chloride for lethal injection executions."

Those last three words were lost on her at the time.

Now . . .

She turns around to stare at Kay, lying on the floor, remembering . . .

Remembering how she'd posted about her brush with fame: having worked at the federal prison where the Oklahoma City Bomber was executed over a decade ago.

But why would she want Tony Kerwin dead?

Because Elena hated him?

Because . . .

Because of the stress he was causing?

Dangerous stress. Stress that could cause a recurrence.

And what about Meredith? Why would Kay ever want Meredith dead? She loved her; everyone loved her. She was

truly shaken up at her funeral; you can't fake that kind of
emotion.

Landry can hear sirens in the distance.

They're coming. Thank God, they're coming.

She and Kay had talked about the dying process the night
of Meredith's funeral. About the so-called blessing that their
friend hadn't suffered a long, lingering death; hadn't wasted
away like Kay's mother, or Whoa Nellie, or so many of the
others . . .

Kay had agreed with Elena, that it was better to go
quickly—to never know what hit you. She agreed that only
dying was to be dreaded, not death itself . . .

The sirens are closer.

Landry walks over to the window and peers out, watching until the red domed lights appear, rotating on the top of
the first police car.

Then she unlocks the door and slowly goes down the
stairs to greet them, no longer frightened that a murderer
lurks somewhere in the house.

Later—much, much later, after the investigators confirmed that Kay's fatal knife wound did, indeed, appear
to be self-inflicted, though further tests are needed to
confirm it; after Landry has repeatedly reassured her
children, via telephone, that she's all right; after Rob has
boarded a flight home from North Carolina—she sits outside on the back porch with Elena, watching fireflies in
the dusk.

There are still several police officers inside the house,
wrapping up the investigation. Bruce is there, too. Earlier,
Landry heard him and one of the cops discussing last week's
three-game series between the Braves and the Reds.

This is merely a day's work for them. They've seen it
all.

But for Landry . . . for Elena . . .

"I keep wondering if Meredith knew what was happening," Landry says quietly. "If she knew . . . you know."

"That it was Kay?" Elena shrugs. "I hope she didn't. I hope she never knew what hit her."

Landry hopes so, too, and yet . . .

Meredith never got to say good-bye.

That her cancer had progressed and was most likely terminal—news Detective Burns shared over the telephone a little while ago, believing it had contributed to Kay's twisted motive—is irrelevant.

She should have died on her own terms—not on somebody else's. Some people fear dying, others fear death . . .

Still others fear nothing more than life itself.

Not me, Landry thinks. *I'll take it. Every scary, glorious minute of it.*

She looks at her watch. It's after eight. Rob is landing in about an hour. She didn't try to talk him out of it when he said he'd be on the next plane home. She told him to hurry.

Landry takes a deep breath, inhaling warm air scented with rain and roses.

Elena slaps her arm. "The mosquitoes are coming out."

"Yes," Landry says, "but so are the stars."

And together, they sit in silence for a while longer, gazing into the darkening sky until the heavens are ablaze with pinpricks of light.

The Day My Life Changed Forever

When the doctor's receptionist called to say that they had the results, it never dawned on me that it might be bad news.

"Hi, hon," Janine said—she calls all the patients "hon"—and casually requested that I come by in person this afternoon. She even used just that phrasing, and it was a question, as opposed to a command: "Can you come by the office in person this afternoon?"

Come by.

So breezy. So inconsequential. So . . . so everything this situation was not.

What if I'd told Janine, over the phone, that I was busy this afternoon? Would she have at least hinted that my presence at the office was urgent; that it was, in fact, more than a mere request?

But I wasn't busy and so there I was, blindsided, numbly staring at the doctor pointing the tip of a ballpoint pen at the left breast on the anatomical diagram.

The doctor kept talking, talking, talking; tapping, tapping, tapping the paper with the pen point to indicate exactly where the cancerous tissue was growing, leaving ominous black ink pockmarks.

I nodded as though I was listening intently, not betraying that every word after "malignancy" has been drowned out by the warning bells clanging in my brain.

I'm going to die, I thought with the absolute certainty of someone trapped on a railroad track, staring helplessly into the glaring roar of an oncoming train. I'm going to be one of those ravaged bald women lying dwarfed in a hospital bed, terrified and exhausted and dying an awful, solitary death . . .

I'd seen that person before, too many times—in the movies, and in real life . . . but I never thought I'd ever actually become that person. Or did I?

Well, yes—you worry, whenever a horrific fate befalls someone else, that it could happen to you. But then you reassure yourself that it won't, and you push the thought from your head, and you move on.

"Would you like to call someone, Kay?"

Call someone . . .

Would you like to call someone . . .

Unable to process the question, I stared at the doctor.

"A friend, or a family member . . . someone who can come over here and—"

"Oh. No. No, thank you," I said.

Because back then, in that moment . . .

There was no one. No one at all. No one to call. No friends, no family.

You know what? I thought that was the unluckiest day of my entire life. But really, in the end, it was the luckiest.

Cancer was, ultimately, my greatest gift—because it led me to you, the only friends—the only family—I have ever known.

—Excerpt from Kay's blog, *I'm A-Okay*

Read on for a sneak peek

at the next thrilling novel

THE BLACK WIDOW

by *New York Times* best-selling author

WENDY CORSI STAUB

Prologue

"Some things," Carmen used to say, "just don't feel right until after the sun goes down."

It was true.

Mixed drinks . . .

Bedtime stories . . .

Turning on the television . . .

Putting on pajamas . . .

All much better—more natural—after nightfall, regardless of the hour or season.

There are other things, Alex has since discovered, that can only happen under cover of darkness. Such endeavors are far less appealing than the ones to which Carmen referred. Unfortunately, they've become increasingly necessary.

Alex opens the door that leads from the kitchen to the attached garage, aims the key remote at the car and pops the trunk.

It slowly opens wide. The interior bulb sends enough light into the garage so that it's unnecessary to flip a wall switch and illuminate the overhead bulb.

Not that there are any windows to reveal to the neighbors that someone is up and about at this hour . . .

And not that the crack beneath the closed door is likely wide enough to emit a telltale shaft of light . . .

But still, it's good to practice discretion. One can't be too careful.

Alex removes a sturdy shovel from a rack on the side wall. The square metal blade has been scrubbed clean with bleach, not a speck of dirt remaining from the last wee-hour expedition to the remote stretch of woods seventy miles north of this quiet New York City suburb.

Into the trunk goes the shovel, along with a headlamp purchased from an online camping supply store.

Now comes the hard part.

Alex returns to the house with a coil of sturdy rope and a lightweight hand truck stolen a while back from a careless deliveryman who foolishly left it unattended behind the supermarket. It's come in handy. Alex is strong—but not strong enough to drag around well over a hundred pounds of dead weight.

Well, not dead *yet*.

The figure lying prone on the sofa is passed out cold, courtesy of the white powder poured into a glass of booze-laced soda that sits on the coffee table with an inch or two of liquid left in the bottom.

Alex dumps the contents into the sink, washes it down the drain, and scrubs the glass and the sink with bleach.

Then it's back to the living room.

"Time for you to go now," he whispers, rolling the hand truck over to the sofa and unfurling a length of rope. The end whips through the air and topples a framed photo on the end table. It's an old black and white baby photo of Carmen, a gift from Alex's mother-in-law the day after their son was born.

"He's the spitting image of my Carmen as an infant, isn't he?"

On that day, gazing into the newborn's face, all patchy skin and squinty eyes from the drops the nurses had put in, Alex couldn't really see it.

But as the days, then weeks and months, passed, the resemblance became undeniable. Strangers would stop them on the street to exclaim over how much parent and child looked alike. At first it was sweet. But after a while Alex started to feel left out.

"He looks like you, too," Carmen would claim, but it wasn't true.

"You're just trying to make me feel better."

"No—he has your nose. See?"

"It's your nose, Carm. It's your face. Everything about him is you—even his personality."

The baby had been so easygoing from day one, quick to smile, quick to laugh . . .

Like Carm. Nothing like you.

Alex leaves the photo lying facedown on the table.

Carmen—even baby Carmen—doesn't need to witness what's about to happen here.

Five minutes later the car is heading north on the Taconic Parkway, cruise control set at five miles above the posted limit—just fast enough to reach the destination in a little over an hour, but not fast enough to be pulled over for speeding.

Even if that were to happen, nothing would appear out of the ordinary to a curious cop peering into the car. Alex would turn over a spotless driver's license and explain that the sleeping person slumped in the passenger seat had simply had too much to drink. No crime in that statement, and quite a measure of truth.

Three hours later the first traces of pink dawn are visible through the open window beyond the empty passenger seat as Alex reenters the southbound lanes on the parkway. All four windows are rolled down and the moon roof is open, too, despite the damp chill in the March wind.

The radio is blasting a classic rock station. Led Zeppelin's "Immigrant Song" opens with a powerful electric guitar; eerie, wailing, lyric-free vocals from Robert Plant.

The fresh air and the music make it better somehow. Easier to forget throwing shovels full of dirt over the still unconscious human being lying at the bottom of the trench.

Easier not to imagine what it would be like to regain consciousness and find yourself buried alive.

Maybe that won't happen. Maybe it never has, with any of them. Maybe they just drift from sleep to a painless death, never knowing . . .

But you know that's not very likely, is it, Alex?

Chances are that it's a frantic, ugly, horrifying death, clawing helplessly at the weight of dirt and rocks, struggling for air . . .

Alex reaches over to adjust the volume on the radio, turning it up even higher in an effort to drown out the nagging voice.

Sometimes that works—with the voices.

Other times, they persist, refusing to be ignored.

Not tonight, thank goodness.

The voices give way to the music, and it shifts from Led Zeppelin to the familiar opening guitar lick of an old Guns N' Roses tune.

Singing along—screaming, shouting along—to the lyrics, Alex rejoices. There is no more fitting song to punctuate this moment.

It's a sign. It has to be. A sign that everything is going to be okay after all. Someone else will come along. Another chance. Soon enough . . .

"Oh . . . oh-oh-oh . . . sweet child of mine . . ."

Chapter 1

"No, come on. That one wasn't good either. You look annoyed."

"Probably because I *am* annoyed," Gabriella Duran tells her cousin Maria, watching her check out the photo she's just taken on her digital camera.

Yes, digital camera.

Gaby had assumed a few snapshots on a cell phone would suffice, and would make this little photo shoot far less conspicuous. But Maria, who took a photography class at the New School not long ago, insisted on using a real camera, the kind that has a giant lens attached. It's perched on top of a tripod, aiming directly at Gaby.

Which might not be a terrible thing if they were in the privacy of her apartment. But in the middle of jam-packed Central Park at high noon on the sunny Sunday before Memorial Day . . .

Yeah. Definitely a terrible thing.

"Can't you please just smile for two seconds," Maria says, "so that I can get a decent shot? Then we can be done."

Gaby sighs and pastes on a grin.

"You just look like you're squinting."

"I *am* squinting." They've been here so long that the sun

has changed position, glaring directly into her eyes. "How about if I just turn the other way?" She gestures over her shoulder, preferring to face the clump of trees behind her rather than the parade of New Yorkers jogging, strolling, and rolling past on the adjacent pathway.

"No, I need the light on your face. Here, just take a few steps this way . . . no, not that far, back a little, back . . . back . . . okay, good!"

A pair of long-haired teenagers roll past on skateboards.

"Say cheese!" one of them calls.

Gaby shakes her head at Maria, who is raising the view-finder to her eye again. "Okay, smile . . . *without* clenching your teeth."

"Maria, I swear—"

"Remember, Mami—" her cousin cuts in, using the Latina term of endearment, "you're trying to attract the perfect guy with this picture. Trust me, he's not going to be interested if you—"

"Okay, first of all, the perfect guy doesn't exist."

"Not true." Maria shakes her head, her dark ringlets bobbing around her shoulders. "He exists. But he doesn't know *you* exist. Yet. And he won't unless you let me take a picture that captures the real you."

The real me . . .

Gaby has no idea who that even is these days, other than knowing that the real Gabriella, who once laughed her way through life, doesn't seem to remember how to smile anymore.

She hasn't felt remotely like herself since last summer before she and Ben split up. After five years of marriage—and three years together before that—life without him was frighteningly unfamiliar. Even now, she begins every day with the momentarily frantic feeling that she's woken up in a strange body in a strange place, having swapped someone else's life for her own.

Then again, she really hasn't felt like herself since . . .

No. Don't go there.

She doesn't dare let herself think about it even three years later—especially not when she's supposed to be smiling.

Dr. Ryan—she's the shrink Gaby has been seeing lately—says it's okay to distract herself when she feels like she's about to burst into tears over morbid thoughts of the past.

"Get yourself out of the moment," the doctor advised. "Read a magazine, go for a run, call a friend—anything that you enjoy."

She nodded at the advice, rather than admit that there's very little she enjoys anymore. Even the things that once gave her pleasure have been reduced to mere obligations.

Yet here she is, allowing her cousin to take photos to create a profile on the InTune dating Web site. Even Dr. Ryan thought it might be a good idea—another positive step toward getting over Ben, making a fresh start.

"Gaby, I wish you'd try to relax," Maria cajoles. "It's for your own good. Try and have fun with it."

"Okay, fine. Let's see how Mr. Perfect likes this." She sticks her thumbs into her ears and wiggles her fingers, rolls her eyes back and thrusts out her tongue.

"Hilarious! I love it!" Maria snaps away.

"Hey! I was just kidding around."

"I know, but this will show him that you have a light side. We can do the sexy shots later."

"Sexy shots?" she echoes, already shaking her head.

"Hey, why don't you romp around on the grass?"

"Romp around on the—"

"You know, maybe do a cartwheel or something."

"A *cartwheel*? Are you insane? Or do you just want people to think that I am?"

"Just do something that shows that you have a light-hearted, fun side. Go!" Maria points her left index finger at

Gaby, her right poised on the shutter. "Come on. It's for Mr. Perfect."

Gaby shakes her head.

She thought she had already found Mr. Perfect, a long time ago.

She was wrong.

She also thought she could live with that. Live alone. Forever.

But then—in a weak, lonely moment, after too many happy hour cocktails on Cinco de Mayo—she allowed Maria to convince her that online dating is the answer to all her problems.

"Everyone does it," Maria told her.

"Not everyone."

"I do."

"You're not everyone."

"But everyone else does, too. Excuse me," Maria called to a pretty waitress scurrying past their outdoor table with bowls of tortilla chips and guacamole. "Can I ask you a quick question?"

"Sure, what's up?" The waitress paused, looking pleased at the momentary reprieve from running around in the heat. Hands full, she blew her bangs away from her sweaty forehead.

"Have you ever been on an Internet dating site?"

"It's how I met my fiancé."

"Really?"

"Really. Look." Balancing her tray with her right hand, she waved the diamond ring on her left. "We're getting married next month."

"That's great. Congratulations. That's all I wanted to know. Oh, and we'll take another round when you have a chance." The waitress walked on, and Maria looked smugly at Gaby. "See that? You can't argue with an engagement ring."

Ordinarily, Gaby might have. But Maria—and the tequila, and the thought of another solitary weekend in her tiny studio apartment—had finally worn her down.

She shrugged. "Oh, why not? I'll give it a try."

That was three weeks ago.

She'd talked herself out of the idea in the cold, cruel light of day on May sixth, but Maria threatened to create a profile for her anyway. And Gaby knew she was quite capable of following through.

Born just a week earlier, her cousin has always done her best to bulldoze Gaby like a bossy big sister.

"*Ella es cabeza dura*, that one," their Puerto Rican maternal grandmother used to say about Maria—meaning, she's hard-headed. "Don't let her push you around, Gabriella."

Most of the time, Gaby didn't. Still doesn't.

But right now . . .

Resigned to the fact that she's going to find herself with an online profile one way or another, she manages to muster a halfhearted smile for Maria's camera.

But the carefree girl she once was—the girl who might actually have turned cartwheels across the grass in Central Park—had died long ago, along with her marriage and her only child.

Having completely forgotten about the long holiday weekend, Alex is alarmed by the sight of a police road block on Main Street on Monday morning.

They know. They know, and they're looking for me.

There's nothing to do but stop and dutifully roll down the window as the cop beside the blue barricade comes walking toward the car.

"Good morning, officer."

"'Morning. You'll have to turn around and detour back

up Cherry Street to get to the other side of town. Memorial Day parade is about to start."

Memorial Day parade!

It's Memorial Day!

Thank God, thank God, it's just a parade, and not . . .

Come on, of course it's not about you. They can't possibly know about you. You've been so careful . . .

"All right, officer. Thank you. Have a great day!"

Was the last part overkill? Alex wonders, carefully making a K-turn and making sure to use directional signals. Was it a blatant red flag to the cop?

Nah. People always tell each other to have a great day.

Even if he were to be summoned back—and for what?—there's nothing in the car that would alert the cop that anything is amiss. Even if the officer were to examine the contents of the plastic drugstore shopping bag on the passenger seat, there still wouldn't be any reason for suspicion. Of course not.

And of course it was his imagination that the clerk back at the store had raised her eyebrow when she rang up the purchases: Advil, Band-Aids, a magazine, a pack of gum—decoy items, all, meant to distract attention from the main objective: an over-the-counter pregnancy test.

"Find everything?" the clerk had asked—routine question, yet Alex worried for a moment that it was a precursor to something more probing, less discreet.

But of course that was pure paranoia. No clerk would ever question a total stranger about something so personal.

No clerk had any way of knowing that a random customer—paying with cash—had purchased the same test countless times before all over the tristate area.

You have nothing at all to worry about. Just get home and take care of business.

Alex keeps the odometer precisely at the speed limit all the way up Cherry Street, past familiar rows of old maples framing well-kept suburban houses. All is quiet this morning. The neighborhood is populated by young families and well within walking distance of Main Street. The stroller-and-leash brigade most likely headed out early to claim prime spots along the parade route.

Noticing the flags flying from poles and porches, Alex makes a mental note to put up a flag, too, back home. There's one somewhere in the basement.

The basement . . .

Ten years ago, when the Realtor showed him and Carmen the house, the basement was a major selling point.

"The family that lived here in the sixties added over seven hundred square feet of living space when they turned this into a rec room," she said, flicking a light switch and leading the way downstairs into a large open area.

Once, years earlier, Alex had forgotten to roll up the car windows at night. It rained, and the carpet and upholstery got wet. Forever after that, the interior was permeated by a strong mildew odor. The basement smelled the same way.

The walls were paneled in brown wood and the floors covered in green indoor-outdoor carpeting that gave way to linoleum in one corner where an old olive-green washer and dryer sat alongside a slop sink. There were windows scattered high on three walls. On the fourth there was just a door.

The Realtor had opened it, and an even stronger dank smell greeted their nostrils. "Wait until you see this," she said, as if she were about to reveal something utterly dazzling: a stocked wine cellar or fully equipped home gym . . .

"What is it?" Carmen asked, nose wrinkled, peering into the dank—apparently vacant—interior.

"It's a bomb shelter!"

Alex and Carmen had exchanged a glance.

"The house was built back in the Cold War era. People were afraid Russia was going to drop a nuclear bomb."

Alex had seen the black and yellow Fallout Shelter signs on sturdy public buildings all over the city, but . . . *"Here?"*

The Realtor shrugged. "New York was considered a major target, and we're right in the suburbs. The assumption was that the radiation contamination would spread if the city were hit. People wanted to protect their families. Back in the day, this room was filled with canned goods, bottled water, lamps, cots, a space heater, even a toilet."

"That explains the smell," Carmen murmured.

"It's a piece of history," the Realtor crowed. "Isn't it fabulous?"

Fabulous wasn't quite the right word. Not back then.

Not now, either.

Alex never imagined, when they bought the house, that the underground bunker would ever be used for anything more than extra storage . . . and perhaps a conversation piece.

But then, there were a lot of things he had never imagined back then.

Online, you can be anyone you want to be.

That's the beauty of these Internet dating sites. You can call yourself by another name, make up an exciting background and glamorous career, even use a photo-shopped head shot—within reason, of course. You don't go and shave fifty pounds off your body or twenty-five years off your age, and you don't claim to be a celebrity or a billionaire, because those are things you obviously can't pull off once you meet someone in person.

But early on, when you're trying to bait the trap, so to speak, you really have to offer something that will tempt anyone who comes across your profile.

The picture he just uploaded to his new page on the

InTune Web site hasn't been digitally altered, but it is a few years old. In it, he's wearing a red sweater. He read someplace that a splash of red attracts the opposite sex when it comes to online photos.

The snapshot was taken a couple of Christmases ago. He was thinner and more handsome then, still hitting the gym every day and getting a good night's sleep every night, back before all the trouble started. He had more hair and fewer wrinkles—issues that can be easily remedied with the right imaging software.

Expensive software—which he can no longer afford, thanks to *her*.

And thanks to her, he didn't even consider taking new pictures for his new online dating profile. When he looks in the mirror lately, he doesn't like what he sees. When he looks at old pictures, he does. Case closed.

He leans back in his chair and surveys his latest profile.

Any eligible female who stumbles across Nick Butler's tall, dark, and handsome picture will most likely click through to read his questionnaire.

First, she'll check out his age, thirty-one; his location, Upper West Side; his occupation, architect.

She'll see that he's never been married and has no children. That will most likely be met with approval because, really, who wants that kind of baggage?

Not me. Not most single people in their right mind.

With Nick Butler, a woman seeking an unencumbered man won't even have to worry about pets. He lied that he's allergic, to keep the crazy cat ladies away.

He couldn't believe how many of those he found when he first entered the realm of online dating. It seemed like such a cliché until he started noticing all the single women who posted photos of themselves cradling kittens or managing to work feline-centric answers into their questionnaires.

Nick Butler's questionnaire just covers the basic favorites in every category.

Favorite Food: Italian. Who doesn't love Italian food?

Favorite Movie: *The Last of The Mohicans.* An oldie but not ancient; suitably rugged, with both historic and literary appeal, plus a romance.

Favorite Music—

Someone clears her throat behind him, and he jumps, startled. Turning around, he sees Ivy Sacks, one of the project managers, standing in the doorway of his cubicle.

"How's it coming along?"

Ivy is referring to the spreadsheet that has, with a quick click of the mouse, replaced the dating questionnaire on his desktop screen.

"It's . . . you know. Coming along."

"When do you think it'll be finished?"

"Soon. Very soon."

"Good."

For a moment she just stands there looking at him. Her expression is impossible to read.

"Anything else?" he asks, hands poised on the keyboard as though eager to get back to work on the spreadsheet.

"I was just wondering . . ."

When she trails off, he doesn't prompt her to continue, afraid that she might be on the verge of asking him out. This wouldn't be the first time, since the divorce, that he's gotten that vibe.

Ivy is the only woman at the firm who happens to be roughly his age and single. But her facial features and build are far too angular for his taste, and her no-nonsense personality makes it impossible to imagine her ever kicking back and having the slightest bit of fun.

"Never mind," Ivy says. "Just shoot that spreadsheet over to me when you're done, okay?"

"Sure, no problem."

He waits for her to leave.

The moment she does, he clicks away from the spread-sheet, back to his online profile.

Favorite Music?

Perhaps the easiest question of all.

Smiling to himself, he writes *Classic Rock*.

SPINE-TINGLING SUSPENSE FROM
NEW YORK TIMES BESTSELLING AUTHOR

WENDY CORSI STAUB

NIGHTWATCHER
978-0-06-207028-9

Allison Taylor adores her adopted city, New York. But on a bright and
clear September morning in 2001, the familiar landscape around her
is savagely altered—and in the midst of widespread chaos and fear,
a woman living upstairs from her is found, brutally slaughtered and
mutilated. Now a different kind of terror has entered Allison's life . . .
and it's coming to claim her as its next victim.

SLEEPWALKER
978-0-06-207030-2

The nightmare of 9/11 is a distant but still painful memory for Allison
Taylor MacKenna—now married and living in a quiet Westchester
suburb. She has moved on with her life ten years after barely escaping
death at the hands of New York's Nightwatcher serial killer. But now
here, north of the city, more women are being savagely murdered,
their bodies bearing the Nightwatcher's unmistakable signature.

SHADOWKILLER
978-0-06-207032-6

Nestled in the warm, domestic cocoon of loving husband and
family, Allison finally feels safe—unaware that a stranger's brutal
murder on a Caribbean island is the first step in an intricate plan to
destroy everything in her life.